W9-AQM-133

Praise for Randy Singer

"Singer, the attorney-author of several solid legal thrillers, turns in another winner. . . . Singer's many fans will be lining up to read this one."

BOOKLIST ON *DEAD LAWYERS TELL NO TALES*

"Singer's latest courtroom drama is full of twists and turns, second chances, and spiritual redemption. The author's experience as a trial attorney is evident in the details and realism throughout. He allows the reader an up-close view into the legal system."

ROMANTIC TIMES ON *DEAD LAWYERS TELL NO TALES*

"This riveting and thought-provoking legal thriller is sure to please Singer's fans and earn him new ones."

LIBRARY JOURNAL ON *DEAD LAWYERS TELL NO TALES*

"Singer skillfully loosens the strings and reweaves them into a tale that entertains, surprises, and challenges readers to rethink justice and mercy."

PUBLISHERS WEEKLY ON *THE LAST PLEA BARGAIN*

"Another solid, well-crafted novel from an increasingly popular writer. . . . Its nonfiction origins lend the book an air of reality that totally made-up stories sometimes lack."

BOOKLIST ON *THE LAST PLEA BARGAIN* (STARRED REVIEW)

"*The Last Plea Bargain* is a superbly written book, hard to put down, and easy to pick back up."

THE VIRGINIAN-PILOT

"Singer's superbly researched plot charges out of the starting gate on page 1 and doesn't rest until literally the last page."

CROSSWALK.COM ON *THE LAST PLEA BARGAIN*

"If you're looking for a mystery full of rich details and realistic scenarios, you will enjoy Singer's latest. It is easy to see why Singer reigns with Christian legal thrillers. You'll be guessing till the end."

ROMANTIC TIMES ON *THE LAST PLEA BARGAIN*

"Intricately plotted, *Fatal Convictions* is . . . an exciting legal thriller with international overtones. In addition to the action and rich cultural information, realistic characters carry the action to its exciting conclusion."

FAITHFULREADER.COM

"Singer's legal knowledge is well matched by his stellar storytelling. Again, he brings us to the brink and lets us hang before skillfully pulling us back."

ROMANTIC TIMES ON *FATAL CONVICTIONS*

"Get ready to wrestle with larger themes of truth, justice, and courage. Between the legal tension in the courtroom scenes and the emotional tension between the characters, readers will be riveted to the final few chapters."

CROSSWALK.COM ON *FATAL CONVICTIONS*

"Great suspense; gritty, believable action . . . make [*False Witness*] Singer's best yet."
BOOKLIST (STARRED REVIEW)

"A book that will entertain readers and make them think—what more can one ask?"
PUBLISHERS WEEKLY ON *THE JUSTICE GAME*

"Singer artfully crafts a novel that is the perfect mix of faith and suspense. . . . [*The Justice Game* is] fast-paced from the start to the surprising conclusion."
ROMANTIC TIMES

"At the center of the heart-pounding action are the moral dilemmas that have become Singer's stock-in-trade. . . . An exciting thriller."
BOOKLIST ON *BY REASON OF INSANITY*

"Singer hooks readers from the opening courtroom scene of this tasty thriller, then spurs them through a fast trot across a story line that just keeps delivering."
PUBLISHERS WEEKLY ON *BY REASON OF INSANITY*

"[A] legal thriller that matches up easily with the best of Grisham."
CHRISTIAN FICTION REVIEW ON *IRREPARABLE HARM*

"*Directed Verdict* is a well-crafted courtroom drama with strong characters, surprising twists, and a compelling theme."
RANDY ALCORN, BESTSELLING AUTHOR OF *SAFELY HOME*

HE DEFIED AN EMPEROR

AND INSPIRED A FAITH

RANDY SINGER

A NOVEL

THE
ADVOCATE

TYNDALE HOUSE PUBLISHERS, INC.
CAROL STREAM, ILLINOIS

Visit Tyndale online at www.tyndale.com.

Visit Randy Singer's website at www.randysinger.net.

TYNDALE and Tyndale's quill logo are registered trademarks of Tyndale House Publishers, Inc.

The Advocate

Copyright © 2014 by Randy Singer. All rights reserved.

Cover photograph of coin copyright © by JosA Carlos Pires Pereira/Getty Images. All rights reserved.

Cover texture copyright © by Lost&Taken. All rights reserved.

Author photograph copyright © 2008 by Don Monteaux. All rights reserved.

Designed by Dean H. Renninger

The author is represented by the literary agency of Alive Communications, Inc., 7680 Goddard St., Suite 200, Colorado Springs, CO 80920, www.alivecommunications.com.

All Scripture quotations, unless otherwise indicated, are taken from the Holy Bible, *New International Version,*® *NIV.*® Copyright © 1973, 1978, 1984, 2011 by Biblica, Inc.® Used by permission of Zondervan. All rights reserved worldwide. www.zondervan.com.

Scripture quotations marked NLT are taken from the *Holy Bible*, New Living Translation, copyright © 1996, 2004, 2007, 2013 by Tyndale House Foundation. Used by permission of Tyndale House Publishers, Inc., Carol Stream, Illinois 60188. All rights reserved.

Some phrases that appear to be Scripture are an amalgam or paraphrase written by the author.

The Advocate is a work of fiction. Where real people, events, establishments, organizations, or locales appear, they are used fictitiously. All other elements of the novel are drawn from the author's imagination.

Library of Congress Cataloging-in-Publication Data

Singer, Randy (Randy D.)
   The advocate / Randy Singer.
      pages cm
   ISBN 978-1-4143-9130-4 (hc) — ISBN 978-1-4143-4860-5 (sc)
   1. Jesus Christ—Trials—Fiction. 2. Jesus Christ—Crucifixion—Fiction. 3. Lawyers—Fiction.
4. Trials—Fiction. 5. Legal stories. I. Title.
   PS3619.I5725A68 2014
   813'.6—dc23   2014001578

Printed in the United States of America

20	19	18	17	16	15	14
7	6	5	4	3	2	1

In memory of Lee Hough, agent and friend.

"Every time I think of you, I give thanks to my God."

PHILIPPIANS 1:3, NLT

Cast of Characters

• *Historical figure*
* *Fictional character*
† *Based on a historical figure about whom little is known*
‡ *Based on a historical figure whose name is unknown*

* **Adrianna**—a Vestal Virgin selected as matron by Emperor Caligula in AD 38

• **Agrippa**—grandson of Herod the Great; appointed to rule over Judea and Samaria by Emperor Claudius

• **Agrippina the Younger**—sister of Caligula, fourth wife of Claudius, and mother of Nero

• **Annas**—former chief priest of Israel who wields influence at the trial of Christ

† **Andronicus**—a leader of the church in Rome

† **Apronius**—Roman senator tried for treason during the reign of Tiberius

• **Caiaphas**—chief priest of Israel during the trial of Christ

• **Caligula**—emperor of Rome from AD 37–41

* **Calpurnia**—a Vestal Virgin, matron of the house from AD 28–38

† **Cato**—Roman senator who serves as consul in AD 36

• **Chaerea**—a member of the Praetorian Guard assigned to protect Caligula

• **Claudius**—emperor of Rome from AD 41–54

* **Cobius**—Roman gladiator from the same school as Mansuetus

• **Cornelius**—Roman centurion in Caesarea

† **Crispinus**—Roman senator who makes his fortune as a *delator*, prosecuting other senators for treason

* **Flavia**—a Vestal Virgin selected by Emperor Tiberius

† **Junia**—a leader of the church in Rome

* **Lucian Aurelius**—a boyhood friend of Caligula who later becomes a member of the Praetorian Guard

• **Lateranus**—Roman aristocrat pardoned and restored to his position by Nero

* **Longinus**—Roman centurion with Pilate during the trial of Christ

• **Macro**—prefect of the Praetorian Guard from AD 31–38

* **Mansuetus, the gladiator**—one of Rome's great gladiators during the reigns of Tiberius and Caligula

* **Mansuetus, the son**—a promising young advocate named after the gladiator

• **Marcus Lepidus**—a leading Roman senator during the reign of Tiberius

* **Marcus Serbius**—loyal childhood friend of Theophilus

• **Nero**—emperor of Rome from AD 54–68

† **Onesimus**—a slave to Philemon of Colossae and companion of the apostle Paul

• **Paul of Tarsus**—an apostle and leader in the early church

• **Pilate**—prefect of the Roman province of Judea from AD 26–36

† **Procula**—wife of Pilate

‡ **Quintus**—Roman centurion in charge of the execution of Jesus

† **Rubria**—a Vestal Virgin selected by the Emperor Caligula in AD 38

• **Sejanus**—a prefect of the Praetorian Guard and de facto ruler of Rome after Tiberius withdraws to the island of Capri

• **Seneca the Younger**—Roman philosopher and statesman

* **Sergius**—Roman soldier assigned to guard Paul

† **Theophilus**—a renowned Roman advocate who serves as an assessore for Pilate in Judea and later represents Paul in front of Nero

• **Tiberius**—emperor of Rome from AD 14–37

• **Tigellinus**—prefect of the Praetorian Guard from AD 62–68 and friend of Nero

THE
STUDENT

CHAPTER 1

IN THE ELEVENTH YEAR OF THE REIGN
OF TIBERIUS JULIUS CAESAR AUGUSTUS

I was fourteen years old when I learned what it meant to be crucified.

We hauled our own crossbeams, the twelve of us, students of Seneca the Younger, dragging them at least five miles down the cobblestones of the Appian Way. The day was hot and dry. Dust settled in our mouths and noses. I ground my teeth and felt the fine particles of dirt. I licked my dry lips, trying to moisten the thick white spit at the edge of my mouth. Sweat trickled down my face. Seneca marched ahead of us, carrying nothing but his waterskin, his sweat-soaked tunic sticking to his thick back. My own tunic was wet and grimy. My sandals squished with every step.

I had started out carrying my crossbeam, hoisting it across my thin shoulders, but I soon gave up and dragged it like most of the other students. It weighed nearly as much as me. The rough wood chafed my back, so I switched it from one shoulder to the other as I pulled it along. The only one who wasn't dragging his beam was Lucian, two years older than the rest of us and built like a gladiator. He balanced his beam on his shoulders, yet even Lucian was starting to stoop from the load.

To make it seem real, Seneca had arranged for a Roman legionnaire to bring up the rear. He was a humorless man, stocky and unshaven with nasty breath and a spiteful attitude. This was his chance to bark orders at the sons of aristocrats as if we were common slaves. If we stopped, he gave us a hard shove and cursed us. He took big gulps of water, taunting us with how refreshing it was, then spit much of it on the ground.

"When my parents learn of this, they'll have Seneca's head," Lucian said under his breath.

I was sure Seneca wasn't worried. His job was to mold us into young men fit to be Roman senators or commanders or magistrates. This was nothing compared to the military training that many of my contemporaries would be facing in a few years. Still, we were the sons of senators and equestrians, so we cast annoyed glances at each other. *Who does this man think he is, humiliating us this way?*

Caligula had the lightest beam to carry. Naturally. He was my age but a few inches taller, with spindly legs and a long, thin neck. His head, topped off with curly red hair, seemed oversized for his body. Caligula had a mean streak, so I generally kept my distance. There was an unwritten rule that he was never to be crossed—not because we feared the spoiled young man himself, but because we feared his family.

His full name was Gaius Julius Caesar Germanicus. He had been born on the battlefield in Gaul, the son of the great general Germanicus and his wife, Agrippina. It was the soldiers who had dubbed him Caligula, which meant "little sandals." He became a good luck charm of sorts for Germanicus's troops, and they would let him march into battle with them, staying near the rear of the lines. He was the great-nephew of the emperor and might one day be emperor himself if his mother managed to poison all the right relatives.

He was also a bully.

He had been taunting my friend Marcus earlier in the walk, taking his frustrations out on the smallest among us. Now he was just plain tired.

"This is outrageous," Caligula said more than once. Unlike Lucian, he said it loud enough for Seneca to hear. Yet our teacher ignored him and kept on walking. A few times Caligula stopped, and the legionnaire pushed him, though not as hard as he shoved the rest of us.

I kept my head down and focused on each step, counting to one hundred and then starting over again. I was in my usual spot at the front of the class, not far behind Seneca.

It was nearly noon when Seneca finally stopped by an open pasture on the side of the road near a small, cool stream. I dropped my beam on the ground and bent over, hands on my knees, trying to catch my breath.

Seneca allowed us to get a drink and told us to sit on our crossbeams. He stood in the middle of our little band. The sun nearly blinded me as I looked up at him.

Seneca wiped the sweat from his eyes and began the day's lesson. The legionnaire stood next to him, arms folded across his chest, scowling.

"You have all heard of the Third Servile War," Seneca said, "when Spartacus led a two-year slave rebellion against Rome. The Senate didn't take the slave rebellion seriously until it became clear that Rome itself was under threat."

Some of my friends fidgeted on their beams, trying to get comfortable after the long walk. Not me. I could listen to Seneca all day. His curly hair, round baby face, and small blue eyes made him seem as harmless as a child. But he had a commanding voice, and I loved his wit and cynicism in the same way that I imagined Cicero's students had once loved him. Armies destroyed people, and gladiators entertained them, but orators like Cicero and Seneca inspired them. One day I would do the same.

"Marcus Licinius Crassus was the richest man in the Senate, perhaps the richest man in Roman history," Seneca continued. "He had more than five hundred slaves and was an expert in architecture. He knew how to control fires by destroying the burning buildings and curtailing the spread of flames to nearby homes. When fire struck Rome, Crassus and his men ran to the flames and offered an option to the surrounding property owners. They could sell to young Crassus on the spot at a discounted rate, or they could watch their houses go up in flames. As soon as they shook hands on the deal, Crassus's slaves would extinguish the fire, and Crassus would reap his rewards."

"Brilliant," Caligula said.

Seneca shot him a look, but I knew Caligula didn't care.

"At the height of his wealth, Crassus was worth more than 200 million *sestertii*. And because he had built his fortune on the backs of slaves, he had a great incentive to quash Spartacus's rebellion. Since Rome's best generals were fighting in foreign lands, Crassus raised his own army to march against Spartacus and the rebel slaves. The first several battles did not go well for Crassus. At the first sign of trouble, his men abandoned their weapons and fled. To improve morale, Crassus revived the ancient practice of decimation. Lucian, what does that mean?"

"I am sorry, Master Seneca. What does what mean?"

Seneca let a few beats of silence show his displeasure. "*Decimation*. What is the origin of that word?"

Lucian frowned. "I do not know."

"Anyone?" Seneca asked.

I knew the answer, but I had learned long ago that it was sometimes better to hold my tongue. I kept my eyes down while Seneca surveyed the group.

"*Decimate* comes from the root word *decimare*, which means to take or destroy one-tenth," Seneca explained. He moved closer to us, and the sun behind him seemed to make him glow. "So Crassus divided his Roman legions into groups of ten and had them draw lots. The one to whom the lot fell would be stripped of his armor and beaten to death by the other nine. The fighting spirit of his troops increased dramatically. Crassus had demonstrated that he was more dangerous to them than their enemies."

Seneca now had everyone's attention. In my mind, I imagined the twelve of us drawing lots and the loser being beaten to death by the others. I didn't think I could bring myself to do it.

"Eventually, Crassus's men cornered Spartacus and his army.

Spartacus wanted to engage Crassus in battle, slaughtering his way toward the general's position. But the overwhelming numbers were too much for the slaves. Spartacus died in battle before he reached Crassus. Six thousand slaves were captured."

I had been taught for as long as I could remember to despise Spartacus and the bloody revolt he had started. The uprising was an affront to every Roman citizen. But there was always a part of me that cheered for the slaves—my natural desire to root for the disadvantaged. I secretly wished that Spartacus had been able to run the gauntlet and engage Crassus one-on-one, the way real men fight.

"Crassus wanted to make sure no slave in the empire would ever revolt again," Seneca said. "And so he perfected the art of crucifixion."

He paused for effect, and we all knew something unusual was coming. It was why our parents paid handsomely for us to attend this school. Seneca was famous for his memorable stunts.

"Even though you're not old enough to attend the games and see the live executions there, I'm sure many of you have seen criminals hanging on crosses outside the walls of the city. Still, I thought it might be interesting for Gallus to tell you how it's done."

The legionnaire named Gallus stepped forward, directly in front of where I was sitting. *Why is it always me?* I stared at the black hair on his legs, the worn sandals, the calloused feet.

"Stand up!" he said gruffly.

I stood, looking him squarely in the eye.

He picked up my crossbeam and placed it in the middle of the group. He pulled a hammer from his belt and a long, sharp spike from his sack.

"Lie down on the beam," he said. "Arms stretched out on the wood."

I looked at Seneca, who nodded slightly.

"Need any help?" Caligula asked the legionnaire.

"You want to take his place?" Gallus shot back.

"Not really."

"Then shut up."

I lay down on the beam, arms stretched wide, keeping an eye on Gallus. The legionnaire knelt beside me, hammer in one hand, spike in the other. "We use six-inch spikes," he said, pressing the point against my left wrist.

"Come here and hold this," he said to another student. It was Marcus, my skinny friend. Because he had struggled carrying his beam, he had been berated by Gallus most of the morning.

Marcus got up and held the spike over my wrist, his hand trembling.

"Nervous?" Gallus asked him.

"Yes, sir."

"You've got nothing to worry about. It's your friend here who should be worried."

Gallus snorted a laugh, but I wasn't concerned. I knew Seneca would only let this go so far. Maybe the soldier would draw a little blood, but Seneca would never let him drive a spike through my wrist.

"We've found," Gallus said, eyeing the other boys, "that when we sever the nerve that runs up your wrist, it causes unbearable pain. Plus, when we put the spike here, it's lodged between two bones, so it won't just rip out of the arm."

"The pain is so severe," Seneca said helpfully, "that a new word was invented to describe it. Our word *excruciatus* literally means 'out of the cross.'"

Gallus went on to explain the details of the process. How the feet would be impaled. How the prisoner would literally suffocate, his body sagging under its own weight as he lost the strength to push up against the nails in order to draw breath. "We usually let 'em hang for about three days. They typically die on the second day, and then the birds have a snack on day three. Any questions?"

There were none.

Gallus swung his hammer. I closed my eyes and cringed. He

stopped it a few inches from the spike and laughed. He allowed me to get up and return on wobbly knees to my original spot as he described all the configurations he and his fellow soldiers had used to crucify prisoners.

"Okay," Seneca finally said, "I think they've got the picture."

Gallus stepped back, and Seneca continued the lesson. "Crassus still holds the record," Seneca said. "He put six thousand men on crosses, every one of the slaves he had captured, and lined the Appian Way with them—from here all the way back to Rome."

The teacher paused and let the enormity of that sink in. We had been walking for miles. At one time this entire distance had been lined with dying men.

"Crassus and his men rode through the gauntlet of the crucified, while the slaves cried out for mercy, begging to be thrust through with a spear. Cheering crowds greeted Crassus in Rome, where he was crowned with a laurel wreath and hailed as a *triumphator*. He sacrificed a white bull at the temple of Jupiter, and the entire city celebrated for days. It was said that three days after the slaves' bodies were discarded, you could still smell the stench."

Seneca looked over our heads, down the Appian Way, as if he could imagine the scene. "And so I have a question for you," he said, his voice lower. "Should Romans crucify people? Is this the type of conduct befitting the most advanced civilization the world has ever known?"

I was looking at Seneca, but I noticed Gallus out of the corner of my eye. He seemed to stiffen at the very suggestion that his cherished method of execution might be open to question.

I hoped Seneca wouldn't call on me. Everything inside me said that crucifixion was not worthy of the glory of Rome. How could we inflict such torture on our enemies? What separated us from the barbarians when we committed such acts? And what about the innocent men condemned to die for something they didn't do? Our system of justice wasn't perfect.

But I didn't want to seem weak in front of my classmates. Seneca's little display, complete with Gallus as a prop, was designed to show us how horrible it was to die this way. Yet we were Romans. We weren't supposed to flinch in the face of death, no matter how horrible. One sign of manhood was being able to stomach this kind of gore, even relish it.

"I'll answer that," Caligula said, standing.

"Very well, Gaius," Seneca replied. He never used his pupil's nickname.

"Have there been any slave revolts since the triumph of Crassus over Spartacus?" Caligula asked. The question, of course, was a rhetorical one, a method of argumentation that Seneca had taught us.

"I was born on a battlefield," Caligula continued. "I have seen wars. Men die. Their heads are cut off and their guts are ripped out. Only the strong survive. There is nothing pretty about it and nothing philosophical to debate."

That last comment was a dig at Seneca, and I wondered what he would do about it. As usual, our teacher didn't flinch.

"The only criticism I have of Crassus," Caligula continued, "is that he wasted a lot of good wood on a bunch of slaves."

He stood there for a moment, proud of his wit. He smirked and sat down.

Seneca scanned the young faces before him. "Does anybody disagree?" he asked.

I knew I should stay seated. Nothing would be gained from picking a fight with Caligula. Lucian would undoubtedly come to Caligula's defense—if not now, then later, when Seneca wasn't looking. Others would join them because they were intimidated by them. The only student who might agree with me would be little Marcus, and having him on my side was sometimes more trouble than it was worth.

But I couldn't be silent, could I? If I held my tongue now, what would I do when the stakes really mattered?

I stood, certain that Caligula was rolling his eyes. "I disagree," I said as forcefully as possible.

"For some reason, Theophilus," Seneca said, "I am not the least bit surprised."

⸺ CHAPTER 2 ⸺

I faced Seneca, trying to block the other boys out of my peripheral vision. I knew I should be careful because Caligula was petulant and didn't like to be made the fool. But when I had an audience, I couldn't resist showing off a little.

I stood to my full height and spoke using my orator's voice, as Seneca had taught me.

"'Let us not listen to those who think we ought to be angry with our enemies and who believe this to be great and manly,'" I said. "'Nothing is so praiseworthy, nothing so clearly shows a great and noble soul, as clemency and readiness to forgive.'"

A few of my classmates groaned at my eloquence. No matter; Seneca had taught me not to be distracted by a hostile audience.

"Those are the words of Cicero, and those are also words of truth and reason," I said proudly. "Roman virtues should include not only justice and courage but forgiveness and mercy."

"Spoken like someone who has never seen a battle, never seen a friend decapitated by a barbarian," Seneca countered. He paced a little, gauging the expressions of the students. "Cicero, not coincidentally, had never seen the battlefield either. So doesn't young Gaius have a point? Rome did not conquer the world with etiquette and Senate resolutions. We extended our civilization, including our cherished adherence to Roman law, by brutal force."

Seneca locked his eyes on me. "How can one claim to honor the law yet not support the forms of punishment that ensure others will follow it?" He pointed behind me to the Appian Way. "Roads like that do not appear from thin air. They are built. Built by slaves, as was your father's estate, Theophilus. There can be no advance without civilization, no civilization without order, and no order without punishment."

I didn't know if Seneca actually felt this way or if he was just challenging my thinking. He was always hard on students like me, ones who thought we could hold our own. In my opinion, he let students like Caligula off too easy, simply because they weren't willing to try.

I wanted to note that Seneca had never been in battle either. He probably wouldn't have lasted one day on a forced march. He had the soft body of a philosopher, though his mind was tempered steel.

"Germanicus Julius Caesar was one of the greatest generals Rome has ever seen," I said. This was Caligula's father, a revered warrior who had died from poisoning when Caligula was only seven, and I noticed Caligula stir. He scowled and leaned forward as if I had crossed some sacred line just by mentioning his father's name.

"Germanicus became consul because of his triumph in Germania. Yet when he traveled to Alexandria, he saw the starvation of the people there, and he opened the granaries so they could eat. They worshiped him like a pharaoh, and if he had stayed, they might have made him a god. But Caesar was angry because Rome would now see less of the corn supply."

"Is this just a history lesson," Seneca asked, "or do you have a point?"

"My point is this: It is the kindness of Germanicus rather than the brutality of Crassus that best represents the heart of Rome. Germanicus would not have crucified those slaves. You can fight barbarians without becoming one."

I stood facing Seneca with my chest thrust out, proud of my little speech. Even though there was an unwritten rule that we didn't talk about the suspicious circumstances of Germanicus's death, I thought mentioning his name in this context would be acceptable. My argument was especially clever because his own son Caligula had been the one who had argued so peevishly that crucifying the slaves was right. Maybe even Caligula would think twice about it now.

All might have been well if Seneca had just allowed it to end there. But the man never let us savor a moment of oratorical triumph. When we felt the most pride, he would cut our legs out from under us and make us feel small again.

"You have chosen an interesting example, Theophilus. But I must ask: Was what Germanicus did legal? Should he have even been in Alexandria? Or have you premised your argument on a violation of the very laws you would have us honor?"

We all knew the answers to those questions, yet I did not want to say them aloud. The orphaned son of Germanicus was sitting less than twelve feet away.

But what was the truth? That's what Seneca had drilled into me in the past two years of training. If we got confused, he said, it was probably because we were considering extraneous issues that were clouding our judgment. His advice was to find the truth and cling to it. He gave us one question to ask, one question to guide our answers to life's most difficult issues.

What is true?

"It was not legal, Master Seneca. Alexandria was important to Germanicus because of his ancestry as a descendant of Mark Antony. But Caesar Augustus's laws forbade the entry of any member of the ruling class into Alexandria."

"Was Germanicus a criminal, then?"

I didn't hesitate. "He was."

It was the truth. But sometimes the truth has unintended consequences.

— CHAPTER 3 —

I didn't see him coming.

Caligula attacked me from the side, cursing about what I had said. He drove me to the ground and climbed on top, punching my face before I could even react. I raised my arms to block the blows, but he pulled one arm away and drove his fist into my cheek. I heard the thud of bone on bone. I tasted blood and saw stars.

I turned my head and tried to block the blows, but Caligula was maniacal, pummeling me with his right fist. The other boys had gathered around, and I thought I saw Marcus trying to help me. But someone was holding him back.

Seneca?

Nobody was going to rescue me, and I wanted to cry. Caligula hunkered over me now, still landing blows. I managed to cover my head with my forearm, curling into a little ball on my side, pulling my knees up to my stomach. Surely if I went into the fetal position, he would stop. Instead, he kicked me in the ribs and drove his fist into my ear. I felt it pop, a sharp pain that made me yelp.

Somehow little Marcus broke through and pushed Caligula in the back, knocking him off-balance. Lucian grabbed Marcus and threw him away from the two of us. But my friend had given me enough of an opening so I could scramble to my feet and lunge at Caligula.

This time I was the crazed animal. I had tasted blood and humiliation. I had nothing left to lose. I had been trained in gymnastics and wrestling, and though Caligula outweighed me by nearly fifteen pounds, I was wiry and filled with adrenaline. I threw him to the ground and put him in a cradle move I had perfected. I wrapped one arm around his head and the other around his legs. He tried to scratch at me, but I squeezed him tighter and put my full weight on top of his body, punching him with little blows in the face with the same arm I had wrapped around his legs.

"Enough!" Seneca barked.

I let go and sprang to my feet, wiping the blood from my mouth. I kept one eye on Caligula, ready for him to jump up and attack.

Instead, he started shaking. At first they were small spasms, but they soon became full convulsions, his hands wrenched at odd angles, his wrists bent forward, fingers clawing at the air. I stood there, my mouth agape. His head was tipped back and he was foaming at the mouth.

"Stand back," Seneca demanded, stepping in to kneel beside his student.

I backed away, shuddering at what I had done. *Was he dying?*

Seneca put a hand under Caligula's head, tilting it back. He pulled out his waterskin and jammed it between Caligula's teeth. He grabbed Caligula's tongue.

"It's parliamentary disease," Seneca said breathlessly. "We need a doctor."

I stared for a moment, horrified and guilt-ridden at the scene before me. "Come on," I said to Marcus and took off running down the Appian Way toward the city. I was probably the fastest kid in the class. Plus, I felt personally responsible for whatever Caligula was going through. *Had I just killed the great-nephew of the emperor?*

I soon outdistanced Marcus, fueled by the fear of what I had done, running so fast my lungs started burning. I passed an array of travelers—merchants with wagons pulled by mules, a lone horseman, a bleary-eyed family trudging along, a group of actors, a small regiment of soldiers. With every group, I breathlessly asked if any of them were doctors or if they knew where one might be found. I barely slowed down long enough to get an answer.

The picture of Caligula squirming on the ground, his eyes rolled back in his head, would not leave my mind. I ran faster, parched with thirst, my muscles beginning to fail. "I need a doctor!" I yelled at every traveler.

I don't know how long I ran. It might have been ten minutes or it might have been thirty. Finally I found a man who claimed to be a physician riding with a small caravan. He was probably the personal physician for the family inside the litter. Gasping for air, I explained what had happened.

When I mentioned the name Caligula, the physician's gray eyebrows shot up and he interrupted me. "Did you say Caligula, son of Germanicus?"

"Yes! And he's having an attack right now!"

The man quickly got permission from the family in the litter, pulled me up on the back of his horse, and spurred the animal into a gallop down the road. I hung on as best I could, being jostled about as we flew by Marcus, who was headed in the other direction. I yelled at him, and he turned around with big eyes and outstretched palms. I waved for him to hustle back and join us.

My mind was racing faster than the horse on the way back to my companions. I could only imagine the worst. Caligula had died. I was responsible. Seneca would be blamed as well for not taking action sooner. I prayed to the gods that they might somehow spare the lives of both Caligula and me.

When we arrived at the site, I was relieved beyond words to see Caligula and the others sitting there talking as if nothing had happened. Sweaty and shaking, I climbed down from the horse, and my knees nearly buckled from stress and exhaustion.

Seneca pulled the physician aside, and they exchanged a few words. Caligula would not look at me.

My relief lasted only a few moments. The physician decided that the only way to be sure the episode had passed was to remove the vicious humor by bleeding. He pulled out a surgical knife and a bleeding cup from a pouch on his horse, and I watched Caligula turn white.

Caligula told Seneca he felt fine. He demanded that the physician not touch him. But Seneca ignored him. The doctor had a determined and calming authority that came from age. Caligula frowned, shot me a hate-filled glance, and did as he was told.

The doctor sat down next to Caligula and clasped the boy's left wrist. He had Caligula look away. Seneca held a bowl under Caligula's forearm. With the knife, the doctor made a surgical slice in the arm that left me woozy as I watched. Caligula winced but tried to play it tough.

The bright-red blood flowed into the physician's bowl until the doctor was satisfied that Caligula had suffered enough. He pressed a cloth onto the wound, and the cloth itself soon turned crimson, staining the hands of the doctor.

I looked away. My stomach was knotted and twisted, the world starting to spin. After everything that had already gone wrong, I didn't want to pass out in front of my friends. I sat down, put my head between my knees, and stared at the ground, forcing myself to think about something else.

The next thing I knew, the doctor's hand was on the back of my neck.

"Just take a few deep breaths," he said.

I looked up, and though the world was still blurry and swimming, I managed to keep myself from passing out. My right eye was swollen half-shut, and my ear ached. My cheekbone hurt as well, and I wondered if it was broken.

The doctor looked me over and told me that I would be fine.

Seneca thanked the man and paid him handsomely. Then he made Caligula and me shake hands and apologize.

I looked Caligula straight in the eye and told him I was sorry for speaking ill of his father. His handshake was weak, and though he had a few inches on me, I felt embarrassed for what I had done to him earlier. He was only sticking up for a father who had been murdered by a coward.

"I know you were only answering the questions you were asked," Caligula said to me. His words were deliberate, and his face still looked white from the loss of blood. I sensed a bitterness lurking just beneath the surface. "I'm sorry for beating you up," he said.

It was a face-saving move. A reminder that until Marcus had intervened, Caligula was getting the better of me.

But nobody who had been there would remember it that way. I had wrestled him to the ground, and he had gone into convulsions. He needed the doctor, not I.

"Apology accepted," I said confidently.

Yet from the look on Caligula's face, I knew I had not heard the last of the matter.

── CHAPTER 4 ──

I slept fitfully that night in the barracks, my mind racing with the implications of what had transpired earlier that day. My emotions pulled me in different directions. I was proud of sticking up for myself, yet I felt sorry for Caligula. It was not easy seeing him writhing uncontrollably on the ground with everyone gawking at him. We had all been sworn to secrecy about the disease, but I knew it would be hard to keep it quiet.

The pain from my swollen face and ear reminded me that I'd had no choice but to retaliate. Seneca had handled things the same way a time or two before—allowed some of the students to fight it out and shake hands afterward. I think Seneca knew I could handle Caligula, or maybe he thought I needed to be toughened up a little. But now, hours later, the problem wasn't with me. Caligula was the one not willing to let it drop.

He had made no attempt to hide his contempt for me throughout the rest of the day. I saw him huddling with Lucian and others, making plans and casting glances my way. Retaliation was in the air, and the other boys started distancing themselves from me—

except, of course, my friend Marcus, who followed me around like a shadow.

I decided to lie awake all night on the theory that Caligula and his friends would strike under cover of darkness. But the day's activities had been taxing, and the steady breathing of the others in the barracks made staying awake difficult. I don't remember when I dozed off, but my exhausted body could not obey the demands of my paranoid mind.

I definitely remember when I woke up.

They dragged me from my bunk and threw me to the floor before I knew what was happening. Somebody wrenched my hands behind my back while one of my attackers stuffed a rag in my mouth. A third tied a blindfold over my eyes. I tried to scream, but my shouts were muffled by the gag. I felt a heavy knee in the middle of my back while somebody else pinned my head to the floor with his elbow. My attackers quickly tied my wrists together behind my back, whispering to each other as they worked. They tied my ankles as well and pulled my gag tight, knotting the cloth behind my head.

I was terrified, my heart beating out of my chest.

They turned me on my side and somebody kicked me in the gut, forcing the wind out of my lungs.

They pulled at the ropes on my ankles and wrists. I kicked and squirmed, but my movements only brought more pressure from all sides, strong hands holding me in place, pressing me against the floor. Someone tied my wrists and ankles together in one big knot in the middle of my back. I stopped squirming and told myself to just breathe.

They grabbed my arms and legs and carried me, facedown, out the barracks door and down the street. It sounded like the footsteps of ten or twelve boys at the very least. I could hear them whispering and laughing and arguing over which direction they should go.

I tried to calm myself by recalling all the pranks we had played on each other. I seldom participated because I was busy studying, but I had been the brunt of some of these in the past, and I told myself that this time would be no different. Seneca had trained us in Stoicism, and that meant I knew how to detach myself from suffering or humiliation.

In theory.

But in fact, my mind raced with fear about what my classmates had in mind. Underneath the blindfold, my eyes watered from the crushing humiliation of being singled out and picked on by everyone else. They were laughing at me, having a grand time at my expense. I was the one who had never learned to fit in. The kid with only one true friend in the whole school.

It seemed like they carried me for a long time, pausing occasionally so they could take turns bearing my weight. Finally they stopped and placed me facedown on the ground. They rolled me on my side and cut the cords binding my wrists and ankles together. I felt the blood rushing back to my hands, and I could straighten my legs again. They cut the rope that bound my wrists, and I jerked my arms free—struggling, swinging—but there were too many of them, and they pinned down my arms. They rolled me onto my back, still blindfolded and gagged, and I felt a beam under my shoulders.

That's when I knew what was happening. I was going to be crucified!

The whispering was more frantic now, and I heard a few voices I thought I recognized. Adrenaline shot through my veins but I couldn't struggle free. Surely somebody would stop this madness! They would laugh at how they had scared me and then had let me go—humiliated but unhurt. They wouldn't really nail me to a cross.

Would they?

I heard somebody mention a hammer, which chilled me and made every muscle in my body contract. The gag turned my cries for help into muffled groans. I heard them nailing a small block of wood to the vertical post of the cross, somewhere below my feet. I was crying harder now, breathing in short sobs. They stretched my arms out to the sides and wrenched them over the top of the crossbeam, tying my wrists to the beam so that my triceps rested on top of the wood. They tied my legs to the vertical post, the ropes cutting into me just below my knees and at my ankles.

"Move that block up a little," I heard someone say. But the others argued that it was fine where it was.

There was no mistaking this for a harmless prank. Seneca had told us that some prisoners hung on their crosses for days while others died within a matter of hours. My shame and humiliation were overcome by the terror that I might actually die. I was fourteen years old. How could this be happening to me?

Then, in the midst of this bone-chilling terror, there was a brief flicker of hope. I was lying there on the cross, tied to the crossbar and vertical beam, gagged and blindfolded, but there were no longer any hands on me. Maybe they were just going to leave me there and let me be discovered by some passerby. My humiliation would be complete, but at least there would be no fear of dying like a common criminal.

I could sense that my attackers had stepped away for a moment and were huddling about something. Would they cut me free and run away before I took the blindfold off, figuring that I had learned my lesson?

But then I sensed somebody leaning over me. I felt the sharp point of something scratch my side and knew they had cut off my *subligar*, the knotted loincloth that I had worn to bed. I was now lying there naked, utterly humiliated, wishing I could somehow cover myself.

Several of them lifted the cross and turned it over so that I was hanging from it facedown. They unknotted the blindfold and took out the gag. It was dark outside, almost pitch-black, and my attackers were all behind me. I tried to look over my shoulder, but they were already lifting the cross up, and I was disoriented.

I didn't cry out. I would not give them the satisfaction of hearing me beg. Tears rolled down my cheeks in the darkness, but I clenched my jaw and kept my silence—anger and defiance pushing aside the fear.

The pressure on my arms and chest made it hard to breathe. I looked down, and I could make out the heads of Caligula and at least a half-dozen other boys. I used to think that some of them were my friends. I had defended them when Seneca pressed too hard. I had suffered with them as we learned to endure hardship together.

But now they were all helping to lift the cross and secure its base into a hole they had apparently dug in the ground earlier that night.

When the cross jarred into place, it felt like my arms tore away from my shoulder joints. My assailants knelt down and packed in the dirt around the foot of the cross, bracing it so it wouldn't lean.

The pressure on my chest and arms was nearly unbearable. The only way I could breathe was to tense all my muscles and pull up using my arms, taking one gasping breath before I sagged back down. When I sagged, there was a small block of wood that my feet could barely touch. I could rest there for a moment, though I couldn't draw a deep breath in that position.

Most of my tormentors lingered in back of the cross, but Caligula and Lucian stepped in front and looked up at me. In the shadows from the moon and stars I could see Caligula's sneer. "Next time," he said, "show a little respect."

I raised myself up, pain burning my chest and shoulders. My arms were already starting to go numb.

"I showed you no disrespect," I said. "Please. I'm not a criminal." I gasped for air. "You have proven your point. Let me down."

Caligula scoffed. "You're a great believer in the Fates. Perhaps the Fates will save you now." He motioned to the others, and they all started walking away.

I raised myself up again and called out after them, naming the ones I had thought were my friends. One of the boys picked up a rock and threw it at me, and a few others joined in. Caligula watched for a moment, then told them to stop. They all walked down the road and left.

I looked around with tears in my eyes, trying to get my bearings.

I was on the side of a dirt road and seemed to be about a half mile from the torches of the city. They had placed the cross in plain sight so that when the merchants came in the early morning with their carts of grain and vegetables, I would be discovered. But I didn't know if I could survive that long. When I sagged down so my feet could rest on the block of wood, I felt like my chest would collapse and my arms would be ripped from their sockets. I had to flex my arms and rise up to take some of the weight off my shoulders. But every time I did that, scraping my back against the rough wood of the cross, I could feel more strength being sapped from my body.

Before long, stabbing pains shot through my triceps, shoulders, and chest with each breath. I forced myself to rise, breathe, cry for help, and sag back down. Each time it got a little harder. Each time I felt myself getting a little more desperate. The humiliation and anger at my supposed friends had been replaced by a relentless pain and a single overriding goal.

I just wanted to survive.

I followed this agonizing routine for what seemed like an eternity. My breathing became shallow. Before long, I couldn't even cry out for help.

I closed my eyes and prayed to the gods. What a humiliating death! Hanging there, exposed like a common criminal or a rebellious slave. I was the son of an equestrian! I was a Roman citizen! Surely if I died, Caligula and his cohorts would receive the most extreme punishment.

But I wasn't ready to die.

I started imagining things. I kept seeing the face of Caligula, at first mocking me and then breaking into convulsions. I thought about my mother and little sister—the pain they would feel if I didn't survive this. My father would be furious, out for revenge.

In that delirious state, when I first heard the voice, it was hard to know whether it was real or imagined.

"Theophilus! Theophilus!"

I felt a stick tap against my shin, and somehow it jolted me back to reality. I looked down and saw him standing there. I recognized the curly blond hair and the reed-thin body. He had a look of shock and worry on his face. He glanced over his shoulder as if my attackers might come back at any minute and put him on a cross as well.

"How do I get you down?" Marcus asked.

"Hurry" was all I could manage.

He shinnied up and untied my ankles first and eventually my wrists. It felt so good just to breathe again.

By the time my feet hit the ground, I was swirling with emotion. Pain still stabbed at my shoulders and chest. I felt gratitude for a friend who had put himself at risk to save me. But mostly I was furious at Caligula, Lucian, and their cohorts.

I wanted revenge. I wanted them to pay. What had I done to deserve being crucified? I knew Caligula and his family were powerful, but how could I keep my mouth shut about this?

"What are you going to do?" Marcus asked.

"I'm going home," I said through gritted teeth. I found my *subligar* on the ground and tied it on. I was in no shape to be walking all the way home, but I wasn't going back to the barracks. "You should come with me."

I could tell by the look in his eyes that Marcus didn't like the tone of my voice. He was willing to risk everything to save a friend, but he didn't really want to squeal on his classmates.

"We can't let them get away with this," I said.

— CHAPTER 5 —

None of the lessons Seneca taught me about Roman justice compared to the lesson I learned following my own crucifixion.

Marcus and I both returned that night to our families and reported what had happened. My two dislocated shoulders, the scrapes on my back, and the scars around my ankles and wrists left no doubt about my story. My mother looked at my swollen face with dismay and shock. My ribs hurt too, and I assumed that was from the beating I had taken from Caligula before I started fighting back.

Yet Caligula's family proved too powerful for the charges to stick. His mother, Agrippina the Elder, was the granddaughter of Augustus Caesar and the stepdaughter of Emperor Tiberius Caesar.

She was the same Agrippina who had lived on the battlefield with her husband while Rome fought the Germanic tribes. It was on those battlefields that the boy nicknamed "Little Sandals" had been born. After Germanicus died, Agrippina claimed that an aristocrat named Piso had poisoned her husband, and all of Rome believed her, though Piso remained in Syria. Agrippina had returned from Antioch with the ashes of her dead husband, Germanicus, in an urn. His body had been cremated, though it was said in Rome that his heart had been untouched by the flames. The emperor bestowed on his widow the title "the Glory of My Country."

My family was no match for the woman whose fame rivaled that of Tiberius Caesar. And in Rome, family status mattered more than justice.

Seneca wanted to ban Caligula from the school, but Agrippina wouldn't hear of it. Caligula denied that he and his friends had anything to do with my crucifixion. "Surely the family of Theophilus has other enemies," he claimed. "Perhaps they broke into the barracks and took him away in the middle of the night."

Lucian claimed that on other nights he had seen me sneaking out of the barracks to engage in some kind of mischief in the city. He said that I would normally return just before dawn. That's why he didn't worry about it when he saw my empty cot. Two other boys confirmed his story. The rest, all except Marcus, claimed they didn't know anything.

The patronage of Germanicus's family was far more important to the school than my own family's, so ultimately Caligula was believed. Seneca resigned in protest, drawing the ire of Agrippina and elevating the entire incident so that the tongues of every gossip in Rome could talk of little else. It was widely reported that Caligula and I had fought and that I had been crucified later that night.

But word of Caligula's parliamentary disease did not leak out.

Though my father pulled me from the school, I had already become notorious. I would be walking down the street and would notice others walking toward me, whispering to each other. I had no doubt what they were talking about.

"That's the boy who got crucified. He'll probably be scarred forever."

Marcus was also yanked from the school formerly taught by Seneca, but unlike me, he followed the great teacher to a new school of rhetoric. My parents decided that I needed a fresh start outside Rome so the controversy could die down. They sold a field adjacent to the Tiber—a piece of land that had been in the family for decades—so they could send me to Greece, where I could complete my training in rhetoric and law.

"You are going to the school founded by Apollonius Molon in Rhodes," my father told me one night. My heart leapt at the news. "It's where Julius Caesar became a great orator and received his education in Roman law. It's also—"

"Where Cicero studied," I interrupted. "Cicero went to Rhodes as a stuttering boy and left as a rhetorical genius."

Since the night of my crucifixion, I had wallowed in self-pity. Seneca had tried to teach me not to trust my emotions. But I couldn't keep from feeling sorry for myself and angry that Caligula and his gang would go unpunished. I had heard my parents talking about sending me out of the country, and I hadn't wanted to leave. But I had never expected this!

"When do I leave?" I asked.

"First thing in the morning."

✝

It took less than a week at the Molon School of Rhetoric for the novelty to wear off. This was going to be a lot of hard work! The Greeks believed in discipline of body, mind, and soul. Unlike Seneca, who seemed to have a halfhearted belief in Stoicism, the Greeks took their Stoicism seriously. Virtue, they claimed, was sufficient for happiness, and nothing except virtue was good.

At the Molon School, they frowned on the emotional and flowery rhetoric of the other great rhetorical institution—the Asiatic School. Our instructors sarcastically called the Asiatic teachers "the dancing masters." We were told to hold our heads high, argue our points with confidence, appeal briefly to their emotions, and then sit down. They told us the same thing that Apollonius Molon had told Cicero more than a hundred years earlier: nothing dries more quickly than a tear.

At first I loved the rhetorical training but hated the grueling physical regimen. Yet after a few months, as my body transformed under the watchful care of my instructors, I came to appreciate the physical aspects as well.

In Rome, training in gymnastics was mostly reserved for young men preparing for military service. Not so with the Greeks. They believed in whipping every young man's body into shape. They embraced gymnastics for its own virtues—self-discipline, the molding of the body, the pure joy of competition. My instructors believed that to be a great orator one must also be in peak physical condition.

We started each day before dawn with a large breakfast of hard-boiled eggs, rare meat, roasted grain, and goat's milk. They had a saying at the school: eat breakfast like a king, lunch like a commoner, and dinner like a slave. After breakfast, we began our studies and voice exercises. We would often recite our passages by the sea so that we could develop volume and project our voices. Later in the morning, once the sun had risen and the heat became a factor, we recited the same passages while walking uphill so that we learned how to maintain our tone and volume even when short of breath.

The afternoons found us training in the gymnasium. I had studied gymnastics and wrestling in Rome, but my previous training paled in comparison to this. Every day brought a new form of competition. I became more than proficient at *pancratium*, the sport of hand-to-hand combat that combined boxing and wrestling. I often dreamed of using my newfound skills against Caligula or even Lucian. My frame was not large enough to beat the best students in the school, but I learned to hold my own against students my size.

In Rome, the sons of aristocrats loved being spectators, watching the slaves do battle in the arena or race the chariots. Romans exercised out of necessity, keeping their bodies in shape because that's what self-disciplined Romans did. But the Greeks still believed in the body beautiful. At least at the Molon School, physical training was an obsession, and it was one I learned to enjoy.

The Molon School also improved my confidence. Here there was no shame in being the first to raise your hand and engage your tutor more pointedly than the others. It was at Rhodes, on the edge of the Aegean Sea, that I learned self-confidence and became a man.

It was there that I learned about the Greek gods. My favorite was Apollo, the god of music, oracles, sun, medicine, light, and knowledge. Apollo was the giver of prophecy and oratory. For example, Epimenides, a Greek herdsman, fell asleep for fifty-six years and woke with the gift of prophecy from Apollo. He later uttered the immortal words about Zeus: "In him we live and move and have our being."

Unlike Epimenides, I didn't get much sleep at Molon. But my shoulders slowly healed by the shores of the Aegean, with the exception of a sharp pain that would sometimes shoot across the front of my left shoulder when I tried to lift something heavy over my head.

Like Epimenides, I was awakened to my own gifts in the Molon School and at the temple of Apollo. My body and soul grew there, and I consider those years to be among the happiest of my life.

PART II

THE
MENTOR

ROME, SIX YEARS LATER

CHAPTER 6

IN THE SEVENTEENTH YEAR OF THE REIGN
OF TIBERIUS JULIUS CAESAR AUGUSTUS

I was twenty years old when I returned to Rome, ready to change the world. Fully trained in rhetoric and a master of laws, I dreamed of becoming an advocate in the Roman courts or perhaps a master teacher like Seneca.

But Rome was not the same city I remembered leaving. Or perhaps I had changed—it was hard to tell. Either way, the contrast between the beautiful island of Rhodes in the Aegean Sea and the bustling and sweaty metropolis of Rome made me look at the city with fresh eyes.

Unlike the relative quiet of Greece, Rome was a cacophony of sounds that made it hard to concentrate during the day or sleep at night. Shopkeepers hawked their goods, beggars recited their incantations, construction workers hammered at all hours, pupils repeated their singsong lyrics as they learned to read in the open-air balconies, and all night long there was shouting from the baths and the creaking and clamor of heavy wagons and carts on the cobblestone streets. I leased a small flat on a narrow street, and my transition back to city life was a sleepless one. The poets said, "God made the country, and man made the cities." Even a glorious city like Rome showed how inferior an architect man had turned out to be.

But for all its drawbacks, Rome was still the capital of the civilized world, and for someone with ambition and dreams, there was no better place to start a career.

During my first week back, I spent my leisure time in the Forum. I marveled at how the citizens of Rome had lost the awe of their own architectural wonders. Merchants set up their stalls in front of the marvelous temples or around the steps of the basilicas. Games played on the marble porticoes sometimes required scratching boundaries or scores into the pillars or steps. In the shadow of the greatest architectural feats of the world, there was no wide-eyed wonder—just the constant hum of thousands of Romans trying to make a living.

Yet I had been away long enough that I walked these same streets with a newfound appreciation for the history and influence of the place.

On one of those days I climbed the steps of the Rostra, a platform about eighty feet long and eleven feet high, adorned with bronze rams pillaged from the bows of the great ships captured in war. It was here that emperors made their pronouncements and politicians argued their cases. Here great eulogies had been delivered. Here the bloody, decapitated heads of conquered kings had been displayed.

I stood in the middle of the platform, ignored by the people scrambling below me. I imagined myself addressing the citizens on a matter of grave importance, employing the same skills that Cicero had exhibited years earlier, skills I had learned in the same school. I was struck by the fact that this one spot might be the most influential place on the face of the earth, that the greatest orators ever known to mankind had stood right here and looked out at these same buildings and changed the course of history. Someday, if the Fates were willing, I would do the same.

But first I needed a job. And for that, I had no greater prospect than my upcoming meeting with Seneca.

During my six years in Greece, my former teacher had navigated his way into far greater prominence than when I had left. He had also assured me, in letters we had exchanged, that he still had a soft spot for one of his most conscientious erstwhile students.

✝

"You look well!" Seneca said, grabbing me by the shoulders and giving me a squeeze.

"As do you," I replied. We both knew I was taking a bit of liberty with the truth. He looked roughly the same as before, except he had put on a few more pounds. His curly hair had retreated farther up his long forehead, and he now sported a double chin and noticeably more wrinkles.

We stood in the center of his house, in a splendid rectangular atrium with marble columns and an elaborate fountain. The floor consisted of slabs of colored marble tiles arranged in geometric patterns and polished to highlight the grain. Near the fountain, Seneca proudly displayed purple marble imported from Egypt, worth more per slab than my entire flat. Expensive paintings lined the walls, and statues adorned the pillars.

I followed Seneca down a long hall and up several steps to the office where he transacted business. The room overlooked a large courtyard, exquisitely manicured. All this for a man who espoused Stoicism and decried the luxuries of life.

We spent the first few hours discussing the training I had received in Rhodes, and it felt like old times. Seneca peppered me with questions, and I was reminded that even at my quickest, I was no match for my former teacher. We lamented the moral decline of Rome and the increasingly bloodthirsty ways of its people. When the conversation transitioned from philosophy to politics, Seneca lowered his voice, and his words became measured.

"Time has erased most memories of your little incident with Caligula, but his family is still paranoid about people finding out about his physical ailments. They fear it might impact his opportunity to become emperor." We were sipping wine, and I sensed that Seneca was about to tell me the real reason I had been summoned. "Agrippina and the house of Germanicus are, unfortunately, as influential as ever." Another sip as he eyed me over his wineglass. "It's a treacherous path to power these days, especially for those of us living in Rome. Much easier to climb the ranks in the provinces and return to Rome at a more opportune time."

The words made my stomach clench, and my dreams suddenly seemed more distant. Perhaps I was naive, but I hadn't thought my fight with Caligula six years earlier would still stalk me.

"What do you know about Judea?" Seneca asked.

Judea? "I know the Jewish people are strong-willed and hard to govern," I said. "I know that Pontius Pilate is hardly equal to the task."

Seneca gave me the type of wry smile that normally preceded something unpleasant. I dreaded what was coming next.

"Which is precisely why he needs a true genius to serve as his *assessore*," Seneca said.

It took me a few seconds to process the implications. An *assessore* was the chief legal adviser to a prefect like Pilate. It was a position typically reserved for men with greater experience and contacts than I had. In that respect, it would be a huge opportunity. But Judea was always on the edge of outright rebellion, and Pilate had a knack for infuriating the Jews. Serving as his *assessore* would be fraught with danger, the possibilities for failure limitless. Yet how could I tell my benefactor no?

Seneca leaned forward, perhaps reading my thoughts. "Sejanus does not trust the family of Germanicus," he said. This was good news. Sejanus was the man Tiberius Caesar had left in charge of running the empire while Tiberius lived on the island of Capri.

"It's only a matter of time," Seneca promised. "You spend three years in Judea, and after that I will help you establish a law practice in the heart of Rome. By then the family of Caligula should no longer be a threat."

We spent several more minutes discussing the potential assignment, and Seneca explained how he could wield his influence to make it happen. I never said yes, but that didn't deter Seneca. By the time he was slapping my back on my way out, it was assumed that Pilate would have a new *assessore* within a few months.

"What happened to the old one?" I asked.

Seneca flicked a wrist as if shooing away a fly. "That's of no importance. Besides, it's easier to follow someone who has been a failure than someone who has been a resounding success."

As we grasped wrists at the portico, Seneca sprang another surprise. "There is one other matter I could use your help with before you leave," he said. "It involves a meeting with Flavia, one of the Vestals, immediately after the Fordicidia ceremonies two days from now. We have an audience with her in the Forum following the sacrifice."

Seneca said this as if it were an afterthought, but a private audience with a Vestal Virgin was no small thing. I tried to contain my enthusiasm like a good Stoic.

"May I ask what this is about?"

He gave me a patronizing smile, the way he had done so often when I asked one of my thousands of questions as his student. "You may ask," he said, "but I cannot tell."

And with that comment, Seneca patted me on the shoulder and sent me on my way.

— CHAPTER 7 —

Hundreds of years before I was born, Numa Pompilius, the second king of Rome, saw his empire devastated by famine. He knew that Tellus, the goddess of the earth, was angry and had to be appeased. Uncertain of what he must do to save his empire, the king prayed and was given the solution in a dream:

> By the death of cattle, Tellus must be placated. Two cows,
> that is. Let a single heifer yield two lives for the rites.

Pompilius solved the riddle by instituting the sacrifice of a pregnant cow—a single heifer yielding two lives—and the Festival of

Fordicidia was born. The sacrifice of the pregnant heifer assured the fertility of the grain already planted and growing in the womb of Mother Earth. The unborn calf was a mediating being—alive but not yet born, innocent but sacrificed. The ritual, like most Roman religious rituals, spawned days of celebration and entertainment.

On the morning of Fordicidia, I met Seneca at the round temple of Vesta, joining thousands who crowded the streets to watch the ceremony. As usual, not many from Rome's ruling class were in attendance. The true worshipers in Rome were the common people, not the artists or the intellectuals or the magistrates. Cicero once said that Rome had one religion for the poet, another for the philosopher, and another for the statesman. He was only partly right. The statesmen, it seemed to me, had no religion at all and used religion only to control the people. Poets and philosophers loved to write about religion but seldom practiced it. Only common citizens and soldiers on the battlefield truly believed in the power of omens and portents and the rites of purification and sacrifice.

Seneca made no secret of his disdain for all this foolishness. "Do you want to propitiate the gods?" he once asked me. "A true worshiper of the gods is he who acts like them."

My own beliefs had been influenced heavily by the skepticism of the Greeks. *Better not to believe in anything at all than to cringe before a god who is worse than the worst of men.*

But here we were, Seneca and I, being jostled about by a mob laced with bloodthirsty adrenaline, straining to see the show unfolding on the great marble portico outside the temple of Vesta.

For the occasion, the temple servants had built a huge circular wooden platform, elevated by eight giant posts. An enormous black heifer stood at the top, anchored by chains attached to an iron collar around her neck and bolted to the platform. Muscle-bound slaves dressed in tunics did their best to keep the heifer calm. Other slaves, thinner and more agile, all wearing ghoulish masks, danced around the outside of the platform to the beat of drums. They gestured wildly, whipping the crowd into a frenzy.

As the music rose and the slaves danced more lasciviously, I became increasingly uncomfortable. The Greeks never acted like this.

To the left of the platform, dressed in flowing red garments, was Sejanus, the man in charge during Tiberius's absence. He was a severe-looking man whose face bore the weathered vestiges of military campaigns. For today, Sejanus was *Pontifex Maximus*.

The man appeared to take no interest in the proceedings. He surveyed the onlookers, barely acknowledging the dancers as they took their gyrations to a new level of vulgarity. Women had now joined the sensual dance, but Sejanus stood stone-faced as if above it all, just waiting for it to end.

Under the platform, a beautiful young woman knelt with her chin held high and her hands open in front of her. She seemed lost in a trance, worshiping. Her long dark hair cascaded over her shoulders, shimmering in contrast to her pure-white robe. "That's Flavia," Seneca told me.

At that moment, most eyes were not on Flavia but were focused on the top of the platform, where the matron of the Vestals, a woman named Calpurnia, had just appeared. Calpurnia had recently turned thirty and was seven years away from completing her service.

"She takes her role very seriously," Seneca whispered as if it were an ignoble thing. He regarded the whole affair as a charade. "I doubt she'll ever marry."

Calpurnia was a slight woman with red hair plaited and fastened by jeweled tortoiseshell combs and pins of ivory. I was sure she had spent hours preparing for this moment. Like Sejanus, she seemed unmoved by the dancers, staring toward the horizon over the heads of the crowd.

Just when I thought the crowd might explode with ecstasy, one of the slaves handed Calpurnia a long-handled knife. She grasped it with both hands and raised it over her head, prompting a full-throated bellow from the onlookers. The drums beat faster, the dancers kept pace, and the crowd pulsed with anticipation of what would happen next.

Calpurnia stepped behind the heifer, holding the knife aloft, staring at it as if it held some kind of enchanting power, and then swung it around with a violent double-fisted stroke that sliced the underside of the great heifer's neck.

The drums stopped, the crowd hushed, and the heifer crumpled to its knees. Blood poured through a hole cut in the platform directly above Flavia's head, drenching her in a crimson shower that matted her hair and covered her face and body. She knelt there as the blood cascaded over her, her palms upturned, blood soaking every inch of the once-white robe that now clung to her body like a second layer of skin.

After a minute, she wiped the blood from her eyes and opened them, a contrast of almond and white against the crimson face. She brushed her hair back, wiped her eyes a second time, and stood to face the crowd, holding her arms aloft. The Forum erupted in cheers, even louder than before. Tellus had been appeased; Mother Earth would yield her offspring; Rome would enjoy its bounty.

Still dripping with blood, Flavia walked over and knelt in front of Sejanus. The crowd quieted again as he placed a hand on her head and mumbled something I couldn't hear. Flavia bowed her head and closed her eyes, soaking in the blessing from the second-most-powerful man in all of Rome.

"Welcome back," Seneca said to me.

We left before the second part of the ritual, where the baby calf would be extracted and burned. The ashes would be saved by the Vestals and sprinkled on a bonfire during the Festival of Parilia.

We elbowed our way through the crowd until we found enough privacy to talk.

"She saw us in the crowd," Seneca said. "We are supposed to meet in the Forum later, but I thought it would be important for her to know we were at the sacrifice."

I was still getting used to being treated as a peer by Seneca. In a few hours he and I would be meeting with one of the Vestal Virgins. A man of my station and age would never have such opportunity apart from the influence of my friend and former teacher.

But I also knew that I could be honest with the man.

"The Greek gods are less bloodthirsty," I said.

"I know," Seneca replied without looking at me. "And the Greeks are not ruling the world."

— CHAPTER 8 —

I had missed the Roman Forum during my time in Greece, even the self-important politicians and greedy businessmen who scurried around at the epicenter of the civilized world. It was a place to see and be seen. I soaked in the energy as Seneca and I waited for our meeting with Flavia under the Arch of Augustus.

A few minutes after we arrived, I saw her entourage proceed up the Via Sacra. She rode in a litter bedecked with silver and jewels, reflecting the sun, carried by four hairy, barrel-chested Ethiopians. Lictors preceded her, clearing the way with shouts and an occasional use of the rod.

People stood aside as Flavia passed, and some onlookers burst into spontaneous applause. Fortune smiled on anyone who came close to a Vestal—her very presence was so powerful that if her shadow fortuitously fell across the path of a condemned prisoner, he was automatically freed.

There were only six active Vestals in Rome, but eighteen women served at the temple of Vesta. The youngest six were students; the next six, including Flavia, were in active service. The six oldest taught the students and presided over the most important ceremonies. Thus, a senior Vestal like Calpurnia slit the throat of the heifer, but a younger Vestal like Flavia ended up taking the blood bath.

All Vestals were selected by the emperor himself for thirty years of service. It was the grandest of all beauty contests. Patrician families from all over the empire brought their young girls, between the ages of six and ten, to the House of Vestal. According to law, the girls had to be free of physical and mental defect and the daughters of Roman citizens. According to custom, the girls also had to be beautiful and blazingly smart.

The Vestal matron filtered hundreds of candidates, narrowing the field to about a dozen. Then the emperor appraised the candidates. It was one of the most harrowing mornings known to our culture, as the young girls responded to the rapid-fire questions of the emperor, withering under the scrutiny of his personal inspection, until he decided on the most worthy candidates.

At that point, the candidates would stand in a line with their parents behind them. The emperor would approach the winners one by one and extend his hand. "I take you, *amata*, my beloved, to be a Vestal priestess, who will carry out the sacred rites on behalf of the Roman people."

Then he would lead the winners away from their parents. Many times the young girls' lips would tremble, their eyes welling with tears. They were not allowed to look back. Their heads would be shaved, and they would move into the temple of Vesta. Their parents would leave the temple with heavy hearts but with the pride of knowing their daughter was a chosen one.

Amata. Loved by the *Pontifex Maximus*.

Flavia had been the very first Vestal chosen by Tiberius Caesar, who was rumored to have an exquisite eye for potential beauty. Even at a young age, Flavia could turn heads, and she was known to have a true zest for life.

I felt a little overwhelmed by the grandeur of the approaching dignitary. "Are you sure it is all right for me to be here?" I asked.

Seneca didn't bother looking my way. "You've been trained by the best Greek rhetoricians," he said, staring straight ahead as if transfixed by the Vestal. "Not to mention the most brilliant Roman tutors. Just do your best not to outshine your teacher."

I tried to convince myself that Seneca was right. I *had* been trained for this. All of that practice by the Aegean Sea, the dissecting and analysis of the great philosophers and orators, even the physical discipline from gymnastics—it would all pay off. I had mastered my subjects. I was more than ready for this moment.

But I had not yet mastered all the social graces required at this level of Roman society, nor had I perfected the art of self-deception. So the closer Flavia got, the more I felt my mouth drying up. My heart pounded so hard I thought it might burst through my toga. At least I had Seneca with me. The man was never at a loss for words.

I couldn't help but stare when Flavia's procession stopped in front of us. She alighted from the litter in her sparkling white robe and long *palla* that was secured by a brooch and draped over her left shoulder. Her hair was fixed in the style of Vestals—separated into six braids and woven on top of her head to form a sort of crown. I had heard the style required waist-length hair.

Flavia shooed away her lictors, and they formed a semicircle around the Arch of Augustus to give us space.

I was immediately drawn to the woman. She had large brown eyes, full lips, and a beautiful smile that came quickly and naturally. She seemed so relaxed for someone of her station. I sensed that I was in the presence of greatness, though she was only two years older than me.

She smiled at Seneca as he greeted her with a customary kiss on the hand, and I followed his lead. "Some say you are the next Cicero," she told him.

Seneca tried to shrug it off. "Some people will say anything to curry favor."

She grinned because he had fallen for her trap. "In my circles, comparisons to Cicero, the champion of the Republic and the critic of all things imperial, are not necessarily compliments."

"The man did have a bit of a populist flair," Seneca said as if it were a crime.

He quickly introduced me and told Flavia how I had studied under the Greeks at the School of Molon. Her face lit up. "I love the Greeks," she said. "They're idealists. They build cultures and philosophies. We build roads."

She moved a half step closer and reached out to touch my arm. "Tell me about the School of Molon. One of the problems with being a Vestal is that we cannot travel much."

At that moment, all my rhetorical training betrayed me. My tongue no longer seemed to fit my mouth, and I stumbled through my first few sentences. Even so, I was amazed at how Flavia listened, soaking it all in, barely blinking, making me feel like the most important man on earth. She had an almost-irresistible charm and a disarming personality. When she spoke, she displayed a quick wit and a convincing tone that had me smiling and nodding.

After fifteen minutes of casual conversation with Seneca and me, Flavia lowered her voice and turned serious. I was ready to do whatever she requested. "Have you been to the games lately?" she asked Seneca.

He frowned. "The games are Rome at her worst. The lowest and basest instincts of our citizens all compressed into ten hours of slaughter."

Flavia nodded, and concern wrinkled her brow. "I'm sick of the bloodshed, Seneca, and I suspected you might share my feelings. As one of Rome's brightest minds, you may be able to help me."

Seneca was wise enough not to answer immediately. He understood the importance of the games to Rome's political system. Tiberius was said to be an emperor of "bread and circuses." He kept the masses happy by supplying free bread for hundreds of thousands and free entertainment that featured the most vicious and bloody games the empire had ever seen. Plus, the executions that occurred during the lunchtime intermissions served as a vivid reminder that crossing Rome meant a painful and scandalous death.

"I've heard that Tiberius is not really a supporter of the games," Flavia continued. "I sit in the box with Sejanus, who can barely stand them himself. And the bloodshed is only getting worse. More men die with each spectacle, and the crowds become bored if the blood doesn't flow faster and faster. Your opinions are highly regarded both here and on the island of Capri. I would consider a letter from you to Tiberius about the games a personal favor. I have asked a few other influential citizens, including three senators, to do the same." She fixed Seneca with her stare, and I marveled at her intensity.

I knew my mentor well enough to know that he was conflicted. He espoused Stoicism but lived as a man of luxury. He preached detachment but craved approval. Seneca needed popularity the way grapes needed rain, and nothing could destroy his popularity more quickly than taking a stand against the games.

"I think you overestimate my stature with Tiberius," Seneca said in a halfhearted attempt at humility. "And I am not sure he dislikes the games as much as you think. But I'm willing to help however I can. Give me a few days, and perhaps I will have something worthy of your request."

Flavia broke into a smile, thanked Seneca profusely, and kissed him on both cheeks. She did the same to me, and I watched slack-jawed as she walked away, mission accomplished. She thanked us again and waved as she climbed into her litter.

As Seneca and I watched her go, I realized that Flavia had done what great orators before her could not—she had rendered Seneca dumbstruck without even trying.

"I never liked the games anyway," Seneca said, still staring after the Vestal's entourage.

"Funny," I replied. "You never mentioned that to me."

— CHAPTER 9 —

After our meeting with Flavia, Seneca asked me to try my hand at drafting a letter for him to the emperor, and I attacked the job with great vigor. I knew that a man like Tiberius would not be repulsed by bloodshed. He had commanded legions in Germania, Pannonia, and Illyricum and had undoubtedly sentenced thousands of prisoners to the cross. On the battlefield, he had seen blood flow like the Tiber. He had tied deserters to horses facing opposite directions, whipped the horses, and watched the men get ripped in half. Surely the deaths of a few thousand gladiators and criminals wouldn't bother him.

But I had an approach that just might work.

Tiberius was exceedingly paranoid. A fisherman had once climbed the rocks of Capri to present a gift of fresh fish to the emperor. Alarmed that the fisherman had made it past his guards, Tiberius ordered the man's face scrubbed with the fish.

Later, the fisherman was purported to have said, "I'm glad I didn't bring him crabs!"

When word got back to Tiberius, he had the man brought before him a second time.

"Scrub his face with crabs!" the emperor commanded.

Such was the character of the man who ruled Rome, the intended recipient of our letter. He wielded great power but secretly believed that half of Rome was conspiring to kill him. He suspected a dagger under every toga.

He was also a man obsessed with his legacy. Rulers were judged by what they built and whom they conquered. Both required a strong economy. So that was where I began.

I spent three days compiling data. I attended gladiator training camps and talked to the *lanistae*—the managers—letting them know I was working for Flavia, though I didn't tell them the nature of my assignment. I checked death records. I pulled together programs of past fights. I talked to friends who were avid fans and closely followed the games. I was building my case, and I wanted to make Seneca proud. I had been his star pupil once. Now he was my benefactor, and we both had a lot on the line.

I started the letter with the customary language honoring Caesar and then turned my attention to Spartacus's revolt. Gladiators had killed their own trainers and battled Rome's legions for three years. Crassus had crucified six thousand of them.

By my calculations, there were at least sixteen thousand gladiators training in Rome as I drafted the letter. That nearly equaled the combined forces of three Roman legions and far outnumbered the imperial troops in Rome. Most of the gladiators were slaves or prisoners of war—enemies of Rome. If Spartacus could mount a rebellion with a few thousand, what could his counterpart do today? And Spartacus had been far outside Rome. Now the gladiators trained in the very shadow of the emperor's palace.

But that wasn't all. The average life span of a gladiator was twenty-two years. Three-quarters of them died before completing ten fights. One out of every six fights resulted in death. I estimated that about eight thousand gladiators died each year throughout the empire at a total cost of more than sixty million *sestertii* to purchase and train their replacements. The games, I argued, were robbing the empire of the capacity to expand and build.

And if eight thousand died this year, it would take ten thousand the next to satisfy the bloodlust of the spectators. It was an enormous expense and a lurking danger to Rome. Why not curtail the games? Why not emphasize the chariot races and other competitions that did not result in death?

For three days I slaved over the letter, writing and rewriting until my eyes grew bleary. During that time, I might have managed a total of ten hours of sleep. It would all be worth it if Seneca read the letter, nodded, and signed it proudly.

When I finally had the opportunity to present it to him, he perused it thoughtfully, and I held my breath. This was, after all, correspondence that would go directly to the emperor! Seneca finished, frowned, and didn't say a word for an unbearable few seconds.

He finally looked up. "What did you learn in Greece about the most effective form of advocacy?" he asked.

We were friends now, but he was still the teacher. I responded confidently, though his frown had already dampened my spirit.

"Ethos, pathos, and logos," I said. "Aristotle. The best advocate is one who combines his personal credibility, an emotional tug, and solid logic."

As the words left my mouth, I knew what Seneca would say. My letter was long on logic and short on emotion. Yet it was intended to be. Classical forms of persuasion wouldn't work on a man like Tiberius. He was unemotional, skeptical, suspicious. He would see through emotional ploys and react negatively. I had considered all of that as I had labored over every word.

Yet Seneca said nothing of the sort.

"You have always been good at the books, Theophilus. But in real life, people are persuaded by stories. Facts get stuck in the head, shielded by our biases and struck down by the swords of our preconceptions. Stories go straight to the heart. Tiberius has not been to the games for a very long time. We must remind him of what it *feels* like there—how it debases the human spirit and shrinks the soul."

Seneca told me to meet him at the Fordicidia games. Like every other patrician trying to find his place in Roman society, I had already planned on attending. The games were Rome's premier social event. There the elite families of the senators mingled with their friends, contracts and alliances were formed, promotions and positions were cemented. If the Forum was the nerve center of the Roman Empire, the games—at least for now, at least until Tiberius could be convinced to decree otherwise—were its blood-pumping heart.

Because I had left Rome before I was old enough to attend, I had never been to the games myself.

"You may want to eat something before you attend," Seneca warned. "You'll lose your appetite by lunch."

— CHAPTER 10 —

The Circus Maximus was the largest arena in the world. Over 2,000 feet long and 387 feet wide, it had a seating capacity that exceeded 150,000. At the height of the games, during a close chariot race or when two gladiators were evenly matched, the roar of the crowd would thunder through the seven hills of Rome, clawing out to the surrounding city and echoing back on itself. Seasoned spectators claimed that the noise made their ears ring for minutes afterward, as if the waves of the Mediterranean were crashing in their heads. The arena, they said, literally shook with the noise.

The Circus was located below the imperial residence on the Palatine Hill and was connected to the palace by an underground tunnel that opened to the emperor's luxurious, shaded box. The sprawling palace, full of arches and frescoes and colored marble, formed a stunning backdrop to the arena. The shadow of the emperor's house loomed over the festivities like a father hovering over his children at play.

Tiberius would not be at the games, of course, but the people didn't care. Sejanus would preside, and Tiberius would foot the bill—what more could one ask of the emperor?

Two days earlier, this same arena had been the scene of the always-popular chariot races, the drivers churning four abreast around the barrier down the middle of the oblong arena. Fortunes were made and lost in the betting.

The night after, thousands of slaves covered the floor of the arena with sand and brought in an elaborate set for today's games, replete with shrubs and trees, transforming the arena into an African landscape. The games would begin with a hunt.

Seating for the event was carefully segregated. Sejanus, a few select senators, the imperial slaves, and the Vestal Virgins would take their seats under the red tile roof of the emperor's box. Other senators, resplendent in their gold-trimmed togas, sat on both sides of the box. Equestrians like me were entitled to the spacious seats closest to the arena floor, stone benches with plenty of leg room. Above us, on wooden seats, sat the other Roman citizens—the freedmen. Women were allowed only in the top rows.

My seat next to Seneca was almost directly across the arena from the emperor's box, and I had the perfect vantage point to watch both the games and Flavia's reaction to them. My own family's seats were several rows higher and farther from the center of the arena, but today I was with Seneca, and friendship had its privileges.

Fashionably late, the trumpets blared, the flutes played, and a colorful procession arrived from the emperor's palace. The sun was low in the sky on my side of the stadium and reflected off Sejanus and his cohorts, the long, polished trumpets blinding to the eyes. Sejanus, wearing a purple toga, led the procession, and the crowd erupted. He was followed by the Senate's two consuls and a handful of other senators. Next came the Vestals, who seemed out of place in their white satin robes and elegantly braided hair. I noticed that Flavia was a few inches shorter than the other Vestals, but she held her head high and looked majestic as she took her place a few seats down from Sejanus. If she abhorred the games, she didn't let on.

After the cheering subsided and the crowd sat down, the condemned criminals were paraded through the arena. They were chained and humiliated, staring at the sand in front of them. The guards held placards over their heads, informing the crowd of their crimes. The good citizens whistled and jeered at the prisoners, though the taunting seemed halfhearted. The criminals were a mixture of freedmen and slaves, all noncitizens, accused of murder or sedition or stealing from the state treasury. There were men of every skin color and nationality imaginable, and my advocate's heart, always the champion of the underdog, assumed they might have avoided this punishment if they could have afforded a better lawyer.

After the parade of the condemned, the gladiators entered. They were all huge, carrying a variety of weapons, looking ready to kill. Their bodies had been massaged, oiled, and well fed—the *lanistae* looking after their investments. A dead gladiator, one *lanista* had told me three days earlier during my research, was an expensive gladiator.

Sejanus stood and announced the name and record of each gladiator, then waited for the traditional salute: "We who are about to die salute you!" Sejanus would nod, and the next gladiator would step up.

Money began changing hands all around me, and friendly arguments broke out about which *ludi* trained the best gladiators and which weapons were the most lethal. *If only the Romans cared this much about law or politics or philosophy.*

Seneca began making his own snide comments, mimicking the others around us, saying he wanted to bet on this man or that man because he liked the color of his shield. I admired the courage of the gladiators and told Seneca as much.

"You want to hear about real courage?" Seneca asked. He told the story of a German gladiator who went off to the lavatory before a show, the only place where he wouldn't be watched, and choked himself to death by jamming one of the lavatory sponges on the end of a stick down his own throat. "That man defied everyone, choosing the manner of his death!" Seneca said.

"And that makes him a hero?"

"My favorite gladiator of all time."

── CHAPTER II ──

The morning games were run with impressive precision. A metal fence was erected around the arena floor, and exotic animals were turned loose, only to be hunted down with deadly efficiency. Archers and javelin throwers showcased their accuracy, dropping lions, panthers, and even bears in their tracks. In one chaotic and colorful moment, twenty-five ostriches were released simultaneously, their wings flapping in a frenzied attempt to escape. They were dead within minutes.

A wild boar gored a hunter midway through the morning, but otherwise the only blood spilled on the arena sand belonged to the beasts. After two hours of slaughter, the place was littered with animal carcasses, and I understood why everyone entering the gates had been handed a small container of incense.

By noon the crowd grew restless, and the lottery began. We had been handed numbers as we entered that morning, and as the morning's set was deconstructed, the master of the games ordered the animals dismembered and called out numbers. This person won an ostrich leg! Another the carcass of a wild boar! The prizes all seemed to go to the freedmen crammed into the third and fourth tiers, which was fine with those of us in the lower seats. We could buy our own wild animals.

The real slaughter started at lunchtime. Soldiers paraded the criminals out again, one at a time, to be executed in front of the crowd. The first was beheaded, a quick and painless death, but that was just a warm-up. Next came a crucifixion. People around me, snacking on nuts and dates, placed bets on how long it would be before the man's legs were broken and he gasped his last breaths. Watching the soldiers pound spikes into the man's wrists and feet nauseated me.

There was a burning as well. The prisoner, who had been covered in oil and tar before he was tied to the stake, let out a bone-chilling scream when he caught fire. The crowd shrugged it off, neither applauding nor turning their heads.

One after another, the prisoners came, men condemned for serious offenses against the state. The only ones who drew the slightest crowd reaction, a smattering of applause or gasps, were the ones attacked and savaged by the wild beasts.

There could be no dispute about the deterrent effect of what I was witnessing—these images would stay with me for a very long time. But unlike most of the crowd, I knew too much about Rome's system of justice to assume that these men all deserved to die.

I knew that many of these men had been represented by the weakest advocates Rome had to offer. The whole affair added more urgency to my desire to be a lawyer. I couldn't stop all the executions—trying to slow down the gladiator games was proving challenging enough—but perhaps I could stop a few of them. At least I could ensure that a few truly innocent men didn't walk into an arena full of Roman citizens and sacrifice their lives in order to provide a few minutes of entertainment over a lunch break.

I diverted my eyes more than once and found myself studying the reactions of Flavia and the other Vestals. While people around her chatted, Flavia watched the proceedings imperiously, never once taking her eyes from the carnage at hand. I pictured her at seven or eight years old, having just been chosen for the honor of being a Vestal, being forced to watch naked men set on fire. While other girls were being tucked into their beds by their mothers, Flavia had been a Vestal in training, and part of that training was learning not to flinch at the worst violence that depraved human minds could conceive.

Halfway through the lunch intermission, Seneca had seen enough. "Come to my house tomorrow morning, and we'll finish the letter," he said. "I've got work to do this afternoon."

Part of me wanted to leave with him. But in truth, another part wanted to stay. I had already endured the worst, and the crowd was starting to file back in. The gladiator fights were at least *sport*. These were men who had a decent chance of surviving, some of whom would earn their freedom. In fact, many of them—those who had been born freedmen—were entering the arena by choice. Since I was working to shut this entire enterprise down, shouldn't I at least experience firsthand what I was up against?

I expected the gladiators to fight one pair at a time but was surprised to hear four sets of names announced for the first round. They each took their spots in different parts of the arena, ensuring that every segment of the crowd had a set of gladiators fighting directly beneath them.

When the contests began, shining metal and glistening bodies locked in deadly combat, and the crowd's energy rose to a fevered pitch. It was hard to take it all in—and I found my head swiveling from one fight to the next, clued in by the roar of the crowd.

As I watched, I couldn't help but put myself in the sandals of the gladiators. What were they thinking? How much adrenaline must be coursing through their veins? What did it feel like to kill or be killed?

In Greece, I had grown to above-average height and had more than held my own in athletic contests with heavier men. I was quick and strong for my size. But the gladiators were cut from different cloth. I had felt small while visiting their training camps three days earlier, intimidated by their chiseled muscles and intense stares.

I knew that I wouldn't last five minutes against any of them.

The first death occurred less than fifteen minutes into the fighting. A Thracian at the far end of the arena had quickly subdued his opponent, who now knelt before him. The victor looked back over his shoulder at the imperial box, and the crowd roared its disapproval. Thumbs were turned down everywhere, even in my section of the arena by men who had barely watched the fight.

The virgins and senators in the imperial box had their thumbs down as well, including, to my surprise, Flavia. Her face was stern and unyielding, no different from the others.

When Sejanus frowned and turned his thumb down, the defeated gladiator lifted his head, exposing his neck. The Thracian placed the tip of his sword against the man's neck, and I diverted my eyes just before he finished his opponent off. An appreciative roar went up from the crowd, and then it was on to the next fight while men around me settled their bets from the first one.

Similar scenes were repeated throughout the afternoon, time after time, until the sand was soaked with human blood.

Naturally, Sejanus had saved the premier match for last—the only match that would occur by itself, the center of attention for all 150,000 screaming spectators. Before this featured match, there was a brief break so the slaves could dump fresh sand over the blood-soaked portions of the arena and rake the surface to give the two combatants a level field.

The first of the two gladiators to emerge was a Gaul—a stocky man with red hair covering his body, his biceps as thick as my thighs. He was heavily armed in the style of a Roman centurion: a straight, double-edged sword; a long, rectangular shield; a belt studded with metal; a scaled arm guard made of leather; and two silver shin guards. The man's name, according to the program, was Celadus, which literally meant "crowd's roar." When he emerged from the tunnel, his helmet in hand, the crowd did exactly that.

Celadus boasted fourteen fights on his record but looked like he had been in the arena far longer than the seven years or so it would have taken to accumulate those fights. His skin was leathery and scarred, his face covered by a ragged red beard. He marched over to the imperial box, raised his sword to the emperor, and did a complete turn so the entire crowd could adore him. As the cheering died down, he put on the helmet—a large bronze headpiece with a red plume crest and an ornate grille that protected every square inch of his face.

His opponent came out next, a taller and thinner man with a clean-shaven face and curly blond hair that seemed strangely out of place in the arena. This man went by the name Mansuetus. I felt immediately drawn to him. His name meant "gentle," which showed he had a sense of humor. He smiled at the crowd—the first gladiator who had done that—as if he might actually enjoy a nice little fight on such a sunny day. He wielded the armor of an ancient Greek warrior from the Thracian tribe: a smaller rectangular shield, a curved sword called a *sica*, leg guards that rose to midthigh, and a helmet with a side plume, visor, and high crest that left his face exposed.

He bowed deeply before the imperial box, swinging his arms out in a flourish. The crowd hissed and whistled while a few men around me shouted their approval. When he straightened back up, I noticed a subtle nod from Flavia and a look of concern that I hadn't seen when she observed the other gladiators. It seemed to me that she started to mouth something to Mansuetus and then thought better of it. Perhaps it was my imagination, but I thought they caught each other's eyes for just a moment.

A satirist once said that being a gladiator was like being Adonis. Women chose them over children, country, and husbands. Yes, women proclaimed loyalty to their families, but steel in the arena, and the gladiators who wielded it, was what they really craved.

Perhaps I was being overly sensitive as I thought about Flavia's reaction to Mansuetus. I had no claim to her affections, no right to be jealous—I had only met her once. But still I felt an intense interest in her well-being. The punishment for a Vestal who violated her vow of chastity was well-known and merciless. Surely she wouldn't risk that! Surely she wouldn't risk her exalted station as one of Rome's most esteemed women for a forbidden affair with a gladiator.

The fight started slowly, both men circling and sizing each other up as the crowd watched in hushed silence. If the lesser fighters had been this deliberate, the crowd would have hissed, and a *lanista* would have whipped the men into action. But here, in this final bout, the champions had earned the crowd's respect, and the audience savored every moment.

It was a classic case of speed and agility against brute force. Celadus stalked Mansuetus, moving relentlessly forward, protected by his oversized shield and bronze helmet. But the gentle Thracian was light on his feet, staying just out of reach of the Gaul's sword, looking for the opportunity to outflank the man and get behind his armor.

When they finally engaged, the Gaul rained down one blow after another on Mansuetus's shield. Mansuetus backpedaled, and the crowd rose to its feet. In a flash, almost too quick for my eyes to follow, the Gaul struck two hard blows. The first, aimed at Mansuetus's head, was deflected by the Thracian's shield. But the second, a backhanded blow that sliced across Mansuetus's calf, exposed muscle and drew blood.

Mansuetus made him pay. In striking the blow, Celadus had leaned too close. Mansuetus pivoted and pounced, slicing the Gaul's shoulder, drawing blood himself. Celadus staggered back a step or two, glanced at the wound, and quickly reengaged. The deadly dance of thrusts and counterthrusts continued, Mansuetus hampered by his wounded leg while the Gaul seemed barely able to hold his shield with his left arm.

The crowd found a cadence with the gladiators, who grunted and growled as they rained their blows against each other, swords clanging against shields, occasionally slicing through to draw more blood. Neither of the men backed down, and I glanced toward Flavia, who was watching with her hand to her mouth, cringing with worry as Mansuetus became streaked with crimson.

Even the jaded men around me realized they were seeing the type of valor that was not to be mocked. "It's a shame," one said soberly, summing up the thoughts of us all, "that one of them has to die."

The end came in a most unexpected way.

— CHAPTER 12 —

Mansuetus was the first to do it. After twenty minutes of fighting, blood and sweat streaked his body, and sand clung to his wet skin. The smile had long disappeared from his lips. He stepped away from the encounter and gave his adversary a subtle nod. As they kept a wary eye on each other, both men slowly removed their left hands from their shield straps and placed the shields on the ground. The crowd hushed, and those around me stood on their toes, shading their eyes from the sun, trying to get a better look. Even Sejanus and the Vestals stood in curious disbelief.

Mansuetus crouched down, keeping his eyes on the stocky Celadus, and placed his curved sword on the sand as well. This brought a few shouts of displeasure, which quickly crescendoed into whistles and hoots of disapproval. A *lanista* who had been stationed near the edge of the stadium took a step toward the fighters. Who would have thought that these two gladiators, of all men, would need to be whipped into action?

Celadus crouched and placed his sword on the sand as well, stepping back from the weapon with his eyes still glued to Mansuetus. Flavia inched forward, almost to the edge of the imperial box.

The crowd turned on the fighters with a vengeance. Jeers rained down from the third and fourth tiers and were soon echoed by the patricians below. "Finish the fight!"

"Battle to the death!"

"Cowards!"

The man in front of me shook his head in disgust.

An ironic grin curled Mansuetus's lips, his white teeth contrasting brilliantly against his grimy face. He circled to his right, as did the Gaul, until they had completed a half circle and stopped in front of the other man's armor.

Each knelt slowly, deliberately, and picked up the other man's sword and shield. The crowd, catching on quickly, screamed its approval. The *lanista* stepped back. Apparently the gladiators had agreed, even before stepping into the arena, that if the fight had not concluded by a designated time, they would switch armor and finish each other off with unfamiliar weapons.

When they reengaged, the crowd was in a frenzy. Romans loved a good surprise. And what could be better than this—gladiators who feigned a truce only to fight more viciously than they had before?

But this time the match was uneven. Mansuetus had a greater reach, a longer and heavier sword, and he was quicker. He was strong enough to adapt to the heavier armor, and even with his wounded leg, he seemed unstoppable. The Gaul, not used to dodging and weaving, continued to plow straight ahead, nullifying any advantage the lighter armor might have afforded. The two men stood within arm's length of each other, exchanging blows, but the advantage now lay entirely with Mansuetus.

Eventually the Gaul's wounded left shoulder wore down, and he lowered the shield enough for the taller Mansuetus to strike a hard blow across his neck, slicing into a vein. Blood came gushing out, and Celadus dropped to his knees, tottered for a second, and then dropped his *sica* and fell on his face.

Mansuetus watched grimly as his adversary fell. He quickly turned to face Sejanus, and I saw a look of relief flash across Flavia's face as she returned to her seat.

Without waiting for a signal from the crowd, and to nobody's surprise, Sejanus turned his thumb up, extending mercy to the fallen Celadus. The only question now was whether it even mattered.

According to custom, Mansuetus would now head to the imperial box, where Sejanus would congratulate him, place a wreath of victory on his head, and hang a gold medallion around his neck. Spectators would shower the ring with *sestertii*, and Mansuetus would scoop them up. Meanwhile, a physician would attend to Celadus to see if he could be saved, stitched up, and repaired in time to fight again in six months.

But just as the crowd was beginning to relax, it was caught off guard again. And this time, so was Mansuetus.

The Gaul—miraculously, it seemed—had rallied enough to grab Mansuetus by the ankle and jerk him back. My breath caught as I watched Mansuetus stumble to the ground. The Gaul rose to one knee and lunged with his *sica*, narrowly missing Mansuetus, who rolled quickly to his right and then sprang to his feet. He grabbed the sword he had dropped just a moment earlier. As the Gaul struggled to gain his footing, Mansuetus struck, the sword landing against the Gaul's side and driving the man to the ground face-first.

The crowd roared again—more bloodshed!—and this time Mansuetus, without waiting for a signal from Sejanus, finished the job. He grabbed the sword with both fists and planted it with all his might between the Gaul's shoulder blades, pinning him to the ground.

That finish, for the first time all day, seemed to take the wind out of the crowd. The moment held, and there was an unsettling silence throughout the arena. Celadus was motionless, lying in a pool of his own blood. Mansuetus bent over, hands on his knees, exhausted.

"Some men just don't know when to stay down," a voice behind me said.

I noticed that Flavia had turned away from the sight. Only Sejanus seemed impressed. It was the first time I had seen him smile all day.

The image that stayed with me occurred a few minutes later, after Mansuetus limped over to the imperial box and Sejanus joined the gladiator on the floor of the arena. Mansuetus knelt before the acting emperor, who crowned him with the victor's laurels. The crowd applauded politely, but I heard none of the lustful cheers that had filled the place earlier.

My eyes turned to the Gaul, being dragged from the arena with his own sword still planted firmly in his back. A brave man, one who had fought valiantly, hauled away to be burned with the trash.

Greece was the cradle of civilization, I thought, *and now Rome will be its grave.*

— Chapter 13 —

I didn't sleep well that night. Gruesome images were seared into my mind—the slice of the neck, the sword in the Gaul's back, the crowd lustily craving more. The executions at noon still bothered me the most. Men hanging on crosses or being torn apart by beasts while the crowd chatted and waited for the main event. I had been on a cross, even if only for a few hours, and it was impossible to see others hanging there without feeling some of their pain.

I couldn't stop thinking about Flavia either. I kept playing the scenes over and over. She and the other Vestals parading into the imperial box, her beauty radiating in the sun. Her impervious expression throughout the day's events. The surprising thumbs-down after the first gladiator fight. The way she had made eye contact with Mansuetus.

Rethinking the day's events, I decided that she had turned her thumb down in the early gladiator fights so that her vote might be taken more seriously if she had to urge Sejanus to extend mercy to Mansuetus. From the way she leaned forward in her seat while Mansuetus fought, and from the look of near panic on her face when he was wounded, I thought that she might have leaped over the concrete wall of the imperial box, if necessary, to keep him from dying.

I woke the next morning exhausted. I shaved, put on my linen tunic and woolen toga, and combed my wavy hair. I was going to spend the day with Seneca, and as always, appearances mattered.

Before heading out, I grabbed a morning snack of bread, dates, honey, milk, and a few olives. I carried my parchment and writing utensils through the narrow streets to Seneca's house on the Capitoline Hill. As usual, his spacious front hall was crowded with morning callers anxious for the man's patronage. His slaves had swept and polished the marble floor, and his head slave grandly announced my presence. Because of the urgency of my mission, I was placed ahead of Seneca's other "clients."

Those who had been waiting longer stared ruefully as Seneca came out and greeted me warmly, escorting me back to his office. We talked about the games and the disquieting conclusion of the last contest, which had seemed to unsettle the crowd. Seneca saw it as fate smiling on us and said we should send the letter to Tiberius right away.

For the next two hours, Seneca composed his letter while I acted as secretary and transcribed it. He gave me a crooked smile when we started and told me I might have to hold my nose for the first part. "Nobody writes the great Tiberius without a certain amount of flattery," he explained. "He will probably skip it, but it needs to be there just the same."

As I transcribed the letter, I marveled at Seneca's command of the language and doubted that Tiberius would skip even a word. Knowing the emperor, it was more likely he would have it carved into the marble of his palace.

Eventually Seneca let the great emperor know that he had a concern and began to describe what he had witnessed.

The games, Most Excellent Tiberius, have become pure butchery. Men constantly cry for more bloodshed. "Kill him! Flog him! Burn him alive!" The bloodlust corrupts, and the valor of the gladiators is lost on the crowd. "Why is he such a coward? Why won't he die more willingly? Why won't he rush to the steel?"

Boys in the street no longer dream of being senators or generals but only of being gladiators. Those who before took the greatest pride in serving in the legions now want only to die in the arena.

Was Rome built by bloodlust or by something nobler? A culture is known by its heroes, O great Tiberius, and how it treats them. What does it say about the impulses of the spectators when they call for the blood of the very men they seem to worship? And what does it say about our country when our slaves have become our greatest heroes, based on their ability to gut another man with the sword?

It was, I thought as I dutifully recorded the words, a subtle and clever appeal to the emperor's paranoia. If the crowds idolized the gladiators but still wanted to see them dead, what did that say about their intentions toward the emperor? And why should we feed this impulse?

Our heroes should not be the strongest slaves we've conquered. Our heroes should be the brave generals who make our empire safe. Our greatest hero should be our greatest citizen, the Princeps, the Son of the Divine Augustus. I beg you, for Rome and her posterity, to evaluate the frequency of the games and decide if they are worthy of the patronage of such an excellent ruler.

The audacity of the letter impressed me. When Seneca finished, I stared at him in near disbelief. Was he really going to send it?

That wry smile appeared on his lips for the second time that morning. "You don't think I'd be so foolish as to send such a letter without first testing the waters, do you?" he asked.

"It does seem rather bold."

"Bold times call for bold action," Seneca said. Then he tilted his head back with a knowing chuckle. "But they also call for well-placed sources who can first engage the emperor about his opinion of the games and hand him the letter only if the wind seems to be blowing in the proper direction."

I marveled not so much at the shrewdness of Seneca but at the revelation that he had a well-placed source on Capri. I was beyond fortunate to have him as a benefactor.

"In the meantime," he said, "make a second copy of that letter so I can present it to Flavia."

I did as I was told and watched as Seneca sealed each letter with his signet ring. I was hoping I would have a chance to deliver the letter to Flavia myself, but Seneca handpicked a different courier. He did, however, have one more surprise for me before he sent me on my way.

"You have two days to pack," Seneca announced. "You'll be receiving your commission as *assessore* in the province of Judea from our good friend Sejanus two days hence."

— CHAPTER 14 —

"Bold times call for bold action," Seneca had said. Those words echoed in my head as I prepared to leave Rome and spend three years in Judea. Seneca had been talking about his letter to the emperor, but I mulled the words in the context of Flavia. Should I write her a letter? What would I say? An equestrian of my rank and age had no business corresponding directly with a Vestal.

But I had been struck. How could I just disappear without letting her know where I was going or making sure she understood that I had helped Seneca with the letter?

Ultimately I decided not to write. Unrestrained courage is sometimes more like suicide than valor. If the Fates meant for me to cross paths again with Flavia, it would happen. But it was not likely. I told myself to forget about her, but my heart wasn't listening.

It wasn't for want of distractions. My future, both immediate and long-term, held more than sufficient peril to occupy my attention. I was going to a troubled province run by a troubled prefect. Pontius Pilate had a reputation for being moody and short-tempered—another equestrian trying to climb the provincial ranks. According to my sources, he was insecure and not at all happy that he had drawn the short straw of Judea.

Pilate had served under Sejanus as a member of the Praetorian Guard during the days when Tiberius still lived in Rome. Though Sejanus was gruff and demanding, he knew each of his men by name and later ensured that each had a chance to make something of himself. Thus, a little over four years ago, when Tiberius withdrew to Capri and Sejanus took over many of the emperor's responsibilities, Pilate had been dispatched to Judea as a prefect. His task was to serve as the personal representative of the great Tiberius Caesar, with strict orders to keep the peace and contain the Jews.

It had not been a smooth journey.

Pilate, a man of infinite bravado and limited patience, made two serious mistakes early in his prefecture. The first occurred shortly after he arrived in Judea. He ordered the troops stationed in Jerusalem to display the standards of the Roman army, including the image of Caesar Augustus, on the walls of the Antonia Fortress, overlooking the Jewish Temple. The standards were mounted at night, under cover of darkness, surprising the Jewish worshipers the next morning.

Pilate's predecessor, mindful of Jewish sensitivities to any graven images in the Holy City, had always left the standards of the army in Caesarea. But in Pilate's mind, the emperor's image was everywhere else in the empire, so why not in Jerusalem? Why not have a graven image of the emperor casting his gaze down at those worshiping in the Temple—one god keeping an eye on the worshipers of another?

It was the middle of the winter, but that didn't stop thousands of Jews from walking sixty-five miles from Jerusalem to Caesarea to confront Pilate. They stood outside his palace for days, begging him to take the standards down. Pilate refused. It would be an insult to the emperor.

After five days of stalemate, Pilate agreed to meet with the Jewish leaders in the great Caesarean amphitheater. He argued with them until his patience grew thin. Neither side was willing to compromise. Exasperated, Pilate ordered his soldiers to surround the contingent and draw their swords. The Jews bared their necks and dared the soldiers to kill them.

Astonished, Pilate backed down and gave an order to remove the standards from Jerusalem. The followers of Yahweh had won the first round.

They would not be so fortunate in the second. It occurred after Pilate built an enormous aqueduct to bring springwater across the Judean desert to the cisterns of Jerusalem. The aqueduct stretched for nearly forty miles, beautiful new pipes that brought pure and cold water to the city.

But the Jews protested again. Pilate had used corban money—sacred tithes from the Temple treasury—to help pay for the construction. This time he was dumbfounded by their protestations. Romans celebrated such engineering feats, heaping honors on the rulers who bestowed them. But the Jews complained! Could nothing satisfy them?

The next time Pilate visited Jerusalem, he took his place on his judgment seat and addressed the naysayers. They seemed even more enraged than they had been about the standards. They pressed close, forming a ring around him, and shouted insults about the way he had used God's money. Pilate maintained his composure but steadfastly refused to apologize—the aqueduct had been built for *them*.

Still the Jewish leaders pressed their point. Why had he used the Temple money? It was sacrilege!

Though it appeared that Pilate was bravely facing the crowd alone, he had in fact hidden his soldiers among them, dressed like Jews yet with daggers under their garments. When he had heard enough and felt threatened by the increasing hostility of those closest to his seat, Pilate raised his right hand and made a slashing motion across his throat. The soldiers struck, slicing their way through the crowd. They massacred hundreds, from the judgment seat through the streets of Jerusalem, even as the Jews scrambled to retreat, trampling each other in the panic.

This was the man I would now serve. I would be his chief legal adviser, his *assessore*, in a province where a strong-willed people hated him with barely restrained passion. Judea was a boiling cauldron, and I was being thrown into the middle of the pot.

I packed my stacks of white togas with the two narrow stripes, my cloaks and sandals, my household items, and my favorite books. Many of those same books had gone with me on the journey from Greece to Rome, and they were now well-worn scrolls, faded and cracked, carefully sealed in boxes designed to protect them on the journey at sea. I packed my wax notebooks and my iron pens. I said good-bye to my friends, made a sacrifice at the temple of Mars, and walked to the coast.

Our ship would sail by way of Alexandria, heading toward the rising sun. As we left port, I stood at the stern and watched the Roman coastline fade away. It would be three years before I would see Rome again, and I already missed her. For all her shortcomings, Rome was still the center of the civilized world and the greatest city on earth. The food, the architecture, the bustling excitement of the Forum, the consolidation of power that took place there—I would find none of this in Judea.

I found an out-of-the-way spot on the massive ship, felt the wind in my face, and listened to the chants of the slaves as their oars slid in and out of the water. I took out my most cherished scroll and read the words again. This one was from Seneca. The eloquent words formed a mission not just for my time in the land of Judea but for my entire life:

"But how," you ask, "does one attain the highest good?" Your money will not place you on a level with God, for God has no property. Your bordered robe will not do this, for God is not clad in raiment; nor your reputation, nor your display of self, nor knowledge of your name spread throughout the world, for no one has knowledge of God. The throng of slaves which carries your litter along the city streets and in foreign places will not help you, for this God of whom I speak, though the highest and most powerful of beings, carries all things on his own shoulders. Neither can beauty or strength make you blessed, for none of these qualities can withstand old age.

What we have to seek for, then, is that which is untouched by time and chance. And what is this? It is the soul—but the soul that is upright, good, and great. What else could you call such a soul but a god dwelling as a guest in the human body? A soul like this may descend into a Roman equestrian as well as into a freedman's son or a slave. For what is a Roman equestrian or a freedman's son or a slave? They are mere titles, born of ambition or of wrong. One may leap to heaven from the very slums. Only rise and mold thyself into kinship with thy God.

PART III

THE
NAZARENE

"The role of a prefect in the province," Tiberius once said, "is to shear his sheep, not skin them." A governor could act with brutal force, if necessary, to keep the peace, but the goal was to be a good shepherd.

Nobody would have used that phrase to describe Pontius Pilate.

He didn't even look the part. He was more Praetorian Guard than provincial governor. He was short and muscular, a committed disciple to exercising in his Caesarean bath complex before his evening meal. He was bald with an oval face, weathered skin, a furrowed forehead, small and close-set eyes, and a natural sneer. He preferred his gold breastplate and scarlet armor from his days as a guard to the long red robes of a magistrate.

Nor was his disposition well suited to the administrative drudgery of running a province. I learned early on that he could be stubborn, inflexible, and petty. He was Roman to the core and never understood, or even tried to understand, the Jewish culture. His sole goal was to serve his time and secure an advancement to a position in Rome. And nothing was more important in achieving that goal than currying favor with Caesar.

Ironically enough, it was this need for Caesar's approval that allowed me to become one of Pilate's closest confidants.

As the personal representative of the emperor, it was Pilate's job to maintain a detailed record of everything that happened in his province. Every day Pilate was expected to add to his *commentarii* and send copies to the provincial archives in Rome along with excerpts to Tiberius at Capri. When I first arrived, Pilate's private secretary wrote the *commentarii* in cursive script on parchment as Pilate dictated.

To prepare for these formal reports, informal notes would be jotted down during the day by Pilate's advisers on wax tablets.

Pilate would scan the reports and data, dictate summaries to his secretary, and then change the wording and start over. He wrote with little confidence and no flair. He was never really satisfied with the report destined for Tiberius, but he would eventually have it copied, seal both copies with his signet ring, and dispatch them with two duplicate couriers to Capri.

That entire process changed when Pilate discovered that I had a way with words. At first, I joined him as he dictated. I watched him pace the room with his hands behind his back, struggling to find the right phrase. I would suggest a certain wording. "Yes! Yes!" Pilate would exclaim. "That's it precisely. Say that again, Theophilus." He'd walk over to his secretary, peering over the man's shoulder, making sure he got the words exactly right.

Before long, Pilate was merely suggesting the substance and I was dictating the entire letter. He would read it afterward and sometimes make changes, though I cringed when I read some of them.

From time to time, Tiberius would reply to one of the *commentarii*, probably just to demonstrate that he actually read them. When he did, he only seemed to have questions about the parts that Pilate drafted. The result was that Pilate began entrusting more and more of his writing responsibilities to me.

After about a year, Pilate insisted that I join him for his morning shave. It was a long and tedious process, and Pilate, being a morning person, didn't want the time to go to waste. Every military man had heard the stories of how Julius Caesar read reports each morning as he shaved, taking advantage of every minute. Hence, it became expected of all magistrates to do the same.

Pilate and I would sit side by side while the barbers clipped my hair and shaved his head, then splashed cold water on our cheeks and the backs of our necks, dragging their razors across our skin. After each stroke, the barber would wipe the blade along a leather strop, and Pilate and I would talk about the challenges of the day, interrupted by an occasional curse when the barber slipped and drew blood.

Unfortunately, it was easier to write about the province than to govern it. And no matter how much I gilded the words and made the sentences dance, the fact of the matter was that things were bumpy in Palestine. Pilate seemed determined to rule Judea from Caesarea, the gleaming city by the sea. The city had been largely rebuilt by Herod the Great, a client king who had reigned in Judea for thirty years, prior to Pilate. Caesarea was magnificent in its architecture and diverse in its inhabitants. For Pilate, it was both comfortable and fitting for a man of his stature. He left only when absolutely necessary.

But staying hunkered down in Caesarea wasn't Pilate's only weakness. He made no effort to understand the Jewish people. For Pilate, they were eccentric and uncompromising, impossible to figure out. Judea was the one province where Rome had been unable to impose its religion and culture. Thus, instead of being forced to adopt the state-sanctioned religion of Rome, which combined the sacrifices to the traditional gods of the Roman pantheon with emperor worship, the inhabitants of Judea were allowed to continue in their Judaism. Accommodation was the order of the day. And Pilate could never understand why the Jewish leaders weren't more grateful.

I knew this was one of Pilate's blind spots, so I made it my mission to study the Jewish religion and to dialogue with their leaders. On more than one occasion, I listened to the great Jewish rabbi Gamaliel teach in the Temple courtyard. I befriended members of the Jewish Sanhedrin and became particularly close to the leaders with substantial wealth—men like Joseph of Arimathea and Nicodemus. Still, the Jewish customs seemed bizarre, antiquated, and inflexible. In Rome, we used our religion for personal gain and favor, bending the rules as necessary to advance our individual agendas. But the Jews took the opposite view. These men would rather die than transgress the thousands of nuanced laws and customs required by their God.

During my first two years in the province, tensions simmered just beneath the surface. Pilate's soldiers were itching for an excuse to attack. The Jews awaited a Messiah who would shatter the yoke of Roman domination. Pilate seethed and sulked, making his reports to Caesar, biding his time, keeping his body in shape, and planning the next set of games for the arena in Caesarea. For my part, I felt trapped in the middle, doing my best to apply Roman law without triggering Jewish sensibilities.

Though we managed to hold it together for two long years, I awoke each morning with a feeling in the pit of my stomach that before long, it would all unravel.

The first thread was pulled in the Roman Senate.

— CHAPTER 16 —

I was with Pilate when the letter came from a friend in Rome. Pilate read the first few sentences, and his face went ashen. A frown furrowed deep into his forehead as he read the rest of the letter and handed it to me without speaking.

According to Pilate's friend, Tiberius Caesar had sent an official letter to the Senate, to be read in the presence of Sejanus. The letter started by praising Sejanus, making it seem like the seventy-one-year-old Tiberius was getting ready to appoint Sejanus as his successor.

But then Tiberius's rambling letter took a strange turn. Without explanation, Tiberius made several accusations against Sejanus, including charges that Sejanus had plotted against the emperor himself. Tiberius's letter, which took nearly an hour to read, dismissed Sejanus as commander of the Praetorian Guard and appointed a man named Macro to take his place. Even as the letter was being read in the Senate, Macro and his guards were gathering outside the doors.

Tiberius had concluded the letter by requesting that the Senate lodge charges against Sejanus and conduct a trial to determine whether he was guilty of treason.

The news sucked the breath out of me, especially when I read what happened next. The Senate ordered the arrest of Sejanus and sent him to the Tullianum, a notorious cesspool where Roman generals had traditionally placed conquered kings or high-profile dignitaries just before their executions. That same night he was convicted in a mockery of a trial on the portico of the temple of Concord. The Forum was packed with citizens, shoulder to shoulder, cheering every charge against Sejanus and drowning out any attempt by Sejanus to defend himself.

Immediately after the senators declared him guilty, Sejanus was executed by strangulation. Two soldiers pulled on ropes looped around his neck until he died, no doubt in agony. His body was thrown down the Gemonian Stairs that led to the temple. And instead of leaving the body there to rot, as was the custom with traitors, the crowd had surged forward and ripped the body to pieces.

Riots ensued as statues of Sejanus were torn down and ground to dust. His wife and children were arrested and held for trial. His friends fled Rome for the countryside.

Visions of the dead ruler flashed through my mind as I finished reading the letter from Pilate's friend. I could recall so vividly Sejanus's regality and stone-faced temperament at the games. The way he had carried himself around Rome—a seasoned commander of Roman legions and the Praetorian Guard. The way people had groveled to earn his patronage, freedmen and senators alike. Like so many others, I had received my first post from Sejanus.

"Did you see this coming?" I asked Pilate.

He shook his head, his thoughts clearly a thousand miles away.

Pilate had served under Sejanus. On more than one occasion,

Pilate had regaled me with stories about those years, about the love/hate relationship between Sejanus and his troops. The stories were interesting in their own right, but for Pilate, I could tell they also had a reassuring undertone. Sejanus was a buffer between Pilate and Tiberius. As long as Sejanus lived, Pilate would never feel the full fury of the emperor's wrath.

Now that buffer was gone.

"Rome lost a friend, as did I," Pilate said.

Maybe. But I never saw him shed a tear.

In the ensuing weeks, Pilate came up with a plan that I knew immediately would not end well. I tried to talk him out of it, and I had a strong ally in his wife, Procula, a most remarkable woman. She was ten years younger than her husband, as close to my age as to his, but was absolutely devoted to him. She had a charming face, a full figure, the slight hint of a double chin, and the smooth skin of a noble, though she too hailed from an equestrian family. Her eyes were her most expressive feature—narrow and elongated, inquisitive and bright. She took great care to accentuate them with makeup and always had her eyebrows done exactly so. The eyes drew you in and held you, and she was smart enough to know it.

Pilate made no secret of his affections for her, a rare exception to his usual gruff demeanor. She was easy to love and a favorite of all the staff—upbeat and energetic, the intellectual equal to any man in Caesarea.

Yet even Procula couldn't talk Pilate out of this idea.

"It's my private residence!" he thundered. "No Jew is going to tell me how to adorn my private residence!"

He was talking, or rather shouting, about the shields. After mourning the death of Sejanus, Pilate had gathered fifty shields, coated them with gold, and consecrated them to Tiberius. He ordered them hung in his private palace in Jerusalem, an extravagant and gaudy building with enormous rooms, high ceilings, and terraces that overlooked the city. I reminded him that Jerusalem was a holy city. "Hang them in Caesarea," I urged him. "It's the capital anyway."

Pilate wouldn't hear of it. Shields like these were hung everywhere in the empire—public buildings, temples, even in lavish private homes. The inscription on the shields was not inflammatory. How could the Jews find it offensive? *Pilate to Tiberius.* It was the least he could do to honor the emperor in a province where, because of the emperor's kindness, the people could worship their own God and were exempted from military service.

"Who could object to it?" Pilate asked.

It was a rhetorical question, and I chose not to answer. Instead, I looked to Procula, who shrugged and shook her head.

There was no reasoning with Pilate when he got like this.

— CHAPTER 17 —

As *assessore*, I stood behind Pilate's seat when Herod Antipas, who ruled the neighboring region of Galilee, presented his petition along with his brother and two other Jewish leaders. Their long beards were carefully trimmed, their flowing robes dutifully pressed. They brought more servants than necessary in a regal display designed to remind Pilate that their ancestor, Herod the Great, was the one who had built the very palace where Pilate was now holding court. Herod the Great had been a true friend of Caesar, they reminded Pilate. And he would never have attempted to desecrate the Holy City.

"Do not arouse sedition; do not destroy the peace," they pleaded.

"You do not honor the emperor by dishonoring the ancient laws. Tiberius does not want our customs to be overthrown. If you say he does, produce a letter so that we can stop pestering you and start petitioning him."

Pilate didn't respond, but I could tell he was boiling. He stared at the ground in front of him, denying Herod even the courtesy of eye contact. The back of Pilate's neck was red, and I prepared myself for an eruption of his infamous temper.

Instead, when Herod finished, Pilate showed no emotion whatsoever. "Finished?" he asked, looking at Herod for the first time.

"If there is no such letter, we will appeal to Caesar ourselves," Herod threatened.

"Do as you must," Pilate responded. He rose abruptly, pivoted, and turned his back to them. He marched into the palace, and I followed, leaving the Jewish leaders staring into space.

Despite Pilate's bluster, the threat was not lost on him. We labored that night to draft a preemptive report, alternating between presenting the incident as a small annoyance on the one hand and making it seem like an affront to Tiberius himself on the other. Perhaps, Pilate said, if we played our cards right, Tiberius would award Pilate the neighboring territory of Herod Antipas in addition to Judea.

We ultimately decided to downplay the incident. Tiberius didn't like prefects who couldn't handle their own provinces. And this time Sejanus wasn't around to provide cover.

The shields weren't coming down. Pilate just wanted Tiberius to know that the delicate sensitivities of his Jewish subjects had been offended once again. But Tiberius was the son of the divine Augustus, and nothing was going to stop Pilate from worshiping him in his own quarters.

Pilate sealed the letter, stared at it for a very long time, and sent it off.

✝

Even a military man like Pilate—no, *especially* a military man like Pilate—could not easily shrug off the sting of a sharp rebuke. And this rebuke, having been sealed by the signet ring of Tiberius Caesar, cut particularly deep, creating a sense of despondency that made Pilate nearly suicidal.

The letter from Caesar contained none of the usual formalities and perfunctory words of flattery. Instead, Tiberius cut straight to the point. He had read the report from Pilate and had received correspondence from the Jewish delegation. He was not pleased. Pilate's job, Tiberius reminded him, was to govern Judea, not start a provincial war.

> *Each of your predecessors was wise enough to respect the peculiar customs and practices of the Jewish people while at the same time firmly enforcing Roman law. I was told you had the wisdom and courage to do the same. Perhaps I was misinformed.*

Tiberias ended the letter with an order that left no room for interpretation.

> *Take down the shields. Send them to the temple of Augustus in Caesarea.*

Pilate hardly spoke a word all day. Even Procula couldn't console him.

That night he showed up at the baths at the normal time. We lifted our weights in silence while other staff members spoke in hushed tones.

"Put on the gloves," Pilate demanded partway through our regimen.

It wasn't an unusual request. Greco-style boxing, using gloves of padded leather that we wrapped around our hands, was part of our routine. Pilate was strong as a bull but not well trained. I could parlay his thrusts with quickness, stamina, and a three-inch reach advantage.

We normally started slow, circling, measuring each other, before Pilate would invariably plunge straight ahead. Tonight he didn't wait. He attacked me with a viciousness I had never before seen. I back-pedaled and jabbed, but he just kept coming, grunting as he landed blows, sweat spraying from his body. His right fist caught the bridge of my nose, and blood spurted. A left felt like it cracked my ribs. I held up my hands and gave him a quizzical look, but the bull just attacked again.

I blocked a few of his punches, and he stopped to catch his breath. Blood was dripping down my face.

"I'm twenty years older, Theophilus," Pilate said, huffing. "I thought you knew how to fight."

When we reengaged, I no longer treated him as the prefect. I caught him with a fist just above his left eye and opened a gash. People gathered around, halting their own exercises to watch. For the next twenty minutes, we put on a show nearly worthy of the arena, attacking each other with anger, grimaces, and cursing until we were both covered in blood and sweat.

Finally, with Pilate too tired to raise his hands for another blow, he took a couple steps back. Blood dripped down his face and dropped from his chin to the marble. He bent over, his chest heaving. I was holding my nose, trying to stanch the bleeding.

Those who had gathered around started clapping, politely at first and then louder. I unwrapped my hands and began to clap myself.

Pilate caught his breath, stood, and unwrapped his gloves. He nodded brusquely at those clapping and brushed past me. "Come on," he said. "You bleed like a pig."

After the slaves dabbed the wounds and stopped the bleeding, we took our turn in the cold bath, the warm chamber, and ultimately the hot marble tub. Afterward, the servants rubbed our bodies, closing the pores of our skin against the cold before they scraped us with a bronze blade.

"Feel better?" I asked.

Pilate thought about the question for a long moment. "Every time I look at those damnable shields in the temple, every time I offer incense or sacrifices to Tiberius, I will hear his words of condemnation."

I didn't press the point or dare remind him that I had recommended against the shields. If he hadn't learned this time, I reasoned, he would never learn.

—— CHAPTER 18 ——

Aesculapius was the god of medicine and healing. He was conceived when Apollo impregnated Coronis. While she was pregnant, Coronis fell in love with another man and for her unfaithfulness was sentenced to burning. Just before Coronis died, Apollo rescued his son, cutting him from his mother's womb. Apollo named him Aesculapius, which literally meant "to cut open."

To compensate for the loss of a mother, Apollo gave his son the ability to heal people, and Aesculapius grew into a renowned physician. In fact, his healing powers became so great, he started raising people from the dead. The healings stopped when Jupiter, jealous about someone else having the privilege of immortality, killed Aesculapius with a thunderbolt.

Even in death, the god's power was not extinguished. Aesculapius had healed hundreds, perhaps thousands, by his touch. He had brought men and women back from the dead. He became a favorite god among the Greeks and Romans. Rulers constructed temples in his name, and the masses called on him for healing.

So it was that Procula, the beloved wife of Pilate and the mother of his three children, turned to Aesculapius in desperate need of healing. She told me about the experience during a long walk by the Mediterranean Sea a few weeks after she had recovered from her near-fatal illness. I knew she had spent the night in the temple. I knew she had miraculously recovered. But she had not told anyone but Pilate about the vision until that day, when she shared her story with me.

✝

For four days, Procula had been running a fever that would not break. She had tried everything. Pilate had offered sacrifices to the usual pantheon of gods, sat tenderly at her bedside dabbing her forehead with a damp cloth, hired Greek doctors to prescribe herbal medicines and drain Procula's blood. She had endured cold baths followed by heated saunas designed to sweat the fever away. But nothing worked, and Pilate was on the verge of panic. "Don't leave me," he pleaded with Procula.

She managed a weak smile, reaching out for his hand. "I'm not going anywhere," she assured him.

It was bravado, and they both knew it. During the first two days of the sickness, she had been vomiting and couldn't seem to get warm even as her forehead was burning up.

By day three she was weak and fading. She just wanted to curl up and cover herself with blankets. Instead, the doctors drew her blood and forced her to endure the cold baths and hot saunas again. She slept fitfully, screaming herself awake in the middle of gruesome nightmares.

On the fourth day, the doctors gave her poppy seeds to reduce the pain. That's when the hallucinations started. That evening, as the fever spiked again, they all knew it was time for her to spend the night at the altar of Aesculapius.

She gathered her strength, took a bath, and put on a simple white linen dress. Pilate and her servants walked with her to the temple at dusk, one servant supporting each arm, but that was as far as they could go. Pilate gave her a kiss, and she entered the temple alone.

She knelt before the altar and the marble statue of Aesculapius. "Heal me, O god of eternal life."

She had brought a nonvenomous snake in a burlap bag. She hated snakes, but she hated the disease more. She would do anything to get rid of the fever, to stop the hallucinations, to feel like herself again.

Snakes were sacred to Aesculapius. He had not only healed many people from poisonous snakebites, but snakes supposedly obeyed his voice, wrapping themselves around a stick at his command. As Procula opened the bag, reaching inside to grab the snake just behind its head, she felt woozy. She wondered if she might pass out on the marble floor.

The snake she had brought, long and green and scaly to the touch, didn't seem to fall under the god's spell. As soon as Procula set it down, the serpent slithered off the altar toward the base of the statue.

Her servants had prepared honey cakes, and she pulled them out of a second bag, placing them on the altar as well. From that same bag, she removed a bottle of wine, poured some of it on the altar, and set the bottle down next to the honey cakes. Her bags empty, she walked to a side wall of the temple and sat on the floor, leaning her head back and repeating the words over and over: "Heal me, O god of eternal life."

She needed sleep, but she was too cold. She knew that those who slept in the temple of Aesculapius had dreams that would describe the cure for their ailments. It was her only hope. She needed to sleep. She needed to dream.

"Heal me, O god of eternal life." She shivered against the stone. She was freezing, her body shaking. It was dark outside, and the temple was lit only by the oil lamps on the altar. She watched the snake explore the nooks and crannies of the stone temple.

At one point, the snake slithered toward her, and she held her breath. It stopped a few feet away and seemed to regard her with curiosity. She couldn't harm the snake because it was now sacred.

She froze with terror as the snake came toward her again. She tensed every muscle and closed her eyes, her skin tingling with fear. She felt the serpent crawl over her left calf, and she nearly shrieked as she looked down to see it draped over her leg. It stayed there for a breath-holding, heart-stopping moment, and then it slithered away.

She wanted to leave herself.

"Heal me, O god of eternal life."

Sometime later, still shivering against the cold, Procula curled into a fetal position on her right side. It was quiet in the temple. The floor was cold and hard. It smelled musty. She couldn't get the snake out of her mind. What if it came back and crawled across her face?

"Heal me, O god of eternal life."

Those were the last words she mumbled before she fell into a fitful sleep. The last words before she had the vision.

The man's face was both beautiful and bloodied. His left eye was purple and swollen nearly shut. His beard and features were Jewish, but he wore a purple robe of royalty. Somebody had wedged a crown of thorns on his forehead—briars that cut into his skin and formed rivulets of blood that streaked down his face and matted his beard.

Yet there was strength in the firm-set jaw and compassion in the eyes. He stretched out his hand and touched Procula. He mumbled something—a prayer in Aramaic that Procula didn't understand. He placed a hand on her forehead as he spoke. When he had finished, he brushed her hair gently behind her ear and smiled.

She wanted to thank him or minister to him. She tried to reach out and lift the thorns from his head or wipe the blood from his face. But she seemed powerless, paralyzed. She could not even speak. The man knelt there for a moment; then he rose and was gone.

At dawn, Pilate came to wake her. Gently he touched her shoulder and whispered in her ear. He placed blankets around her shoulders.

"How are you feeling?" he asked.

It took her a minute to process the question. She was still freezing and she felt weak, but somehow she knew that her strength was returning. She wasn't dizzy anymore, and it seemed she could focus on her husband for the first time in days.

"Better, I think."

Together, they made their way to the altar. Pilate had brought a rooster, its wings and beak tied with leather. He placed it on the altar and handed Procula the knife. She gathered her strength; she would need all of it for the next moment of chaos and flurry. With her left hand, she grabbed the legs of the rooster and squeezed. As Pilate helped hold the bird in place, Procula sliced the leather that tied the bird's beak, and it immediately squawked. Quickly, she cut the leather cord on the bird's back and its wings flailed out, feathers flying. She squeezed the legs harder, holding on, the adrenaline flowing, and drew the knife across the rooster's neck.

Another flap of the wings, a warm stream of blood that covered her hand, and then the stillness was back.

She handed the knife to Pilate, and they left together. He pressed a cheek to her forehead and told her that he thought the fever might have broken. For the first time, she realized that her body was soaked with sweat.

There was a litter waiting outside the temple, and Pilate helped her in for the jostling ride back to the palace. She closed her eyes and tried to picture the face of the man who had come to heal her. Had the healing already taken place, or did she need to do more?

That question was answered in the next two days. The fever subsided. Her strength returned. Three days after she left the temple of Aesculapius, she returned with more honey cakes and a prayer of thanks. She stared at the face of the statue. She tried to imagine the statue brought to life, battered and bruised, a crown of thorns on its forehead. But no matter how hard she tried, she couldn't make that face resemble the one she had seen in her dream.

Nevertheless, she said her prayer of thanks and left.

✝

When she finished her story, she looked at me with inquisitive eyes. "What do you make of this?"

In truth, I had no idea. "I'm just glad you are well," I said.

And none too soon. In seven days, we would be heading to Jerusalem. It was time for the great Jewish feast of Passover. Pilate and his soldiers would be needed to keep the peace. And Procula would be needed to help keep Pilate in check. He was still seething about the shields.

We took a few more steps in silence, and I thought about the healing power of Aesculapius. "With power like that," I said, "I can see why Jupiter wanted him dead."

"Yet even Jupiter could not destroy a god with the gift of eternal life," Procula said.

We were deep into legend now, and I decided to let it go. I wasn't sure that I believed any of it, though I had witnessed Procula's healing like everyone else.

Who can comprehend the ways of the gods? I wondered.

—— CHAPTER 19 ——

After two days of travel, we entered Jerusalem late in the afternoon on Sunday, five days before the Jewish celebration of Passover. As always, we entered in grand style. Pilate first, sitting erect on the back of a large white stallion, its harness trimmed with gold and silver. He wore a white tunic with maroon sleeves and the dark-green armor of a legionnaire. A sword glistened at his side. For occasions like this, he had found that the armor garnered more respect than the toga.

Our entire procession was designed to impress and intimidate. The captain of the provincial troops, a burly veteran of the wars in Germania, rode next to Pilate. Three thousand soldiers marched behind, lining the roads six abreast, their swords and shields polished, their sandals kicking up a small dust storm.

Procula and I rode behind them all, eating the dust with the other civil servants and the wagons weighed down with supplies. Hundreds of slaves brought up the rear. It wasn't easy moving the capital of Judea for a week.

During our sixty-five-mile journey, we had passed a steady stream of Jewish pilgrims making their way to the Holy City. They traveled in small family units, fathers and children walking, mothers sometimes riding a mule or a donkey. They moved slowly, carrying cages with pigeons and pulling along sheep or goats. They would get off the road and stand aside as we passed, gawking at those of us on horses, sometimes averting their eyes when I looked at them. Some of the children waved. Procula and I waved back.

By the time we entered the gates of the city, the streets were bursting with pilgrims. Normally the city housed seventy-five thousand residents. During Passover week, according to our best estimates, the population swelled to nearly two hundred thousand. Add in a few hundred thousand animals, and it was easy to understand why Passover, with its frenetic slaughtering of animals and crowds teeming with patriotic and spiritual zeal, was Pilate's least favorite week of the year.

The crowds made way as we marched through the center of the city. I was constantly mindful of the looks and murmurs of the Jewish inhabitants. We ended our march at the Praetorium, the fortresslike palace that Herod the Great had built on the western edge of the upper city. The western side was fortified by the wall of the city as well as an inner wall forty-five feet high with towers at regular intervals. On the north side, there were enormous white marble block towers topped with battlements. The Praetorium loomed over the city and was, by all accounts, impenetrable.

There were more than one hundred guest rooms in the palace and dozens of huge banquet halls built with rare stones and cedars from Lebanon. Elegant furniture and gold artifacts adorned the various rooms. Bronze statues, Corinthian pillars, and mosaic marble floors graced the large halls. The lush, green grounds of the palace contained gardens and ponds, patios and groves, with running water gushing out of marble statues.

Pilate hated the place. He couldn't get over the odor drifting up from the city—the carcasses of animals, the sweaty masses of people, the smell of burning flesh from the animal sacrifices, and the grease from the tens of thousands of cooking fires. We would burn incense inside the palace all day long to cover the smell. We planned to stay until the day after Passover and not a minute longer.

The feast itself had ominous undertones. Passover was the Jews' most sacred holiday, a celebration of Israel's delivery from slavery in Egypt more than a thousand years earlier. On the last night before their release, an angel of the Lord had instructed Moses to have his people slaughter lambs—pure lambs without any blemish—and spread the blood on the doorposts of their homes. An angel of death, according to the Jewish legends, then killed all firstborn males of the Egyptian households but passed over the Israelites who had taken refuge under the blood. The next day, there was wailing in Egypt, and the Israelites went free.

As far as I was concerned, the story was pure myth, but the ramifications were real. This was the time of year when the Jewish people celebrated God's victory over their oppressors. Throughout Judea, there were always murmurs of freedom and revolution. But this week, more than any other, brought those murmurs into the open.

The Passover ceremony incorporated symbolism of bloodshed,

sacrifice, and rebellion. Young boys, at the end of the Passover meal, ran to the front doors of their homes to look for a prophet named Elijah, the forerunner to the Jewish Messiah. The Messiah, their long-awaited deliverer, would supposedly do to the Romans what Moses had done to the Egyptians. He would usher in a new golden age for Israel, bringing justice that flowed like a river and righteousness like a never-failing stream.

I was all for righteousness. And I had devoted my life to justice. But for obvious reasons, I wasn't fond of the ancient Israelite prophecies that talked about the overthrow of Jewish oppressors.

"There have always been God-fearing Gentiles who are friends of Israel," Joseph of Arimathea once told me. He was perpetually trying to get me to worship the God of the Jews. "Even some of the great leaders of Persia, during the time of Daniel, once worshiped our God."

"I can handle the worship," I quipped. "It's the circumcision that makes me nervous."

Joseph didn't smile. He took his religion very seriously.

This year, the rumors had reached the Praetorium before we did. Another entourage had apparently arrived in Jerusalem prior to us. It was led by a man named Jesus, a miracle worker, riding on a donkey, his feet scraping the ground. The crowds had surged toward him, placing their cloaks and palm branches in his path.

Pilate's Jewish sources reported the scene breathlessly. "People pressed in and shouted, 'Hosanna! Blessed is he who comes in the name of the Lord!' Women were crying. They held their children out to him, asking for a blessing."

"Was he armed?" Pilate asked.

"No, Your Excellency."

"Did he have any soldiers?"

"No, Your Excellency."

"Was he giving speeches or inciting hatred for Rome?"

"He is not that kind of leader, sir."

Pilate smirked. Perhaps he was replaying the scene in his mind. "And he was riding a donkey?"

"Exactly."

Pilate dismissed the men and shook his head. "A donkey," he said to me as if he couldn't believe it. Pilate had fought in real battles against ruthless barbarians. Now it was his job to protect Rome from a commander who charged into town on a donkey.

"Let's hit the baths," Pilate said.

It sounded like a good idea to me.

— CHAPTER 20 —

The magnificence of Herod's Praetorium was surpassed in Jerusalem only by the grandeur of the Temple. Even for a person like me, raised in the gleaming city of Rome, the sight was breathtaking. The Temple complex was the center of the Jewish universe, the place where all culture and religion ultimately found its expression. If Herod's Praetorium was the moon, the Temple was the sun. The former was a dwelling place for an egocentric provincial governor; the latter was a dwelling place for God.

Herod had rebuilt the Temple during his reign, throwing ten thousand workers and over a thousand priests at the task. You could see it from miles away, a great white structure framed by a granite courtyard spanning thirty-five acres. It was surrounded by great porticoes consisting of two rows of huge marble columns, thirty-eight feet high, supporting cedar beams and a red-tiled roof. Only the purest white stone was used in the Temple construction, and it gave the building and its courtyard an incandescent feel. To see the Temple, said the Jews, was to glimpse the glory of God.

At the center of the massive outer Temple courtyard, commonly referred to as the Courtyard of the Gentiles, was the sacred core of Temple buildings. Those buildings were separated from the Courtyard of the Gentiles by a stone wall about four feet high and a gate with signs in both Greek and Latin, warning Gentiles like me that we could proceed no farther on pain of death.

The lowliest Jewish peasant from the smallest crag in the land of Galilee could enter, but Pilate and I could not go past that gate. Rome might rule the entire Mediterranean world, yet Romans couldn't set foot on this small piece of real estate at the center of Herod's Temple.

Inside the stone wall were other barriers that filtered more people out—the Courtyard of Women and the Courtyard of Priests. The Temple itself stood in the very middle, its white granite carefully polished, its gold overlay flashing in the sun. It had a flat roof with gold spikes to keep the birds away. And inside the Temple, behind an enormous double curtain, was a place the Israelites called the Holy of Holies—so sacred that it could only be entered by the high priest once a year on Yom Kippur, after the priest had ritually purified himself and offered appropriate sacrifices. It was, according to the Jews, the place where their God, Yahweh, dwelled. Entering the Holy of Holies was so dangerous that they tied a rope to the priest's ankle in order to drag him out if he died while performing his tasks.

I was fascinated by the transformation of the Temple during Passover. Dusty travelers and dirty animals turned the marble Courtyard of the Gentiles into a farmyard. The smell of blood and incense filled the air for an entire week, mixed in with the peculiar smell of serious money being made.

The first time I had wandered through the courtyard during Passover week, I realized that the Romans could learn a thing or two from the Jews about taxation. For starters, the Temple tax could only be paid using Tyrian coins, meaning that tables of money changers were spread throughout the courtyard to convert common coinage into Tyrian shekels. All at an appropriate premium, of course. And that was just the beginning.

The Passover pilgrims were also required to bring an animal deemed acceptable for sacrifice. For even the poorest Jews, this meant at least a pigeon. But there was a catch. The bird had to be spotless and pure, with no bruises or imperfections from the journey. As I watched, the Temple priests solemnly inspected the birds and sadly shook their heads. Not good enough. Fortunately for the traveler, however, the priests had a whole cage of pigeons that were preapproved. The traveler traded his damaged bird for an approved bird, again at a steep premium. Once the worshiper sulked away, the priest took the defective bird, inspected it again, and realized that the animal was more pure and spotless than originally thought. Into the cage it went to be sold to the next road-weary worshiper.

†

The second day of our week in Jerusalem, I was standing on the balcony of the Antonia Fortress, a fortified tower that hovered over the northwest corner of the Courtyard of the Gentiles. I was watching the soldiers play a game with knucklebones that they called *basilinda*, the Greek word for *king*. The events in the courtyard below happened so quickly that I nearly missed them.

There was shouting and pointing, a commotion under the porticoes at the north end. In the center of the action was a single man, a furious Jew who was creating all kinds of chaos, overturning the tables of the money changers and releasing pigeons from their cages.

The soldiers saw it and started fastening their armor. I held out a hand to the captain. There were Temple guards down there; let them handle it.

The Jew at the center of the havoc was shouting something, his white robe flying behind him. He was thin and sinewy, but he had the hardened look of a laborer. He sent tables flying with explosive strength. A crowd formed in his wake, and the Temple traders scrambled around on the ground, chasing after coins that were rolling on marble. They cursed at the interloper. Others packed up their tables and moved out of the way before he could get to them.

The crowd behind him started cheering, and I found myself relishing this spontaneous rebellion against the money changers. "It's about time," I mumbled to myself.

The man had no weapons, and the Temple guards started closing in. Despite my attempts to delay them, the Roman soldiers from the fortress had sprung into action as well, rushing toward the steps of the Temple courtyard. They were bored. They wanted action.

As suddenly as he started, the madman stopped. He caught his breath and turned this way and that as if he were daring anyone to challenge him. The crowd fell back; the priests and guards gave him a wide berth.

"My house shall be called a house of prayer for all nations!" he shouted at the priests. He swept his arm in a great arc. "But you have made it a den of thieves!"

For a moment there was silence, and it seemed like the crowd held its collective breath, waiting for the religious leaders to respond. But the priests just sneered and walked away. The Temple guards put their swords back in their sheaths. One or two folded their arms across their chests.

A member of the crowd shouted, "Hosanna!" and others echoed the cheer. People began pressing toward the man, approaching from all areas of the courtyard—thousands of them, trying to get close enough to touch him. He talked to them and smiled, reaching out to place a hand on a beggar's head, stopping to pray for a man who appeared to be blind.

From the balcony, I witnessed a strange phenomenon. The inner courtyards and the Temple proper, with all its polished marble and gleaming gold, were attracting little attention. The center of gravity had shifted to this table turner, this fearless maniac who seemed to have a grudge against the religious establishment. At the very least, he was now a folk hero.

Or perhaps he was more. The crowd gathered close around and listened in hushed silence as he talked, hanging on his every word. A stillness spread out from him in every direction. At one point, he apparently called for the children, and they scrambled up into his lap.

Was he a threat to Rome? I didn't think so. A Temple reformer? Maybe. The priests and the Temple guards were certainly keeping their distance, gathering in small huddles and casting sideways glances at him.

Our own soldiers stayed on the edges of the crowd, letting the people see that the Roman guards were there to keep the peace. Yet the man who had started it all didn't seem to notice or care. He looked like he was having fun now, a man of the people.

I wanted to find out more about him. I needed information. And I needed a good glass of wine. Once the sun went down and much of the city went to sleep, I knew a place where I could find both.

—— CHAPTER 21 ——

This was the life. The great estate of my friend sprawled out before me on a vast hillside a few miles outside the city, wheat fields and vineyards stretching in every direction. The air was cooler and crisper here, a nice reprieve from the stale air that hung over Jerusalem.

I sipped the wine, Judea's best, from a silver cup. We stood on a marble terrace, leaning on a railing of carved stone, staring mind-lessly at the thousands of oil lamps that still burned in the city.

I was surprised when Nicodemus told me that the volcanic rabbi in the Temple, Jesus of Nazareth, had stood on this same terrace before. Nearly a year earlier, he had come at night, at the request of Nicodemus, and shared a cup of wine with one of Israel's wealthiest rulers.

"I've become a disciple," Nicodemus said. "Though I haven't let it be widely known."

"Your rabbi certainly has a flair for the dramatic."

"You could say that."

I took a deep breath of night air and felt myself relax. I had learned a long time ago that Nicodemus was my intellectual equal. Neither of us felt the need to impress the other. Our growing friendship transcended cultural differences.

"What did you talk about when he was here?" I asked.

"He's a rabbi, Theophilus. We talked about religion."

"Is he a threat to Rome?" I asked, getting right to the point.

Nicodemus took his time thinking about it. When he spoke, he seemed to be measuring his words. "Have you heard about the way he healed the centurion's servant?"

"No. My Jewish sources seem to be failing me."

Nicodemus ignored my little barb and told me the story of how Jesus had allegedly healed the servant of a Roman centurion. "He didn't even need to go and see him, Theophilus. He just said the word and the man was healed."

"Sounds impressive," I said. "If it's true."

Nicodemus chuckled. "Always the skeptic."

"I'm Roman. It's in my blood."

"The point, my friend, is that even after the healing, Jesus never tried to get the centurion to leave the service of Rome. In fact, Jesus told his own followers that he'd never seen such great faith in all of Israel. Does that sound like somebody intent on overthrowing Rome?"

I enjoyed another swallow of wine and relaxed a bit more. Perhaps it was the drink. More likely it was the relief of knowing we didn't have a major problem on our hands.

"Why would a rabbi like you—someone revered throughout all of Israel—become the disciple of another rabbi?" I asked.

"Ah," Nicodemus said as if I had finally stepped into his trap. He looked out over the hills and began telling me about Jesus—the things Nicodemus had heard before inviting the man to his estate. The man could cast out demons, heal the lame, cause the blind to see, silence his critics, multiply food. "Some say he walked on water," Nicodemus said, turning just in time to see me smirk. "I know," he quickly added. "I didn't believe that one at first either."

Nicodemus filled me in on their conversation. The rabbi's strange response when Nicodemus asked him about all the miraculous signs he was performing: "'Unless a man is born again, he cannot see the Kingdom of God.'"

Nicodemus paused as if the rabbi's statement was incredibly profound.

I shrugged. What did that even mean? For obvious reasons, I didn't care for the mention of a kingdom, but the reincarnation aspect seemed harmless enough. It was the essence of Eastern religions, and I was surprised Nicodemus had bought into it.

"I don't understand," I said.

"Nor did I," Nicodemus admitted. "When I asked what he meant, he told me that unless a man was born of water and the Spirit, he could not enter the Kingdom of God. He said that what was born of the flesh was flesh, but what was born of the Spirit was spirit."

Again Nicodemus paused as if measuring my reaction. He seemed to be describing the separation of body and soul, a concept familiar to me. It was why in Rome we cremated our dead. The soul journeyed on, but the body did not. A man's soul soared to heaven when it was freed from his body, or it descended through the corridors of the underworld if his life did not measure up.

We talked for nearly an hour. Everlasting life. Immortality. Didn't we all strive for that? Augustus Caesar had lived the kind of life that achieved immortality. And during my time in Greece I could feel the spirit of Cicero coursing through my veins, the man's words and achievements outlasting him. This was why I trained to be an advocate, to develop strength of character, to lead a moral life. But immortality was a rugged climb and not for the faint of heart. In my way of thinking, it was for a select few—those who had the blood of the right ancestors flowing through their veins, who proved themselves in turbulent times. It was not something that could be achieved by normal men.

Nicodemus respectfully but enthusiastically disagreed. Even in the dark, I could see the spark in his eyes. He claimed that Jesus was the Son of God. That whoever believed in him could have eternal life. Even lowly peasants.

I swirled my wine, letting the sweet smell of the grapes fill my nostrils. I reminded my friend that the "Son of God" title had already been taken. The great Tiberius Caesar, son of the divine Augustus.

Nicodemus told me that I should go listen to the rabbi teach. "The leaders of the Sanhedrin are planning to set a trap for him tomorrow in the Temple courtyard," Nicodemus said. "They're going to ask him whether we should pay the imperial tax to Rome."

The imperial tax, paid only by those who lived in the provinces and not by Roman citizens, formed the backbone of Rome's economy. The trap for Jesus was obvious, though no less clever for its transparency. Answer yes and lose the crowd—what kind of Messiah supports the imperial tax? Answer no and lose your life. What kind of Roman ruler would allow such sedition?

Nicodemus had my attention. "What do you think he'll say?"

"Why don't you come and see for yourself?" Nicodemus asked.

I told him I just might. I finished my wine and thanked him for his hospitality. As I was leaving, he put a hand on my shoulder, appraising me with earnest eyes. "You've been a good friend, Theophilus. That's something I cherish. But I cannot put our friendship above the words of the prophets. If this man is the Messiah—and I believe he is—Rome won't be able to stop him. He's not a threat in the way you're worried about. He's not going to take up arms against Rome. But the prophecies are clear. The rulers of the world will all eventually bow to the Jewish Messiah. I don't want you to be on the wrong side of fate."

The words were nearly treasonous, but I figured it was just the wine talking. One thing was certain—Nicodemus would follow this new Messiah anywhere. Yet right now, his main concern seemed to be my welfare.

I decided to shrug it off. "We are Romans, Nicodemus. We make our own fate."

CHAPTER 22

The Temple courtyard was back to normal on Tuesday. It was as if the Nazarene had never passed through the day before, leaving fear, resentment, and a mad scrambling for coins in his wake.

There were a few changes. The Temple guards had proliferated, and the money changers looked wary, glancing around occasionally to see if the wild man was going to make another run at them. But the priests were still inspecting lambs, goats, doves, and pigeons, frowning and shaking their heads, and travelers were still digging into their purses to buy a better animal.

The hum of exploitation had returned.

I wandered around in my white Roman toga, sweltering in the afternoon heat, getting jostled by the busy crowd. At one point I helped a young child of five or six who was standing next to one of the huge Corinthian columns with big tears in his eyes. We scoured the crowd and searched around until we located his parents in another part of the courtyard. His mother thanked me profusely and tried to pay me. I refused with a polite smile. The little boy endured a good tongue-lashing from his father and then scrambled over to give me a hug before they went on their way.

Seneca would have been proud.

At a few minutes after noon, I followed the flow of the crowd to the place where Jesus was teaching. Most of the people were mesmerized by what the rabbi was saying and didn't pay any attention to me.

I found an inconspicuous place in the back and listened. My Aramaic was passable—certainly much better than Pilate's—and I could understand enough to catch the drift.

Jesus was a storyteller. "A man had two sons. . . ." "There was a landowner who planted a vineyard. . . ." "A king prepared a wedding banquet. . . ."

And he wasn't much for happy endings. The son disobeyed his father. The tenants killed the landowner's agents and ultimately even the landowner's son. Nobody came to the wedding. Finally, when somebody did, not wearing proper wedding clothes, he was tied up and thrown out by the king.

"Many are invited but few are chosen," Jesus said.

What intrigued me was the man's presence, the authority with which he taught. He walked around and engaged the crowd, his piercing brown eyes transfixing his listeners. He used the full arsenal of advocacy I had studied in Greece—voice inflections, facial expressions, fluid movement of his rough hands, a smile for a mother holding her child, a hard stare as he delivered a line aimed at the religious leaders. These were things that took me years to learn, yet this man—supposedly a carpenter's son—evidently came by them naturally. The crowd leaned in, silencing anyone who dared talk.

Jesus' eyes snagged on me at the back of the crowd, or so I thought, if only for a brief moment. It seemed like he recognized me from someplace.

"Beware of the teachers of the law," he said, raising his voice. I bristled. Perhaps he thought I didn't know the language. Perhaps he didn't realize my role as Pilate's *assessore*. I could crush him with a word.

"They like to walk around in flowing robes," he continued, surveying the crowd again. "They love to be greeted with respect in the marketplaces and have the most important seats in the synagogues."

I realized that his words weren't aimed at me, and I felt a little silly for momentarily thinking otherwise. He was addressing the Pharisees—the teachers of the Jewish law—standing to his immediate right. They knew it too and scowled back at him, their long faces and glue-stiffened beards registering their disapproval. They wore long black robes, just like Jesus said, prayer shawls with long tassels, and phylacteries, each containing a verse of Scripture, on their foreheads.

The rabbi accused them of devouring widows' houses and told the crowd that the Pharisees would be punished severely by God. Around me, there were murmurs of agreement, and I realized the crowd had grown. I was no longer tucked safely away in the back.

"Teacher," a young man called out from the middle, not too far from where I stood, "we have a question."

The Nazarene walked toward the man and his friends. The crowd parted to let Jesus pass, then came together behind him, encircling him and the young man who had called him out. I could sense a growing tension, like storm clouds at sea ready to make their assault on the land. I knew these men were the ones Nicodemus had told me about, preparing to ask the one question that would bring Jesus down.

I tried to catch the eye of Nicodemus, standing on the other side of the crowd, but he was engrossed in what was happening.

"Teacher, we know that you are a man of integrity and that you teach the way of God in accordance with the truth," the young man said, acting as a spokesman for the group of young Pharisees. "You aren't swayed by others, because you pay no attention to who they are." He paused, speaking loud enough for the entire crowd to hear, though Jesus was right in front of him. "Tell us then, what is your opinion? Is it right to pay the imperial tax to Caesar or not?"

Jesus shook his head. "You hypocrites, why are you trying to trap me?" he asked. "Show me the coin used for paying the tax."

One of his questioners reached into his sack, pulled out a denarius, and gave it to Jesus. The rabbi held it up to the sun, turning it over in his hand.

Exhibit A.

"Whose image is this? And whose inscription?" he asked.

"Mm," some people next to me murmured. His point had not been lost on them.

His questioners worked to maintain their stoic expressions, though you could see a brief flicker of panic in their eyes. The denarius, a silver coin created at the private mint of Tiberius, had a profile of the emperor on one side along with the inscription, *Tiberius Caesar, worshipful son of the god Augustus*. On the other side was a picture of the Roman goddess of peace and the words *Pontifex Maximus*—high priest, the greatest bridge builder to God.

Whose inscription indeed! Jesus held it there, showing it to the crowd as if they'd never seen it before, and his questioners seemed to shuffle away from the suddenly poisonous coin. *You can't tolerate shields in Pilate's private residence but you can bring a graven image of Caesar into the Temple courtyard?* I thought. And from the looks of the faces in the crowd, I wasn't the only one thinking that way.

"Whose image? Whose inscription?" Jesus repeated.

"Caesar's," the young man answered.

Jesus grinned. He handed them the coin. "So give back to Caesar what is Caesar's, and to God what is God's."

✝

It wasn't until the crowd had dispersed and I had a chance to talk with Nicodemus that I fully grasped what had just happened. "Our rabbis have a certain style of interacting with their students," Nicodemus explained. "The rabbi answers a question with another question, referencing the Torah to show the weakness of the student's position. Only then does he actually answer the underlying question. As you know better than most, our commandments say that we shall have no other gods besides Yahweh and we will make no graven images of any other god. When Jesus asked about whose image was on the coin, his audience immediately thought about the commandments and their prohibition of such images."

I nodded. That much I had figured out.

"Jesus also asked about the inscription," Nicodemus continued. "That called to mind the Torah's command to inscribe Yahweh's laws on our hands and our foreheads, on our doorposts, and on the gates of our cities. The most important inscription of all is the *Shema*— 'Hear, O Israel, the Lord is God, the Lord alone. You must love the Lord your God with your entire heart, soul, mind, and strength.'"

I thought about this for a moment, but it still didn't answer my primary question. "Why didn't the crowd seem more upset when he sanctioned the imperial tax?"

Nicodemus looked past me at the activities in the courtyard as if weighing whether he should answer the question at all. Finally he turned to me, and I sensed he was taking a big risk. "In our religion, do you know what belongs to God?" he asked.

"For starters, a whole lot of pigeons, doves, and lambs."

"I'm not just talking about sacrifices," Nicodemus said. As usual, my sarcasm had been lost on him. "'The earth is the Lord's and everything in it.'"

"The Torah again?"

"A psalm of King David."

"*Everything in it.*" This was why it was so tough to govern the Jews. "So you're saying that Jesus was really telling the Jews not to pay the imperial tax?" I asked. My head was swimming a little now.

"I never said that," Nicodemus insisted. "And Jesus didn't either."

Maybe. But I could no longer be sure. And maybe that was the whole point of what Jesus had said, slipping through the jaws of the trap. One thing I did know—the man was a clever advocate.

And perhaps a dangerous one as well.

⸺ CHAPTER 23 ⸺

Two mornings later, I awoke when the cock crowed. I swung my legs over the side of the bed, and the soles of my feet landed on cool marble.

I opened the shutters and looked out at the moon still casting shadows through the tree limbs, the darkness struggling to fight off the first heralds of dawn.

I washed. A servant came and lit the fire. Jerusalem was beautiful from here, peaceful in the first pale rays of sunrise. The dimly lit sky masked the blemishes of the thatched mud homes surrounding the glory of the Temple, illuminating only the intriguing contours of the city—the spikes on the Temple roof, the massive supporting columns, the porticoes surrounding the Temple courtyard, the great wall of Jerusalem winding to the horizon.

There were still fires smoldering from the previous night. Later that day, the day before Passover, the sacrifices would be in full swing. The slit of the knife across the throat of the heifer, the gutting of the lambs, the stabbing of the pigeons and doves. Everywhere you went, you would encounter the reek, so pungent you could taste it in the dry desert air—the odor of death, the stench of burning carcasses. Crimson ribbons of blood would streak the inner Temple courtyard.

Romans engaged in bloodletting for sport. The Jews sanctified it, calling it propitiation.

I yawned. It had been a late night, and I didn't sleep as well in Jerusalem as I did in Caesarea. At least yesterday the Temple had been relatively quiet. The Nazarene and his followers were nowhere to be found.

The sun peeked over the horizon, its rays of hope awakening the city from its slumber. Pilate would be up by now. I would meet him in a few minutes for our morning shave. There were reports to write, disputes to settle, rumors to be investigated.

I put on my toga and sandals, grabbed an oil lamp, and headed to the barber.

In the distance I heard it, not as loud this time, but still unmistakable.

The cock crowed for the second time. The beginning of a new day.

✝

Twenty minutes later, the servants interrupted our morning shave. Pilate and I were deliberating whether we should say anything to Tiberius about the latest Jewish Messiah, the donkey-riding man from Nazareth who had single-handedly cleared the Temple. It was always a delicate balance between telling Caesar too much and telling him too little. Too much and he thinks the province is out of control. Too little and he might hear about the unrest from other sources and think Pilate was keeping something from him. We had decided to mention this latest rift among the Jewish religious leaders while at the same time reassuring Tiberius we had things well under control.

We never got a chance to start the letter.

"The Sanhedrin met in the middle of the night," one of the servants said breathlessly. "They've convicted a man who was leading a rebellion and want to bring him before you."

The barber ran the cold blade down my cheek and wiped it off. I glanced at Pilate and saw the annoyed look on his face.

"Tell them I'm shaving," he said with a flick of the wrist.

But the servant held his ground. The high priest was insistent, demanding an audience. He had most of the Sanhedrin trailing behind him, followed by a large contingent of the Temple guards. A mob was forming. "With respect, Your Excellency," he said, "it may be best to address this quickly."

Pilate looked at me, and I shrugged. This was why we had come to Jerusalem for Passover. Things would only get worse if we let them fester.

"They tried him at night?" I asked. A nighttime trial was prohibited by Jewish law.

"Apparently."

"Did they post notice of the charges in the Temple and send them to us?"

The courier shook his head. "I don't know, sir. I just know that they have already found him guilty and meted out punishment."

Pilate and I exchanged another look. He knew my commitment to the law, my obsession with proper procedures. Roman justice, not our engineering or our military feats, was what separated us from the barbarians, the toga-clad people from those with loincloths.

"Bring them to the judgment seat," Pilate said.

The servant looked down and shuffled his feet.

"What is it?" Pilate asked sharply, making no effort to hide his annoyance.

"It's the day before their High Sabbath," the man said meekly. "They're not willing to come inside."

Pilate grunted. The Jews didn't want to defile themselves by coming into the home of an unclean Roman. It was an ongoing insult that I thought Pilate abided too lightly.

"Set up the judgment seat in the Stone Pavement Courtyard," Pilate commanded. He reached for a bowl of water and began washing his face. "I'll be back in ten minutes," he told his barber.

✝

The Stone Pavement Courtyard was surrounded on three sides by the walls of the palace and lined with enormous Corinthian columns. Roman guards were stationed on both the ground floor and balcony and stood at attention, red-and-yellow rectangular shields in their left hands, the emblem of their battalion in their right. Their full-body armor gleamed in the morning sun, contrasting against the red capes hanging on their backs. There were hundreds of them and a few thousand more ready to storm the courtyard if necessary. It was an impressive display of Roman power.

Pilate stood in the marble portico at the top of a huge flight of steps twenty feet above the courtyard. I stood behind him to his right. A tall Samnite centurion named Longinus was on his left. Pilate had put on full military regalia—body armor and a red cape—to remind the Jews that he had been on the battlefield before and was not afraid to shed blood.

The enormous wooden gates on the opposite side of the courtyard swung open, and the Jewish leaders marched through, dressed in their ceremonial robes, looking grim and determined. They were followed by members of their Temple guard, dragging the prisoner like a dog with a chain attached to a metal collar around his neck, pulling and yanking him toward the portico. Hundreds of Jews followed and spread out on the massive stone pavement, filling the courtyard and spilling out beyond the gates.

The guards jerked the prisoner to the bottom of the steps and thrust him forward. He had the dark-olive complexion of a Jew and the sinewy build of a laborer. His hands were bound behind his back, and his robe had been torn so that it hung awkwardly on one side, revealing welts and bruises on his shoulder and arm. His lips and nose were swollen, he had gashes on his forehead and cheeks, and his long dark hair was matted with blood and sweat. A dark bruise had already formed under one eye, and there was dried blood and spittle caked on his beard.

A guard jerked on the chain to move him. The man caught his balance, firmly planted both feet, and raised his penetrating brown eyes to look at Pilate.

It was Jesus. The one who had cleared the Temple and overturned the tables of the money changers. The one who had healed the sick, who had supposedly walked on water. He stood there with a quiet dignity, his face calm, while others snarled around him.

"What charges do you bring against this man?" Pilate asked. He posed the question in Greek, the official language of the imperial legal system.

Caiaphas, the burly high priest, stepped forward, his eyes burning with contempt. "If this man weren't a criminal, we would not have handed him over to you." The crowd murmured its approval and seemed to surge toward the steps, a great, heaving mass of humanity.

Pilate had been through worse.

"Then take him yourselves and judge him according to your own law," he said with a dismissive wave. He took his seat, signaling an end to the proceedings.

The crowd reacted angrily, and the leaders all started talking at once. They quieted when Annas, the former chief priest and arguably the most influential man in all of Jerusalem, raised his voice and called for silence.

"It is not legal for us to put someone to death!" he said, his face twisted in anger. Those around him shouted their approval.

I marveled at how quickly the tables had turned. Just a few days earlier, Jesus was running roughshod through the Temple courtyard, and no one dared oppose him. Now, as far as I could see, he didn't have one friend in the entire crowd.

Pilate stood and raised his hand, hushing the crowd. The Roman soldiers, making their presence known on the outskirts, leaned their standards against the walls and put a hand on their swords. Some of the Jewish men glanced nervously at the soldiers. Nobody had forgotten the slaughter of the Jews following the aqueduct dispute. Pilate stepped to the edge of the stairs, his eyes meeting those of the rabbi. Then he turned to Annas.

"Isn't this the same man who was welcomed to the city by the fanfare of your own people just five days ago? And now you want him dead?"

Annas stiffened. "Your Excellency, this man is the leader of a dangerous element. He claims to be the king promised to the Jews." Annas looked around and seemed to be debating how far to take this. He took a step forward and lowered his voice. "We have no king but Caesar."

The comment hung in the air for a moment with all its complex implications. Just as nobody had forgotten the slaughter of the Jewish civilians, nobody had forgotten the incident of the shields. *"We have no king but Caesar."* It was, among other things, an implied threat to pull rank on Pilate again—to appeal directly to Caesar if the Jewish leaders didn't get their way.

For the first time that morning I saw Pilate hesitate. He still kept his shoulders square in a posture of defiance. But he paused, looked again at the prisoner, and then, with a curt nod, said simply, "Bring him back."

Pilate pivoted and walked into the great judgment hall of the Praetorium, his red robe billowing behind him. Roman soldiers stepped forward and took charge of the prisoner, dragging him up the steps. I watched for a moment, then turned and followed Pilate.

This was going to be a long morning.

— CHAPTER 24 —

The soldiers dragged Jesus into the room by the chain attached to the collar around his neck. Pilate dismissed everyone except me and the centurion Longinus, who took his place by the door.

Pilate circled Jesus, looking him over. The prisoner stared straight ahead.

"Are you the king of the Jews?" Pilate asked. It was a scornful question, mocking the appearance of the man.

"Are you asking this on your own, or have others told you about me?"

I had to suppress a smile. This was the same rabbi who had dumbfounded the religious leaders just a few days earlier in the Temple courtyard. Now he was playing cat and mouse with Pilate. *"Are you asking this on your own?"* Was Pilate operating on hearsay? Had Pilate himself seen any evidence that Jesus was establishing a kingdom? Of course not.

Pilate's visage darkened, and he stood directly in front of the Nazarene. He didn't like being questioned. "I'm not a Jew, am I?" he asked. His voice was more caustic this time, less inquisitive. "Your own nation and chief priest handed you over to me. What have you done?"

"My kingdom is not of this world," Jesus said slowly, deliberately, as if explaining something to a child. "If my kingdom were of this world, my servants would fight so that I wouldn't be handed over to the Jewish leaders. As it is, my kingdom does not have its origin here."

"You are a king then?"

The question brought a pause from Jesus, as if he had all the time in the world. "You say that I am a king. I was born for this, and for this I have come into the world: to testify to the truth. Everyone who is of the truth listens to my voice."

Pilate looked Jesus up and down again as if he were appraising a visitor from another world. Jesus was talking about religion, but Pilate was an eminently practical man. He seemed torn between admiration for the prisoner's self-assurance and frustration at the man's insolence.

"What is truth?" Pilate asked with a snort, and I thought of the lessons drilled into me by Seneca. This was the right question, though Pilate asked it flippantly, not expecting an answer.

Accommodating him, Jesus chose not to respond.

Pilate nodded to Longinus, who called in the guards and led the prisoner away.

When the massive wooden doors closed behind them, Pilate shook his head in frustration. "The man is arrogant," he said.

"He's also innocent, Your Excellency."

"He claims to be a king."

"He may be delusional, but he's no threat."

Pilate frowned, deep furrows carved into his forehead. "Maybe he isn't, but the men who hate him are."

He walked over to a window and stared at the city for a long time. When he turned back to me, I could see the tension lining his face.

"He's one man," Pilate said. "And the truth is, I have an entire province to consider." With that, he headed for the portico. I dutifully followed.

"What is truth?" I mumbled.

✝

This time, Jesus stood at the top of the portico steps, facing the crowd. Pilate and I huddled behind him.

"There are no grounds for charging him," I said.

Pilate agreed, but I could see uncertainty in his eyes. "Do they think I'm their slave?" he asked. "That they get to tell me when the power of Rome will be brought to bear?"

He stepped to the edge of the portico, and the crowd quieted. "I find no grounds for charging this man," Pilate announced.

The words were met with shouting and jeering. The mob, which seemed to have grown while we were inside, pressed toward the stairs. Soldiers on the portico descended a few steps, and those on the exterior walls stood a little more erect, eyes trained on Pilate, waiting for his signal.

Pilate allowed the uproar to die down. He was still standing, a sign that he had not yet pronounced final judgment. "Let me hear your testimony," he commanded.

For twenty-five minutes, the rabbi's accusers called witnesses. Jesus had threatened to destroy the Temple and rebuild it in three days. He had disrespected the Jewish leaders, calling them white-washed tombs and vipers. He had told the Jews not to pay taxes, a charge which I knew had no foundation. The testimony was all over the place, but Jesus just stood there the entire time, like a statue, never disputing any of their charges.

I had been through hundreds of trials with Pilate. Together we'd seen grown men beg and argue and curse. We'd seen them lunge at their attackers. I had watched one man clutch his chest and die. But I had never seen this kind of stoicism in the face of such vitriol.

"Are you not answering anything?" Pilate asked at one point. "Look how many things they accuse you of."

But Jesus didn't even cast a sideways glance toward the prefect. He kept his gaze fixed on the crowd, his face showing no emotion, as if he were in a trance.

I found my sympathies shifting toward the Nazarene. I had watched him with admiration in the Temple courtyard and been drawn in by his advocacy skills. It was professional respect, one orator to another, the same way a great gladiator might develop grudging respect for a valiant foe. I had been intrigued by the things he had reportedly said to Nicodemus. But it was there on the portico of the Stone Pavement Courtyard that I saw the type of stoicism Seneca had preached about when I was just a boy.

As the witnesses paraded forward, one by one, I was only half-listening. The words of Seneca were foremost in my mind:

To see a man fearless in dangers, untouched by desires, happy in adversity, composed in a tumult, and disdainful of those things which are generally coveted or feared, all men must acknowledge that this can be from nothing else but a divine power that has descended on that man.

I had seen that divine power in my few short interactions with Jesus. And I had no idea what to do about it.

I was brought back to the moment by a particularly adamant witness who testified with flailing hands about all the trouble the prisoner had caused. "He stirs up the people," the man yelled, "teaching throughout all of Judea, from Galilee, where he started, even to here."

It hit me like a lightning bolt from Jupiter. *Did he say Galilee?*

"Your Excellency," I said.

Pilate held up his hand to stop the witness, and I stepped forward for a brief conference. In criminal trials, a prisoner could be transferred from the *forum apprehensionis*, the place where he was arrested, to the *forum originis*, his home region. Pilate apparently hadn't noticed the reference to Galilee, but I had. And now, in this brief moment, I was torn between my duty toward the law and my desire to help this prisoner. Galilee was the jurisdiction of Herod Antipas, the bizarre son of Herod the Great. We could send Jesus there—we *should* send Jesus there. But there was no telling what would happen.

"The man said *Galilee*," I whispered to Pilate. "He said the prisoner was from Galilee."

Pilate's eyes lit up. I didn't have to spell it out for him.

He turned and looked down at the witness. "Say that again," Pilate demanded.

The man seemed to wilt. "I think I was saying that he was stirring up trouble, um, pretty much everywhere."

Pilate bored into him. "Go on. What else did you say?"

"From Galilee all throughout Judea," the man admitted. His voice could barely be heard.

"This man is a Galilean!" Pilate exclaimed. "Take him to Herod!"

— CHAPTER 25 —

Two hours later Jesus was back, looking worse than before. I was struck by the contrast between his battered appearance and the elegant purple robe Herod's men had draped around his shoulders. A guard told me Herod had mocked him, disdainfully calling him the "King of the Jews." But he had found no fault in the man, so he had sent him back to Pilate. Technically, Herod could have released him. But Jesus had been our problem from the start. It would now be up to Pilate to render a final decision.

The crowd crammed even tighter into the Stone Pavement Courtyard, growing to nearly a thousand. There was a sense of desperation in the air. The soldiers paraded Jesus to the bottom of the steps, forming a wedge around him, using their shields to keep the crowd at bay. Around the perimeter, troops were being jostled by the crowd, and I could see the hatred fomenting in the eyes of the soldiers. They looked at Pilate and Longinus with exasperation. *How long before you give the order?*

Many of these same men had been involved in the attack on the Jews following the aqueduct fiasco. I wasn't there for that debacle, but I thought it must have begun just like this. Tensions simmering until Pilate became so aggravated that he issued the order he would later regret. Once the bloodshed started, there was no stopping the soldiers.

Pilate stood motionless as he prepared to address the crowd, announce his final verdict, and take his place on the judgment seat. Even as his closest adviser, I had no idea what he was going to say.

While Jesus was gone, Pilate had been nearly despondent, speaking in a low, gruff voice about the choices before him. He was convinced the entire trial was a setup by Caiaphas and Annas, a ruse so that they could write another letter to Tiberius and end Pilate's reign.

Procula had weighed in, and she wasn't making it easy for him. She had watched the proceedings from a second-story window and recognized the face of the prisoner with astonishing clarity. It was the same face, she told Pilate, that she had seen in the temple of Aesculapius on the night she was healed. This man was innocent! She begged Pilate not to sentence him to death. "Have nothing to do with that innocent man," she pleaded. "How can you execute the one who healed me?"

Pilate had looked at me.

"She's right," I said. "The man is innocent."

But now the decision belonged to Pilate and Pilate alone.

He took his time and surveyed the courtyard, mindful that his next words might well start a massacre. He held his head high, the imperial look that he had learned so well in Rome, and thrust his chin out. "You brought this man to me and accused him of leading a revolt. I have examined him thoroughly on this point in your presence and have found him innocent. Herod came to the same conclusion and sent him back to us."

A malicious murmur rippled through the crowd. The faces of the leaders darkened with rage. I thought the crowd might rush the portico.

Pilate glanced up toward a second-story window on the west side of the courtyard, and I could see the shadow of Procula there. He seemed to gain strength from her and continued, his voice rising. "Nothing this man has done calls for the death penalty. I will have him flogged and then release him."

Pilate took his seat, signaling an end to the matter, but the crowd wasn't having it. Someone in the back yelled, "Crucify him!" Others joined in. The crowd found a rhythm, and a collective chant of "Crucify him!" rolled from one end of the courtyard to the other. A soldier on the outskirts scuffled with a man and knocked a Jewish woman to the ground. Other soldiers were being taunted and bumped from behind.

I decided the time had come to make my final recommendation. I had been thinking about an alternate strategy the entire time Jesus was with Herod. I didn't want to suggest it until we had tried everything else.

"Pilate," I called out.

He stood and huddled with me again.

I looked down at the stoic prisoner, the cause of so much turmoil. He was about to be flogged, the skin ripped from his back, yet when his eyes met mine, I sensed that he was at peace with his destiny. If he only knew that I was about to gamble with his life.

"There is an old custom, Your Excellency," I said. "And it may be time to revive it."

"Go on."

"Your predecessors used to release a prisoner every year at Passover. It was a symbolic concession to the Jewish holiday. I suggest we reinstitute that now and give them a choice: Jesus or Barabbas."

"Barabbas?" Pilate asked disdainfully. He kept his voice low, his eyes on the crowd. Barabbas had killed a Temple guard and tried to lead a revolt against Rome. He was one prisoner Pilate couldn't wait to put on the cross. But more important, the Jewish leaders hated him too.

"We've got to make it easy," I said.

Pilate glanced at the second-story window, but Procula was gone. He stepped away from me and raised his hand. For a long time, the crowd chanted on defiantly, ignoring him. Eventually their own leaders urged them to stop so they could hear Pilate out.

"Bring out Barabbas!" he ordered Longinus.

A few minutes later, the wild man was dragged to the bottom of the portico steps, hair disheveled, a maniacal look in his eyes. They stood him next to Jesus. As if on cue, Barabbas cursed and tried to attack his Roman guards. They beat him into submission and drove him to the ground.

"We have a custom," Pilate shouted. "Historically, at the Passover, we have released one prisoner. Do you want me to release Jesus or Barabbas?"

The words were no sooner out of his mouth than the crowd started shouting the name of Barabbas. I searched for my Jewish friends—Joseph of Arimathea, Nicodemus, a dozen other leaders with whom I had developed relationships. I saw a few of them on the edge of the mob, looks of concern on their faces. But not one person shouted the name of the rabbi.

Pilate was as stunned as I. He shot me a look, and I knew this entire debacle would now be my fault. Longinus was getting antsy, shifting his weight from one foot to the other as if he couldn't control his troops any longer.

"Release Barabbas," Pilate ordered. A cheer rose up, and the soldiers unchained the man. He stood there for a moment in his loincloth, his body covered with hair. He rubbed his wrists where the shackles had been. He squinted at the sun. He looked at Pilate, then at Longinus. He laughed. He started backing away, then turned and pushed his way through the crowd.

"What should I do with Jesus?" Pilate asked.

Again the chant resounded: "Crucify him! Crucify him! Crucify him!"

I stared in hatred at the high priest and his cohorts, men with arrogant smirks on their faces. My stomach was in a knot. I realized that my desperate gamble might have cost an innocent man his life.

Pilate rose to his full height. "I will have him flogged, and then I will release him," he said for the second time. Most of the crowd couldn't hear, their chants drowning out the words of the prefect. But the soldiers at the foot of the steps had heard.

They forced the crowd back, clearing out a space immediately in front of the steps where the flogging would occur. There was a hole in the pavement there. Two soldiers brought out a whipping pole that they slid into the hole and anchored it by chains to two iron rings bolted to the pavement. The entire time the crowd continued its chant.

Pilate took his place on the judgment seat, and the Syrian guard in charge of the punishment unwound his whip. It had jagged pieces of metal woven into the end. The crowd gathered closer, those in back standing on their toes. The chants died down as the guards tied the hands of Jesus to the whipping post.

The Syrian looked up at Pilate, and the prefect nodded. Under Roman law, only the prefect possessed the power to spill blood, the right of the sword, the responsibility to pronounce the exact number of lashes. Pilate would have to count them out until the bright flow of blood spattered the stone pavement. Only Pilate could stop them.

My job would be to stand behind the prefect and never flinch, never take my eyes off the pitiful sight of the prisoner being torn to shreds. My job was to watch the punishment my reckless gamble had caused.

I had never been so ashamed of being a Roman.

—— CHAPTER 26 ——

One.

Pilate sat stone-faced as the whip whistled through the air and landed on the prisoner's back.

Jesus flinched and gasped; the metal shards dug in and took their bite of flesh.

Two.

The Syrian guard seemed to be enjoying himself and leaned into the lash with his entire body. The whip wrapped around Jesus' torso, and its tips tore into his flesh, drawing blood from his back, chest, and side. I winced and wondered just how much the prisoner could stand. He stared straight ahead, hands tied tightly to the post, his upper body and legs exposed.

Three.

It was easy now to spot his followers in the crowd. A few women, standing near the front of the circle of onlookers, with tears flowing down their cheeks. The oldest one had her head in her hands, sobbing. *Was that his mother?*

Four.

A man next to the woman shook his head and placed an arm around her. He covered her face with his hand, and she buried her head in his shoulder.

Five.

Even some of the leaders who had been calling for the prisoner's crucifixion just minutes ago could no longer watch. They looked at the ground or stared at Pilate as if wondering when the torture would stop.

Six.

Jesus' back was already crisscrossed with ragged red lines, the torn skin exposing muscle.

Seven.

And so it went. Thirty-nine lashes in all. Thirty-nine times the whip whistled through the air, landed, and ripped flesh and muscle. The last few times the Syrian hesitated before unleashing the next blow and glanced at Pilate, thinking that the prefect would call a halt. Finally Pilate raised a hand, and I felt the bile rising in my throat. Somehow, after thirty-nine lashes, the prisoner was still standing. His back was lacerated into ribbons of flesh, muscle, and blood. Would they even need to crucify him now?

As they untied Jesus' hands, he looked up at Pilate. He struggled to straighten but seemed disoriented and dropped to one knee. A soldier on each side grabbed an elbow and jerked him to his feet. Another soldier appeared with a circle of woven thorns and jammed it on Jesus' head like a crown. A third picked up the purple robe that had been provided courtesy of Herod and placed it around the prisoner's shoulders, then pressed the cloth against his gaping wounds. The soldiers laughed, bent at the waist, and brought their arms down in adulation for a great king.

Some of the crowd egged them on. Others were silent and had seen enough.

"Hail! The King of the Jews!" the soldiers said.

"Enough!" Pilate snapped. "Bring him up."

They pulled Jesus up the stairs, leaving a trail of blood behind. When the prisoner reached the top, Pilate gave an order to turn him around. Pilate stood next to him and surveyed the crowd. The chanting had stopped. The flogging seemed to have taken the wind out of some of the main accusers.

"Behold the man!" Pilate said. He pointed to Jesus. Blood trickled down the rabbi's face and collected around his swollen eyes and lips. His beard was matted with it. I hardly recognized the man I had first seen just a few short days ago.

What more do you want us to do?

This time the crowd hesitated. But the chief priest and officers of the Temple started the relentless chant again. "Crucify him! Crucify him!"

Pilate shook his head, disgusted and saddened.

"We have no king but Caesar!" Annas shouted.

"I need to speak with him again," Pilate said. Once more, he turned and headed inside.

A moment later, for the second time that day, I found myself inside the Praetorium with Pilate and the Nazarene.

Pilate was desperate. "Where are you from?" he asked, his voice strident.

The prisoner stared at the ground, the same way that Roman governors did in order to show no emotion.

"Where are you from?" Pilate took a step closer. "Talk to me!"

Still, the purple-robed prisoner said nothing.

"Don't you know what power I have? Don't you understand that I have the power to set you free? Give me something to work with."

Jesus looked up, his face streaked with blood and sweat. He took a breath and spoke softly, yet still loud enough that I heard it a few feet away. "You have no power except that given you from above. The one who turned me over to you has the greater sin."

Pilate seemed startled by the answer. This man's life was about to be taken from him, and yet here he stood, judging the prefect of all of Judea? Telling Pilate how much sin he committed because of his role in these proceedings?

"Take him back out," Pilate ordered.

When the guards and Jesus exited, we were left alone. Through the open doors we could hear the reaction of the crowd when Jesus reappeared. The people seemed to have regained their bloodlust and roared insults when they caught sight of him. Quickly the jeering and angry shouts coalesced into a chant. "We have no king but Caesar."

Pilate looked stricken, ashen with worry. I was afraid the riot would begin before we returned to the portico. The crowd would press too tight, and the soldiers would strike out, starting the slaughter. Whatever we decided, it had to be quick.

Pilate walked to the smooth marble wall, and I followed him. He touched the holes in the concrete seams of the enormous stones. "You know what these are?" he asked.

"No, Your Excellency."

"This is where we mounted the shields," he said. "Every time I walk this hall, I think about the letter from Tiberius."

The crowd outside seemed to be more in sync now, their chants ringing louder.

"We have no king but Caesar!"

"You are no friend of Caesar!"

"How would I explain this one to him?" Pilate asked. "If I set the man free, if we slaughter half that crowd when they protest, how would I explain it?"

"He's an innocent man, Your Excellency. Tell Caesar that we upheld the glory of Roman law. Tell Caesar that we refused to be intimidated by a mob, that we did what was right."

Pilate snorted at the answer, and it wasn't hard to read his thoughts. *What is right? What is truth? Don't give me platitudes, Theophilus; give me solutions.*

The chants crescendoed as if somebody had incited the crowd anew. They sounded so close that I wondered if they had somehow moved just outside the door.

"We have no king but Caesar!"

"You are no friend of Caesar!"

The noise distorted my thinking. I was anxious to return to our place at the top of the steps. Longinus could not be trusted to control the soldiers or the crowd.

"Play it out, Theophilus," Pilate said. "If I stand my ground, what happens?"

"We lock up the prisoner. The crowd eventually goes away."

"Or perhaps they don't. Somebody panics. Somebody pulls out a weapon," Pilate said. "Our guards react, butchering hundreds. Annas writes to Tiberius and tells him that the man I protected claimed to be a king."

I didn't respond because I didn't know what to say. Pilate was right; there was no honorable way out.

"Speak to me!" he demanded between clenched teeth. "Tell me where I'm wrong."

Like the prisoner, I maintained my silence. Pilate wasn't wrong.

If I told him he was, he would explode in anger. Freeing the rabbi would be costly, perhaps devastating. Pilate's mind was made up. I could see it in his eyes.

"Sometimes," Pilate said, his voice suddenly calm, "one man must die for the good of a nation."

I wanted to argue the point, to tell Pilate that the law required an innocent man to be set free regardless of the cost. But the prisoner wouldn't even speak in his own defense. It was almost as if he wanted to die. If Jesus wouldn't defend himself, why should I stick out my neck to take up his cause?

"This is the shields all over again, isn't it?" Pilate asked.

The chanting continued as I weighed the question. The Jewish leaders had been willing to lay down their lives to protest the shields—harmless symbols honoring Caesar that were hanging in Pilate's own palace. How much more would they be willing to die for this—to punish a man who had ridiculed them and upended their Temple? And how would Tiberius react when he learned that Pilate had refused to condemn a man who claimed to be a king?

"Yes, Your Excellency," I said. "It's the shields all over again."

It must have been the answer Pilate needed. He steeled himself and turned toward the door.

"Let's go," he said.

— CHAPTER 27 —

Pilate brushed back his cape and took his place on the judgment seat for the final time. He waited for the defiant chant of the crowd to stop, and even then there were a few stray cries of those who wanted Jesus crucified.

Pilate ordered a bowl of water brought to the top of the steps. It was not a normal request for the middle of a trial, and it took several minutes for the servants to return. The crowd waited, murmuring about what the request might mean.

The silver bowl was placed on top of a pedestal a few feet away from the judgment seat. With his eyes on the crowd, Pilate rose and stood behind the bowl.

"I am innocent of this man's blood," he declared loudly. He dipped his hands in the water and scrubbed them together. He shook off the remaining water, and his servant handed him a towel.

"His blood be on us and our children!" someone shouted. Others quickly joined in. Pilate said nothing, dried his hands, and handed the towel back to his servant.

The man loved ceremony, but the words of Cicero confirmed what I felt in my heart. *A stain on the soul can neither be blotted out by the passage of time nor washed away by any river.* Much less, Cicero might have added, by a small bowl of water. I knew Cicero was correct just as surely as I knew one other thing: Pilate's soul was not the only one being stained. I was right there with him, having refused to stand my ground for an innocent man.

Pilate returned to his seat and asked for the *titulus* board, a rectangular piece of wood about two feet long, coated with white gypsum. He passed the board to me, and I took a seat. A servant handed me a reed that I dipped into the black ink.

"Three languages," Pilate said. "Jesus of Nazareth, King of the Jews."

I began the first inscription in Greek. Next would come Latin. Lastly, the same words written in Hebrew.

Annas placed a foot on the bottom step, and a guard moved toward him. The former high priest narrowed his eyes.

"It should say, 'He *claimed* to be king of the Jews,'" Annas insisted. A few of the other leaders voiced their agreement, but I kept on writing, finishing off the Greek.

"What I have written, I have written," Pilate said.

When the *titulus* was complete, it was hung with a rope around Jesus' neck, and the crowd jeered. But the shouts were less insistent now. The *titulus* was a clear sign that the prisoner stood condemned and would soon be executed.

Pilate remained in his seat, and my mind seared the scene before me into my memory. The bloody rabbi, standing at the top of the steps, gazing toward heaven, a wooden sign around his neck. The chief priests in the front row of the crowd, still scowling. Pilate sitting above the fury, pretending to be a man in charge, though everyone knew he had been emasculated. And the empty second-story window where Procula had stood earlier that day, symbolizing the futility of even a dream from the gods.

"He is condemned," Pilate said. "Let him be crucified."

The crowd roared, and the soldiers wasted no time descending on the prisoner and pulling him down the steps. In the next few moments, despite the dozen or so guards surrounding Jesus, the crowd seemed to swallow him.

I watched with my stomach in my throat as the band of soldiers and the crowd pushed the prisoner across the courtyard and through the gates at the other end of the stone pavement. I knew they were heading for the area the Jews called Golgotha, the place of the skull, where the soldiers would nail his body to a cross as soon as possible. Two others were scheduled for execution as well—thieves who were supposed to be the bookends for the crucifixion of the notorious Barabbas. Instead, they would hang on either side of Jesus.

I watched until the last person left the courtyard and the soldiers swung the massive gates shut and secured the large iron lock.

The silence that followed was disorienting. There was still a trail of crimson baking in the sun, a trail that marked the prisoner's movements that day—up and down the stairs, into the Praetorium, across the courtyard. There was a large puddle on the stones at the foot of the whipping post. But the servants were already scurrying about, anxious to scrub the floors of the palace and the steps of the portico.

Others would take down the whipping post, storing it until it was needed again.

The silence gave me a moment to reflect. When I closed my eyes, I could still see him—his face bloodied, bruised, and swollen; the crown of thorns pressed low on his brow; that ridiculous purple robe hanging from his shoulders, the cloth sticking to his wounds. I could still hear his voice and feel his eyes piercing my soul. "I was born for this," he had said, "and for this I have come into the world: to testify to the truth."

He had a sense of destiny, which shamed me even more.

I once had a sense of destiny too. Or at least I thought I did. I was born to be an advocate for the truth, to fight for justice, to speak for the powerless. But in my greatest test I had failed miserably. I had lost my nerve and at a critical moment abandoned my principles.

Now the rabbi would pay with his life.

What is truth?

It hadn't been Pilate's finest hour either. Yet he had escaped another explosive incident and didn't seem to care about one man's life. The truth of Pilate's legacy was this: His past misdeeds had hemmed him in. He could no longer do what was just.

He seemed determined to shrug it off. He rose from the judgment seat and unhooked his red cape, handing it to his servant. He dismissed the remaining guards and cast one last glance at the window where Procula had once stood.

"I'm hungry," he said. "And I need to finish my shave."

I was grateful that he didn't ask me to join him. I headed straight for my room, my thoughts consumed by the role I had played in the death of Jesus. I replayed the flogging, the stoic prisoner absorbing each blow as Pilate counted them out. I knew the whole affair would have turned out differently if not for my gambit with Barabbas.

The thought of it sickened me, and I reached for the washbowl, leaned over it, and threw up.

— CHAPTER 28 —

I couldn't stay away.

At the fifth hour, with the sun almost at its peak, I walked to Golgotha, a rocky crag north of the Damascus Gate, just outside the city limits. It was the preferred spot for executions because the criminals would be seen by everyone entering the city and because there was a cemetery nearby. On the sheer face of the hill, two small caves in the rocks resembled the eye sockets of a skull.

I arrived and climbed the small dirt road that led to the top of Golgotha. The crowd had thinned, but there were still a few hundred people loitering around, watching the criminals suffer. Jesus was in the middle, with one thief on each side.

I stayed on the fringes of the crowd, trying not to draw attention. One of the soldiers, playing a game of dice at the foot of the cross, caught a glimpse of me. He twisted his face into a question. I nodded in reassurance and he returned to the game. I had never shown up for an execution before, but I had no power to stop one unless I was acting on orders from Pilate.

I knew the centurion in charge, a Roman named Quintus, who had made the trek with us from Caesarea. He was a member of the Italian Regiment, a decorated and loyal soldier. He had seen plenty of men die, but unlike many of Pilate's other commanders, he did not lust for it.

He and his men had driven long spikes through Jesus' wrists, just below the palm, between the two bones of the forearm. I had seen them do it to other prisoners in the arena. I had watched the blood spurt out. Even now, as Jesus hung there, blood trickled to the ground.

An angled block of wood had been attached to the cross as a footrest, and Jesus' feet had been placed one on top of the other, then nailed in place. He hung, for the most part, with his head down. Periodically, he would pull himself up, rubbing his flayed back against the coarse wood of the cross. He would gasp for air and grimace as the nails pressured the nerves in his wrists and ripped the tendons in his feet. I found myself catching my breath with him, thinking about the pain and humiliation I had suffered as a boy, gasping for air and feeling the shame.

I had been there—where he was—but this was no prank. There would be no friends to save him, no reprieve or pardon. He would hang there until he didn't have the strength to take another breath. Or, if the guards were merciful, they would break his legs with a steel rod and put him out of his misery.

I had to look away.

Most of the crowd was decidedly less sympathetic. "He saved others, but he cannot save himself!" one of the leaders of the Sanhedrin said.

Another joined in. "He's the king of Israel! Let him come down from the cross, and then we'll believe in him. He's the one who claimed to be the Son of God!"

I made my way to a group of women standing with a solitary man. They were all crying, though the bearded Jewish man tried to wipe away his tears. I recognized one of the women from the Stone Pavement Courtyard, the one I suspected of being the rabbi's mother.

"What does this mean," I asked the women, "that he saved others?"

The one closest to me was a beautiful young woman with dark knotted hair, smooth skin, and almond eyes. She wore none of the makeup favored by Roman women, but even in her misery she possessed a raw beauty seldom seen in Caesarea or even the great capital city of Rome. Her eyes were red and puffy. Tears rolled down her cheeks.

She looked at me, and I couldn't tell whether she recognized me from earlier or not. "He saved me," she said. She didn't sound indignant or defensive. Only sad.

"How did he save you?"

She stole a sideways glance at the other women as if seeking their permission. "I was caught in the act of adultery by those men," she explained, motioning to the leaders at the foot of the cross. "They dragged me before Jesus and reminded him that the law of Moses required that I be stoned. They asked him what he thought."

I waited, shoving a small pebble with my sandal. The silence prompted her to continue.

"He told them that the man who had never sinned should be the one to throw the first stone," she said. "It's another precept of the law of Moses."

"And that stopped them?"

"It probably wouldn't have. But then he knelt down and wrote in the dirt."

She paused and stared at the rabbi as if she had forgotten all about our conversation.

"What did he write?" I prompted.

She turned back to me. She didn't exactly smile, but there was the slightest upturn of her lips as she remembered the moment. "The names of the women the leaders had been sleeping with. Jesus wrote them very deliberately, one by one, starting with the oldest man's affairs first. They dropped their stones and left."

He saved others, but he cannot save himself. I wanted to tell this young woman that the rabbi seemed like a good man, but I knew those words would ring hypocritical and hollow. I wanted to tell her that I was sorry, yet I couldn't bring myself to say that either. So we stood there in silence as Jesus tensed and raised himself up for another labored breath.

"After the religious leaders left, Jesus told me that he wouldn't condemn me either," she said. "He told me to go and not sin anymore."

"He sounds like an amazing man."

"He is." There was a long pause. "Or at least he was."

She turned to the cross, and I took it as a cue that the conversation was over. I moved a few feet away and turned my attention back to the three crucified men hanging there, laboring to breathe. Every few minutes, more onlookers would peel away and head down the hill.

Travelers on the road sometimes stopped and stared for a moment, but not many of them came up the hill.

Men had been known to hang on the cross for days before they died. Tomorrow was the Sabbath. The Jews had work to finish before the evening.

The defections were slow at first, a small group here or there. But by noon, the crowd had thinned to less than a hundred.

For some reason, I couldn't walk away. The sign I had written with my own hand had been nailed above his head: *Jesus of Nazareth, King of the Jews.* His face was marred and bruised. He grimaced in pain and had an awkward way of sliding up and down the wood, tensing every muscle to catch his breath. I wanted to give an order to put an end to the man's suffering.

"So you're the Messiah," one of the thieves said. He pulled himself up for a breath. "Prove it by saving yourself—and us, too, while you're at it!"

Jesus looked at the man with sad eyes. But he didn't defend himself.

"Don't you fear God?" the other thief asked, gasping. "We deserve this, but this man hasn't done anything—" he stopped to catch a breath—"anything wrong."

The argument drew me closer. I had been there during the second thief's trial. He had perjured himself and tried to intimidate the witnesses. He had shown no remorse. And now he had found humility?

He lowered his voice, but I still heard what he said: "Jesus, remember me when you come into your Kingdom."

Jesus glanced at him with great sympathy. I could have sworn the rabbi tried to smile.

He raised himself up, inhaled, and spoke with calm assurance. "Today you will be with me in paradise."

That was all he said, but it seemed to be enough. The thief dropped his head on his chest and muttered something that sounded like a prayer.

And then, without warning, the sky went dark.

— CHAPTER 29 —

I had experienced an eclipse before, and I knew there was nothing miraculous about it. The moon covered the sun, creating a few hours of darkness at midday. It could all be explained rationally.

But all Romans, myself included, believed there could be supernatural causes as well. When Augustus died, an eclipse of the sun—greater than any previously known—so darkened the skies that the stars came out at the sixth hour. The body of Augustus rose from the funeral pyre to become one of them.

The son of god ascending.

And now, with another man who called himself the Son of God, hanging on a cross, the sky had grown black again. Could it be just coincidence? Of course. But something deep in my troubled spirit told me there was more to it than that. The gods were angry.

Perhaps they were angry at me.

I stood there, like the others, trying to get my bearings. Nobody had prepared for this. Soldiers don't bring torches to a midday execution.

For a moment, I considered the possibility that when the sun reemerged, the cross would be empty. That the rabbi would pull off the greatest disappearing act in history, wiggling his way down under cover of darkness. It was ludicrous, I knew, but so was darkness at noon. Imaginations run wild when the darkness disorients.

I instinctively moved closer to the cross, near where the Roman soldiers stood guard. I bumped into a few people along the way. I didn't think the followers of Jesus were numerous enough or strong enough to take advantage of the darkness and pull the rabbi down. And if they tried, I wasn't sure whether I would help them or resist them. Either way, I wanted to be close to the action just in case.

I waited, but nothing happened. In the silence, you could hear the labored breath of the condemned men as they pulled themselves up, inflated their lungs with a few gasps of air, moaned, and then slumped back down. There was a rhythm to it, punctuated by an occasional curse from the recalcitrant thief.

The darkness had an intriguing effect on the crowd. A few of them talked about trying to return home. The soldiers no longer played games. Quintus dispatched two of the men to bring back torches.

There was whispered conversation about what the darkness meant. The soldiers tried to shrug it off—this was not the first eclipse in history; it wouldn't be the last. But the religious leaders had been silenced. Nobody mocked the rabbi now.

As the silence lingered, I edged closer to Quintus.

"Have you ever seen anything like this?" I asked.

He had been on the battlefield. The man had experienced some things. Still, I wasn't shocked by his answer.

"Never."

A half hour later, the soldiers returned, and Golgotha danced with the shadows of firelight. Most of the crowd had left, except for some members of the Jewish religious establishment, the band of soldiers under the command of Quintus, and a few friends of the rabbi.

Time passed slowly.

I thought about a lot of things. Strangely, I remembered the story that Seneca had told me about the German gladiator who killed himself in the lavatory, choking himself to death by jamming a sponge down his throat. "That man defied everyone, choosing the manner of his death!" Seneca had exclaimed.

Romans were fascinated with death. Who could face it with courage, and who would shrink away? What bizarre things could we concoct to prolong the agony of it? And most important, as Seneca had noted, who could choose the manner of his own death?

I sensed that the rabbi, nailed to the cross and slowly suffocating, was still somehow in control.

Three hours after the darkness descended, long past the time that an eclipse should have lifted, Jesus rose up one last time and pierced the darkness with an anguished shout. *"Eli, Eli, lema sabachthani?"* My limited Aramaic didn't keep me from understanding the words. *My God, my God, why have you forsaken me?*

I stared at him, waiting for more. They were the first words he had spoken in three hours. One of the soldiers thought he had asked for a drink and filled a sponge with sour wine. He held it on a reed stick so the rabbi could quench his thirst. Jesus tasted it, turned his head, and spit it out.

He then cried out at the top of his lungs. "Father, into your hands I commit my spirit!"

It sent chills down my spine. A young woman gasped. The woman I thought was the rabbi's mother covered her mouth with her hands, sobbing. Jesus dropped his head to his chest and said, in a barely audible voice, "It is finished."

And just like that, he stopped breathing.

I was holding my own breath, watching his chest, and realized that the man was finally at peace. The silence was broken only by the sobs of his mother and the other women who had followed him to the cross.

That's when it started. First a small rumbling, followed by a low growl as the ground shook beneath us, as though the entire hill on which we were standing might be swallowed into the bowels of the earth. I struggled to maintain my balance and kept an eye on the crosses as they shook, the blood spraying from the prisoners and sprinkling those of us below. People around me gasped and shouted for mercy. Quintus fell to his knees while the other soldiers crouched in readiness as if preparing to do battle with the gods themselves.

The earthquake ended as abruptly as it started. The ground became firm again, and people struggled to catch their breath.

"Surely, this man was the Son of God!" Quintus exclaimed.

I kept my eyes fixed on Jesus, half-expecting him to shoot to the heavens like a comet in reverse, the way Augustus had done. But he just hung there, motionless, his struggle finally over. The earth did the same, as if it had struggled along with him and, with him, found its peace.

Gradually, inexorably, the light returned. The soldiers regained their composure, and Quintus looked at me with a wary eye as though I might tell Pilate that he had given the title of Augustus to this beleaguered Jewish rabbi.

I noticed in the sunlight that my own toga had been stained with a few drops of the rabbi's blood. It brought to mind the image of Flavia at the Festival of Fordicidia, soaked with the blood of a pregnant cow. Or the way physicians would have a patient suffering from parliamentary disease drink the blood of a slain gladiator. Romans knew one thing: there was power in blood, especially the blood of a sacrifice.

I walked alone back to the Praetorium. I hardly noticed the damage from the earthquake along the way.

It wasn't until the following day that I first heard the news. The earthquake had damaged the four-inch-thick curtain that separated the Holy Place of the Jewish Temple from the Holy of Holies, the place that only the high priest could enter once a year. The curtain had been torn in two. The earthquake must have shifted the structures holding the curtain in place.

They said it had been torn from top to bottom.

—— CHAPTER 30 ——

Things quieted down after the crucifixion of Jesus of Nazareth. The Jews celebrated the Passover without further incident on the fifteenth day of their month Nisan. We used the day to prepare for the long trip back to Caesarea.

On Sunday, we left at dawn. We went out the same way we came in—an impressive entourage with a few thousand soldiers marching in formation, reflecting the sun from their shields and armor. Anyone who watched would have thought Pilate was still in charge. Those of us who had been there for the trial of Jesus knew better.

It took Pilate and me two days to refine the letter we sent to Tiberius Caesar reporting the incident. As usual, Pilate had asked me to prepare the first draft. But when he read it, he accused me of including too much detail and making the prisoner seem innocent. "He claimed to be a king. That's the main point," Pilate said.

He redrafted the letter himself. The trial of Jesus merited only two paragraphs. The Nazarene had called himself a king. He had a huge following. Mindful of the prior admonition from the great Tiberius to keep peace in Judea, Pilate had given Jesus every opportunity to recant.

When he found out that Jesus was a Galilean, Pilate had sent him to Herod. But Herod merely made fun of the man and sent him back to Pilate. Eventually, Pilate ordered that the man be crucified, demonstrating to the Jews that the great Tiberius had no rivals.

There was no mention of Barabbas. There was no mention of the multiple times Pilate had found the man innocent. There was no mention of the prisoner's stoic insistence that although he was a king, his Kingdom was not of this world.

And not surprisingly, there was no mention of the eclipse or earthquake.

I had carried my guilt back to Caesarea. My unease over my role in the trial had intensified by watching the brave rabbi die. Even the gods had been displeased with the injustice of it all.

Cicero wrote that guilty men are tormented and pursued by the Furies not with blazing torches as in the tragedies but with the anguish of remorse and the torture of a guilty conscience.

Cicero could not have been more right. It took me weeks just to regain my appetite. I thrashed in bed at night. When I did sleep, I was visited by images from the trial and crucifixion of Jesus. I relived and rehashed my lack of courage under pressure. What if I had stood strong with Pilate when he first decided to find the man innocent? What if I hadn't insisted on that ploy of offering up Barabbas? What if I had stood up to Pilate when he waffled at the end and put his own self-interests first?

What if I had been the one on trial and my life had depended on somebody being courageous enough to apply the law impartially?

Pilate made it clear that such questions were off-limits during our time together. I brought the subject up once, indirectly, by commenting on how upset the verdict had made Procula.

"What I have done, I have done," Pilate said. "The gods will decide whether I played my part well."

"Do you ever wonder yourself?" I asked.

He gave me a look of annoyance that told me I had already pushed the matter too far. "What I have *done*, I have *done*."

It was the last time I mentioned the incident to him.

But he couldn't stop people outside the Imperial Palace from talking about it.

A month after we returned to Caesarea, the rumors still floated like leaves on the wind, stirring up the Jews in our city. The followers of Jesus claimed he wasn't really dead. He had been seen alive after the crucifixion in the city of Jerusalem and at one time had taught a group of five hundred on the hills outside the city.

I put no stock in the rumors. I had watched the man die, seen him give up the ghost with my own eyes. He might have been, as Quintus himself had exclaimed, the very Son of God. And his soul might have been immortal, vying right now with the other gods for his place in the pantheon. But dead men didn't come back to life. Certainly not in the way that the Jews were describing Jesus. He supposedly looked the same, except for the nail wounds in his wrists and feet and a hole in his side where the soldiers had pierced him with a spear to make sure he was dead.

I was a little concerned, from a political perspective, that the movement had not died with its alleged Messiah. But this was not the first time such things had happened. Perhaps his disciples had stolen the body from the grave as some of the religious leaders were claiming. Pilate had placed guards at the tomb, but I knew Roman soldiers were not infallible and not above being bribed. In any event, we still had a province to govern.

I never had a chance to return to Jerusalem. Three months after the trial of Jesus, and six months ahead of schedule, I was replaced with another *assessore* and sent back to Rome to begin my career as an advocate. I knew the hand of Seneca was behind the maneuver. With Sejanus now dead, alliances had shifted, and Seneca's star was again on the rise. Agrippina's family was no longer the threat it had been previously. The time was ripe for Seneca's allies and friends to make their influence felt in the capital city.

I knew I was only a minor player in the drama unfolding in Rome. Nevertheless, I was excited to return at a time of such great turmoil because turmoil spawned opportunity. Tiberius would soon be gone, and the jockeying to succeed him as emperor was already taking place. I could read about it from afar, or I could be on the fringes of the swirling intrigue unfolding at the center of the civilized world.

I was tired of writing formulaic letters to Tiberius and helping Pilate judge the same types of cases over and over. The law was made in Rome. There, I would be free to carve a name for myself as an advocate, not just serve as an adviser to a hotheaded and unpredictable prefect.

I left Pilate on good terms, though our relationship was never the same after that trial in Jerusalem. He wished me the best and told me I had served him well. He drafted a letter touting my virtues, and I packed it carefully among the other books that I kept in the boxes impregnated with cedar oil. My scrolls were well-worn and cracked because I constantly unrolled and read them before tying them up again and stuffing them away.

But my favorite letter I had left unopened for the last three months. I opened it once, with great reluctance, during the voyage home. The words that had inspired me on my trip to Caesarea now filled me with sadness and regret.

What we have to seek for, then, is . . . the soul that is upright, good, and great. What else could you call such a soul but a god dwelling as a guest in the human body? A soul like this may descend into a Roman equestrian as well as into a freedman's son or a slave. For what is a Roman equestrian or a freedman's son or a slave? They are mere titles, born of ambition or of wrong. One may leap to heaven from the very slums. Only rise and mold thyself into kinship with thy God.

As the winds battered our ship and prolonged the journey home, I thought long and hard about my time in Caesarea. I had demonstrated a great capacity for writing, and I had mastered the intricacies of Roman provincial law. But on the point that mattered most, I had failed most profoundly. I had not risen to the occasion as Seneca had encouraged me to do. And because of my cowardice and failure, my soul felt a long way from kinship with God.

PART IV

THE
SENATOR

CHAPTER 31

IN THE TWENTIETH YEAR OF THE REIGN
OF TIBERIUS JULIUS CAESAR AUGUSTUS

I returned to Rome to find a different kind of city than the one I had left behind. Not much had changed by way of architecture or economy, but there was a certain tension in the air that you could almost taste. After the fall of Sejanus, the leading senators had turned on each other with a spate of treason trials, invoking the crime of *maiestas*, which included any behavior offensive or hostile toward the majesty of the state or the person of the emperor.

From his remote post on Capri, Tiberius fostered a climate of distrust that led to a proliferation of these trials. They were conducted in the Senate chamber, and it was said that the commander of the Praetorian Guard, Naevius Sutorius Macro, would attend the trials and watch the faces of the senators as the evidence was presented. Even a look that seemed to suggest sympathy with those accused of *maiestas* could be grounds for suspicion and subsequent charges.

The trials gave rise to a new class of parasite that fed off Tiberius's fears and the wealth of others. The *maiestas* laws provided that the persons who successfully prosecuted the cases would inherit the estate and political offices of the accused. Such men were called *delatores*, and they wormed their way into power by prosecuting others for crimes of alleged malice toward the Roman people or the emperor. All of Rome despised them, and the most hated *delator* of all was a man named Caepio Crispinus. As a result of several successful cases, he now served in the Senate, where he could keep a close eye on the men who would be his next victims.

I found safety in keeping a low profile. I set up a law practice and, with Seneca's help, developed a fairly robust client base. I spent my time pleading cases in the Roman Forum at the Basilica of Julius, where seven civil courts conducted proceedings simultaneously. When the basilica opened for the day, there was such a crush of litigants and advocates you could barely move. All day long, spectators flocked from one proceeding to the next, depending on the status of the litigants and the types of issues being tried. My cases seldom attracted a crowd. I specialized in representing borrowers when their lenders exacted more than the 5 percent interest allowed or when the lenders tried to compound interest illegally.

There were two problems with my nascent practice. First, I seldom got paid. Clients who have to borrow money at usurious rates do not have the funds to pay lawyers. Instead, they tried to barter with me. As a result, I was promised more goats, pigs, and bushels of barley than I could possibly devour in the next decade.

Second, I tended to make powerless friends and powerful enemies. Alienating the Roman citizens who had the most money was not helping my long-term ambition to make a lasting impact in Rome.

That all changed on a cold February morning when Seneca summoned me to his house for the *salutatio*, a formal morning reception. As he had done several years earlier, Seneca's servant called my name first, and I skipped over nearly sixty others who had come for a favor that morning. We retired into Seneca's office, where he had a fire going in the hearth.

He poured some wine, rubbed his hands together over the fire, and filled me in on the latest gossip from the Judean front. Pilate was on his last legs. He had brutally suppressed another religious uprising, this time in Samaria, and the Samaritans had complained to Rome's prefect in Syria.

"Pilate has been ordered back to Rome to answer the accusations of the Jews and Samaritans," Seneca said.

The news rocked me. I had been making good progress in my quiet new endeavors in the civil courts, but this added a level of dangerous uncertainty to my future. Would Pilate return and be sanctioned for his numerous shortcomings? Would a hearing in front of the Senate reflect poorly on my own role? It seemed like every act of misconduct was now somehow turned into an affront against Tiberius Caesar. Would they do the same with Pilate? And if they did, could I possibly escape guilt by association?

"He's lost control," Seneca said as if the matter were not open for debate. He threw a few logs on the fire and took a seat. "A new religion is spreading like wildfire through his province. The captain of the Italian Regiment, a man who reports directly to Pilate, is now a follower of the Way. He's been trying to convert the provincial troops."

"Cornelius?" I asked.

"I don't know what his name is. But it doesn't look good for Pilate."

I knew the man Seneca was talking about. Cornelius was a respected soldier with a lot of influence in the province.

I had been hearing some things about the spreading influence of the Jews who were committed to the teachings of the Nazarene, but I had no idea that the movement—if that's what it was—had infected Pilate's own troops. For some reason I felt a flicker of joy at the thought of it. The Nazarene and his followers deserved better than what happened that day before the Jewish Passover.

Seneca took a sip of wine and changed the subject. He leaned toward me and lowered his voice. He had dark and swollen pouches under his eyes. His skin sagged and already showed some age spots. He was feeling the pressure of the times.

"The people are sick of these treason trials," Seneca said. "The Senate is like a pit of vipers, turning on each other, sentencing each other to death, stealing each other's families and possessions." Seneca shook his head and frowned. His jowls added ten years to his appearance. "Tiberius is seventy-five and in poor health. The tide will turn soon. The only question is whether any of us will live long enough to see it."

He lifted the cup to his lips again. After drinking, he set it down very deliberately, as if this was one of the few enjoyments he had left in life. "The conventional wisdom is to keep a low profile and be careful what you say even to your friends," Seneca continued. "Have you heard about Plautius?"

I nodded. "Everybody's heard about Plautius."

The poor man was a bizarre example of how ludicrous the *maiestas* laws had become. Plautius had made the mistake of carrying coins bearing the image of Tiberius into the bathroom. It turned out to be a crucial error, deemed by the courts to be an affront to the emperor. Plautius was condemned to death, though his sentence was later commuted to one of exile.

"Lucius Apronius is the latest victim," Seneca said. "I believe he's a friend of your father's."

He was indeed. Apronius had an estate outside Rome, not far from the land farmed by my family. He was known to be a kind and generous man but unyielding when it came to matters of principle.

"He's being prosecuted by Crispinus." Seneca spat the words out as if the very name were a curse. "For obvious reasons, Apronius is having a hard time finding a capable advocate to defend him."

I immediately knew where this was going, and Seneca must have read the look of concern in my eyes. "I know what you're thinking," he said with a dry smile. "But you must trust me on this. You can spend the rest of your life representing tenants in the civil courts, or you can rise to the occasion and plead a case in the Senate. And, Theophilus, before you give me your answer, you need to understand two things.

"First, there is no doubt that Apronius is guilty as charged. He thinks Tiberius is usurping the role of the Senate, and he thinks the old man needs to step down. So nobody is asking you to win this case. But if you put up a good fight, people will notice. Senators will notice. They'll learn what I already know—that you are one of the best advocates at your age in all of Rome."

His flattery was taking its intended toll. I should have said no before he could draw the next breath. Instead, I asked a question. "What's the second thing?"

"You have a chance to be on the right side of history," Seneca said. "*We* have a chance."

He hesitated for a moment, and I could tell he had been wrestling with this issue for a long time. "If I'm right, when Tiberius dies, there will be a tremendous backlash against his legacy and against *delatores* like Crispinus. Those who stand up now to his reign of terror will be heroes when that day comes, their names on the tip of every man's tongue. That could be you, Theophilus. That could be me."

"And what if you're wrong? What if Tiberius hangs on for another five years and they come after me because I had the audacity to represent someone who criticized him?"

Seneca smiled. He lifted his cup in a toast, apparently a toast of me. "Then I'll deny we ever had this conversation."

When I didn't return the smile, Seneca turned serious again. "My only request is that you meet with Lucius Apronius one time. I think you'll find him to be an honorable man. If you can tell him no to his face in good conscience, I'll honor that decision."

I agreed to the meeting because Seneca was a good friend and benefactor. I also agreed because I was intrigued. My tenants were underdogs in the cases I handled. But their lives were not at risk.

I was ready for a bigger stage. Perhaps it was time to take my place in the sun.

— CHAPTER 32 —

The wind bit through my cloak that night on the way to the estate of Lucius Apronius for dinner. He lived four miles outside the city, not far from my childhood home.

His house was warm and comfortable, the food delicious and exquisitely prepared. Apronius was a gracious host but insisted that we should wait until after dinner to talk about his upcoming *maiestas* trial. He looked a little like the statues I had seen of Cicero—receding gray hair, deep-set eyes framed by bushy gray eyebrows, and a mouth that fell into a natural frown. He asked about my family and my time in Greece and Judea.

I was struck by the common decency of the man. He treated his servants with the kind of respect seldom seen in Rome. He looked them directly in the eye and addressed them by name. At one point, his grandchildren raced into the banquet room and interrupted us, a serious breach of etiquette. He apologized but didn't seem at all embarrassed. He introduced his wife, who was right on their heels, and for the next several minutes I had a rather pleasant conversation with the grandchildren. I wondered what would happen to them if Apronius were convicted.

After dinner, he insisted that we go for a walk in his torchlit gardens. "The brisk air will wake us up."

Brisk? October was brisk; February was biting! We put on our cloaks, and he showed me around the gardens, his hands behind his back as we walked side by side. He glanced up at the stars and waxed philosophical.

"Theophilus, we're not living in the Rome of my childhood. Augustus Caesar gave lip service to the Republic while slowly stripping the Senate of all but ceremonial power. Tiberius has taken the next step, reducing our once-august body to a pack of fools anxious to curry favor with an emperor who has not even set foot in this city for ten years. But do you know what disappoints me most?"

I wasn't sure I wanted to know. I was already a little uncomfortable with a client so freely confessing his disdain for Caesar. If he was willing to criticize the emperor in front of me, a young advocate whom he hardly knew, what had he said to his friends in the Senate?

On the other hand, I admired his frankness, a character trait sadly lacking in Rome.

"I'm most disappointed by my fellow senators. We fall all over each other making resolutions to impress the emperor. We grovel to Macro, commander of the Praetorian Guard. We turn on each other and accuse each other of thinking bad thoughts about the mighty Tiberius. Whatever happened to the dignity of a senator?"

"I don't know," I said lamely.

He stopped and turned. He looked for a long moment at his house, perhaps thinking about his wife, children, and grandchildren. The man had a lot at stake.

"If you decide not to take my case, I won't blame you," he said. "I'm up against Caepio Crispinus, and he hasn't lost a *maiestas* trial yet. And I'm not willing to lie."

Seneca had already filled me in on the specific charges. Apronius had been invited by one of his close friends from the Senate, Papius Mutilus, to a lavish dinner. With the wine flowing and the two of them alone, Mutilus had started complaining bitterly about Tiberius. The emperor was a hothead. He didn't have the brains to govern. He was nothing like Augustus Caesar. He had conquered no new territories. And what had he built?

Apronius had taken up the cause, reciting his own litany of complaints. He suggested the Senate should take action. Rome would be better served if Tiberius were no longer Princeps. Even better if the Republic were restored.

The next day another senator approached Apronius, voicing his own disgust with Tiberius. This senator, a man named Junius Otho, served as a *praetor* in the law courts where I practiced. He claimed that Tiberius had overstepped his legal authority and that the emperor's paranoia was ruining the country.

Thinking he had found another ally, Apronius suggested that he, Otho, and Mutilus get together and talk about actions the senators could take.

Unfortunately, it was all a setup. Both Mutilus and Otho reported their conversations to Caepio Crispinus. Mutilus and Otho claimed that they revered Tiberius and were just trying to test the loyalty of Apronius. Charges were filed, and the outcome seemed sure. It was rumored that the three men involved in the prosecution of Apronius had already decided the best way to apportion his estate.

"What's the worst thing you actually said about Tiberius?" I asked. I was shivering—partially from the cold and partially from being so nervous about the prospect of representing a man who had freely insulted the emperor.

Apronius gave me the sly smile of someone slightly amused at his own hubris. "I may have mentioned the case of Plautius and the coins Plautius took into the privy," Apronius said. "I may have said that in my own privy, I have Caesar's image engraved on the end of the sponge we use when we finish our business."

This coaxed a smile from me as well. "You told the other senators that?"

"I probably used a little coarser language. But that's the essence of what I said."

†

There were a thousand compelling reasons why I should have stayed away from the defense of Apronius. We couldn't possibly win. And I wasn't willing to take Seneca's advice and handle the case just for the notoriety. I knew myself too well for that. If I got involved, I would go to every extreme to prevail. Serving as Apronius's advocate would place me firmly in the camp opposed to Caesar. Maybe Seneca was right and the tide was turning, but if it didn't turn fast enough, I could soon be accused of treason myself and washed out to sea with the rest of the traitors.

A year ago, Tiberius had ordered that everyone in prison convicted of treason be piled in the street and killed at one time. Those who saw the spectacle talked about the cries of agony as the prisoners were speared through by the Praetorian Guards. They were left to rot there for seven days, their bodies devoured by wild dogs. Then, at the order of Tiberius, their remains were dragged by hooks to the Tiber River and flung into the current. Loved ones and relatives were prohibited from rescuing the remains and giving the men proper funerals.

My knees nearly buckled at the thought of it.

But fear is not the most powerful motivation.

In a strange way, the courage of Apronius reminded me of the courage of the Nazarene. Both men faced powerful and corrupt accusers without flinching. Both had been betrayed. Both seemed to answer to a higher call.

I had turned my back on an innocent man once. The guilt of doing so had dogged me for the last two years. Having come face-to-face with my own cowardice, I had a strong desire for a second chance to prove my valor. Perhaps that's why I admired men of courage so much—because I had such a hard time mustering it myself.

I left the house of Apronius late at night, the moon lighting my way back to Rome. I had a bag full of money—the largest retainer I had ever charged a client. I held my head high because I knew I was doing the right thing.

But I also had an awful feeling in the pit of my stomach. Between the wrath of Caesar and the stubbornness of my new client, there would not be much room for error.

— CHAPTER 33 —

I regretted my decision almost immediately. Word spread quickly in the tongue-wagging city of Rome, and I soon became infamous—a hero to the freedman but a pariah to the senatorial class. Details about Apronius's snide criticisms of Tiberius had already leaked out. Under their breath, Roman citizens had dubbed the case "The Sponge Trial."

Nobody in Rome believed that Apronius had a chance at acquittal. The common people loved his audacity. But they also knew there was a reason such courage was in short supply in Rome. Most men who possessed it were already dead.

When I went to the baths, the other aristocrats treated me as if I had a contagious disease, granting me a wide berth. Seneca might have been right that the citizens of Rome were sick of the treason trials. And maybe history *would* vindicate us. But at this point, none of the aristocrats seemed willing to take that bet.

There was one small benefit from my newfound notoriety. I had been proceeding toward marriage with a woman from a respectable equestrian family who was even-tempered and as intellectually curious as me. But there was no flame in our relationship. Once it became public that I would be representing Apronius, this woman and her family decided we would not be a good match. Rather than being distressed, I found myself relieved. Marrying her in the first place would have been a huge mistake.

During the three weeks leading up to the trial, I might have withdrawn from the case had I truly believed that doing so would unravel the damage to my reputation. But in a moment of empathy and courage, I had made a decision that I could no longer undo. The only choice now was whether to proceed as Seneca had suggested—represent Apronius halfheartedly with an eye toward losing—or do everything within my power to win.

Five days before the trial of Apronius, I found myself sharing a meal with Pontius Pilate and Procula in the Aventine Hill section of the city. Though I couldn't really afford a night off this close to the trial, I couldn't bring myself to turn down the invitation from the former prefect of Judea. Since returning to Jerusalem with the malfeasance charges pending against him, Pilate had become a virtual outcast in Roman society. Right now, more than anything else, he needed a friend.

Pilate was a mere shadow of the man I had known two years earlier. He still looked the same—the bald head and oval face, the tanned and weathered skin, the close-set eyes, and the forehead that so quickly furrowed into a show of displeasure. He was still in the same excellent physical shape he maintained in Caesarea. But after spending a few hours with him, I could tell that he was a far different man emotionally.

All of his smug self-assuredness had vanished. He was despondent throughout dinner, despite the best efforts of Procula and me to cheer him up. We tried to get him reminiscing about our time in Judea, but the truth was that Pilate and I were both trying to forget those days.

He had obviously been drinking even before I arrived, and he continued nonstop through the dinner. The more wine he consumed, the more he turned inward, though he did ask a lot of questions about Apronius's trial. Perhaps he saw it as a preview of his own trial, scheduled to take place a few weeks later.

By the last course, Pilate was slurring his speech. He fell asleep before dinner was over. Procula apologized for her husband and offered to walk me out.

We were standing on the front portico when she asked the question that I sensed she had been waiting to ask all night. "Did you hear about Cornelius?"

"That he became a follower of the Nazarene?"

"Yes." She looked down for a moment as if trying to judge how far she should take this. "Did you hear how it happened?"

"Not the details."

"Would it interest you?"

"Sure."

She told the story with a certain sense of awe in her voice. It started when Cornelius had a vision. That led to a meeting with a Jew named Peter, who told Cornelius about Jesus and his miracles. Peter described the crucifixion of Jesus and how he had supposedly come back to life on the third day and been seen by many witnesses.

"Cornelius told me about this himself," Procula said. "Peter baptized Cornelius and a few of his soldiers, and they became followers of the Way."

"I heard the talk about Jesus coming back from the dead even before I left Caesarea," I said. "At the time, I wrote it off as just another Jewish myth. Still do."

Procula considered the matter. "All I know is that the face of Jesus is the same face I saw in the temple of Aesculapius when I was healed. I know Jesus was innocent of the charges against him, and I warned Pilate not to have him crucified. He didn't listen, and we've had nothing but trouble since."

"I regretted that decision too," I admitted. "It's one of many things I would do differently if I ever had the chance."

The conversation seemed to have run its course, and we both said our good-byes. I was halfway down the steps when Procula stopped me.

"Theophilus?"

I turned and looked at her.

"My husband really needs help," she said, her voice brittle. "He doesn't stand a chance at trial without an advocate who knows what he's doing. He's approached a few others but they all have their excuses. . . ." Her voice trailed off.

I sensed where this was going. It was the last thing in the world I needed. Another unwinnable case in front of the Senate. Another stubborn man's life in my hands.

"Would you take his case, Theophilus?" Procula asked.

I hesitated. "Does he even want me to represent him?" From what I had heard, Pilate planned on representing himself. He had been putting on a brave public face. He had been justified in every one of his actions, he claimed. He would proudly explain himself to the full Senate and take whatever sentence they dished out.

She sighed, her eyes fixed on the pavement. "We talked about it a few nights ago. Pilate said he would never ask you; he doesn't want to drag you into this. He doesn't want the claims being made against him to rub off on you."

I couldn't tell whether Procula was making this up or not. Truthfully, it didn't seem like something Pilate would say, at least not the Pilate I knew. He never seemed to worry about anybody but himself. Maybe somehow facing these charges had changed him.

"Tell him I'll be back to meet with him after I finish the trial of Apronius," I said. "But, Procula, if he wants me to represent him, he'll have to ask me himself."

"I'll tell him," Procula promised. "But some people have a harder time asking for help than others."

CHAPTER 34

In putting together Apronius's defense, I first tried to draw on my vast knowledge of Cicero. The man had been Rome's greatest orator and had stood undaunted in the face of overwhelming odds. But that's not where I ultimately found my inspiration.

My dinner with Pilate had drawn my thoughts back to the Nazarene. Something about the way he had seemed resigned to his fate stirred me. The way he had lectured Pilate about destiny. *"You say that I am a king. I was born for this, and for this I have come into the world: to testify to the truth."* Jesus had stared Pilate down, despite the fact that Pilate had the authority to order his execution. What was it the Nazarene had said? *"You have no power except that given you from above."*

I mulled that over for a moment, marveling not just at the supreme self-assurance of Jesus but at his assertion that Pilate had no jurisdiction over him.

That's when it hit me. A way to defend Apronius that might actually work!

I wasted no time before getting to work on my new theory, toiling late into the night. The next day, I had Apronius pull records from prior treason trials. I started going for long walks up and down the Seven Hills of Rome, shivering against the cold, practicing my argument. Those closest to me must have thought I had gone a little mad—walking around, talking to myself, not bothering to shave.

Two days before the trial, I practiced my argument in front of Seneca. When I finished, he leaned back, crossed his legs, and rubbed his chin. I could tell he was deep in thought. His eyes looked past me as he watched the scene play out in his mind.

"It's brilliant," he said. "It just might work."

He coached me on some minor adjustments. A voice inflection. The way I held my hands. A need to pause or a change in the wording of a few sentences. But he didn't touch the substance of my speech.

Before I left, he grabbed me by both arms and told me he was proud of me. "I always knew you had this in you," he said. "When you talk to those senators, remember that they are merely men, the same as we are. But maybe you can spark them to rise above the petty jealousies that have inflicted that group recently. And even if you don't, you have made your teacher proud."

†

The wave of optimism I felt coursing through my body that night all but disappeared by the morning of the trial. My toga was freshly washed, but it was the toga of an equestrian. My entire defense was contained in the small box that held my wax notebooks with my closing argument and a few exhibits I intended to introduce. Later that morning, I would walk to the Senate alone, without even a servant trailing behind me.

Others would arrive in grander style. Crispinus would be carried to the Senate in a litter with a huge entourage of servants and well-wishers following along. His very passing would create a stir on the streets of Rome. His entrance into the Senate chamber would be followed by the glad-handing of other senators as they masked their animosity toward him with nervous smiles. Junius Otho, the *praetor* who would testify against my client, would have lictors precede his entourage, announcing his arrival. Mutilus would merit the same kind of reception.

Thinking about it, I lost my appetite. My stomach was in such an uproar that I decided to skip breakfast and head straight to the Senate. My nerves were on edge, and it would do no good to try to rehearse my argument again.

But just as I was putting on my cloak, help arrived in the form of a loud and insistent knock.

I opened the door, and he was standing there grinning. He was taller now—I no longer looked down on him. But it didn't seem like he'd gained a single pound since childhood. He was all skin and bones, elbows and knees, and his cloak hung on a rail-thin frame. Somehow, his bone-sharp face had retained its boyish innocence.

"Marcus!"

"I thought you might need somebody to carry your bag," he said.

We embraced and patted each other on the back. Marcus explained that he was a physician practicing medicine in Sicily. But when a friend needs help, he said, you drop everything and come.

"I can't believe you're here," I said.

"You never could stay out of trouble."

We left ten minutes later, the two of us walking side by side through the streets of Rome, past the busy shops where people conducted their daily affairs. A few recognized me and, under their breath, wished me luck. Others stared from the opposite side of the street.

I had arranged to meet Apronius at the lower end of the Forum so that we could review some last-minute details. He appeared to be in good spirits.

I introduced him to Marcus, and the three of us huddled in the cold while a few light flakes of snow started to fall. Apronius's servants stood at a respectful distance. Some onlookers stopped and stared.

When we finished our meeting, we headed down the long plaza of the Forum toward the Senate.

As we approached, I saw a huge crowd of people braving the cold. They had apparently come to show their support for a senator who had the courage to take on Tiberius. They clapped as we drew near, and Apronius took time to stop and shake hands, greeting some of them by name, embracing others.

The plaza outside the Senate door was packed with men, women, and children, bundled up as if they intended to stay all day. These were freedmen—some who had been helped by Apronius financially, others who knew his family, still others who might have worked for the man. They were our people, and I knew that today, like every day when important Senate business was transacted, the massive chamber doors would remain open so that the citizens on the street could hear the proceedings.

Inside I might be persona non grata. But out here, I was quickly becoming a hero.

I dove into the crowd along with Apronius, shaking hands, thanking people for coming. A few held my grasp longer than necessary, garnering my full attention. "He's a good man," they said. "We're counting on you."

By the time we were ready to enter the Senate, I was glad that

I had ignored Seneca's initial advice. My remarks were not tailored merely to showcase my advocacy skills. My argument was designed to win.

As an equestrian, Marcus would have to wait outside along with the rest of the crowd. At the threshold, he gave me a parting pat on the shoulder. "The gods be with you."

"Perhaps the people already are," I said.

He nodded. "It's quite a display."

I looked past him at the faces of the crowd. Some of the countenances were dirty and sooted, sheltered by tattered hoods. Others were men and women of distinction, just like Marcus. They were all Romans, here to take a stand for justice.

"That's the Rome I dreamed about as a boy," I said to Marcus, nodding at the crowd. "That's why I became an advocate."

But Marcus was facing the opposite direction. Behind me were the scowling senators, milling around the Senate chamber, preparing to decide the fate of my client.

"And that," Marcus said, motioning to the men who composed the Roman Senate, the most prestigious legislative body in the history of the world, "is why I became a doctor."

CHAPTER 35

The Senate chamber was cold, magisterial, and expansive. The ceiling was nearly sixty feet high, supported by huge Corinthian pillars. The floor was composed of marble of various colors, imported from around the world, strategically placed to form crisp geometric patterns. The place was heated by subterranean fires; unseen servants fed the flames, circulating warm air through vents. Still, a chilling breeze came in through the doors that opened out to the Forum.

Opposite the doors was an elevated platform with seats for the consuls who would oversee the day's activities. A few members of the Praetorian Guard stood in front of the platform, keeping an eye on the senators.

Nearly six hundred senators sat in elegant wooden seats with rounded backs that fanned out in a semicircle. The first few rows were reserved for the advocates, their clients, and the senior senators. On a crowded day, the youngest senators would have to stand behind the last rows of raised seats in the back. Today, not surprisingly, there was standing room only.

There was a considerable amount of open floor space between the senators and the consuls. Like a recessed stage, this was where Crispinus and I would examine witnesses and make our arguments. We could pace and gesture; we could pivot this way and that. It would make for great entertainment. Not quite the arena, but still a lively piece of drama.

A few of the senators nodded at Apronius as he and I took our seats in the front row. Then the presiding consul, a senator named Porcius Cato, called the proceedings to order.

Cato was a mountain of a man, weighing close to three hundred pounds, and his frame seemed to consist of one mound of flesh piled on another. He had an oval face, fleshy jowls, full lips, and protruding eyeballs with large, dark circles under them. It was said in Rome that it was better to be a condemned man in the arena than a slave carrying Cato's litter.

The trial of Apronius was not the only matter on the Senate's docket that day. First, Cato presided over an hour of tedious administrative business.

I looked around and tried to study the body language of the senators. My strategy depended on the courage of a few key members, and I zeroed in on them. Unfortunately, I saw none of the grim-faced determination I hoped to see from men who might be prepared to take a stand against the mob mentality of this place. Marcus Lepidus, for example, whispered amiably to the senator sitting next to him, as if he didn't have a care in the world.

When our time came, Cato read the charges against Apronius and called on Caepio Crispinus to make his case.

Crispinus rose and nodded at the senators. He walked to the middle of the floor and began telling the story of my client's alleged treason. He cut quite an imposing figure, his skin smooth, his gray hair neatly styled, his toga folded just right. He spoke with the eloquence of Cicero, intertwining humor and anger and self-righteousness into a flawless fabric that cloaked my client with the garments of guilt.

Apronius had earned a reputation as one of Rome's outstanding senators, Crispinus admitted, but his hatred for Tiberius had overwhelmed his good sense. The man now presented a grave danger to the state of Rome and to the emperor himself.

Like a trained actor, Crispinus could change his tone in a second from accusatory to sad. The friends of Apronius had become concerned, he said ruefully. Reluctantly, they had put together a plan that would ascertain their friend's true intentions. Papius Mutilus had invited Apronius to dinner. Yes, Mutilus had spoken disparagingly about the emperor, but as every senator knew, the emperor had no stronger advocate than Mutilus. The good senator had spoken badly of Caesar only to see if Lucius Apronius would do the same.

And Apronius did just that. He claimed to Mutilus that the emperor had usurped the power of the Senate, an assertion that was patently false.

I glanced at the senators as Crispinus spoke. All of them knew my client was right about Caesar, yet ironically, the intimidation by Tiberius was so great—and his usurpation of power so complete—that the senators looked shocked that one of their colleagues would dare speak such a thing. And I wasn't the only one watching. Naevius Sutorius Macro, the commander of the Praetorian Guard, stood just below the consuls' dais, arms crossed, studying every senator for even the slightest indication that they might be sympathetic to our cause.

For nearly an hour, Crispinus railed against the treasonous comments of my client. When speaking with the *praetor* Junius Otho, Apronius had actually mocked the emperor. He had mentioned the case of Plautius, the man condemned to die for carrying coins with the image of Tiberius into a bathroom. At this, Crispinus paused, his eyes scanning the entire chamber. "And then this man," he said, pointing at Apronius, "said that he detested the emperor so much, he would have the image of Caesar stamped on the end of his bathroom sponges."

If the accusation weren't so ludicrous, and if my client hadn't admitted to saying it word for word, I would have found the whole thing humorous. But none of the senators were laughing. The words of Apronius had been repeated on the streets of Rome over and over. If the Senate left such a statement unpunished, citizens would feel free to vilify Tiberius the same way satirists had pillaged so many of his predecessors, making a mockery of Rome's most venerated leaders. The senators didn't want to return to those days. Or if they did, they were smart enough not to show it.

Crispinus followed his opening argument by calling both Papius Mutilus and Junius Otho as witnesses. They both spoke in solemn tones, feigning disappointment and indignation at the things Apronius had said. Crispinus had them pile it on thick, praising Tiberius for his excellent administration of the empire and his benevolence in allowing the Senate to continue in its current role. Weren't these very *maiestas* proceedings an example of Tiberius trusting the Senate to decide matters of critical importance to the future of Rome?

When it came my turn to cross-examine the illustrious senators, I asked only a few questions.

"Did you actually intend to enter into a conspiracy to overthrow the emperor?"

"Of course not."

"Did you see Apronius take any deliberate steps to overthrow the emperor, or were these mere words?"

"So far, they were merely words. But he seemed ready to act if others would join him."

As the senators testified, I noticed the crowd outside the doors pushing a little closer when I asked my questions. I sensed their disappointment that I hadn't done more to make both Mutilus and Otho appear to be liars.

Be patient, I thought. *Everything is going according to plan.*

⟶ CHAPTER 36 ⟵

When Apronius got his chance to testify, he rose from his seat and approached the dais looking grim and determined. The pressure of the *maiestas* proceedings had driven other senators to suicide. Some had been reduced to groveling and muttering abject apologies, full of tears and drama. But Apronius stood tall and raised his right hand to take the oath.

Cato swore him in, and Apronius promised, "in the name of Tiberius himself," to tell the truth. If he testified falsely, he called a curse upon himself, including "the destruction and total extinction of my body, soul, life, children, and descendants."

Apronius stood below the dais, and Crispinus began pacing between him and the senators, firing questions.

"Did you tell Papius Mutilus that Tiberius Caesar was not worthy of the title of Caesar?"

"Yes, I said words to that effect."

"Did you criticize Tiberius Caesar, son of the divine Augustus, for his failure to continue the building programs of Augustus?"

Apronius didn't blink. "Essentially, yes."

"Do you affirm those accusations today?" Crispinus asked, his tone showing his incredulity. Crispinus undoubtedly thought my client would at least deny his prior statements. If nothing else, our strategy surprised him.

"I am affirming that I said those words to Papius Mutilus," Apronius said calmly. "Today, I acknowledge that my words were rash and ill-advised. Tiberius Caesar is a fair and honorable principate and one who would welcome honest disagreements with his policies."

At this, Crispinus moved toward the witness, the lines on his face turning into a harsh scowl. "Did you not claim that he had abandoned the empire? Did you not claim that the man suffered from delusions and paranoia?"

He had claimed all of that and more. While preparing for today's trial, Apronius had been absolutely unmovable on one point—he would tell the truth, no matter the consequences. But that was easier to say when the room was not full of judgmental senators staring into your soul, wondering how anyone so measured could be so reckless in talking about the emperor.

Apronius swallowed hard.

"Your fellow senators are waiting," Crispinus mocked. "It seems that your fabled memory has had a lapse. Did you or did you not call the divine Tiberius both delusional and paranoid?"

"I did."

It went on this way for quite some time. Statement after statement made by my client came to light, and I had no power to stop it. Sometimes Apronius would begin to answer and Crispinus would cut him off with another question. Meanwhile, Macro surveyed the senators, occasionally glancing in my direction. The targets, I knew, were being selected for the next prosecution.

Crispinus ended his examination, as both Apronius and I knew he would, on the matter of the lavatory sponges.

"Senator Apronius, tell your fellow senators whether you claimed that you had engraved an image of Tiberius Caesar on the end of your lavatory sponge."

For the first time, Apronius looked down, his voice a low rattle. "I should not have said that. But I did."

"I'm sorry," Crispinus said loudly, "but I am not sure that all the senators heard. Did you indeed say such a thing?"

"I said that I regretted saying those words. But I admitted that the words were mine."

Crispinus shook his head in a grand show of disgust. He made a spectacle of returning to his seat while a soft murmur of feigned disbelief floated through the chamber. The senators all knew Apronius had made those statements. Why were they playing such a ridiculous game and acting so surprised?

Cato squirmed in his seat in a vain attempt to get his enormous body comfortable, then called on me. "Any questions for the witness?"

I had several but was suddenly having second thoughts about the first few I had planned. In preparing for trial, I had explained to Apronius the philosophy of Cicero: use humor to lower their guards, logic to engage their minds, and emotion to win their hearts. Thus, we had designed our first questions to elicit a chuckle and simultaneously demonstrate how ridiculous these charges were.

I carried a small box as I strode to the middle of the floor in front of Apronius. In it were his lavatory sponges. My plan was to show them to Apronius, ask if they contained any images of Caesar, and mark them as an exhibit. It would demonstrate what everyone knew—the statements by Apronius were only satire. It would also show a level of feistiness that I hoped would inspire some senators to stiffen their spines.

But I had badly miscalculated what the mood might be. There was no hint of humor in the air. Fear, yes. Disgust, perhaps. And a healthy degree of surprise that Apronius had not at least attempted to deny his statements. I was afraid that if I tried to introduce these exhibits now, it would be seen as mere mockery.

Apronius, to his credit, must have sensed the same thing. He glanced at the box and gave me a quick shake of the head.

"I have only a few questions for Senator Apronius," I said. "My first one is this: Have you ever *done* anything to harm the state of Rome or the emperor? For example, have you taken any *actions* to conspire against the authority of Tiberius Caesar?"

"No, I have not."

"When you said that the Roman Senate should do something about the state of affairs of Rome, were you advocating anything illegal?"

"No. I was only saying that, as senators, we should exercise the jurisdiction that is properly ours, jurisdiction given to us by the laws of Rome and affirmed by Caesar."

"Do you regret your criticism of Tiberius?"

We had planned this question and gone over it a dozen times. That's why it surprised me when Apronius waited so long before he answered. He was supposed to issue a full and heartfelt apology. But now that the moment had come, I wondered whether he could bring himself to do it.

"I regret the hyperbole and sarcasm with which I expressed my sentiments. But I believe I have a duty, both to the state of Rome and to Caesar himself, to express concerns about the well-being of our empire."

His answer, though not in the script, was expressed with such conviction and certitude that it made me proud to have him as a client. Behind me, a cheer went up from the gallery outside the Senate doors. Cato frowned and turned to the guards. "Keep them quiet or I'll order the doors closed."

Apronius stared straight ahead, jaw firm, unflinching.

I had seen this kind of courage in the face of the Nazarene. I had seen it in the best of the gladiators. I had read about it in the annals of Roman history. But today I was witnessing something truly historic—a Roman politician unafraid to die.

"I have no further questions for the defendant," I told Cato.

~ CHAPTER 37 ~

When it came time to make our arguments, Crispinus strutted to the well of the chamber and held nothing back. He jabbed his finger at Apronius as he derided the traitor, and the spittle forming at the edge of his mouth made him resemble a rabid dog. He turned, paced, and gestured, his toga flapping this way and that. It was a classic example of the Asiatic school of rhetoric, the orators we had derogatorily called "the dancing masters" during my days at Molon. Unfortunately, it seemed to be having its intended effect.

Many of the senators, mindful of Macro's watching eyes, made a show of registering their agreement. They murmured their approval and nodded along and occasionally even interrupted Crispinus with applause. He thrived on the feedback, his voice becoming more bombastic, his flourishes more exaggerated. I could hear the crowd outside the Senate doors growing restless, and a few shouts of disgust penetrated the chamber. Seneca's instincts had proven right. The common citizens of Rome were fed up with the treason trials, especially when they endangered a man as reputable as Apronius.

Crispinus finished strong, claiming that Caesar's very honor was at stake. A vote for not guilty would be a vote to open the floodgates to all sorts of vile and scandalous things that could be said against Tiberius.

"Do we not owe the emperor greater respect than that? Should we allow men to sneak around behind his back and make vile accusations against him? This is an emperor who fought in Armenia and recaptured the Roman standards from the Parthians. This is an emperor who initially refused the titles of Imperator and Augustus, a man so humble he declined to wear the civic crown and laurels. This is a man who has filled Rome's treasury to the greatest level in her august history and has ensured that all her provinces are ruled fairly and well.

"Are we to allow traitors who skulk around in the shadows to besmirch his name? For the sake of Rome, for the sake of Caesar, for the sake of this institution, we must be willing to punish one of our own members who engages in such treasonous conduct."

The clapping, I noticed, did not start immediately. It actually seemed that the great Crispinus had fizzled somewhat. He had tried to rouse the senators to their feet but it fell flat. When he stopped, Mutilus stood to clap and was quickly followed by Otho. A few others joined them and then a few more, until the standing ovation had rippled through the entire Senate. For a senator to remain seated, I knew, would have drawn the ire of Macro.

I allowed time for the clapping to run its course and for the senators to sit back down. Then I stood and glanced toward the Senate doorway, where Seneca was standing.

"*You're ready,*" he mouthed.

I felt strangely calm as I took my place in front of the consuls. I noticed, of all things, a pigeon that flew overhead and perched on a rafter. It seemed that for this moment, all of nature had an interest in what I was about to say.

Cato gave me a nod, and I began slowly, hesitatingly, as I tried to get comfortable with all the senatorial stares. "How can we be so sure about what the great Tiberius himself might say if he were sitting in your seats?" I asked. "Reading the mind of Caesar is fraught with difficulty. This body should vote based on its own convictions, not based on what you think Caesar might want you to do."

I could tell from the looks on their faces that the senators were not buying it. With someone as volatile as Tiberius, you had better err on the side of protecting his reputation.

"But if you are insistent on voting the way you think Tiberius would want you to vote, then you should surely acquit my client."

The remark brought a few snickers from the senators. One or two smiled snidely at the insanity of such a comment. I pointed to one of them. "You doubt the truth of that?" I asked. But I didn't give the man a chance to respond.

"There is one thing that all the witnesses in this case have agreed on. My client never took any *action* against Caesar; he merely spoke disparaging words. So the question becomes: Is that enough? Can a conviction for *maiestas* be sustained on mere words?"

I allowed that thought to hang in the air for a moment. I was nervous, and it was hard not to talk continually and fill the silence. But my training in rhetoric had taken over. The senators no longer intimidated me. In my mind they had become my fellow pupils in the Molon School.

"Have you so quickly forgotten the case of Gaius Lutorius Priscus?" I knew that nobody had forgotten about Priscus. The man was a wildly popular poet and satirist who wrote a disparaging poem about Tiberius's son Drusus just before his death. Priscus read the poem to several high-ranking women at a raucous banquet. The Senate charged Priscus with *maiestas* and convicted him based on conflicting testimony. One senator, Marcus Lepidus, argued vehemently that Priscus's punishment should be commuted. Instead, the Senate ordered that Priscus be executed immediately.

When Tiberius heard about this, he complained of the senators' hasty punishment and praised Lepidus. He also issued an edict—from that point forward, the Senate had to wait nine days after conviction before a prisoner could be executed.

"You, Marcus Lepidus," I said, pointing to the senator, "gave an impassioned defense of Priscus. And that man's satire makes Senator Apronius's comments look mild by comparison." Lepidus stared stoically at me, making it impossible to read his thoughts. "You had the courage to stand against the entire Senate once. And when Tiberius heard about it, he praised you. Do you remember what he said?"

Lepidus gave me a slight nod, and I knew I had him as I continued. "He complained that the Senate had been too hasty to convict Priscus for mere words and that you alone had exercised commendable restraint."

I turned away from Lepidus and lifted my voice so that every senator could easily hear. "Mere words," I said. "That's what Tiberius called such stinging satire. *Mere words.*

"Is Tiberius so weak that the honor of his office and the nobility of his person cannot withstand an attack of *mere words*? Are his accomplishments so meager and his policies so misguided that they cannot hold up to the slightest amount of criticism? Does he need you to police every word spoken because his reputation cannot stand on its own two feet?"

I noticed that the chamber had grown quiet. Perhaps the senators' lack of courage could be used to my advantage. I tried to tighten the rope another twist.

"This chamber's authority to conduct treason trials was granted to you by Caesar himself. But that authority came with a very crucial limitation.

"Mere words cannot be the basis of a conviction for *maiestas*. To say otherwise is to say that the great Tiberius can be injured by nothing more than what a man says. That his office and honor are so fragile that one snide comment from a misguided senator will cause the emperor to come crumbling down. A vote of guilty says that you believe Tiberius is weak. But a vote of not guilty says that mere words, harmless puffs of air from a human mouth, cannot destroy the impenetrable house of Caesar.

"Mere words," I said. "Which of you has never uttered a single word critical of Caesar?"

I left the question dangling and returned confidently to my seat. Nobody inside the chamber clapped. Instead, the senators were damning me with their eyes. Perhaps I had just made an easy decision a more difficult one.

But outside, the freedmen were cheering.

─ CHAPTER 38 ─

It didn't take long for the Senate to dash my hopes. In an hour of debate, only Marcus Lepidus argued in favor of acquittal. When he sat down, a string of senators rose to challenge what Lepidus had said. It was a game of one-upmanship, each senator sounding more indignant than the last. My heart sank as I listened to the men who were supposed to be the leaders of Rome. Apronius handled it stoically, resigned to his fate. He held his head high and turned in his seat, impassively watching each senator as he spoke.

Cato finally ended debate and called for a vote. The senators in favor of guilt were instructed to move to the right side of the great Senate chamber and those in favor of acquittal to move to the left. The senators rose en masse and shuffled to the guilty side of the chamber. Only Lepidus and Apronius crossed over to the other side, surrounded by empty seats.

"The accused will come forward," Cato said.

Apronius walked to the front and stared straight at Cato, chin held high. I stood next to him.

"The full Senate, having heard the evidence against you, finds you guilty of the charge of *crimen maiestatis* and sentences you to death by strangulation nine days hence. All of your possessions and titles shall be equitably distributed among those who brought and prosecuted the charges."

Shouts of protest erupted outside the chamber. The guards moved quickly. They put chains on Apronius's ankles and wrists and escorted him toward the door. He stopped for a moment and stared at his former friends, Papius Mutilus and Junius Otho. It was a chilling sight. His eyes promised them that the beast they had unleashed would one day turn back and devour them. A guard jerked the chain and moved Apronius forward. Other guards created a human alleyway to escort Apronius through the crowd and across the Forum. He would spend the next nine days in the Tullianum.

He turned and looked at me before he left.

If I read his lips correctly, he said, *"Thank you,"* and then he was gone.

The scene took me back to the day that the Nazarene had disappeared from the Stone Pavement Courtyard. This time I felt the same despondency the rabbi's followers must have felt then—an innocent man condemned for political reasons. A fresh stab of guilt ripped the rewoven fabric of my spirit. I had been a coward in Jerusalem. Today I had reaped a coward's reward.

A few of the senators whom Apronius and I had thought would vote in favor of acquittal looked ashen-faced. I could tell they were wondering who would be next. There was none of the usual huddling and good-natured chatter that typically filled the chamber.

I surveyed the melancholy scene, shaking my head at what had become of Rome. The only senator in the entire chamber who was smiling was the despicable Caepio Crispinus. In his head, he was probably counting the money.

✝

That night Marcus and I shared dinner at my flat, and I was nearly inconsolable. My entire life I had dreamed of a moment like today where I would be called on to muster all my skills of advocacy, arguing in support of a worthy cause. I had stood on the floor of the Senate and acquitted myself well. Accolades from friends and supporters of Apronius made it clear that I had won their admiration. Yet none of that mattered.

In nine days, a good man would be put to death. The Senate had turned the majesty of Roman jurisprudence into a mockery of petty jealousies and opportunism.

To his credit, Marcus was a good listener. He did his best to cheer me up during the first glass of wine. The second and third glasses loosened my tongue and dissolved my inhibitions. I was angry, lashing out at the cowards in the Senate and the greed of men like Crispinus.

Marcus suggested that we go for a walk. I made the mistake of taking the wine flask with us.

It was dark and threatening more snow as we made our way down the narrow streets of Rome. Occasionally we were stopped by people who knew me, and they expressed their condolences about the day's events. We twice saw members of the Praetorian Guard patrolling the streets and made a point to pass on the other side.

By the time we wandered into the Forum, it was almost midnight, and the wine was nearly gone. Most of Rome's respectable citizens were no longer strolling around the epicenter of the city, surrounded by temples and the Roman Treasury and the Senate building. But the creatures of the night were out in full force. Prostitutes, beggars, swindlers, and drunkards.

Drunkards like me, I thought, though my mind had long since turned foggy.

A part of me realized I was stumbling on both the cobblestones under my feet and the words tripping off my tongue. More than once, Marcus tried to take the flask of wine from me, but I wouldn't let it go. Several times he grabbed my arm to keep me from slipping. When we walked by the Senate building, I grew more agitated and finished off a few final gulps from the flask. My voice must have been rising because Marcus kept telling me to keep it down.

"Fat, fat Cato," I said, my voice hoarse, the words rolling slowly off my tongue. "Gutless, gutless Cato."

When Marcus steered me away from the building, I had another idea. Clumsily, I climbed the steps of the Rostra. I stood there on the platform and looked out at the blurry figures of Roman night dwellers milling around. I raised my voice to be heard.

"Romans, citizens, listen to me!" I shouted.

Marcus rolled his eyes. "Ignore him!" he said loudly.

"Ignore me at your own peril!" I shot back. I took a sideways step and caught myself. "The evil that men do lives after them," I hollered, "and today this Senate—" I pointed with a broad, sweeping motion in the general direction of the Senate building—"committed evil on an epic scale."

I liked the way that sounded. *Epic scale.* Brilliant. I was really good.

Marcus grabbed my arm and pulled me sideways, but I dug in my heels. "Today was a day for great traitors, men who put Brutus to shame, men who will now claim the wealth of noble—" The name, just for a moment, escaped my memory. I looked at Marcus. "What's his name again?"

Marcus just shook his head.

"Apronius!" I cried, my memory suddenly replenished. "*Apronius* is the best senator, but now he is going to be a dead one."

People had gathered at the foot of the Rostra. They seemed to be swimming in the night air. I could see the soldiers listening to everything I said. Good! Now that I had everyone's attention, I could finish my defense. The things I wished I had said in the Senate chamber earlier that day.

"And as for Tiberius, let me tell you a secret," I said, speaking softly for emphasis. Maybe I could be one of those Asiatic speakers after all.

"Don't make fun of Caesar," I warned, my voice gruff and low. I shook my head, wagged my finger, and a few people laughed. "You want to know why?"

"Yeah, tell us why!" someone shouted.

I held up my right hand, the pose of a master lawyer. "I'll tell you why," I slurred out.

"Shut up," Marcus said under his breath. "Just shut up."

But I had no intention of shutting up. I was on a roll. The wine was speaking, allowing me to say everything I had wanted to say all day.

"Because Caesar is—"

I saw a flash on my side and then felt pain crack across my jaw, both sharp and distant, just before the world went black. I didn't have time to protest, time to ask Marcus why he would punch somebody he considered a friend.

By the time I woke up, I no longer cared.

—— CHAPTER 39 ——

The day after the trial, I woke with a blazing headache, a sore jaw, a dry mouth, and a stomach that was in full-scale revolt. My head felt swollen and full of pressure; loud noises were like a hammer to my skull.

I rallied enough to offer sacrifices in the temples with the hope that somehow Tiberius would intervene and spare Apronius.

In the meantime, Seneca had learned about my drunken rant and summoned me to his house. We might now be friends, but he was still the teacher and I was still the headstrong pupil. He was fuming mad and lectured me for nearly ten minutes. I had been taught better than that, he said. "Are you trying to get yourself killed? Because if you are, you're doing an excellent job."

A good advocate knows when to defend himself and when to simply grovel and ask for forgiveness. After I had said I was sorry about a dozen times, Seneca's anger finally burned itself out. He lowered his voice, and the throbbing in my head subsided a little.

But Seneca was the least of my problems. If Seneca had found out about my drunken exploits, who else might know? I fretted that word had somehow leaked back to Macro or Cato.

Seneca's sources on the island of Capri no longer seemed to be in favor with the emperor, so he didn't know if Tiberius would commute Apronius's sentence or not. "In some ways," Seneca said, "it might be better if he doesn't. You saw how the people love Apronius. His execution would only fuel the anti-Tiberius sentiment."

It seemed like a heartless comment to me. Apronius was a decent man, honest and courageous. How could his execution be good for Rome? Nevertheless, I was in no position to argue with Seneca. Actually, I was in no state of mind to argue with anyone.

Before he dismissed me, Seneca let me know that he was working on a backup plan to save Apronius. In a final dig at my wine-fueled conduct the night before, he said he couldn't share the details with me. "Loose lips could get us all condemned," he said.

Out of everything he said that day, this last comment was the one that hurt the most. He no longer trusted me with confidential information. It wasn't bad enough that I had alienated most of the Senate or that my client was scheduled to be executed in eight days. On top of all that, I now had to rebuild trust with the one man who had believed in me when nobody else had.

†

That night I met with Pontius Pilate at his estate and agreed, at his request, to represent him in his upcoming malfeasance trial. We talked about the charges against him—the way he had used sacred tithes from the Jewish Temple to pay for the aqueduct, the slaughter of the Jews by his soldiers who had hidden daggers in their cloaks, the impertinent display of the shields in the Praetorium, and the slaughter of the Samaritans when they tried to worship. He was also being charged with releasing the notorious Barabbas and not reporting that release to Caesar. I felt personally responsible for that one, though Pilate was kind enough not to remind me whose idea it had been.

Ironically, my greatest regret from my time in Judea, the trial where we had sentenced Jesus of Nazareth to die, was not listed among Pilate's charges. Yet somehow, like Procula, I couldn't help but think that all these calamities we were experiencing were tied to that one event.

"We have no chance of winning, do we?" Pilate asked. The conviction of Apronius was hanging heavy in the room. If the senators were so quick to convict one of their own, what would they do with an outsider like Pilate?

My research wasn't encouraging. A man named Gaius Junius Silanus, a prefect in Asia, had been recalled and tried on remarkably similar charges. Extortion. Brutality. General offenses against the divinity and majesty of Caesar.

I described the trial of Silanus for Pilate. The man's lawyer had brought in revenue scrolls and account books to defend against the extortion charges. But the other offenses were murky and open to interpretation. Former members of his staff testified against him. His slaves were tortured until they confirmed the allegations. That trial had been held before Tiberius retreated to Capri, and Tiberius himself had presided. Silanus was found guilty.

Pilate listened intently and took another drink from the wineglass that seemed to be perpetually in his hand. "What happens if I lose?" he asked.

I explained the consequences in the same straightforward manner that Pilate had always appreciated. He would probably be exiled. His will would be invalidated. His possessions and wealth would be confiscated and divided among those who had prosecuted him.

"I spent my entire life trying to appease Caesar," Pilate muttered. "And look where it got me."

We spent several hours that night talking about our defense—witnesses we would call at trial, accomplishments that could offset some of the charges, and senators who could be counted on to help argue our case. But I could tell that Pilate's heart wasn't in it.

It occurred to me that night how thoroughly the tables had turned. The prefect was now the defendant, facing his own unjust tribunal. The charges against him were as vague and politically motivated as they had been against some of the Jewish defendants whom

Pilate had sentenced to death. I hoped that my friend could muster half the courage I had seen displayed by Jesus of Nazareth.

Pilate would soon be judged by six hundred senators, most of whom were not willing to stick their necks out for an innocent man. Unbidden, the sight of Pilate washing his hands at the trial of Jesus flashed before me. It was exactly what the senators, other than Marcus Lepidus, had symbolically done at the trial of Apronius. In a few weeks, it would probably happen again, and we both knew it. The only thing that would be missing at the trial of Pontius Pilate would be the bowl of water.

✝

The news came the next day, and it hit me hard. I tried to re-create my prior night's conversation with Pilate, second-guessing everything I had said and beating myself up for not extending my client more hope. My own despondency at losing the trial of Apronius had affected my view of Pilate's chances. I desperately wanted to talk with him again and put a better spin on it. I would promise him victory. I would tell him that we needed to keep on fighting. I would remind him that true Romans faced their accusers with the courage of Apronius. Romans were willing to die for the truth.

I would never have a chance to tell him any of those things. After our meeting, Pilate had donned his armor from his days as a Praetorian Guard. He had polished his breastplate and sword. He had put on his helmet and sandals and belt.

He had written a new will, leaving enough to Tiberius that the will wouldn't be invalidated. He had left everything else to Procula. He had ended the will with a profession of his virtuous service as prefect of Judea and a declaration of his love for his wife and children.

He had sealed the will, left it on his desk, and marched into his gardens. There, like a good soldier, he had removed his breastplate and placed it on the ground. He had taken out his sword, grabbed the hilt, and pressed the point up under his ribs so that when he lunged, it would go straight into his heart.

I learned these things from Procula, who was beside herself with grief. She had found the lifeless body of her husband, his sword rammed into his chest, lying in a pool of his own blood. She sobbed as she told me the news, her words anguished and broken. There was nothing I could do to console her.

—

— Chapter 40 —

The day set for Apronius's execution began with a pounding rain, accompanied by cold and biting winds. A few degrees colder, and Rome would have been covered by snow. Even after the rain stopped, the clouds hung low, blanketing the Seven Hills of Rome. In a desperate move the prior day, I had gone to a fortune-teller, and she had checked the entrails of a goat. It was not good news. There were dark clouds hanging over the entire empire, she had said, and the execution of Apronius was just the beginning.

She had spread the entrails on the table in front of her, squeezing the intestines, examining the liver, running her index finger along the stomach. She bent over to get a closer look, her nose a few inches from the putrid smell of the goat innards. She sat back and frowned.

"I see a noble prince on the horizon who will usurp the evil head of the empire," she said.

I assumed she was referring to Caligula, who was now living with the emperor and being whispered about as the heir apparent, despite the fact that his mother had died in exile. I would hardly refer to him as a "noble prince."

"But first there must be much shedding of blood."

She said it with great drama, as if this would be something new and unprecedented in the empire. It occurred to me that nobody had to check the entrails of a goat to guess that there would be shedding of blood when a new emperor took his place.

The woman was unsure if some of the blood would be mine. Either way, I put little credence in what she said. When I left, I wasn't sure what had possessed me to go to the woman in the first place. She was supposed to be one of the best, and I had paid a full day's wages to buy her prophecy. But all I learned was that there would be no reprieve for Apronius.

I arrived at the Forum nearly an hour before the scheduled execution at the fourth hour of the day. The sun was starting to slice its way through the clouds, shards of sunlight casting shadows. The Praetorian Guard made their presence known, and the Roman police force showed up in great numbers as well. I found myself stuck in the middle of the crowd, being shoved around as people tried to get a better view of the proceedings.

In sixty minutes, Apronius would be led out of the Tullianum and paraded across the Forum to the temple of Augustus. There his sentence would be read. Then he would be marched back to the Gemonian Stairs, where he would be strangled. By decree, his body would be left where he died until the birds and dogs had picked it over. After a day or so, it would be dragged to the Tiber and tossed in.

When the prisoner finally emerged at the top of the Gemonian Stairs, a gasp went up from those around me. I had last seen Apronius in his regal toga, leaving the Senate, staring down those who had condemned him. Now, nine days later, he was hardly recognizable.

His gray hair was disheveled, and despite the cold, he wore nothing but a loincloth, exposing the bony body of an old man who probably hadn't eaten since the day of his sentencing. I could count his ribs, and they expanded with every breath as he shivered and shuffled his way down the steps, led by members of the Praetorian Guard. He was unshaven, and his scruffy gray beard seemed to add ten years to his visage. Unlike the proud senator who had been led from the Senate chamber, Apronius kept his eyes glued to the ground in front of him.

The guards created a gauntlet to shield him as he passed through the Forum on his way to the temple of Augustus. Macro led the death march, his armor gleaming, muscles flexed, his sunken eyes darting around to pick out any sympathizers.

The temple of Augustus was built entirely of Carrara marble and had eight enormous columns supporting the portico and a similar number on each side. On the marble at the top of the elaborately decorated columns was a relief of Mars, the war god, leaning on his lance. There were numerous marble statues on pedestals around the outside of the building, including a statue of Augustus himself riding a triumphal chariot. Even though I had seen the place ten thousand times, its grandeur was still a little overwhelming.

Cato, in his role as consul, stood at the top of the steps and waited for the disgraced senator to join him so that he might pronounce the sentence.

Slowly Apronius climbed the stairs. When he reached the top, he turned to face the crowd, his body curled against the cold, a humiliating display for everyone in Rome to see.

Cato read the formal verdict—guilty of treason—and added that Caesar had seen fit not to commute the punishment.

I could sense the teeming restlessness of the crowd, a pot ready to boil, but the soldiers were everywhere. The men around me murmured curses against the Senate and a few women dabbed at tears.

Apronius was led down the steps and paraded the length of the Forum a second time, passing in front of the Basilica Aemilia, the Curia, and the Basilica Julia, where I spent most of my time trying civil cases. I was far enough back that I could no longer see him. The next time I would lay eyes on him would be when they led him up the Gemonian Stairs for his execution.

When he passed the temple of Vesta, a disturbance arose at the front of the crowd. Shouting ensued and guards rushed forward, surrounding Apronius, pushing the crowd away. I stood on my toes but couldn't tell what was happening. I heard more arguing and shouting, and then we were all being pushed back. People around me asked each other if they had seen what had happened. Rumors started flying.

I didn't notice the Vestal until someone pointed to the top steps of the round temple of Vesta. I caught only a glimpse of her back as she entered the temple. Several bare-chested lictors formed a semicircle around the door, guarding against anyone who might try to make a run at her.

I would not learn until later that it was Flavia.

Confusion bordered on chaos as the Praetorian Guards began clearing out the Forum. Using their shields and occasionally their whips, they chased the crowds down the narrow streets that led away from Rome's capital square. I tried to go against the flow of people, but the guards weren't letting anyone past.

"Is it true?" people asked. "Did the shadow of a Vestal free Apronius?"

"That's what they're saying."

The guards held their tongues, but it became obvious there would be no execution that day. The news rippled through the streets of Rome, a wave of excitement bringing smiles and embraces and shouts of relief.

And so it was that on the last day of February in the twenty-third year of the reign of Tiberius Julius Caesar Augustus, the shadow of a Vestal Virgin set a condemned prisoner free. Of course, the law required that the event be accidental on the part of the virgin. But who would challenge the word of a high priestess of Rome?

✝

That night, I celebrated by going to the public baths. The talk was all about the events of that day. Flavia's name was on the tip of every

Roman tongue. Some of my friends suggested that she had been moved when she heard about my stirring speech in the Senate chamber. I smiled at the thought, though I didn't believe it.

I exercised hard in the gymnasium and made my way to the *calidarium*. The massive room, with its high-vaulted ceiling covered with colored stucco and paintings of mythological scenes, was filled with steam, making the atmosphere surreal. Under the floor of the *calidarium* were huge furnaces, fed by the efforts of hundreds of slaves, generating the hot air and steam that filtered up through vents. The furnaces also heated the water that filled the massive tubs of the *calidarium*, water that hovered around 120 degrees.

The torches that provided lighting were muted with glass that was colored red, blue, yellow, and green. It was impossible not to relax here. I found a solitary place in a hot tub where I could lean back and allow myself to unwind from the events of the last ten days.

Because the room was built of marble, voices echoed and reverberated here. But the voices blended in with the constant sound of running water from the dozens of fountains that adorned the place. All of that background noise, combined with the steam and the relaxing feel of the hot water, nearly put me to sleep. I closed my eyes and savored the moment.

"Enjoy it while you can," a voice said, rousing me from my half slumber.

I looked up to see that I had been joined by the last person in Rome I wanted to lay eyes on. I was struck by how unimpressive he looked without his toga. He had pale skin, an almost-sunken chest, thin arms, and a small paunch of a stomach. The man obviously didn't make his living from physical labor.

"Today was a good day for Rome," I said, closing my eyes again.

"There will be other defendants," Crispinus said casually. "The virgins won't be able to save them all. We've taken precautions so that these *accidental* crossings won't occur in the future."

"I'm sure you have."

Crispinus sat down next to me in the hot bath. I opened my eyes, sighed, and resisted the urge to move away in order to keep my distance.

"Normally a man of your slight reputation and low economic standing would not be a target for a *maiestas* proceeding," Crispinus said, his voice hoarse and threatening. He moved a little closer to my ear. "But for you, Cato might make an exception. You remember Cato? Fat, fat Cato? A man who does not like to be mocked."

I used every ounce of self-discipline to keep from showing a reaction. It might have been 120 degrees in the *calidarium*, but the remarks sent a chill down my spine. Crispinus knew about my tirade on the Rostra. This was a man who would stop at nothing to get revenge.

"Most of us are not really interested in you," Crispinus continued, pulling away from my ear. "We know Seneca is the one pulling the strings. You are just the puppet. Testify against Seneca, and we'll cut you in on a fourth of his wealth."

I sat there motionless for a second, letting the audacity of what he had just said sink in. Without warning, in a flurry of water and motion, I turned on him, grabbing his throat with my left hand and squeezing his neck back against the edge of the bath. His eyes bugged out in terror.

"Make a move against Seneca and I'll personally hunt you down and make sure it's the last thing you ever do," I said. I held him there for a moment, pinned against the bath, and then released my grip.

He sniffed, touched his neck, and twisted it from side to side as if making sure he was uninjured.

"You had your chance," he said pleasantly. He stood so he could loom over me again. "Just remember: you never see the knife that lands between your shoulder blades."

Crispinus walked away, and I let him go. The man had powerful friends in the Senate, and I would probably regret this encounter for the rest of my life. But at that moment, I was proud of what I had done.

Apronius had been set free. I wouldn't let his tormentor ruin this night. The Roman system of justice had worked. Perhaps I had declared its death prematurely.

— CHAPTER 41 —

Despite my bravado in the public baths, I spent every minute of the next two weeks on edge. I couldn't sleep, and I had lost my appetite. More *maiestas* charges were filed, this time against some high-ranking officials in the Praetorian Guard. There were whispers that I would be next. Crispinus and his cohorts were building a case against both Seneca and me, and I feared it was only a matter of time. I met with Seneca about it, but we both knew there was nothing we could do.

"It will help if you stay sober," he reminded me, as if I could have forgotten about my drunken tirade.

My law practice had picked up again, fueled by the notoriety I had gained. I was even approached by one of the commanders in the Praetorian Guard who had been accused of *maiestas*, but I decided to sit this one out. I had already made enough enemies to last a lifetime.

I desperately wanted to thank Flavia for what she had done, but I also sensed that I was being watched. By law, the intersection between her and Apronius had to be accidental. If I met with her to thank her, it would fuel suspicions that the whole thing had been orchestrated. I figured Seneca was the one who had convinced Flavia to take the action, but he never admitted it to me. And after my little episode on the Rostra, who could blame him?

With all of Rome already in an uproar, tensions notched even higher when the news arrived during the second week in March. Seventy-eight-year-old Tiberius was coming back to the capital city!

On the sixteenth day of March, I was trying one of many cases in the main hall of the Basilica Julia, an enormous atrium 270 feet long and 60 feet wide. As usual, large curtains had been dropped from the ceiling so the central nave could accommodate four trials simultaneously. There were wooden benches for dozens of spectators in each section, and depending on the case, other observers might stand behind them. In Rome, trials were spectator sports for the intellectually curious.

I was cross-examining a witness who had been lurking on the stairwell outside the basilica earlier, a man obviously willing to sell his testimony to the highest bidder. The crowd was enjoying my dissection of the witness, the exchange punctuated by clapping when I asked certain questions and whistles when they didn't like his answers.

A commotion arose in the section behind me, followed by enough murmuring that the magistrate called the court to order. I turned and noticed people filing out quickly. Within minutes the court was emptied of spectators. A servant came running down the aisle and waited behind me until he was signaled forward by the magistrate. He whispered to the magistrate, and I watched the man's face go pale. He stared into space for a moment, and then he stood.

"This court stands adjourned indefinitely," he announced. He paused as if he couldn't believe what he was about to say.

"Tiberius Julius Caesar Augustus is dead."

✝

The celebrations began almost immediately. Roman citizens poured into the streets—shouting, dancing, singing. It was as if we were celebrating Saturnalia in March. As the day wore on, they draped garlands on the public buildings and broke out instruments. Wine flowed, and the crowds grew.

I sat on the steps of the Basilica Julia and watched the celebration spin out of control. Rome could breathe again, and the bottled-up passion that had been so carefully constrained during the reign of Tiberius spilled out into a riotous party. The crowd began to chant, "Tiberius to the Tiber," the same fate that had awaited anyone accused of conspiring against the emperor. I marveled as I watched the predictions of Seneca come true. I could almost feel the shifting of the tide, and I knew that by the time the evening sun disappeared over the hills, the power in the Senate would have changed—those loyal to Tiberius would be the ones looking over their shoulders.

There was talk about how Tiberius had died, all from reliable sources, but the accounts conflicted with each other. The most credible versions claimed that Tiberius had seemed to die peacefully in his sleep. But then, just as his closest aides were preparing to declare Caligula the new emperor, the old man regained consciousness, sat straight up in bed, and asked for food. Macro, who was outside the emperor's tent, was told about the sudden resuscitation and had everyone except himself and Caligula clear the bedchamber. Macro then smothered the emperor and pledged the support of the Praetorian Guard to Caligula, the adopted grandson of the emperor.

As Rome partied the night away, this much was clear: Tiberius's reign of terror was over. Caligula, the fabled son of the beloved Roman general Germanicus, was the choice of the military to become the new emperor. It took the Senate less than two days to fall in line and invalidate the last will of Tiberius, a document that would have left half the empire to his natural-born grandson Gemellus.

†

Caligula rode into Rome ten days later, dressed in the black and tattered garments of mourning, and the populace fell at his feet in worship. They had built altars all along the road to Rome, calling out to him as their "son" and their "star."

I watched from a distance as my childhood tormentor entered Rome and the crowds along his path exalted him. I hadn't seen the man in over a decade, but he had barely changed. He still had the unruly red hair, the buggy eyes, and the head that seemed too big for his body. He was still tall and gangly. He had the smooth skin of a sixteen-year-old boy, and I was amazed that the time he'd spent with Tiberius—the man responsible for killing Caligula's brother and mother—hadn't aged him more.

As the new emperor slowly made his way through the Forum, I could tell he was trying hard not to enjoy the moment too much. He didn't allow his face to break into the kind of beaming smile that he must have been feeling inside.

Out of their disdain for Tiberius and love for Germanicus, the Roman mobs were offering Caligula absolute power. Even Augustus had not been deified in his lifetime. But watching the fervor on the faces of those who adored their new "son"—tears streaming down the cheeks of the women, mothers holding their children out toward him for a blessing, men cheering lustily for this new Roman savior—I knew that Caligula could just say the word and become a god.

But I also knew the man in a way that others did not. And the smug look of satisfaction on his face as he waved at the crowd terrified me. If this was Rome's new savior, may the gods help us.

CHAPTER 42

In an unprecedented move, selected representatives of the equestrian order and common citizens were invited to the Senate for Caligula's inaugural speech. Because of my role in the treason trial of Apronius, I was one of the chosen ones who received an invitation.

I arrived early and found a spot in the back, against the wall, squeezed in with more than a hundred others. It was a good vantage point from which to watch the senators parade in. There was a lot of backslapping and hand shaking as they milled about waiting for Caligula's arrival. The mood was much lighter than the last time I had been here.

Apronius came by and chatted with me. Marcus Lepidus greeted me as well. Crispinus, Mutilus, and Otho shot me a few threatening looks from the other side of the chamber, but I ignored them. The power had shifted like the sands of the Mediterranean. Nobody quite knew how it would shake out, but there was a general feeling that senators like Crispinus and his ilk would be on the outside looking in.

Cato eventually called the meeting to order, and the senators took their seats. All eyes turned toward the huge bronze doors in the back. The trumpets blared, the guards parted, and Gaius Julius Caesar Augustus Germanicus entered the chamber.

The senators stood as one and burst into enthusiastic applause. Caligula walked down the center aisle, nodding at the men as he made his way to the front. He stopped for a few minutes at the polished marble floor where I had made my defense of Apronius. He glanced around and acknowledged the senators and equestrians he knew. He didn't notice me in the back of the chamber. I didn't expect him to.

He took his place between the two consuls on the dais, and I was struck by how calm he appeared. Cato seized his moment in the sun and introduced the new emperor with flowery oratory that would have made any normal man blush.

Caligula looked regal enough. His crisp white toga had a gold brooch on the shoulder, reflecting shafts of light from the high windows in the chamber. When he rose to speak, there was another round of thunderous applause. He basked in it for a while and then motioned for the senators to take their seats.

He began his speech by complimenting the senators and lauding the importance of their august body. Because of my training, I couldn't resist the urge to grade his delivery. I found it to be somewhat pedestrian. He had the entire speech memorized, and it lacked spontaneity. His eyes darted this way and that, reflecting his nervousness. His hand motions were short and abrupt.

He promised to share power with the Senate in a way that Tiberius had not. Twice he referred to himself as their son. His pronouncements, though poorly delivered, were punctuated with standing ovations as even the senators who had looked skeptical at the start of his speech seemed to be warming to the young Caesar.

As he grew increasingly comfortable, his voice lowered half an octave and he became more animated. Caligula announced with great confidence that he was putting an end to the *maiestas* trials altogether. Applause broke out, but he spoke over it. All who had been exiled or imprisoned under Tiberius would regain their status and freedom immediately. All documents connected with the trials would be destroyed. Those trials were a disgraceful chapter in Rome's history, and it was time to move on.

During this part of his speech, the applause grew louder with each sentence. By the time he announced his pardon for those who had been exiled, the senators were standing. When he declared that it was time to move forward, there was a sustained standing ovation inside the chamber, echoed by cheering in the streets outside. Even Crispinus, Otho, and Mutilus were standing and clapping, though they didn't look happy about it.

By the time the applause died down and the senators took their seats, I was starting to think that maybe Caligula had changed from the self-centered and spoiled fourteen-year-old I had known. Whether he had or not, I could still breathe easier, less concerned about Crispinus's threats of legal revenge.

Caligula next addressed the issue of Tiberius's will. Even though the Senate had invalidated the will, Caligula decided to honor the bequest by Tiberius to grant each member of the Praetorian Guard one thousand *sestertii*. I glanced at the soldiers, and they were all smiles. Caligula promised that within a week they would be paid that bonus, which was roughly an entire year's salary for each soldier.

And he didn't stop there. Each member of the Roman police force and each firefighter would receive five hundred *sestertii*. Not only that, but every single citizen in the Roman Empire would receive three hundred.

Needless to say, the cheering was more boisterous than ever, and my ears rang from the sound. I clapped along but secretly wondered how much money Tiberius had left in the public treasury. Could Rome afford all of this benevolence?

Caligula next requested that the Senate consider granting Tiberius the same honors that Augustus Caesar had received after his death, including elevation to the status of a god and inclusion in the Roman Pantheon. This time, the senators held their applause.

I wondered if Caligula had anticipated that response. There could be no love lost between Caligula and the man who had killed his mother and brother. Perhaps Caligula wanted to make a request he knew the senators wouldn't accept so that they would feel like they had already regained some of their authority. At the same time, Caligula could say that he had done everything possible to honor Tiberius but the Senate had overruled him.

It was clever. And it reminded me of the types of double-crossing Caligula had engaged in when we studied together under Seneca.

By the time he finished, I might have been the only person in Rome with mixed emotions about the new emperor. He announced that Tiberius would be given a proper burial, followed by one hundred straight days of chariot races, plays, and gladiator games. He had already begun making the arrangements for importing the exotic animals.

Caligula walked out of the Senate chamber to more deafening applause, and he was followed closely by senators now savoring the afterglow of his glory. By the time I filed out of the Senate, the emperor had been swallowed up by the wildly enthusiastic crowd. There was not a cloud in the sky as Caligula worked his way down the Forum.

"What do you think of our new emperor?" a voice behind me asked.

I turned to make sure that Seneca was alone before I answered. "I think I'd like to go back to Judea," I said.

"Only if you take me with you."

PART V

THE
VESTAL

— Chapter 43 —

It had been years since Flavia had seen a man inside the House of Vestal. By law, the only man allowed in the Vestal dwelling was the spiritual ruler of the household, the *Pontifex Maximus*. For the past eleven years, that man had been ruling from the island of Capri. Though Tiberius had technically designated the functions of *Pontifex Maximus* to Sejanus for some of those years, Sejanus had seldom set foot in the House of Vestal.

It took Caligula less than three days to pay a visit.

He came with an hour's notice, and Flavia had never seen her colleagues more flustered.

Calpurnia, the head of the Vestals, barked out orders to ensure the place was spotless and that the ladies themselves were ready to be seen by the Princeps.

It took Flavia nearly thirty minutes just to prepare her hair on the off chance that she would actually get to meet the young emperor. On most days, if she was not going to be seen in public, she just gathered her hair into a bun on the back of her neck or coiled it into a knot on top of her head. But today she had her hairdresser tie her hair tightly into the braided style of the Vestals, complete with ribbons on the crown of her head and a few ringlets that she allowed to fall and frame her face.

She applied her makeup and appraised herself in the mirror. She thanked her hairdresser and put on her perfumes.

Caligula had been at the house for an hour before a servant came to Flavia's room and requested her presence. Earlier, Calpurnia had promised the women that she would try to introduce them to Caligula. Accordingly, the servant's request wasn't unexpected, though it still made Flavia's palms wet with anxiety.

When she arrived at the main meeting hall and realized she was the only Vestal who had been summoned, she had a hard time catching her breath.

Flavia looked the young emperor in the eye, struck anew by how out of place Caligula looked. She had a hard time picturing him as a supreme ruler. He was tall with spindly legs and a thin neck. His eyes were round and a little buggy. He had curly red hair that was trimmed so that it sat on his head like a crown. And especially in comparison to Tiberius, he seemed *so* young. His face was as smooth as a young boy's, and he was sunburned on his arms, neck, and face, bringing out his freckles. Could anyone his age really be prepared to rule the empire?

Flavia bowed, waiting for Caligula to extend the hand bearing the signet ring. "Hail, Caesar."

"Please," he said, reaching out his hand to take hers and pulling her upright. "I'm not one to stand on formal greetings."

Flavia stole a glance at Calpurnia, their eyes both reflecting the same message. *How refreshing.*

"I just wanted to meet the Vestal brave enough to intervene in the execution of Lucius Apronius," Caligula said.

Flavia murmured something in response, not really sure if it made sense. "I was looking forward to meeting you too," or something like that.

He asked if they could go for a private walk in the gardens, and Flavia's face grew hot. She looked at Calpurnia, who nodded.

And just like that, Flavia found herself taking a private stroll in the Vestal gardens with the young emperor, knowing that every other Vestal was peeking at them through the windows.

She warmed up to him quickly when he insisted that she dispense with the formalities and call him Caligula. She complimented him on his speech to the Senate and particularly his abolishment of the *maiestas* trials. He asked a dozen questions about life in Rome, primarily focused on the political climate and the leanings of certain senators. He seemed to be nervous and consequently talked fast. Flavia knew she had that effect on men in general but never thought that an emperor would be among them.

They found common ground when it came to Greek culture, particularly the plays. It was almost scandalous to hear a man in Caligula's position profess a love for drama and a desire to be one of the actors. "It's the only thing that kept me alive on Capri," he said.

"Greek drama?"

"No, my ability to act."

They sat under a marble statue of one of the most revered Vestal Virgins from the Republican era, and Caligula unburdened himself. Though in his inaugural speech he had urged the Senate to deal gently with Tiberius's legacy, he now revealed the agony he had gone through living with the man who had ordered the deaths of his mother and brother. Intrigue was rampant on the island, and Tiberius had watched his grandson like a hawk. Caligula had to remind himself every day that he was just an actor in a play. The slightest sign of sorrow at the death of a family member might lead to his own execution.

Flavia had known that Caligula was trapped on Capri with Tiberius but had never really thought about the psychological torture the young man had endured. Even from a distance, Tiberius was feared for his short temper and arbitrary punishments of imagined conspirators. She couldn't imagine living with that kind of person every day.

Sitting under the statue and listening to Caligula describe the house of horrors on Capri in such matter-of-fact tones drew out an emotion that Flavia never thought she would experience with the new emperor. She actually felt sorry for the man. He seemed like he needed a friend. He seemed overwhelmed by his new responsibilities and scarred by the past. And who wouldn't be?

They started walking again, this time more slowly, and Caligula sought her counsel.

"It's been two days since I spoke to the Senate," he said. "My advisers tell me the Senate is ready to issue a decree of *damnatio memoriae,* damning the memory of Tiberius and expunging him from all public records. They say the Senate will also grant me whatever additional powers I request. That the people will revolt if the Senate offers any resistance."

They took a few steps in silence. "Is that what you want?" Flavia asked. "The same kind of power that your grandfather had?"

The question seemed to catch Caligula off guard. He looked at Flavia for a moment and then turned his attention back to the path in front of them. "That's the problem. I'm not entirely sure how to navigate this."

You've come to the right place, Flavia wanted to tell him. She had a few opinions on how the empire should be run. And now here, as if served to her on a golden platter, was an opportunity to influence the most powerful man alive.

"Would you like my advice?"

"Absolutely."

Something deep in her spirit told her not to trust the man, but she decided to take a risk. What if this was her one opportunity, brought to her by the gods themselves, to help set things right?

"Follow through on your promise to end the *maiestas* trials," she said. "They turn senators into cannibals, eating each other alive and redistributing fortune and power to the most greedy and deceptive among them. Those trials have turned perjury and conspiracy into an art form."

She waited for a reaction, but Caligula just kept walking. "Okay, what else?"

Flavia glanced over the shoulder of Caligula and saw a head pull away from a window. This was fun! Every other Vestal would be asking her later to recount the conversation word for word.

For the next thirty minutes, she discussed politics and policies with the new emperor. Caligula had clearly given these matters a lot of thought, and he impressed Flavia with his desire to usher in a new era in Rome.

But just when she started to drop her guard, Caligula stopped walking and stared at her for a moment, an awkward gaze from head to toe like he was sizing her up. She felt more than a little uncomfortable, though she quickly reminded herself that the young man had been bottled up on Capri and shouldn't be expected to possess normal social graces.

"We didn't have women like you on Capri," Caligula eventually said.

Flavia blushed and didn't know how to respond. Men didn't speak to the Vestal Virgins that way. But this was the emperor. Who knew what the rules were with him? "I'll take that as a compliment," she said.

"As you should." The statement itself was innocent enough, but his tone was foreboding.

When he left the house later that morning, Flavia had mixed emotions. On the one hand, she hoped he would follow her advice and become the kind of emperor Rome needed. On the other, she couldn't help but worry about a man like Caligula when he possessed such unfettered power.

✝

That night, a full moon shone in a clear sky over the city, a sure sign that the gods were smiling on the new reign of the popular son of Germanicus.

Flavia was enjoying a night in the Vestals' private baths with three of the other Virgins. Adrianna was talking about what a breath of fresh air it was to have a new emperor. A young emperor. A man of the people.

Flavia kept her thoughts to herself. She too was hopeful that

Caligula would restore some of the decency and glory of Rome. But it was easy to make speeches. There was still a lot of work to be done.

It was nearly midnight when Flavia saw a figure on the cliff of the Palatine Hill, on the grounds of the emperor's palace overlooking the House of Vestal. She could see the outline of somebody squatting there, staring down at them.

"Don't everyone look at the same time," Flavia said, "but there's a man watching us from the cliffs of the Palatine Hill."

The other two Vestals stole a glance and said they didn't see anything. By the time Flavia looked up again, the figure was gone.

"I'm going inside," Flavia said.

There were strict rules about honoring the privacy of the Vestals. During the entire reign of Tiberius, nobody had been allowed on the palace grounds that overlooked the bath complex. Yet now, during the first few days of Caligula's reign, that barrier had been breached.

Perhaps it was just coincidence. Flavia certainly hoped so. But her instincts, and her interaction earlier that day with Caligula, told her otherwise.

She lay awake for a long time that night, staring at the ceiling. She waited until the house was perfectly silent and the only Vestal awake would be the one assigned to the eternal flame in the temple of Vesta. She waited until she knew the public baths in Rome had shut down for the night and most of the city would be sound asleep.

It was perhaps four hours before dawn when she rose and quietly dressed. She made sure no one was following as she left the house, her sandals in her hand, careful to make as little noise as possible. She stayed in the shadows and made her way across the Forum and down the hill. She stopped in an alley and put on her sandals.

She met him on the banks of the Tiber. She fell into his arms as if she hadn't seen him in years.

"Want to know what our new emperor did today?" she asked Mansuetus.

He answered with a kiss and she leaned into it, pressing her body against his. By the time their lips separated the first time, she had forgotten all about the question.

﹣ CHAPTER 44 ﹣

Caligula had a style all his own, and Flavia wasn't quite sure what to make of it. She had never imagined an emperor could be so popular with the Roman people. And why not? He passed out money. He paid for a hundred straight days of entertainment. He traveled to the island of Capri and retrieved the remains of his mother and brother, bringing them back to Rome to be placed in the mausoleum of Augustus. There were speeches made and laurel wreaths given, and the remains of his family were laid to rest with dignity.

The Roman nobles privately criticized the young emperor's public behavior, but the masses loved it. Caligula sat in the front row of the theater and became a vocal critic. At the conclusion of a play he would stand and cheer or shout insults at the actors if he didn't like their performances. Many times the other spectators would follow suit, even if they sometimes disagreed.

But the theater wasn't Caligula's first love. That was reserved for the chariot races. At the Circus Maximus, Tiberius and Sejanus had been impartial observers. It was a serious breach of etiquette for anyone in the imperial box to favor one team over the other. Caligula changed all that. He not only cheered his team on but insisted that the riders stop by the imperial box so he could give them pointers. He cursed when his team lost and claimed the manager didn't know what he was doing. Once he went from the races straight to the stable and lectured the trainer.

As a Vestal, Flavia had ample opportunity to see a side of the emperor the general public did not. He liked to ridicule his servants, especially a young commander of the Praetorian Guard named Chaerea. Though an experienced soldier, the commander was pudgy and light-skinned, and his voice was an octave higher than one might expect. Caligula told people that Chaerea would make a fine wife for someone. Whenever Chaerea served as Caligula's main bodyguard, the emperor made up embarrassing passwords that Chaerea had to use when giving orders to the other soldiers.

What's more, Caligula was full of vulgar stories that he insisted on telling in front of the Vestals. Flavia did her best to ignore them. Adrianna took the opposite approach and tried to ingratiate herself with the emperor by laughing along.

Despite Flavia's refusal to laugh at the emperor's lascivious humor, she became one of his favorites. He invited her to sit next to him at the theater, chariot races, and gladiator contests, and she reluctantly accepted. Occasionally Caligula would stop by the House of Vestal and ask Flavia to go for a walk. He even sought her advice on policy matters of great importance, something that Sejanus and Tiberius would never have dreamed of doing. Which was why it didn't strike Flavia as entirely out of the ordinary when she received an invitation from Caligula, exactly six months after he became emperor, to join him for dinner.

†

She arrived at the palace in her usual grand style, preceded by lictors and carried in a litter by slaves. She had dressed in the traditional style of a Vestal Virgin—spotless white robe, hair braided, makeup perfectly applied. She had expected to attend an elaborate dinner in the grand dining hall of the palace with Caligula and hundreds of other honorary guests. Instead, he escorted her, followed by a few slaves, down the winding halls of the palace, through the underground tunnel, and into the imperial box of the Circus Maximus.

It was the fourth day of September, and the night air was cool and crisp. The Circus Maximus was empty, the racetrack lit by torches, and the imperial box had been transformed into a luxurious dining room.

There were two couches on which to repose—one for her and the other for Caligula. He had brought in marble statues of the Roman gods from the palace. Silver dining utensils lined the table, and he poured wine into ornately carved cups produced by the new Roman glass industry in the southern half of the city. The mythological images depicted on the cups celebrated Bacchus, the god of wine, along with *maenads* dancing around him.

The food arrived in well-planned courses and included pheasant, raw oysters, lobster, venison, and peacock. Musicians stood in the back of the box and played flutes. Just before the main course, Caligula stood and recited Greek poetry.

For Flavia, the entire affair was both bizarre and a bit overwhelming. She had heard about Caligula's lavish banquets, each upstaging the last, but she had never dreamed she would be experiencing one firsthand for just her and the emperor.

This banquet was such a departure from tradition that it made her extremely uncomfortable. Flavia was a Vestal Virgin, committed to serving the people of Rome. Yes, she would sneak away to the Tiber and spend nights with Mansuetus. But nobody knew about that. Tonight, in front of a dozen or more servants, she was having a private meal with the emperor of Rome. Everything about this was wrong. It would soon be the talk of the city. But to whom could she complain?

No one. So she politely listened as Caligula talked about himself and stared at her. He was trying so hard to impress that it was painfully awkward.

When they finished the last course and Flavia thought she might escape with her dignity intact, Caligula announced his idea for the grand finale. "I know that you love the chariot races as much as I do," he said. "So tonight, I've prepared something special."

He stood and held out his hand. Flavia took it, and he escorted her to the front of the imperial box, offering her the seat he normally sat in at the chariot races. He smiled. "Wait here. I'll be right back."

He disappeared out the back of the box, and Flavia sat there for several minutes. Her attention was eventually drawn to the opposite end of the oval track, where she heard a commotion. The stable doors opened, and two enormous stallions emerged, dragging a chariot that seemed unsteady as it lumbered toward her. At first it was hard to see the driver in the dim light from the torches, but then her jaw dropped as she realized it was him.

Caligula was wearing the green sash of his favorite team and holding the reins of the chariot in a death grip. He looked unsure and awkward, stiff as a rod, with none of the fluidity she was used to seeing from the real chariot racers. He managed to bring the giant stallions to a stop in front of the box and peered up at Flavia, making no effort to conceal his pride.

He held out a hand. "Join me," he said.

Flavia stood and moved to the edge of the box. The horses pawed at the ground, anxious and skittish. Caligula looked like a man who had no idea what he was doing.

"Hurry up!" he said. "I can't hold them forever."

She knew she should just say no, but this was uncharted water. How do you tell the emperor of Rome that you don't trust him to drive a chariot?

She hitched up her robe and walked down the steps onto the arena floor. Caligula impatiently waved her over, and she kept an eye on the horses. Their enormous back and leg muscles rippled and looked twice as big up close as they did from the imperial box. When she got next to the chariot, Caligula told her to jump on behind him and put her arms around his waist.

"Why don't I just watch from here?"

"We're just going to take a few laps."

"I'd really rather not."

His face turned red. "One lap," he insisted.

She started shaking her head. One of the horses reared up, almost knocking Caligula out of the chariot. He pulled on the reins. "Get on!"

Flavia took a deep breath and climbed up behind him, putting her arms around his waist. Her face was at the nape of his neck, and there was barely room for her feet in the small chariot.

Caligula wasted no time snapping the reins, and the well-trained horses took off, jerking the chariot forward. Flavia nearly fell out the back.

"Hold on!"

Flavia had watched the races for years, but she had never been in the back of a chariot before. The arena floor was hard-packed sand that looked smooth from the imperial box but in reality contained a thousand bumps and ruts. The chariot bounced and swerved, and Flavia held on in desperation. Why had she ever agreed to climb on board?

Of course, the young emperor couldn't resist showing off a little. At the opposite end of the track from where they had started, just as he prepared to round the obelisk and take the sharp corner, he snapped the reins again, and the horses picked up speed. Flavia knew they would never make it around the turn upright.

Sure enough, the angle was too sharp, and the horses pivoted at breakneck speed, whipping the chariot behind them. Before she could even think, the chariot was on its side, sending Caligula and her sprawling across the sand.

Like the real chariot racers, Caligula had wrapped the reins around his waist and was now entangled in them as the horses continued to run, dragging both him and the chariot halfway down the track before they finally came to a stop.

Flavia scrambled to her feet and ran to where Caligula was lying.

She reached him at the same time as a couple of his slaves. She crouched over him while the slaves cut the reins loose and shooed the horses away.

His arm, shoulder, and knee were scraped and bleeding. He seemed stunned and a little out of it.

"Are you hurt?" Flavia asked, gasping for air. She ignored the pain in her own shoulder and knee.

Caligula moved his arm and right leg. He brushed some of the sand off and stood with the help of his slaves. "Did we win?"

Flavia laughed, and her mothering instincts took over. She told him to sit down and wait until more slaves arrived with water and herbs to rinse out his wounds. When they did, she played the physician and gently washed away the sand and grit from the cuts while he winced and complained.

"Maybe you should remain focused on being emperor," she said.

"Maybe you should remain focused on being a Vestal Virgin."

They eventually made it back to the imperial box, where he insisted on one more glass of wine. He made the slaves leave when the wine was poured, and he offered a toast to himself as the world's greatest chariot racer.

Flavia touched his wineglass with her own. She liked the man's spirit but felt uneasy as he watched her drink.

When she placed her cup down, he rose and held out his hand. She took it and stood in front of him. He was looking at her, eyes half-closed, and she felt chills down her spine. He put a hand behind her shoulder and leaned in to give her a kiss.

She let him, only for a moment, and then pulled abruptly back.

"What are you doing?" he asked. His voice had gone from playful to threatening, his face darkening. He took a half step closer.

She placed her palms on his chest. "This has been a wonderful night," she said, her own voice steely. "Let's not ruin it."

She saw the flash of anger in his eyes, and he pushed her hands to the side. He pulled her against him, but she wrestled free and stepped back. "Get your hands off me."

He stood there for a long second, looking sideways at her. She thought for a minute that he might try to grab her and overpower her. She had heard the stories.

And she was ready to fight.

But he just looked her up and down, undressing her with his eyes. Then he stepped back and picked up his glass of wine. He took another sip and placed it carefully on the table. He dipped his finger in the cup and traced that finger along Flavia's lips while she stiffened and gave him a hard stare.

"You know what I love?" he asked.

She shook her head.

"I love the Festival of Fordicidia," Caligula said. "The sacrifice of the pregnant heifer. You sitting under that platform waiting to be soaked in the blood of the sacrifice."

As he talked, he picked up his cup of wine. He held it over her head and slowly poured it out. The wine soaked her hair and poured down her face. She wanted to lash out and slap him, but she held back. Why give him the satisfaction of any reaction? Instead, she wiped the wine away from her eyes and stared at him, her jaw fixed in defiance. If he touched her, if he tried to rape her, she would resist him with every ounce of her being.

But Caligula just laughed. "It's been a long day," he said. "I think you know the way home."

✝

The next morning, Flavia heard the rumors from one of the other Vestals. Two of the best stallions on the green chariot-racing team had died during the night. It was believed they had been poisoned. Caligula himself had ordered a thorough investigation.

She shuddered when she heard the news. She looked up at the

Palatine Hill and tried to convince herself that last night had never happened. For years she had prayed to the gods that the tyranny of Tiberius would end. That the *maiestas* trials would cease and this new ruler, the son of Germanicus, would take his place.

Yet now, only six months into the reign of Gaius Julius Caesar Augustus Germanicus, Flavia longed for the days of Tiberius.

— CHAPTER 45 —

The gods struck back with a vengeance, just as Flavia prayed they would. Less than a month later, the emperor fell sick. Rome's best physicians were called to the palace. Sacrifices were offered to the gods day and night. The freedmen of Rome surrounded the Palatine Hill each night waiting for news, observing a solemn candlelight vigil.

The entire palace seemed to be under quarantine. There were no details given on Caligula's condition. Some believed the emperor was already dead. Flavia followed the intrigue closely as senators schemed and Macro decided to take matters into his own hands.

Gemellus, the other grandson of Tiberius Caesar, was the logical choice to follow Caligula. Macro let the senators know he would support the accession of Gemellus.

A day later, news leaked from the Palatine Hill and fluttered around the temple of Vesta. On his sickbed, Caligula had named his favorite sister, Drusilla, to inherit the imperial property and throne. When the people heard this, they rallied to the side of their fallen emperor. Whatever Caligula wanted, the people wanted as well.

Flavia watched from a distance as the senators tried to read the winds. Would the emperor recover? Did they dare cross Macro and the Praetorian Guards? Which way should they jump?

Flavia had already made up her mind. Every night she prayed to Tellus, god of earth, and Apollo, god of both disease and healing, that Caligula might die. Perhaps Gemellus was not fit to be emperor, but anybody was better than Caligula and his arrogant sister Drusilla.

But it was not to be. One night Flavia heard Adrianna burst through the door and announce that Caligula had recovered.

"He came out to the balcony and spoke to the people!" she shouted. "He threw coins into the crowd and watched them scramble for the money. The emperor is back!"

✝

Caligula wasted no time putting things in order. He dispatched a military tribune to the island of Capri and forced Gemellus to commit suicide. He appointed Macro as prefect of Egypt and sent him away.

In the days after the sickness, when Flavia was with the emperor at public ceremonies, she detected a look of madness in his eyes. His actions became even more impulsive and obsessive.

He fell in love with a woman named Livia Orestilla. But there was a small problem. She was already engaged to a senator named Gaius Calpurnius Piso. This didn't stop Caligula. He abducted her from her own wedding ceremony and forced her to marry him that same day. A few months later, he obtained a divorce.

When his sister Drusilla died unexpectedly, Caligula retreated to the country and let his beard and hair grow in grief. He required the Senate to pass a resolution making Drusilla a goddess so that she could join the ranks of Julius Caesar and Augustus.

After a month of mourning, Caligula shaved, returned to Rome, and scheduled a speech in the Senate. In a thirty-minute diatribe, he criticized the senators for the way they had treated Tiberius after his death.

The great Senate hall fell silent as the emperor dressed them down. He pulled out documents from the *maiestas* trials—documents he had supposedly destroyed—and quoted statements the senators had made. He reminded them of their votes to condemn their colleagues for saying anything against Tiberius and then contrasted those votes with their votes to condemn Tiberius after he died. He told the senators that no emperor could trust them and that the treason trials would be resumed immediately. He walked out of the stunned hall, and the consul in charge declared a recess.

The next day, the Senate reconvened and passed resolutions bestowing lavish praise on Caligula as a sincere and pious ruler. They voted to offer annual sacrifices on the anniversary of his speech. They did exactly what Caligula had accused them of doing—flattered a man they would rather see dead.

But the emperor was not done humiliating the Senate. He held a grand banquet at his house and invited all of the high-ranking senators. When they had finished dining, Caligula said that he had an honored guest he wanted them to meet. He had his stable hand bring in his favorite racehorse, and he toasted the horse with golden goblets. He told the senators that he planned to appoint the horse as one of the two consuls in charge of the Senate and asked if there were any objections.

The hall was silent. "Are there any objections?" Caligula asked a second time.

None of the senators said a word.

Caligula laughed.

A few months later, he ended the preferred seating at the theater and at the games so the aristocrats would have to fight with everyone else for the open seats. He invited senators to lavish banquets so he could humiliate them. Instead of the traditional kiss on both cheeks, he offered them his foot and made them bow down to kiss it.

He declared himself a god and constructed a temple in his own honor. Real and imagined conspiracies against Caligula were harshly punished. The *maiestas* trials took on new life as the senators turned on each other with a viciousness not seen since the last days of Tiberius Caesar.

In all of this, Flavia kept a low profile, biding her time and staying out of the emperor's way. It was not hard. There were plenty of things to distract Caligula. But there were certain events that brought them in unavoidably close contact—public ceremonies, festival sacrifices, and the games, where they both sat in the imperial box.

Moreover, Caligula was still *Pontifex Maximus*, head of the House of Vestal, and he was entitled to select the new Vestal Virgins. Just the thought of him doing so knotted and twisted Flavia's stomach with contempt.

— CHAPTER 46 —

On the appointed day, Caligula arrived at the House of Vestal and greeted Flavia and the other Vestals with cold indifference. They were surrounded by hundreds of servants and the aristocratic families of a dozen young girls who had been chosen as finalists. In addition, Caligula would appoint the new matron of the house from among Flavia and five other women who had served as Vestals for the past twenty years. Today would set the course of the house for the next decade.

After what had happened at the Circus Maximus, Flavia was certain she would not be the new matron.

When Flavia first awoke that day, her mind had raced back twenty years to her own selection by Tiberius Caesar. It had been a day of overwhelming emotion for a nine-year-old. Pride at being selected. Shame at having her head shaved. Fear and sadness at being pulled away from her family at such a young age. Ten years later, when a new set of Vestals were selected, Flavia's heart had gone out to the young girls. She could see the fear in their eyes when Tiberius had placed his hand on their heads and selected them. It was impossible to watch the scene and not relive the emotions she had felt at her own selection.

Now, as she watched the young girls milling about, exquisitely dressed with their long hair elaborately braided, soaking in everything with big eyes and fearful looks, she felt her emotions rising to the surface all over again.

Flavia had her eye on a girl named Rubria Corvus Sergia, who seemed to be the youngest candidate of the lot. She was thin as a rail with long dark hair and big brown eyes that took everything in. Her features were delicate and tiny, and her teeth seemed a size too big for her mouth. She was shorter by a few inches than the others, and Flavia could tell she was barely old enough to qualify.

When she talked, Rubria was full of drama, and Flavia knew right away that Caligula would like her. Every sentence carried the joy and innocence of a six-year-old. She looked around the House of Vestal, asking questions and listening with great awe as Flavia and the others explained the statues and the garden and the eternal flame.

There were no hard rules about how an emperor would make his selection, but Tiberius had kept it simple. He had asked the girls a number of questions and then made his choice based on looks and intellect. Flavia could remember the feeling of having the emperor silently walk in front of her and the others, looking them over. She remembered the questions he had asked and her nervous responses. Most of all, she remembered his smile when he placed his hand on her shoulder and called her *amata*, "my beloved."

Not surprisingly, Caligula adopted a different approach. He lined up the twelve finalists and had their parents stand behind them. He went down the line, leaning down and getting in their faces. He gave a running commentary as he evaluated them, and Flavia shot

Calpurnia a look, as if the Vestal matron could somehow chastise the emperor and tell him that he was doing it wrong.

"Your nose is too pudgy," Caligula said to the second girl. Big tears formed in her eyes.

"Your ears are too big. Maybe you'll grow into them," he told the next girl.

The next one had crooked teeth, and when he pointed that out, the rest of the girls stopped smiling.

"You laugh too much," he told the next one.

Flavia couldn't take it anymore. She watched the girl's shoulders slump and her lips tremble.

"Sometimes we need a little levity in this house," Flavia said. All eyes turned toward her, and the room held its collective breath. "And besides, none of us is perfect."

Least of all you, Flavia wanted to add.

Caligula stared at her for a moment, the veins in his neck pulsing. "Perhaps if my predecessors had been more careful, perfection would not be such a distant goal," he said.

Flavia's cheeks flushed. If she hadn't been so angry, she might have laughed at the irony of the comment. Here he was with his spindly neck, close-set and buggy eyes, and round, oversized face, critiquing the looks of others! Flavia could think of a thousand insults to hurl at the emperor. If he wanted to trade barb for barb, she could show him who had the quicker wit.

But she bit her tongue. You didn't humiliate the most powerful man in all of Rome and live to talk about it.

Satisfied that he'd had the last word, Caligula returned to his examination of the trembling little girls. "You need to eat more," he said to Rubria.

"That's what my father says too," she quickly responded.

She was the first girl who had talked back, and it seemed to catch Caligula by surprise. He had already started to move on, but he turned his head back and smiled. "Then you need to listen to your father."

After he concluded his inspection, Caligula posed questions to the girls, testing their knowledge of politics, drama, art, history, and languages. After that, he had everyone follow him to the Imperial Palace and his private parade grounds, where he put each of the girls on his favorite stallion, Incitatus. The horse was well trained, and even the girls who were absolutely terrified because they had never ridden a horse managed to hold on. Rubria and a few of the others looked like they had been born to ride and even spurred Incitatus into a brief trot. They all looked so tiny on the back of the huge and magnificent beast.

After seeing the girls on the horse, Caligula had the families wait in the palace and took the candidates and the existing Vestals out to a manicured courtyard in the middle of the palace grounds. There, to Flavia's surprise, were a number of baby lambs. They were pure white, literal balls of wool with tiny faces that regarded the intruders with suspicion. And with good reason.

Caligula told the girls that an important part of the honor of being a Vestal was to perform sacrifices on behalf of Roman citizens. "Sometimes, it will be a pregnant heifer. Sometimes a goat. Sometimes a lamb." He looked at the girls' shocked faces. "You must learn to slit their throats and let their blood flow on the altar. If you cannot do that, you don't belong here."

He had his servants hand long knives to each of the little girls. "I'll show you how it's done," Caligula said. "Then I want you to find a lamb and show me that you can do it."

Flavia stepped forward. "Is this really necessary?"

This time, before Caligula could respond, Calpurnia backed Flavia up. "Your Excellency, we have a process for instruction. With great respect for your role in selecting the Virgins, the art of sacrifice is something that must be learned over time."

For the second time that day, Caligula stiffened. "I have a method of teaching as well. They watch me do it and then they do as I do."

With that, he turned his back on Calpurnia and walked slowly toward one of the lambs. He lunged, got a handful of wool, and picked it up. He brought it over in front of the girls, cradling the lamb in his arms. The lamb was trembling and bleating. He placed it on the ground, held it there, and made the girls watch as he slit its throat.

With blood on his hands and the lamb dead at his feet, he looked up at the Vestal candidates. "Who's next?" he asked.

A few of the girls were crying. Rubria turned and buried her head in Flavia's robe. Not one of the girls stepped forward.

But a furious Calpurnia did. "As I said, we have ways of teaching the girls the art of sacrifice. You have just set that process back several years."

Flavia wanted to applaud. At last, someone with the spine to stand up to the emperor!

Enraged, Caligula looked at the bloody knife in his hand and stared at Calpurnia. He surveyed all the Vestals as well as the twelve little traumatized girls. He threw the knife at his feet, and the blade stuck in the ground.

"Meet me at the House of Vestal," he snapped.

✝

Things were no less tense an hour later at the selection ceremony. All twelve candidates stood in a line with their parents behind them. One by one, Caligula approached the winners and held out his hand. "I take you, *amata*, my beloved, to be a Vestal priestess, who will carry out the sacred rites on behalf of the Roman people."

Because of the trauma they had experienced earlier that day, the first two girls sobbed when they were chosen. When Caligula moved in front of Rubria for his third choice and extended his hand, Flavia was not at all surprised. The child had acquitted herself well.

Rubria held her head high and bravely fought back tears. She tried but couldn't force herself to smile. As Caligula finished speaking the prescribed formula, Flavia could tell that Rubria wanted to look behind her and hug her parents one last time. But she knew she wasn't allowed. Instead, once Caligula had finished, Rubria walked purposefully to the side of the room occupied by the Vestals and stood in front of Flavia. Flavia put her hands gently on the girl's shoulders and whispered so that only Rubria could hear. "Everything will be fine. I will take care of you."

When he finished his selections, Caligula faced the Vestals and looked them over. It was time for him to select the new matron of the house. His eyes lingered on Flavia for a brief moment. He had a look of smug satisfaction, as if he was about to take great pleasure in rejecting her.

When his gaze then turned to Adrianna, Flavia was not surprised. There were already rumors about Adrianna's late-night escapades in the palace. She smiled at the emperor, and there was no doubt that Adrianna knew exactly what was coming next.

"In my role as *Pontifex Maximus*, I select you to be the matron of the Vestals," Caligula said to her. She held out her hand, and he took it in his palm and kissed it.

Flavia wanted to vomit.

Adrianna stepped forward and stood next to Caligula, facing the other Vestals. For the next ten years, this woman would be in charge. She beamed at the thought of it.

But Caligula wasn't done. "I have another announcement to make," he said proudly. "An announcement that also falls under my role as *Pontifex Maximus*."

Flavia felt her heart beating in her throat. Given the look on the emperor's face, she knew she wasn't going to like this.

"You are the most powerful women in the empire," Caligula said. "And some of the most beautiful. Yet there are other women just as highly regarded, and I do not want to split our citizens into factions. Some preferring you. Others preferring them. In the interest of unity and to ensure that all Romans hold the position of Vestal Virgin in highest esteem, I am bestowing the privileges of a Vestal on my grandmother, Antonia, the daughter of Mark Antony and the faithful friend of Tiberius. I am also bestowing these same privileges on my sisters—Agrippina and Livilla. They will not be living with you, but they will have all the privileges of a Vestal."

It was a dagger to the gut. Every one of the Vestals had earned her position the same way. Each had endured the selection process that Rubria had just gone through. Each had dedicated her life to the task of faithfully serving Rome.

And now Caligula, with just a word, was bestowing the same privileges on members of his own family?

Flavia knew immediately there was no use protesting. The emperor had already beaten the Senate into submission, and Rome would do whatever he wished. But the House of Vestal would never be the same.

"We will welcome them as Vestal priestesses on the same terms as any other Vestal," Adrianna said.

Speak for yourself, Flavia thought.

✝

That night, Rubria sneaked into Flavia's bedroom and crawled into bed with her. Flavia hugged the young girl and rubbed her back, reassuring her that everything would be okay. Rubria's head was shaved and she missed her family. But something else was bothering her just as much.

She looked up at Flavia, her eyes full of tears. "Why do we have to kill the lambs?" she asked.

There was no good answer, at least for a six-year-old. "Let's talk about it tomorrow," Flavia said. "Just try to sleep. Things will be better in the morning."

— CHAPTER 47 —

TWO YEARS LATER
IN THE THIRD YEAR OF THE REIGN OF
GAIUS JULIUS CAESAR AUGUSTUS GERMANICUS

The games were not what they used to be. There were empty seats, and the crowd was on edge. Flavia could only hope the deterioration would continue, that people would lose interest. Perhaps one day the games would be no more. Maybe Rome could become more like Greece, and sport could be celebrated without bloodshed.

For now, it all came down to money. Caligula's games were struggling because the imperial treasury was running dry. Exotic animals were terribly expensive, as were gladiators. Caligula had already burned through more than two billion *sestertii* that Tiberius had left in the state coffers. Recently, the emperor had turned desperate in an attempt to raise more public funds.

He increased taxes. He found new things to tax, including prostitution. He set up a brothel in a wing of his palace. Any wills that named Tiberius as a benefactor were interpreted so those same bequests went to Caligula. If any rich Roman citizen died without leaving Caligula a large bequest, the will would be invalidated for lack of generosity. That way everything could go to the state.

But still, the revenues could not keep up with Caligula's lavish spending, and the games suffered. On this day, the crowd had jeered during the halfhearted animal hunts in the morning. The arena didn't begin filling until the gladiator battles after lunch. Halfway through them, Caligula made his noisy entrance.

Flavia was already in the imperial box when the trumpets and flutes announced the emperor's arrival. There were scattered catcalls throughout the arena, though most people stood and applauded. Flavia could still vividly recall the games six months earlier when a section of freedmen had booed the emperor and been immediately arrested. Caligula had ordered that their tongues be cut out. They were fed to the wild animals the next day in front of the entire arena. His entrances after that event had been met with nearly unanimous, albeit perfunctory, applause.

Caligula arrived at these games, held in honor of his late sister Drusilla, dressed like the god he claimed to be. He wore a long blue silk robe covered in jewels. A large seashell hung from a gold chain around his neck, reminding the Romans that a year earlier he had marched an army north to Britannia, stopping at the very shores of Gaul, where he had ordered his soldiers to collect seashells before coming home.

Over his robe, Caligula wore the breastplate of Alexander the Great, which he had purloined from the man's tomb and brought out for special occasions. The smooth skin of Caligula's round face had been transformed by a fake beard decorated with gold. He held a trident in his right hand, a sign of his deity.

He walked deliberately to the front of the imperial box and stood there for a long time, enjoying the applause. He smiled disdainfully at his subjects, the benevolent grin of a god with limitless power. Finally, long after the people had tired of cheering, he stepped back and took his seat.

Flavia returned to her own seat two rows behind him. Even being that close to the man nauseated her. He had made a mockery of everything she stood for. She detested every leader in Rome who enabled the emperor and his boorish conduct. But right now, Flavia was less concerned with the emperor than she was with a certain gladiator match.

Mansuetus would be fighting for the first time in six months, and it had her emotions on edge. Typically, certain types of gladiators were paired against other types. Mansuetus was a Thracian and fought with a small shield and a curved *sica*. His speed and quickness was typically matched against a heavily armed gladiator such as the *hoplomachus*.

But Caligula loved to defy tradition, and so today he had cast

Mansuetus against a type of gladiator he had never fought before—a *retiarius*. Those fighters were Caligula's intriguing favorite, the most lightly armed of all. The *retiarius* had a ribbed metal guard protecting his left shoulder and leather on his arm, but his only weapons were a large net and a trident. His tactics were simple: ensnare his opponent in the net and spear him with the trident.

Flavia had seen it numerous times before. A gladiator fighting a *retiarius* would make a single wrong move, and with a flick of the wrist the *retiarius* would cast his broad net and cover his opponent. He would pull the net tight, leaving his opponent thrashing on the ground to be finished off by the three-pronged tip of the trident.

Mansuetus should win. But the fight would be unpredictable. And if he lost and found himself thrashing on the ground, caught up in the net, Flavia felt certain that Caligula would turn his thumb down.

By the time Mansuetus and his opponent entered the arena late in the day, Flavia felt like she might explode from the nerves. She refused to join the lusty cheer of the crowd when the gladiators were introduced.

Though he was supposed to be the villain, wearing the armor of the ancient Greek Thracian tribe, Mansuetus was a crowd favorite due to his cheery demeanor and curly blond hair. He walked to the middle of the arena and waved, turning in a circle so that he could be adored by everyone. He had won thirteen straight fights. If he won three more, he would earn his freedom.

He and Flavia had discussed that very possibility the prior night on the banks of the Tiber. She knew how much Mansuetus loved the arena. Like most champions, he considered himself invincible. He had always maintained that even after he earned his freedom, he wanted to keep fighting, that it was in his blood, that the gods would protect him. But last night he had finally said the words Flavia had been aching to hear.

"I love the arena, Flavia. But I will give it up for you. When I win my freedom, that fight will be my last."

They had spent most of the night together and talked about the future. He would become a *lanista*, training other gladiators. When she completed her service as a Vestal, they would marry. Three more fights and it would all be possible.

Mansuetus approached the imperial box and cast a not-too-subtle glance at Flavia. She gave him a sideways look, chastising him with her eyes. They took enough chances sneaking out late at night. He didn't have to make it obvious to the entire watching world.

But the man was incorrigible. Flavia's scolding look only made him smile more broadly, locking his eyes on hers. She would give him a piece of her mind later that night. Assuming, of course, that he prevailed.

Mansuetus bowed with his usual flair in front of Caligula. "We who are about to die salute you!" he said.

Flavia had never told Mansuetus about the night Caligula kissed her and tried to molest her. She knew if Mansuetus found out, he would take matters into his own hands. But even if he found a way to kill the emperor, he would never survive the fallout.

Flavia couldn't imagine living without him. In eight more years, she would have completed her service to Rome. She dreamed of living with Mansuetus and withdrawing from public life. They could start a family. Raise children. Pursue a life of happiness.

Her thoughts snapped back to the present when Caligula stood. He turned and his eyes fell on Flavia. She pretended not to notice, staring ahead at the gladiators.

"Flavia, why don't you come join me?" Caligula asked. He pointed to the seat next to his.

Even though the emperor had married a woman named Caesonia a year earlier in a lavish ceremony, she rarely attended the games with him. Instead, the seat on Caligula's right was always occupied by Adrianna.

Flavia feigned surprise at the emperor's request. "Your Excellency, I wouldn't dream of taking Adrianna's seat."

But Caligula insisted. He humiliated Adrianna, sending her to the rear of the imperial box.

Reluctantly, Flavia moved next to the emperor. The gladiators were in position, waiting on a signal to begin.

"Whom are you picking in this one?" Caligula asked, leaning toward Flavia.

"Mansuetus."

"Everybody loves Mansuetus. I wonder why that is."

The comment chilled Flavia. The emperor knew something. This was his style—conniving, underhanded, playacting the fool.

"Perhaps people like those bulging biceps," Caligula suggested.

Flavia didn't respond.

"Perhaps it's that nice scar on his left shoulder or perhaps those cute blond curls," Caligula said.

Again Flavia ignored him. The best way to interact with Caligula was the same way one would treat a spoiled child. As if he didn't exist.

"Or perhaps those beautiful, white, smiling teeth."

Was it jealousy? It had to be more than that. This was the first time Caligula had paid attention to Flavia in the past two years.

"Let's hope he doesn't get distracted by his frequent glances in your direction," Caligula said.

Her heart stopped.

The emperor raised his hand, and the fight was on.

The crowd started cheering immediately, many rising to their feet. Fights involving a *retiarius* were notoriously short-lived. Mansuetus danced around, looking for an opening. His opponent's trident was eight feet long, and Mansuetus had to keep his distance. The *retiarius* thrust the trident a few times, but Mansuetus easily blocked it with his shield. Twice he sidestepped the *retiarius*'s cast net.

The entire time, Flavia's heart was pounding with the fear that, like every other time he stepped into the arena, this fight could be his last. She had her hand to her mouth and could hardly force herself to watch.

"He's so close," Caligula said. "Wouldn't you say?"

It seemed to Flavia that he was keeping a respectable distance. "No, Your Excellency."

"Oh. You thought I meant to the *retiarius*'s net," Caligula said.

"I'm sorry?" Flavia asked, keeping her eyes on the fight.

There was another toss of the net and another dodge by Mansuetus. This time he lunged at his foe, but the man stepped back and flipped the net a second time. It wrapped around Mansuetus's knee, and the *retiarius* jerked on it, pulling the big man's legs out from under him.

Flavia gasped.

"Yes!" Caligula yelled, jumping to his feet.

Mansuetus rolled as the *retiarius* lunged with the trident, spearing the ground inches from him. The gladiator sprang to his feet, and Flavia exhaled.

There had been close calls before. And every one of them took ten years from her life.

Mansuetus smiled and brushed his forehead with an arm as if the call had been a little close even for him. The crowd roared its approval, and Mansuetus stole a quick glance in Flavia's direction.

Keep your eyes on your opponent.

"Back to my point," Caligula said as the gladiators resumed their death dance. "I meant that Mansuetus is so close to buying his freedom. Three more matches, if my math is correct."

Flavia shrugged as if it were news to her. "He seems like a noble fighter," she offered.

"Not just noble—undefeated. It would be a shame if the man never had the opportunity to taste freedom and become a citizen."

Flavia wanted to reach over and strangle the emperor. What in the world was he talking about?

"I don't understand, Your Excellency," she said. There was steel in her voice.

Mansuetus seemed as if he had grown bored with the fight. He stood at a safe distance from his opponent and lowered his sword and shield, practically begging the man to come and fight him toe-to-toe. But the *retiarius* was having none of it. He continued to circle with his net, poking here and there with the trident. The crowd began to get restless, and there were a few disgruntled yells from the fans.

"If he wins today, will you meet him at the Tiber tonight to celebrate?" Caligula asked.

He said it with a teasing tone, yet the comment stunned Flavia. She turned and looked at him, though the emperor kept his eyes on the fighters. She could hardly breathe, much less respond. Her thoughts whirled in her head. How did he know?

"What do you mean?"

"You know exactly what I mean. Adrianna told me that you have been sneaking out. It's my job to protect the dignity of the Vestals, so I had you followed."

Caligula, like a master actor, let the accusation hang in the air for a few seconds. Flavia felt the bile rising in her throat as her mind raced with the implications. Vestals who violated their oath of virginity were buried alive. Their lovers were whipped to death in the Forum. And most disturbing of all, the judge of their guilt and innocence was the *Pontifex Maximus*, the man sitting to her immediate left.

"Mansuetus looks rather strong," Caligula observed. "I wonder how many lashes it would take before he expired."

The question almost became irrelevant. Mansuetus had become careless, taunting his adversary and smiling at the crowd. The *retiarius* had been biding his time, distracting Mansuetus with poorly executed casts of the net. Just when Mansuetus fully relaxed, the *retiarius* thrust the trident low and hard, like a spear. The middle point penetrated Mansuetus's right foot. He cried out in pain and tried to pull back to avoid the swiftly cast net. But he stumbled, and the *retiarius* caught him in the net.

Flavia screamed as the *retiarius* retracted his trident and raised his arm to spear Mansuetus.

But Mansuetus grabbed the net that now covered his body and

gave it a mighty pull, yanking his opponent off-balance. They became entangled together on the ground, engaged in hand-to-hand combat, their weapons of little use. Through his superior strength, Mansuetus torqued the body of his opponent into an unnatural position.

Flavia wanted to look away but couldn't will herself to do so.

With all the spectators now on their feet, Mansuetus flexed his powerful muscles and with a loud grunt snapped his opponent's neck.

The crowd roared, and Flavia sat down, feeling disoriented. The move had been a gruesome sight, but the battle in the arena was the least of her worries.

Mansuetus stood and shrugged off the net. He drank in the cheers of the crowd and hobbled over to the emperor's box. He dragged his right foot as he walked, leaving a trail of blood in the sand.

Caligula stepped down from the imperial box and joined Mansuetus on the floor of the arena. He placed the laurel wreath of victory on Mansuetus's head. The crowd showered the gladiator with money and other objects of affection. Mansuetus limped around, stoically collecting as much of the booty as he could, but Flavia could see that her lover had turned pale. She worried about his loss of blood.

Somehow Mansuetus held it together until he exited the arena. Only then did Caligula sit down next to Flavia and lean toward her as he whispered his ultimatum.

"Come spend the night with me in the palace, and your indiscretions along the Tiber River will be forgiven," Caligula said. "Find out what it's like to make love to a god. Refuse me, and both you and Mansuetus will pay the price."

PART VI

THE
GLADIATOR

FOUR MONTHS LATER

CHAPTER 48

IN THE FOURTH YEAR OF THE REIGN
OF GAIUS JULIUS CAESAR AUGUSTUS GERMANICUS

It was October, the air chilly and wet, on the night I was summoned
to the temple of Vesta. I was thirty years old, no longer a wide-eyed
young idealist, but I still had the same swarm of butterflies in my
stomach that I did the first time I met Flavia. Her messenger had
provided very little information. *"The Vestal would like to see you. She
requests the honor of your presence at midnight at the temple. She will
be tending the Vestal flame."*

I shaved twice that day. Once, as customary, in the morning. A
second time late in the evening. My toga was pressed and clean. Over
it I wore a *paenula*, a sleeveless hooded cloak that added an extra layer
of protection against the autumn chill.

When I told the temple guards my name, they allowed me to pass,
saying that Flavia was expecting me. I climbed the steps of the temple
nervously and entered the large circular atrium without knocking,
removing my hood as I did so. The atrium was dominated by the
sacred flame that burned in the hearth at the center. The flame was
tended around the clock by one of the Virgins. If the fire went out on
a Vestal's watch, she could be sentenced to death. Once a year, every
household in Rome would light a torch at the temple to kindle a fire
in their own hearths. The Vestals were, therefore, in a symbolic sense,
the mothers of all of Rome. There was no ritual more sacrosanct than
tending the eternal flame.

Flavia sat on a step next to the fire, her face illuminated by the
sacred glow. As I approached, she stood and thanked me for coming.
Her eyes were sad, which merely accentuated their beauty. Her face

was drawn and gaunt; the strain of Caligula's reign was taking its toll. Like the rest of us, she had witnessed unrestrained evil.

"You look well, Theophilus," Flavia said. It was only a polite greeting, but it made me feel like I could soar.

"As do you."

Flavia smiled. "I'm fortunate it's dark in here, or you would know that's not true."

She invited me to sit next to her, and I took off my *paenula*. I waited for her to explain the reason I'd been summoned. My mind raced with speculation.

She didn't waste any time on formalities. "I don't know how to say this," she began, her voice hollow and uncertain, "but I'm fairly certain that I will be charged soon with violating the vows of a Vestal."

She paused as I took in the news. Did she mean what I thought?

"Caligula is convinced that I've had sex with the gladiator Mansuetus," Flavia continued. Her bluntness surprised me. So did her desire to speak with me, of all people. I suspected she might be blushing in the dark.

"I took note of the work you did at the trial of Apronius," she continued. "He was a good man, a courageous man. That's why I took it upon myself to set him free. But he was also well represented in the Senate."

I swelled with pride at the assessment even as I tried not to react to the admission that she had acted intentionally to free Apronius. Others had said I had done a good job, but there was nobody I would rather have heard it from than Flavia. "Yet still we lost," I said, attempting to sound appropriately self-effacing.

"Or maybe you didn't. Maybe a certain Vestal was so inspired by your defense that it compelled her to act."

"If that's the case, both Apronius and I owe her our undying gratitude."

"Good. Then perhaps you will be open to my request."

Flavia turned and faced me, placing a hand on top of mine. I knew I would be powerless to turn her down.

"Will you take my case—plead my cause in front of the emperor? Will you advocate for both me and Mansuetus the way you did for Apronius?"

A clear-thinking man might have better appreciated what this woman was asking. Hadn't she just said that Caligula was the one instigating the charges? And yet, as *Pontifex Maximus*, he would be the sole judge of whether the charges were true. And I already knew what happened when men crossed this tyrant.

But none of that mattered. I was not a clear-thinking man. Cleopatra had nothing on Flavia.

"It would be an honor."

She squeezed my hand, leaned over, and gave me a light kiss on the cheek. "I was reluctant to ask," she confessed. "I didn't want to put your life in danger."

Thanks for the reminder, I wanted to say. But this was no time for sarcasm. "I will do my best. I can promise you that."

"I know you will. That's why I asked. You're the only advocate I felt I could trust."

We spent the next several minutes discussing the case. How did she know that she was about to be charged? What were the specifics? Who would be the witnesses? What was her relationship like with the emperor?

The last question hit a nerve. She stiffened, and even in the shadows cast by the fire, I could see anger spark in her eyes. "I've rebuffed some of his advances. Even after his marriage to Caesonia, he still pursued me. Part of this is a lust for revenge."

According to Flavia, the night in question was the night after the gladiator games honoring Drusilla. A high-ranking captain of Caligula's Praetorian Guard, a man named Lucian Aurelius— Caligula's friend from our boyhood days—had been stationed outside the House of Vestal with instructions to follow Flavia if she tried to sneak out. Lucian was prepared to testify that he had followed her to the Tiber and witnessed her liaison with Mansuetus. I knew Lucian from my days as his classmate under Seneca's tutelage.

"Is it true?" I asked. "Did you meet Mansuetus that night?"

She hesitated, and I thought I had my answer. When she spoke, her voice was hoarse and it sounded like she was choking back tears. "I've pursued Mansuetus. He's a noble man and should not have to forfeit his life because of my need for affection."

She had been looking down as she talked, but now she turned to me and I could see the tears wetting her eyes. "But is it true?" she asked, repeating my question. "Not on that night, Theophilus. And that's all you really need to know."

─ CHAPTER 49 ─

The day after my meeting with Flavia, her predictions came true. She and Mansuetus were both arrested and charged with the capital offense of violating Flavia's vows as a Vestal. If convicted, Flavia would be buried alive in an underground chamber in the Campus Sceleratus with a few days' supply of food and water. Mansuetus would be flogged in the Forum until he died.

I heard from reliable sources that Mansuetus did not go down without a fight. It took six Praetorian Guards to arrest him. Two were seriously injured.

According to those same sources, Flavia was roused from her sleep by Lucian and a dozen other members of the Praetorian Guard. They read the charges against her, bound her hands, and led her away to the dungeon at the top of the Gemonian Stairs.

I was not allowed to see either of my clients, but I was told the guards had cut Flavia's hair—butchered it, really—so that it was cropped close to her head and scissored off in uneven chunks. She was given a long black tunic and stripped of her jewelry. I would not be allowed to see her or Mansuetus until six days from now, on the eve of the trial.

Word traveled quickly about my role as advocate for both the gladiator and the Vestal, and I suddenly became an incredibly popular man. I went to the market to buy some produce and listen to the gossip. The shopkeepers wouldn't let me pay. "Put up a good fight," they said under their breath.

For the next few days, I ignored my other clients and devoted every minute of my waking hours to Flavia's case. At night, I went to the baths so I could work out my frustrations in the gymnasium and then strategize with Seneca in a corner of the *laconicum*, discussing trial tactics while filling our lungs with steam.

Lucian Aurelius would be the main witness. He claimed he had followed Flavia the night in question and watched her and Mansuetus having sex on the banks of the Tiber. Caligula had assigned my old nemesis, Caepio Crispinus, to prosecute the case. Crispinus was bragging all over town that his case was unassailable.

Even if my clients denied the charges, which Seneca and I both presumed they would do, it would be their word against Lucian's.

"Do you know how Caligula will determine who is telling the truth?" Seneca asked.

I shrugged. "He will obviously accept the word of Lucian. He'll claim my clients are lying just to protect themselves."

"No, he's far too clever for that," Seneca said. "There's a legend about a Vestal named Tuccia who was also accused of violating her vows—must have been more than a hundred years ago. The testimony was unclear, and she was ordered to prove her virginity by carrying water to the Tiber in a sieve. The water didn't spill, and Tuccia was found not guilty. My sources tell me that Caligula will follow that precedent and use the same test if the testimony is contradictory."

"Thank you for the encouragement," I said.

By the fourth day after my clients' arrest, it became obvious that Caligula had miscalculated the popularity of Mansuetus. Though I was not in attendance myself, I heard that when Caligula and Caesonia were introduced at the Circus Maximus that day, there was a chorus of jeers and whistles from the crowd. The emperor looked angrily about and surely would have ordered the perpetrators killed, but he couldn't pinpoint where the noises were coming from. Then, as if on cue, a low and rumbling chant of "Free Mansuetus!" erupted from all sections of the great stadium. Caligula shouted at the crowd, called off the games, turned on his heel, and stalked back to his palace.

But that night at the baths, Seneca was not encouraged. "We are not dealing with a rational man," he said. "He will now be more determined than ever."

On Wednesday, two days before the trial, I was so nervous I couldn't eat. I sat in my study for hours trying to think of a plausible defense. I went on long walks. I tried to practice my arguments, but I had a hard time focusing. I kept thinking about Caligula's exquisite cruelty, the many creative ways he had humiliated and tortured his enemies. The day he hung me on the cross flashed before me. I had this terrible feeling in the pit of my stomach that if I did my job well, I would become just as much a focus of Caligula's wrath as Mansuetus and Flavia already were.

If it had been any other client, that fear would have paralyzed me. But this was Flavia. Thoughts for my own safety were eventually overcome by the prospect of saving *her*. It didn't make sense; I hardly knew her. Yet she was all I could think about in the days leading up to the greatest challenge of my life. Raging love casts out fear, even if that love might never be reciprocated.

My first break came as I was walking home from the baths late Wednesday night after another long meeting with Seneca. I heard the footsteps behind me turn from a walk to a run. I pivoted quickly, my paranoia triggering all kinds of thoughts.

My pursuer was a thin young girl dressed in a long black robe. A hood shadowed most of her face.

"May I walk with you?" she asked, her voice high and frightened.

She couldn't have been more than eight or nine. The streets of Rome were dangerous for someone like her this late at night.

"Do I know you?" I asked.

She fell into stride and we both kept walking. "No. My name is Rubria. I am one of the newest Vestals."

I stopped in my tracks and looked at her.

"Let's keep walking," she suggested. "It will look more natural."

I did as she said, amazed at how mature this young girl seemed, and we turned down a side street. I glanced around to see if anybody followed.

"I need to talk to you about Flavia's case," Rubria said. "She did not do what they have accused her of. I am willing to testify for her."

In the next ten minutes, she told me her story. We walked slowly, crossing the street once at my urging to make sure the two men half a block behind us weren't following us.

Rubria said that she had been in attendance at the games honoring Drusilla. She had watched Mansuetus snap the neck of his opponent. She had seen the crucifixions at lunch. She had seen men—and this time, two women—torn apart by wild animals. She hated being a Vestal Virgin, she told me. And that night, like many other nights, she had slipped down the hall and crawled into bed with the woman who was like a mother to her.

I held my breath as I waited for her to say the name. This was powerful. A young and innocent Vestal who could be our star witness.

"Flavia helped me go to sleep," young Rubria said. "She rubbed my back and sang a song to me and we slept together in her bed that night."

"All night?" I asked. "How do you know she was there all night?"

"I sleep lightly. If she left, I would have known. She was there when I woke up in the morning."

I was immediately in lawyer mode. Crispinus might be able to poke a few holes in Rubria's story, but only if he knew she was going to testify. If not, perhaps I could nail down Lucian with a precise time for when he watched Mansuetus and Flavia by the Tiber. He wouldn't know that Rubria would be testifying in my case.

"This next question is very important to our case," I said. "So I want you to think about it carefully. At what precise time did you first go to Flavia's room?"

Rubria didn't hesitate. It was as if she knew the question was coming. "I was with her all night. She stayed with me after dinner in my room until the end of the first watch, about the third hour of darkness, because she knew it had been a hard day for me. She kissed me on the forehead and told me to try to sleep. I was awake for another thirty minutes before I went down to her room. I spent the rest of the night there."

Perfect! My blood was pumping harder, and I picked up the pace. At last, something to work with. But this poor little girl had no idea what was coming. She was about to make some very powerful enemies. In my heart, I knew I should tell her that. Yet I couldn't take the chance of running her off.

"Are you sure you're ready to testify about this at Flavia's trial?"

"Of course."

"Caepio Crispinus will ask you a lot of questions. He'll try to make you look like a liar."

"I do not care."

I was proud of her. She had more courage than most of the politicians in Rome, men who were old enough to be her grandfather.

"If Flavia were here, she would tell you how much this means to her," I said. "You might just save her life."

The young Vestal did not respond for a long time. When she did, her voice was frail and barely audible.

"I could not survive without her," Rubria said. "Please, sir, don't let anything happen to her."

CHAPTER 50

The day before trial, I was finally allowed to see my clients. I first visited Mansuetus, who was locked away in a dungeon on the outskirts of Rome. The small, dank cell smelled of excrement.

"Watch where you step," Mansuetus said as the guards clanged the iron gate shut behind me. The gladiator's wrists and ankles were shackled. The guards had used a short chain on his ankles, forcing him to walk with small steps.

I had never been this close to the man. He was an impressive specimen. He was at least three inches taller than I, and his powerful muscles rippled. But he also looked like he was at death's door.

He hadn't shaved in six days. His blond hair was long and gnarled. His eyes were bloodshot, and his skin was covered with grime, sores, and black soot. His right foot, the one that had been speared by the trident four months ago, was red and swollen, with pus seeping from the wound on top. When he spoke, his voice had the gruff sound of a man fighting off a serious illness. If we won, I knew I would have to get my friend Marcus to treat him immediately.

"Are they feeding you?"

He snorted. "I wouldn't call it food. But I eat it."

"We need to talk about your case," I said. I removed my wax tablets and stylus to take notes. I found a place to sit against one of the walls. I noticed a few rats on the other side of the room, and my eyes watered from the smell.

I'm not sure what I expected heading into that dungeon, but it wasn't this. The place was so foul it seemed to have broken even the resilient spirit of Mansuetus. There was no defiant smile in the face of death, no resolute assurance that he knew we would win the case. Even when I told him I had a witness who would testify that Flavia had never left the House of Vestal on the night in question, he hardly reacted.

I watched him shiver, occasionally wrapping his arms across his chest in a futile effort to keep warm. His eyes blinked slowly as if it were a struggle to keep them open.

This man was sick. It made me wonder if they were poisoning his food.

He denied ever having sex with Flavia. As his advocate, I encouraged him to tell me the truth. I was sworn to secrecy. I just needed to know the facts so I could deal with them.

"That is the truth," he insisted.

Flavia had certainly implied otherwise. I jotted a note, hoping the silence would pry loose a more forthcoming response, but it didn't seem to affect him.

"Have you seen Flavia?" Mansuetus asked.

"Not yet. But I will later this afternoon."

He squinted—with some effort, as if trying to focus.

"Do you have a message for her?" I asked.

I watched him think about this for a moment. I had seen the two of them exchange looks at the games. And even now, just from watching the man's bloodshot eyes, I could tell how desperately he wanted her to know that he loved her. Yet he had learned all too well that you couldn't trust anyone.

"Tell her that I am doing fine," he said, measuring each word. "Tell her I hope that she's doing well."

We talked for a few more minutes, and Mansuetus asked questions about the trial. Would he be shackled? Where would he be standing? Where would Caligula be? He didn't come right out and say it, but I knew he was dreaming about getting his hands around the emperor's spindly little neck. Even though he was sick, I knew Mansuetus could kill Caligula in a second.

I also knew that the noble gladiator would never get that chance.

†

Flavia's first question was about Mansuetus. "Have you seen him?"

"Yes. A few hours ago."

"How is he?"

I wanted to lie and reassure Flavia. But she would see the man tomorrow, and I didn't want her to be shocked just before the trial.

"He appears sick. He'll make it through the trial, but it's been a long six days."

"Are they torturing him?"

"I don't know."

The Tullianum, where Flavia was being held, was located on one end of the Forum, at the top of the Gemonian Stairs. Prisoners were dropped in through a hole in the ceiling, and I had been lowered the same way so that I could have this private meeting with my client.

I only had a few seconds of light to appraise Flavia before they placed the large carved stone over the opening and the place became entombed in darkness again. Her cut hair stuck out in short, jagged strands. Her eyes were red and puffy as if she had been crying. Her face looked even more drawn than it had six days earlier. Her cheekbones were protruding, and her eye sockets were hollow. Her skin was blackened with grime, and there were welts on her collarbone and arm. It was a picture I seared into my mind in the brief moments we were given.

After the darkness descended, she reached out and took my hand, and we both sat down on the cold stone.

"Are you eating anything?" I asked.

"No. I thought they might try to poison me."

"What are you drinking?"

"The water. I have no choice."

My eyes tried to adjust to the darkness, but no light came through at all. That was the point of the place. No hope. No way out. Only complete and utter blackness while prisoners contemplated their inevitable deaths.

And it was cold. I hadn't needed a cloak that day, but I could have used one in this damp dungeon.

I stood and unwrapped my toga. "You must be cold," I said.

"I'll be okay."

I reached over and touched her shoulder. "Stand up for a minute."

When Flavia stood, I wrapped my toga around her. I could feel the bones of her shoulder blades, the coolness of her skin. The soldiers would laugh at me when they pulled me out in just a tunic, but it would be worth it.

"You didn't have to do that," she said.

"I know."

I heard a noise on the far side of the dungeon. "Rats," she said.

I couldn't imagine how Flavia kept her sanity down here. We both sat back down on the wet stone.

"At least they're well fed," she said. "And the fact that they're alive means there's not too much poison in my food."

When I started talking about the upcoming trial, Flavia placed a hand on my arm. "Thank you so much for coming," she said, interrupting me. It sounded like she was on the verge of tears. "I didn't know if you would."

I wanted to tell her that nothing could have kept me away. I wanted to let her know the way I really felt about her. But I couldn't. She and Mansuetus were both my clients. I owed it to both of them to keep my feelings out of it.

I gave Flavia a preview of what might happen the next day. I told her I had some good news. Rubria was prepared to testify that Flavia had not left the House of Vestal on the night in question. I tried to sound upbeat. Rubria would be the unbiased witness we needed.

Flavia didn't respond.

"Are you okay?" I asked.

"You cannot allow her to testify," Flavia said. "I wasn't at the House of Vestal that night. You can't let Rubria lie under oath. If she does, she'll die too."

Before I could respond, Flavia let out a shriek and grabbed my arm.

"Sorry," she said quickly. "One of the rats."

"Let's stand up," I suggested.

"It's all right," she said. "You get used to them. I'd just forgotten about them for a second."

I stood anyway. "What do you mean you weren't there that night?"

She let out a deep breath. "I was with Caligula," she said. Her voice seemed devoid of emotion. "He told me that if I spent the night with him, he would leave me and Mansuetus alone."

The confession staggered me. I couldn't picture Flavia giving in to the emperor's blackmail. "You believed him?"

Her answer was preceded by a long pause. "I was a fool, Theophilus. But I knew how easily he could destroy us. He had already had Lucian follow us. I knew he would try us, find us guilty, and make me watch Mansuetus die. Then they would bury me alive. I guess I thought . . ." Her voice broke off.

I sat next to her again.

"I thought Caligula might keep his word," she said.

"But he didn't?" I already knew the answer.

"No. Once was not enough." Her voice was stronger now, rage edging out the shame. "No matter how many times I went, it would never have been enough. I refused to go back. A few days ago, he gave me a new ultimatum. If I didn't return to the palace within two nights, he would have me and Mansuetus charged. That's when I called for you."

"So Rubria is willing to lie for you?"

"Some of the other Vestals know that I was gone that night. Adrianna knows, and she would testify against me. You can't let Rubria get caught up in this."

I wasn't sure what to say. My best defense had just been stripped away.

"Let me testify, Theophilus. I'll tell the entire world about my night with the emperor after the games. At least Mansuetus will go free."

"And Caligula will claim you're lying. He'll make you carry water in a sieve or some other impossible feat to prove your testimony."

"If I tell the truth about that one night, perhaps the gods will smile at me and the water will stay in the sieve. It has happened before, you know."

I didn't believe the myth, and I was pretty sure Flavia didn't either. But right now she needed a ray of hope, however improbable.

"I know," I said.

When my time was up, Flavia tried to give my toga back. I didn't take it. I could survive a few stares and snide comments. But I didn't know whether she could survive another night in this cold, hard place.

The guards removed the stone cover, and I could see Flavia's face again. We both stood as the guards dropped down the rope.

"I can't promise a good outcome tomorrow," I said. "But I can promise a good fight."

She stepped forward, placed her hands on my arms, and gave me a kiss on both cheeks.

I put the rope around my waist, and the guards hauled me out of the dungeon.

— CHAPTER 51 —

I was still at my desk working when the sun came up. I had spent the entire night with the oil lamps burning, scratching my argument onto papyrus and then throwing the scrolls away. As I always did when I lacked inspiration, I had turned to Cicero. I read some of his most famous speeches and arguments but came up empty. By morning, I had concluded that it was a lost cause.

Lucian would testify that he had caught the lovers in the very act. Adrianna would testify that Flavia had been missing from the House of Vestal all night the evening of June 9. And Crispinus had probably bribed gladiators who shared barracks with Mansuetus to testify that he had been missing that night too.

In truth, he probably had been. He was probably waiting all night by the Tiber for a woman who was in the bedchambers of the emperor.

I stared out the window. Flavia was prepared to die nobly, testifying that she had broken her vows with the emperor, not Mansuetus. Thinking of her willingness to sacrifice her life for another, I remembered the Nazarene. Even while being crucified, he had reached out to others.

Which triggered another thought. The woman I met at the foot of the cross. The description of the rabbi defending the woman caught *in the very act* of adultery. She had no chance at acquittal, but Jesus had turned the tables. He had put her accusers on trial. He had found a way to signal that a trial would be more embarrassing for them than it was for her. They had dropped their stones and walked away.

My mind started racing. Could the same strategy work here? Caligula wouldn't be embarrassed by an accusation that he had slept with a Vestal Virgin. In a perverse way, he was probably proud of it. Besides, he was the judge, and he could simply reject Flavia's testimony out of hand.

But there was one thing he *would* be embarrassed about. One thing he was determined to keep hidden. Something diametrically at odds with his claim to be a god. If I threatened to air it in the most public way . . .

I wrote quickly now, with time running short. The trial would begin at noon, and suddenly there was a lot to get done. I wouldn't stoop down and write in the sand, but if the gods were willing, my defense would be just as effective.

†

For starters, I decided to pack the judgment hall with supporters of Mansuetus. I sent a servant to his gladiator school with a letter for his *lanista*, imploring the man to help rally supporters for the trial. I stopped at the Basilica Julia, where the *praetors* were holding court. I passed the word among my lawyer friends.

You won't want to miss this one. Maybe I'll ask for a battle to the death between Mansuetus and Lucian to see who is telling the truth. Perhaps I'll suggest that Flavia carry water in a sieve. Maybe it was a different Vestal who was caught with Mansuetus.

I stopped at the market and hinted at the same things. I seeded every rumor I could think of, fueling a fire of speculation about the trial that had already been blazing throughout Rome.

An hour before the trial I returned to my home exhausted. Even without my meager efforts, the judgment hall in the Imperial Palace probably would have been packed. But I was hopeful that the crowd would spill out through the great bronze doors onto the portico and down the street. I was hoping the crowd would rival the throngs that had waited breathlessly outside the Senate for Caligula's first speech. The emperor might be a madman, but he wanted to be a popular one. Today, he would have his chance.

✝

The quickest route from my house to the Imperial Palace on the Palatine Hill did not go through the Forum, so I took a detour. It was a perfect autumn day. The air was cool enough to be refreshing but not biting. The leaves had turned from a glossy green to tinges of brown and yellow. Pedestrians didn't kick up dust like they did in the summer, and a breeze from the northwest shook a few leaves loose and gave flocks of birds a pleasant ride.

I took my time walking the length of the Forum, greeting people I knew with a big smile, telling them they didn't want to miss the grand trial that would start in about thirty minutes. I urged them to bring their friends. When I left the area, I had at least fifty people in tow.

Word spread quickly, and I also had human nature working in my favor. The Romans loved a good show! By the time I started climbing the hill to reach the Imperial Palace, there were hundreds of people behind me.

I could have saved my energy. When I turned a corner halfway up the cobblestone path, I caught my first glimpse of the crowd already waiting. I could barely see the huge portico that formed the entrance to Caligula's palace. There were thousands of people spread out in front of me. They were all pushing and cramming as close as possible to the entrance of the great judgment hall. I could sense the excitement in the crisp autumn air. I tried to squeeze my way through, announcing that I was the advocate for Mansuetus and Flavia, but it was slow going.

About halfway to the steps, two gigantic men blocked my way. When they learned that I was the advocate for Mansuetus, they grasped my forearm and thumped me on the back. They introduced themselves as gladiators from Mansuetus's school and decided they would serve as my personal escort. They cleared a path through the rest of the spectators, shouting at people to move aside, pushing them out of the way if they didn't part quickly enough. Common citizens slapped my shoulders and wished me luck. Some reached out to touch the gladiators, and I marveled at the popularity these men had.

The judgment hall itself was crammed with spectators, though the Praetorian Guard had wisely limited the number they let inside. As an advocate, I had never tried a case before the judgment seat of Caesar.

The hall itself was at least five times as big as the Stone Pavement Courtyard back in Jerusalem. Marble, gold, exquisitely carved statues, and massive pillars created an imposing setting. It was at least four hundred feet from the entrance of the judgment hall to the dais where the judgment seat was located. There would be no fewer than ten *assessores* standing behind Caligula, ready to provide advice. Larger-than-life statues of the great Roman emperors lined the front of the hall. A wraparound balcony was filled with trumpeters who would announce the entrance of the great Caesar. The dais that held Caligula's seat was thirty feet tall. Everything about the place was designed to make the accused seem small and the emperor seem powerful.

It was doing a pretty good job on me.

A large semicircle of empty floor space in front of the judgment seat had been cleared by the Praetorian Guards, who stood watch, lining the perimeter of that space, using their large rectangular shields to keep the crowd at bay. I was allowed past the line of guards and took a seat facing the great platform where Caligula would sit. Caepio Crispinus, with his smooth gray hair and handsome smile, was already in place on the other side. I noticed that even Crispinus appeared to be nervous, fingering through the papyrus rolls he had brought, fretfully glancing behind him at his witnesses.

I went over and greeted him. "I brought a few of my friends," I said.

Crispinus smiled. "One of my friends will be coming too. When he does, he'll sit up there on the dais."

At noon, there was a commotion outside as a group of men forced their way through the crowd at the huge open doors of the judgment hall. Mansuetus was surrounded by at least twenty fully armed members of the Praetorian Guard. His ankles and wrists were shackled. He shuffled slowly to the front of the hall.

Behind him, with a soldier on each side, came Flavia. She was chained in the same manner, but at least they had given her a clean white robe, though her jagged haircut, sore-infested skin, and large almond eyes made her look crazed.

As the two of them took their places at the front, the crowd on the perimeter began to clap. The applause rippled out the doors, down the portico, and across the great lawns surrounding the palace, where it erupted into a sustained roar. When the initial noise began to subside, a chant of "Man-sue-tus!" took its place and echoed back inside, resounding off the stone walls of the hall.

The big man, dressed only in a tunic, lifted his head and smiled.

The guards made the two prisoners stand in the middle of the floor at the foot of the great dais on which Caligula would sit. A row of soldiers stood at attention behind them. This was where Flavia and Mansuetus would remain throughout the trial—where everyone could stare at their backs and try to gauge their reactions.

Flavia looked over her shoulder and caught my eye. She nodded a thank-you, and I nodded back. She was standing just a few feet away from her lover, and I could tell she desperately wanted to reach out and touch him.

Mansuetus did not look good. His right foot and ankle were swollen and discolored. It didn't take a doctor to know that he might be facing amputation even if he were somehow acquitted.

But there was no time to worry about that now. The trumpets blared, filling the hall with sharp notes that made my ears ring. The shrill sound of the flutes followed. A lictor cried out, and the giant gold-plated doors behind the gilded judgment seat opened.

In walked Caligula, dressed in a purple robe, a laurel wreath on his head. He moved to the front of the platform and surveyed the packed hall.

He had several *assessores* standing right behind him. My mind flashed back to the trial of the Nazarene. So this was what it felt like to be on the other side. I feared my knees would buckle.

"Let the charges be read and the proceedings begin!" Caligula said.

A lictor read the charges, and the emperor took his seat. Unlike the prefects in the provinces, the mighty Caesar did not stand during trials.

He nodded to Crispinus.

"I'll hear from the prosecution first."

— CHAPTER 52 —

Caepio Crispinus rose from his seat and glared at the prisoners. "Becoming a Vestal Virgin is the highest honor we bestow on women," he said, his voice gravely serious. "They are the keepers of the eternal flame, the sacred guardians of the hearth for all of Rome. In exchange, they take a sacred vow."

He turned to Caligula. "Your Excellency, this woman swore on the name of the divine Caesar that she would remain chaste while she performed her duties.

"In our history, the Vestals have understood that thirty years of chastity is a small price to pay for the exalted position they hold. The best seats at the games. A central role in our sacrifices. They are the keepers of our most important documents, including your will, Most Excellent Caesar. And they even hold, as this woman has so vividly demonstrated, the power over life and death."

Crispinus stalked the prisoners as he talked, circling them as he made his argument. This would be Crispinus at his narcissistic best, the courtroom as theater, the prosecutor serving as Rome's star actor. No rhetorical flourish would go untapped. The air would be jabbed by his finger; his right arm would sweep in a broad, flamboyant arc; his voice would go from a whisper to the sound of thunder in an instant.

"When Apronius was scheduled to die because of scandalous remarks he made about your grandfather, the shadow of Flavia fell on him, and he was immediately freed. That is an incredible amount of power for one person to have." I could see the resentment still smoldering in Crispinus's eyes. All of Apronius's fortune had been snatched away from him in an instant by Flavia's actions.

"In light of what we know today, does anybody really believe that meeting was accidental—the Virgin's crossing of paths with Apronius? If she is acquitted today, how many more traitors will she pardon by the same type of unconscionable action?"

I noticed that Crispinus was spewing most of his venom at Flavia, and the freedmen lining the back walls were already beginning to grumble. Like me, they probably sensed that the attacks were having their intended effect. Caligula sat still as a statue, his eyes following the pacing Crispinus, though occasionally he cast a disdainful look at the prisoners.

"As Your Excellency well knows, because a Vestal is married to the state, sexual relations with any citizen of the state is the same as incest. And incest has always been punishable by execution.

"Now the word of a Vestal is sacrosanct," Crispinus admitted. "But there are exceptions. When Flavia testifies in her own defense—*if* she testifies in her own defense—her words must be viewed with the greatest suspicion. Especially when Your Excellency will hear the sworn testimony of another Vestal, the matron of the Vestals, who will tell us that Flavia was not at the House of Vestal on the night in question. Instead, she was with this man, breaking her vows on the banks of the Tiber River."

As I watched, I worried about Mansuetus's smoldering rage. His muscles flexed each time Crispinus moved closer. The enormous trapezius muscles would go taut, the fists would clench, the calves tighten. I prayed he wouldn't strike. I knew that Crispinus would like nothing better.

"We know that Your Excellency saw something in the eyes of Mansuetus the day of Drusilla's games when his gaze lingered on Flavia. Something told Your Excellency that there was more to his look than simply admiring the beauty of the Vestal. And so you asked Lucian Aurelius, a commander in the Praetorian Guard, to wait outside the House of Vestal that night and follow Flavia if she left. Under oath, he will describe what he saw when he did so.

"Mansuetus has fought with incredible valor in the arena. He is rightly adored by much of Rome. But like all men, he has a weakness."

At this, Crispinus stopped talking and walked directly in front of Flavia, halting inches from her face. I noticed Mansuetus, standing next to her, raise his shackled wrists to his waist. The back of his neck turned dark.

"Shamelessly, this woman took advantage of that weakness. Flaunting her beauty, seducing her prey, beckoning Mansuetus into her web. She was supposed to be a mother for Rome, but instead, she became Rome's whore!"

The words were still on Crispinus's lips when Mansuetus lunged at him, driving Crispinus to the floor. Mansuetus tried to loop his arms over Crispinus's head so he could strangle the man with the chains binding his own wrists. But Crispinus curled into a ball, tucking his head. In a flash, a dozen guards jumped on Mansuetus as if Crispinus had told them in advance that this moment might happen.

I leaped to my feet and tried to join the melee but was pushed back by some of the guards. Others pulled the two men apart, and I noticed that a gash had opened on Crispinus's forehead where he had struck the marble floor.

The crowd surged forward but was held in check by the shields and spears of the Praetorian Guards.

In the chaos, Caligula shouted, demanding that the judgment hall come to order.

When things eventually settled down, Mansuetus was surrounded by six guards, one with a knife at the gladiator's neck. His chest was heaving, his muscles straining. His eyes were still fixed on Crispinus, a murderous stare that sent chills down my spine.

"For the rest of the proceedings, the prisoner will kneel," Caligula ordered.

Mansuetus didn't budge.

Caligula nodded at a guard located on the platform. He walked down, carrying a large wooden club. "Break his knees," the emperor said.

There were shouts of protest from the crowd, and I thought the entire place would erupt in a riot. I looked behind me and saw people pressing forward, raising their fists, ready to make a mad rush to save their hero. They would die at the hands of the soldiers if they tried.

But just as the guard prepared to take a swing with the club, Mansuetus dropped to his knees and hung his head. One of the guards looped a rope around the gladiator's neck. Two other guards, one on each side of Mansuetus, more than an arm's length away, held the ends of the rope. Another guard stood behind Mansuetus, his sword drawn.

The commander gave a simple order to all three. "If he tries to move, kill him."

Crispinus straightened his toga, dabbed at the blood on his forehead with a cloth that had been handed to him, and returned to his seat. The crowd began to chant the name of Mansuetus, and Caligula demanded silence. The soldiers roughed up a few of the men who had started the chant, and the noise died down.

Finally Caligula turned to me. "You may begin your defense."

— CHAPTER 53 —

"I was going to suggest a gladiatorial death match between Mansuetus and Caepio Crispinus to decide this case," I said, "but I see that's already been tried."

Caligula didn't smile, and I didn't expect him to. I just wanted to demonstrate a little irreverence to signal that I was not afraid. Even though, in truth, I felt like I could barely stand.

I tried to imagine myself on the banks of the Aegean. I took a deep breath so I could use my diaphragm and better project my voice.

"Our case is simple," I said. "The charges are false. My clients are innocent. Lucian Aurelius is mistaken."

I moved forward so that I was even with Flavia and Mansuetus. I had no intention of turning this into theater the way Crispinus had. My approach would be far more subtle.

"Mansuetus will testify that he did not have an improper

relationship with Flavia. I would respectfully suggest to Caesar that this man has proven his valor and that his word can be trusted."

I turned and made a sweeping gesture toward the crowd. "He has no shortage of fans. I am sure that many of the unmarried women here would be happy to spend a night with Mansuetus. Does Your Excellency really believe that somebody this popular needs to chase a Vestal Virgin?"

The question was really about Caesar, not Mansuetus. But the implications seemed to be lost on the emperor.

"Caepio Crispinus has the audacity to call this man a liar," I said, feigning disbelief. "A man who has already earned the respect of all of Rome."

Mansuetus was still on his knees, but he lifted his head and looked at Caesar. Caligula had already shown he was not afraid to take on the popular gladiator. But I was hoping that Caligula would at least understand that if he freed both prisoners it would boost his popularity.

"We will not dispute, Your Excellency, the testimony of Adrianna that Flavia spent all night away from the House of Vestal on June 9. We are well aware that the testimony of a Vestal is sacrosanct and should never be questioned unless there are compelling reasons to do so.

"The truth is that Flavia was someplace else that night. But I would ask Your Excellency not to be too hasty to conclude that it was for illicit purposes."

I paused and slowed down. I didn't want Caligula to miss this.

"Allow me to suggest another explanation, one that is entirely legal and even laudable. What if Flavia had a meeting with a very prominent citizen of our city? What if there was a medical emergency because this man had an attack of parliamentary disease that required immediate medical attention?"

I watched Caligula's eyes narrow as I painted the scenario. Veins spiderwebbed on his temples, and I hoped that he was even now recalling the attack he had as a young boy and his family's determined attempt to cover it up. Nearly three years ago, when I heard that Caligula was sick, I knew immediately what the illness was. But again he hid behind a shroud of secrecy because of the stigma associated with parliamentary disease. Caligula considered himself a god. He couldn't allow anyone to think he had such a dreaded weakness.

"What if she saw this person writhing on the ground, paralyzed, his mouth agape and his eyes rolled back in his head? What if she had to hold his tongue until the attack was over so he wouldn't swallow it, wedging his mouth open with a piece of wood? What if she stayed there late into the night to make sure he would survive until morning?"

Caligula pressed his lips tightly together, blood rushing to his face. He was seething, and I could see his devious mind racing, trying to figure out how to condemn my client without exposing himself.

"As I mentioned earlier, the word of a Vestal is entitled to great weight. But I would also corroborate her testimony with other witnesses who have seen the same thing with this man. Perhaps not that night, but on other occasions."

I didn't stoop down and write the names in the dirt, but my list had the same effect. I named the emperor's private physician and his close bodyguards. I named Marcus Serbius, my childhood friend who had seen Caligula's first episode of parliamentary disease when he was fourteen years old. I said that Marcus, as a physician, would testify about the effects of parliamentary disease on those who suffered from it and whether Flavia's description fit the symptoms. For good measure, I also listed Seneca.

When I finished listing the names, there was a stony silence inside the hall. Caligula gave me the same look he had years earlier, the slit eyes harboring a smoldering desire to exact revenge. I could tell he wasn't sure whether any of the witnesses would actually have the courage to testify about the emperor's bouts with parliamentary disease. In truth, the only one I had even talked to was Marcus.

And even if Flavia testified about spending the night with Caligula, he could still reject her testimony and the testimony of any witnesses I paraded forward to talk about his parliamentary disease. But once the words had been spoken in front of such a vast audience, he would never be able to undo the damage. People would put the big picture together. Caesar would be stigmatized. I was gambling everything, including my own life, on the belief that he was too prideful to call my bluff.

"Flavia full well understands her sacred vows as a Vestal Virgin," I continued. "Those vows are no less sacred than the vows Your Excellency swore when you were named Princeps. She has faithfully performed her duties as a Vestal, and I would respectfully submit that she has been every bit as faithful to her vows and her office as the most noble and high-ranking officials of this great empire. May Your Excellency exercise great wisdom as you consider the fate of one of Rome's most revered priestesses."

I stared down Caligula for a moment before I returned to my seat. The applause started behind me, near the back wall, and then rippled around the room until a frustrated Caligula again demanded silence.

He stood and called for a recess.

"Bring the advocates," he ordered. He left the dais and disappeared behind the gold-plated doors. Two guards came and escorted me back to join him.

I stood next to Caepio Crispinus, staring straight ahead, while Caligula paced around the room and berated us. We had turned these proceedings into a farce, Caligula said. Crispinus had goaded the prisoner and turned the crowd against the prosecution. Caligula accused me of soliciting perjured testimony and said I ought to be whipped to death along with Mansuetus.

"The entire city is in an uproar because you two imbeciles don't know how to do your jobs!" Caligula screamed. He knocked over a small statute and sent golden goblets flying off the shelves. It was a temper tantrum of unrestrained proportions, and I feared for my life.

At one point, he stopped directly in front of me. "Do you remember what happened to your hero Cicero?"

"He met an undeserved fate," I said, trying to keep my voice calm.

"He got *exactly* what he deserved," Caligula shot back. "And I have half a mind to do the same thing to you. Display your head and hands on the Rostra, and we'll see how that silver tongue dances then."

His face was red with rage, spittle spraying from his lips. "I could kill you right now." He motioned to the guards around him. "I have plenty of witnesses who would testify that you attacked me first."

I stared past the man and tried not to flinch. He was smart enough to realize that he would have an outright revolt on his hands if he reappeared in the judgment hall having killed the advocate for Mansuetus. At least I *hoped* he understood that.

He turned to Crispinus. "And you. I give you a simple job to do, and you turn it into a mockery." He looked at us both, back and forth, and for the first time in my life I felt a certain kinship with Crispinus. Even the best advocates were powerless in front of the tyranny of a madman.

"Mansuetus and Flavia are both guilty. I should have all four of you executed together." He turned his back on us. "Get them out of here."

✝

The guards escorted us back into the judgment hall, where the crowd was in a state of agitation. There was a lot of murmuring and restlessness and soldiers casting wary looks at the mob behind them. If Mansuetus was convicted, there would be a massive amount of bloodshed.

A few minutes later, the trumpets sounded, a lictor called the court to order, and Caesar reemerged. He took his seat, and a hush fell over the vast hall. His face was still clouded with anger, and I felt like I might explode with tension.

The emperor sat there for a moment as if deep in thought, then surveyed the crowd and stood. He looked at the two prisoners—Mansuetus kneeling and Flavia standing beside him. The emperor took his time and let the drama build.

"I have conferred with the advocates, and I see no need to hear testimony," Caligula said at last. "The prisoner Mansuetus has proven himself to be a courageous warrior in the arena, and I get the sense that more than a few citizens would love to see him fight again."

The emperor smirked. "And perhaps someplace other than in this judgment hall."

People laughed nervously while a few shouted their agreement.

"As would I. At best, the testimony against this prisoner would consist of one member of the Praetorian Guard who believes he saw the prisoner having sex with a Vestal Virgin on the ninth of June. But it was dark, and the witness was watching from a distance. Against that testimony, the advocates have told me that I would have the sworn word of Mansuetus that it was not him."

Caligula looked down at Mansuetus. "Would that be your testimony?"

The gladiator raised his eyes to Caesar. "It would."

"Very well. Because I am inclined to believe a man like you, a man who has displayed unsurpassed valor in the arena, I see no need to take formal testimony. I am declaring Mansuetus not guilty of the charges presented against him."

The place erupted, and Caligula made no effort to stop it. The roar echoed through the hall and spread outside. For a few glorious minutes, the entire Palatine Hill resounded with the glee of a crowd who had just witnessed a miracle.

Mansuetus slumped forward as if overcome with emotion. Flavia reached down and placed a hand on his shoulder.

But Caligula wasn't done. When the crowd's hollering and back-slapping and embracing had stopped, he spoke to Flavia. "I find your proffered testimony about spending the night with a man who had parliamentary disease to be preposterous. My suspicion is that you have violated your vows as a Vestal Virgin with some man other than Mansuetus."

As he spoke, the jubilant crowd tensed up again. They cared most about Mansuetus, but they also loved the Vestals. I got the feeling that, having tasted victory, they would not settle for half a loaf.

"However, I have already determined that Mansuetus did not engage in an illicit relationship with you on the night of June 9. And because those are the only charges before me today, I must therefore dismiss the charges against you as well."

Flavia bowed her head in appreciation, and another roar rose from the crowd, though not as loud as the first. Patiently, Caligula again waited for the cheering to subside.

"Ten days from now, at the games in honor of Caesar Augustus, we will all celebrate by watching Mansuetus fight again. May the gods be with you."

Caesar raised his scepter, and the trumpeters in the balcony brought their trumpets to their lips.

"Set them free!" Caligula ordered. Then he spun on his heel and headed out of the judgment hall.

The trumpets blared, or at least they must have. But from where I stood, every note was drowned out by the loudest cheering I had ever heard.

— CHAPTER 54 —

The rest of that day was a blur. The three of us left the Imperial Palace to a thunderous roar. We walked the gauntlet of well-wishers, Mansuetus limping and wincing with each step.

Word of our victory arrived at the Forum before our little entourage got there, and the place exploded in celebration. Flavia seemed self-conscious and, along with her lictors, worked her way through the crowd toward the House of Vestal at her first opportunity. Mansuetus was carried away by his fellow gladiators to the cheers of his adoring fans. That left me to mount the steps of the Rostra and give a speech to the assembled crowd.

I swallowed hard and praised Caligula for his great discernment. I talked about the critical role of the Vestals in Roman society and how seriously Flavia took her duties. But it was my segment about the gladiators that produced the greatest ovation. They taught us valor and courage, I said. Determination and persistence. And Mansuetus, the greatest gladiator of all, taught us that we could smile in the face of life's greatest difficulties and attack the deadliest dangers with joy in our step.

The crowd loved it, but the irony was not lost on me. Several years earlier, I had been trying to shut down the games. Now I was praising the heroes those games had produced, heroes who rose from the bloodlust.

That night, I lay awake in bed with the same foreboding thoughts I had nurtured sixteen years earlier, contemplating the consequences of what I had done. I was drained from the day's proceedings and mellowed by the wine we had consumed in celebration. But I had no illusions about my own safety. The crowds might have hailed our victory, but I had enraged the emperor, not to mention Caepio Crispinus and other powerful men. Sixteen years ago, Caligula had wasted no time before striking back. Would it be any different now?

There were a thousand ways he could mete out revenge. A charge of *maiestas*. A random mugging by his hirelings on the streets of Rome. An assignment to a far-flung province. Or perhaps it would be something more spectacular, something that would humiliate me so he could watch me suffer. If that was the case, it would at least buy me a little time while he planned it.

I kept a dagger next to my bed that night. Not because I thought I could fight off a band of soldiers dispatched by Caligula to arrest me. But so that I might use it to slit my own wrists before they got the chance.

†

The next morning, I was summoned to Seneca's house for the *salutatio*, the formal morning reception. I skipped both breakfast and my morning shave and joined Seneca's other clients in his spacious front hall.

Unlike on prior visits, his head servant did not bump me to the front of the line. Instead, I watched as one client after another was ushered back for a meeting with the great philosopher while I waited my turn.

Unlike the freedmen who had greeted me in the Forum yesterday as a hero, the aristocrats in Seneca's hall averted eye contact. A few offered a forced word of congratulations, but the mood was generally sour.

Even before yesterday's trial, Seneca's star had started to decline. It was rumored that Agrippina the Younger had taken up her mother's feud with Seneca and was influencing Caligula. As a result, Seneca had stopped receiving invitations to the emperor's lavish banquets, and his counsel was no longer welcome in Caligula's inner circle. I noticed that the men who were here this morning were fewer in number and lower in stature than the men I had seen on previous occasions.

When the hall was empty, Seneca came out to meet me. He dismissed his slaves and waited until they had left before saying what was on his mind.

"I suppose congratulations are in order for your magnificent performance yesterday," he said.

"I had a good teacher," I said.

"Then perhaps you should have listened to him," Seneca said dourly. His eyelids looked heavy, his expression pained. "I taught you to follow the truth. Yesterday, you built your case on a lie."

"You taught me to fight for justice. When the judge is a tyrant, I'll do whatever is necessary to save my client."

"Including risking the life of your mentor?"

"Is that what this is about?"

"Don't play the fool," Seneca said sharply. He lowered his eyebrows in anger. "You listed me as a witness without talking to me about it first. After everything I've done for you, you brought the wrath of Caesar on me and my household. Who gave you authority to use my name as a bargaining chip?"

His resentment caught me off guard. But I wasn't about to apologize for defending my clients. "What happened to you?" I asked. "What happened to the man who stood up for me sixteen years ago against this same family?"

Seneca scoffed at the question. "Rome is what happened to me. Do you have any idea what I've had to do just to survive? You think you can reap the largesse of everything I've earned and never make any compromises? If you loved Rome as much as I do, you would understand that the only way to save her is to navigate her treachery and outlive madmen like Caligula. *I* will decide when to sacrifice my life for the principles I believe in! *I* will choose the manner of my death! I don't need people who call themselves my friends doing that for me!"

I had realized Seneca might be upset, but I wasn't prepared for the sharpness and intensity of his rebuke. I stood there speechless. I had so much respect for this man. Perhaps he was right. What basis did I have to enlist him in my deadly cause without his permission?

"We spent nights together strategizing," Seneca continued. "Just by being seen with you in the baths I was endangering my life. Yet never once did you tell me that you intended to sacrifice my good name in support of your cause."

"That's because I didn't know myself until—"

"Spare me," Seneca said. "I don't want your rationalizations or excuses. What's done is done."

We both took a breath, and I lowered my voice. "I'm sorry. I'll do whatever I can to make it right."

"There's nothing you can do to 'make it right.' I've had plans in place, Theophilus." He shook his head, and his look went from frustration to disappointment. "Plans to install the right man in the palace. At the right time, in the right way. I was willing to put my life on the line for Rome when it would make a difference. Thanks to you, those plans are over."

I didn't say anything; there was nothing left to say. I had hurt the man most responsible for every good thing that had ever happened to me. My feelings for Flavia had blinded me. I had used Seneca, and I had been wrong to do it.

"I'm sorry," I said again.

He stared at me for a moment as if trying to determine whether my apology was sincere. "What happened yesterday was not the end of the matter," Seneca said. "All you did was poke the lion. Watch your back, Theophilus. We are both in mortal danger now."

— CHAPTER 55 —

I left the house that evening with a dagger tucked under my toga and headed to a dark corner of the city. I walked down a narrow street filled with *insulae*, the high-rise apartment buildings that dominated the city, numbering more than fifty thousand at last count. Seneca once told me that the city was so dense with these buildings that if all the apartments in Rome had been built at ground level, the city would have stretched 120 miles to the Adriatic coast.

As I walked, my nostrils filled with the pungent odor of human and animal waste, oil and grease, and the stale remains of the day's meals. It reminded me how fortunate I was to be able to afford my own house now, one detached from other buildings, with a small garden area in the center. There were less than four thousand homes like that inside the city walls, though mine was certainly one of the smallest.

I found the address I was looking for, a building more elegant than most. It was made of brick, not wood, and had a decorative stripe of Pompeian red about five feet off the ground. There were balconies on the upper floors filled with flower vases, hanging plants, and climbing vines that wrapped themselves around the railings and framed the windows.

I walked past the shops on the ground floor and took the steps to the second-floor landing. There I found the engraved oak door and used the brass knocking ring. I shifted my weight from one foot to the other while I waited.

The woman who answered was younger than I had imagined, thin and wiry with a hooked nose and a face that looked like it had been put in a vise and squeezed to make it long and narrow. Her jaw stuck out, and her eyeballs seemed a size too big for their sockets.

She greeted me warmly and escorted me into a large waiting room. There were vases of flowers lining the walls and paintings with vivid colors—orange, purple, red, and yellow. A large marble table with a statue of a man I didn't recognize dominated the room. A few throw rugs were scattered about. This wasn't the home of a wealthy person, but she was clearly getting by. Business was apparently good.

Her name was Locusta, and she had been recommended to me by a former client.

She beckoned me to a seat and promised that she would keep the meeting confidential.

"How did you get my name?" she asked, crossing one leg over the other and shifting in her seat. The woman brimmed with energy.

"I'd rather not say."

"That's fine. You're aware of my terms?"

"Yes." I took out a pouch of money and handed it to her.

She took it and spread the coins on the table, counting them carefully. When she was done, she scooped the money back into the pouch and looked at me.

"You must want my top grade," she said, smiling. Her teeth were crooked on the bottom.

This whole transaction was unsettling. I had expected to do business with Locusta in the dark, in hushed tones, never getting a good look at her face. Instead, the apartment was well lit, well furnished, and she acted like she was selling me an expensive piece of art.

"I want it to work. And I don't want to suffer."

"Yes, yes, that's what they all say."

She paused for a second as if she had heard someone or maybe just remembered something. "Can I get you a drink?" she asked.

"No thanks."

She gave me a crooked grin. "For some odd reason, nobody ever says yes to that question."

I didn't smile.

"Let's see, where was I? Ah, yes . . . you've come to the right place. Others will sell you potions that don't work. Bull's blood, toads, salamanders, snakes, spiders, scorpions, mercury, arsenic—you might as well drink your own urine." As she spoke, she flipped her wrist, dismissing her inferior competitors.

Then she leaned forward a little and narrowed her eyes. "The best poisons are all vegetable-based—mandrakes, hemlocks, opium. Do you want it mixed in honey, or would you rather drop it in wine?"

I had no idea poison came in so many varieties. "I want it to fit in as small a container as possible."

"Then let's skip the honey. That takes up room."

"Sounds reasonable," I said, though there was nothing at all reasonable about this conversation. "How will it work?"

"The opium will hit first. Dulls the senses. Makes you happy. The other poisons do the usual things—stop your heart, choke your breathing, tie your intestines into knots. The good news is that with opium you won't feel any pain."

She stopped again and gave me a quizzical look. "This is for you, right?"

"Yes."

"Good. If it's for an enemy, I leave out the opium."

I had been told that Locusta made the best poisons in all of Rome. She was known for her mushrooms. But it didn't seem to me that she should be quite so enthusiastic about her products.

"I'm in a bit of a rush," I said, as if I had important meetings in the middle of the night. "Can I just get what I came for and leave?"

"Well, of course," she said, standing. "I'll be right back."

She disappeared into a back room for a few minutes and came out with two vials of liquid. "Put this into somebody's wine, and they'll never know what hit them." She handed me the first one.

"Can I take it without wine if I have to?"

"Naturally. Just make sure you swallow it quickly."

I nodded.

"Do you want to know what this second vial is for?" she asked.

"Not really."

"Most of my clients like to make sure the product works. We can go out to the streets together, find a stray dog, and watch it kill him in just a matter of minutes."

That seemed like a horrible idea. "No thanks. I trust you."

She howled in laughter. "A lot of people have made that mistake," she said after regaining her composure. She chuckled again at the thought of it.

"Thank you very much," I said as I stood and headed for the door.

I had one hand on the doorknob when she spoke again. This time, there was no merriment in her voice.

"All of Rome is talking about your victory. But nobody embarrasses the emperor and lives for long."

I opened the door and turned back to look at Locusta. Her pleasant expression was gone, and her face was grim and anxious. She walked over to me, handed me the second vial, and squeezed my hand around it.

"This one is free of charge," she said, staring through me with those buggy eyes. "The emperor likes his wine strong. If it was me and I was dealing with a man who harbors such insatiable grudges, I might want to use them both in one glass."

I thanked her again and retreated toward the steps.

I had not lied to the woman. My intent was to carry around the most potent poison possible at all times. I already knew how creative Caligula could be when he tortured people. Seneca had taught me well—I was determined to choose the manner and timing of my own death. If the Praetorian Guards arrested me, I wanted the ability to take my own life. Without pain, if possible.

But as I walked down the steps, I also considered this other possibility. What would life be like in Rome without Caligula and his maniacal reign of terror? His uncle Claudius was considered by most to be an imbecile, incapable of ruling. But could anything be worse than the madman ruling now?

Other conspirators had tried and failed. What made me think I could get close enough to slip something into his wine? And even if I could, was it the right thing to do?

There was one other question that had to be answered—perhaps the most pertinent question of all: Did I have the courage to go through with it? I thought I might if it was kill or be killed. Perhaps I didn't really have a choice.

──── CHAPTER 56 ────

The letter came by courier three days after the trial. It was written on parchment, and the handwriting was flawless.

> *From Flavia, a grateful priestess at the temple of Vesta, to the Most Excellent Theophilus:*
>
> *Words cannot begin to express my gratitude for what you have done. I owe my very life to your courage and wit. Every breath that I take reminds me of a debt I will never be able to repay.*
>
> *I am ever mindful of the fact that you put your own life in great danger to save mine. Please be careful, Theophilus. There are rumors that revenge is in the air. I offer prayers and sacrifices every day, to both the Greek and Roman gods, for your safety.*
>
> *Though it pains me to ask for an additional favor, particularly under the current circumstances, I know of no other man who commands the respect and admiration of Mansuetus as you do. As you know, he is scheduled to fight in the games one week from today. He is in no shape to do so. The entrails of my sacrifices do not portend well if he tries. Would you be so kind as to talk to him? Like me, he owes you a debt that cannot be repaid. Perhaps he could make a small down payment by finding a way to postpone his fight until he fully recovers.*
>
> *Whether you see fit to grant this request or not, please know that you have my undying gratitude and unending love.*

I read the letter three times, savoring every word. My emotions were a jumbled mess. I pictured Flavia offering prayers for me as the morning sunlight illuminated her face. She would sprinkle blood on the altar, and my name would pass her lips. She would pour out the wine and beg the gods for my safety. It was not exactly the beginning of a relationship—something I had dreamed about for a decade—but it gave me hope nonetheless.

On three earlier occasions, my parents had found the woman they thought I should marry. It happened once before I headed to Judea and twice after I returned, including the woman who broke off the relationship just before the trial of Apronius. In my eyes, none of those women could measure up to my dreams of Flavia. She was a goddess. Steeped in Greek literature, esteemed by all of Rome, the intellectual equal of any man. She had elegance and valor like no woman I had ever met. Plus, her beauty far exceeded that of other women who might have caught my eye.

Perhaps it was my unrestrained idealism, or perhaps, like Caligula, I always wanted the one thing I could not have. But even before I left for Judea, I had dreamed that I would somehow make a name for myself and then wait for Flavia to complete her service as a Vestal. We would marry and start a family. I had replayed the fantasy in my mind so many times that it had nearly become part of my reality.

Yet at a time when my dreams seemed closer than they had ever been, I also felt them slipping away. Yes, Flavia said prayers for me each morning. And yes, I had her "undying gratitude and unending love," words that I read over and over. But Mansuetus had her heart. If I truly cared for Flavia, which for some inexplicable reason I did, I would do everything within my power to ensure that Mansuetus earned his freedom and stayed alive long enough to become her husband.

The glorious wedding would take place, just as I had imagined, and the bride would be stunningly beautiful. But it would be Mansuetus, rather than me, waiting to take her hand.

✝

I took Marcus with me to visit Mansuetus the following day. Marcus had never watched the gladiators train, but I thought his medical expertise might be helpful in persuading Mansuetus that he wasn't yet ready to fight.

The training camp was located a mile outside the city and was nothing like I had envisioned. Years earlier, when helping Seneca write the letter to Tiberius, I had visited the most distinguished *ludi* in Rome. Some of the schools housed up to two thousand gladiators in elaborate dorms with extensive training facilities. The Ludus Magnus was the largest and most important one. It had recently been purchased by Caligula himself. Three other schools each boasted more than a thousand gladiators with first-class facilities financed by their sponsoring patrons.

But Mansuetus's school was in a state of sorry disrepair. There were less than a hundred gladiators crammed into two small barracks. The fighters slept on thin mattresses on the floor. Many of the blunt wooden swords they used in training were broken, and I learned that the men had to share weapons when they took their turns in the arena. Other than Mansuetus, who was the only real champion from this school, the gladiators looked thinner and less muscled than the ones I had seen in the schools in Rome.

We arrived just before lunch, as the gladiators were concluding their late-morning exercises. Mansuetus sat on the sideline, his leg elevated, leaning back on both arms while yelling at the younger gladiators. None of them looked older than twenty-five.

"Theophilus!" Mansuetus called out when he saw me. He rose with difficulty and didn't put any weight on his bad foot. "Get over here!" he barked.

I approached him, and he grasped my right forearm, embracing me like an old friend. I introduced him to Marcus as well.

"I owe this man my life," Mansuetus said to Marcus.

We talked for a few minutes before I mentioned that Marcus was a physician.

"That foot looks pretty bad," Marcus said.

Mansuetus claimed that the swelling was going down and the

discolored area was receding. But Marcus bent over, studied the injury, and frowned.

"You won't be ready to fight in six days," Marcus said when he straightened. "You need to stay off that foot. Wash it out every day. Keep it elevated."

Mansuetus passed it off with a smile. "I'll be fine," he claimed.

Before I got a chance to talk to him about Flavia's letter, the *lanista* came over and thanked me for saving the life of his most important gladiator.

"I shouldn't say this in front of him because I don't want it to go to his head," the *lanista* said, "but if we lose Mansuetus, we'd have to shut down this school. He brings in fifty times what the other men make."

The *lanista* called the younger men together for a few sets of pull-ups before lunch. Many of them had been at the trial and expressed their appreciation for what I had done.

I watched as they pumped out their pull-ups. "Are those things hard?" I asked a gasping gladiator after he had finished a set.

"Only for advocates," he said.

He had taken the bait. These men were dog tired, and I had watched them hammer out two sets of pull-ups each. This same exercise had been part of my daily gymnastics training at the Molon School, and I had continued to do them in both Judea and Rome.

"Maybe you and an advocate should have a little contest," I suggested.

That brought the intended catcalls and insults from the other men. They goaded the young gladiator, whose name was Cobius, into going first. He grabbed the bar and heaved his big body up and down while the men counted. In his prior set of pull-ups, I noticed that he had only done about twenty. But now, with the other gladiators goading him on, he managed nearly thirty.

He dropped from the bar, exhausted but pleased with himself. "Your turn, equestrian. Try not to roughen up those smooth hands."

I girded up my tunic and spit on both hands. I turned and winked at Mansuetus, then jumped up and started knocking out pull-ups.

During my first ten, Cobius counted as loud as everyone else. By the time I hit twenty, his face had gone red. At thirty, the other gladiators started nudging him and giving him a hard time. I dropped from the bar at thirty-three.

The other men slapped me on the back and poked fun at Cobius. The young gladiator glared at me.

"Let's see how he does with a sword and shield," Cobius suggested.

Even though the weapons were wooden, there was not a chance in the world I could go toe-to-toe with this guy and not get hurt. Fortunately, the *lanista* bailed me out. "We don't want to embarrass you twice in one day," he said to Cobius.

But Cobius wouldn't let it go. "I'll fight without a shield," he said. "Give this pretty boy any weapon he wants."

"Gentlemen!" Mansuetus called from behind me. Heads turned in his direction. He stood and hopped over to the circle the men had formed near the pull-up bar.

"This man put his life on the line for me in a different kind of arena," Mansuetus said. He limped over to me and put his arm around my shoulders. "Anybody who wants to fight him comes through me first."

And that was the end of the matter. The young gladiator stared at Mansuetus but remained silent.

The *lanista* stepped into the middle of the circle and looked around at the men. "Everyone relax," he said. They were all covered in sweat and grime. Many were nursing visible injuries. Their hair was matted, their beards untrimmed, and I could read the desperation in their eyes. I wondered how long it had been since someone from this school had earned his freedom. Mansuetus was only three fights away. I knew what the other men were thinking. If he could do it, there was hope for them too.

"The emperor has asked four of you to fight in next week's games in honor of Augustus," the *lanista* announced. There were groans all around the circle. One hundred gladiators and only four chosen!

"He's holding the games in the Forum and is building the wooden bleachers as we speak," the *lanista* continued. "The same place where Augustus himself hosted the games during his reign. It means spectators will be closer to the action and only one pair of gladiators will fight at a time. The larger *ludi* in Rome got most of the slots."

The men didn't argue. They knew their *lanista* was doing everything he could for them.

"As you know, the emperor has already requested Mansuetus. I'll announce the other three right after lunch."

With that, the men broke into small groups. Marcus and I ate with Mansuetus under the shade of an olive tree. I had seen the training tables of the *ludi* in Rome and had watched the men eat massive amounts of barley, boiled beans, oatmeal, and dried fruit. But here, the men were portioned a plateful of oatmeal and a few dried figs.

"It all comes down to money," Mansuetus told us as he scarfed down the oatmeal. "We were barely hanging on before the trial, but now the emperor will be determined to keep our men from fighting."

I took advantage of the time to tell Mansuetus about the letter from Flavia. There would be other games in a few months, I said. He had come this far. Three more fights and he would earn his freedom. I pleaded with him to wait until he was fully healed. How could the emperor force him to fight if he couldn't even walk?

"Do you see these men?" Mansuetus asked. His eyes took in the small swatches of fellow gladiators. "These are my brothers. We've endured more together than the closest legionnaires. We've suffered together, bled together, faced death together. If I don't fight in six days, none of these men will survive."

I told Mansuetus that I might be able to raise funds for his school if he postponed his fight, but he wouldn't consider the idea. Gladiators had a code of honor. You earned money for your *ludus* in the arena. Besides, he said, they were taking precautions. He would forgo his normal light armor and use the weapons of a *murmillo*, including a tall, oblong shield and a long sword called a *gladius*. It was defensive armor, and it wouldn't require him to be very agile.

When it became apparent that I couldn't talk him out of it, I quit trying. Marcus picked up the conversation, enthralled by the strategy of the gladiators and what Mansuetus thought about his various opponents.

The only man who could give him a good fight, Mansuetus claimed, was a seasoned gladiator named Flamma, a man who had won more than thirty fights and been offered the *rudius* on four separate occasions. Each time, he had refused the wooden sword from Caesar that would have automatically made him a freedman because of the valiant way he had fought.

"I want to face him in my last fight," Mansuetus said. "After that, I'll retire and train other gladiators. But before I finish, I must defeat the best."

I wondered if he had ever discussed those plans with Flavia. I couldn't see her being married to a *lanista*. But then again, I now understood why she was drawn to Mansuetus. He wasn't just a warrior. He was a man with a huge heart who cared more about his fellow gladiators than about his own well-being.

After spending time with him that day, I could no longer regard him as simply a rival for the affections of a woman I loved. He was a good man. He had earned my respect. He deserved someone like Flavia.

When it came time to leave, I wished him the best, and I sincerely meant it.

On the way back to the city, Marcus gave me the bad news. The foot was badly infected. If Mansuetus had been a soldier on the battlefield, Marcus would have amputated the leg just below the knee.

"He's in no condition to fight," Marcus said.

— CHAPTER 57 —

Romans know how to build things. It took thousands of slaves less than two weeks to turn the stone pavement of the Forum into a thirty-thousand-seat arena. They constructed enormous wooden stands on each side that extended almost to the majestic height of the surrounding temples.

I walked past the construction nearly every day. The slaves worked like ants, covering the Forum, and the sound of construction drowned out the legal proceedings. It made a strange sight, the oval-shaped arena sitting in the middle of Rome's historic monuments—the temple of Concord, the temple of Saturn, the Basilica Julia, the House of Vestal, and the temple of Augustus. The architect had been astute, incorporating the Rostra into the design, using it as the foundation for the emperor's box.

Caligula's decision to host the games in the Forum rather than the 150,000-seat Circus Maximus had caused no small amount of grumbling. Caligula said he was doing it to honor Augustus Caesar, who had hosted his own games there. But the citizens of Rome knew the real reasons were financial ones.

Caligula had squandered an enormous amount of money. Long before he became emperor, a soothsayer once said that the son of Germanicus had no more chance of becoming emperor than of riding a horse across the Bay of Baiae. Recalling that prophecy after he became emperor, Caligula had ordered that a temporary floating bridge be built across the two-mile Bay of Baiae, using ships as pontoons. The emperor proudly rode across the bay on his racehorse, Incitatus. The stunt had cost millions of *sestertii* that the government couldn't afford.

And Caligula found other creative ways to waste public funds. He built a large ship that functioned as a floating palace, complete with marble floors and plumbing. In an attempt to preserve his popularity, he periodically gathered the freedmen of Rome around the Imperial

Palace and threw money from the balcony. His frequent banquets were elaborate, gaudy, and expensive.

All these expenditures occurred at a time when many in the empire were starving. The last games in the Circus Maximus had not gone well. The exotic animals were less numerous than before and not well fed. Even some of the gladiators had seemed malnourished. So when Caligula announced that the games for Augustus would be held in the Forum and, accordingly, there would be no wild-animal safaris in the morning, the citizens were skeptical. It cost less to build the wooden seats than it did to buy the lions and panthers and ostriches.

My instincts told me I should stay away from these ill-fated games. But the thought of sitting at my house and waiting for news of whether Mansuetus survived was something I could not bear. I respected the man too much. I had to see this one for myself.

✝

On the morning of the games, Flavia might have been the only person in Rome excited about the weather. It was mid-November, and the day promised rain, plenty of wind, and the possibility of some late-season thunderstorms. A perfect day for Flavia's disguise.

She woke early and met secretly with Rubria. She could see the fear in her young protégé's eyes and had to talk the young girl through the plan all over again.

"There are plenty of wigs I can wear while it grows back," Flavia told her. "Besides, it can't look worse than it does now."

Rubria's hands shook as she held the scissors and started cutting. When she finished, Flavia ran her hand through her uneven hair. She checked herself in the mirror.

"Shorter. You've got to make it shorter."

Reluctantly, Rubria cut Flavia's hair again, this time much closer to the scalp.

"Perfect," Flavia said.

Next Flavia mixed a thin layer of foundation with black soot made from roasted dates and spread it on the lower part of her face, mimicking the one-day growth of a man's beard. She scrubbed the paint from her fingernails and toenails. She put on a tattered black cloak with a deep hood.

"How do I look?" she asked.

Rubria looked her up and down. "Like my father," the little girl said proudly.

"Promise to keep this a secret," Flavia said.

"I promise."

Four hours later, when the games began, Flavia shuffled in with the freedmen. She spoke to no one as she climbed the stairs and took a seat in one of the highest sections on a side of the stadium where she had a good view of the Rostra and the makeshift imperial box. Her hood covered most of her face, and she shivered against the cold. It had already rained for a few hours earlier that morning, and now the sand on the arena floor looked wet and sticky. Flavia prayed it might somehow be an advantage for Mansuetus.

Caligula entered the arena at the fifth hour, shortly before midday, to the sound of trumpets, flutes, and muted applause from the people. Fittingly, the dark clouds had returned, and a few drops of rain arrived at the same time as the emperor.

He stood at the front of the Rostra and announced the opening of the games in honor of the great god Augustus Caesar. To mark the occasion, Caligula was dressed in the white flowing robes of Jupiter, and he appeared to be freezing. His curly red hair was crowned with a laurel wreath, and his pudgy and pasty white arms were bare. Three years of living luxuriously had earned him a noticeable potbelly.

The rain picked up as the criminals were paraded before Caligula with placards around their necks announcing their crimes. A giant bull was led out to the floor of the arena as a sacrifice to appease the gods. The priests danced, the drumbeat grew faster, the throat of the bull was slit, and he crumpled to the ground. In response, a peal of thunder rocked the stadium. The rain blew sideways in sheets.

Let the games begin!

— CHAPTER 58 —

The speed of the executions might have been a record. I counted no fewer than fifty men crucified or burned to death in less than an hour. The soldiers were pounding spikes into wrists and feet as fast as they could. They quickly erected crosses and set the prisoners on fire—no small feat in the driving rain—or they broke the prisoners' legs so they could no longer breathe.

There were two centurions whose only job was to certify the deaths of the crucified prisoners who had not been set on fire. The first rammed a spear into the sides of the men hanging from the crosses. The second followed with a branding iron on a long pole and seared the flesh of the prisoner to see if he had any reaction.

The crowd grew restless as the rain pounded us. A few people left before the gladiator fights even started. Caligula shouted orders at his troops, commanding them to hurry up and get the dead men out of the arena. A bolt of lightning flashed across the sky, followed by another peal of thunder. Everybody jumped.

As soon as the soldiers removed the bodies of the dead men, the gladiators marched in front of Caligula. The emperor announced their records, and they saluted him, though their words were lost in the wind and rain.

I noticed that the young gladiator who had lost the pull-up contest to me, the man named Cobius, was scheduled to fight. He carried the armor of the *murmillo*, a Greek word for a certain type of fish, and his name literally meant "minnow." One thing I learned at the school where Mansuetus trained was that they gave all of their gladiators absurd names, as if the entire enterprise were a clever joke.

Mansuetus stood before the emperor as well, but he didn't flash his customary smile when he saluted. He was definitely limping, though he did his best to hide it. Like Cobius, he carried the large, oblong shield and long sword of a *murmillo*, having traded in his usual Thracian gear. He had armor on his left leg and wore a helmet with a broad brim and single plume that exposed his face. His right arm, the sword-bearing one, was covered with leather and metal. He would be slower today, fighting defensively. I prayed he might win.

The last gladiator introduced was the man known as Flamma—the man Mansuetus had described as his only equal in the arena. He was younger than Mansuetus and every bit as tall but much thicker. He had long black hair and a wild-eyed look. His entire body was covered with hair, and his muscles looked as if someone had carved them from travertine stone.

Flamma saluted the emperor but never acknowledged the cheering crowd. He put on a helmet that covered his entire face with a metal grille. His hair stuck out the back and flowed over his shoulders. I knew Mansuetus wanted to fight Flamma before retiring. I was glad it wouldn't be today.

The first few fights started slowly, and the *lanistae* had to whip the men into action. Caligula seemed to be watching the crowd more than the gladiators. He must have sensed that people were losing interest. The rain let up for a few minutes but then started again with more fury than before. Men headed for the exits at every break in the action.

After an hour of fighting, Caligula took charge. He stood and called a halt to the contests. He told the guards that nobody else was allowed to leave. He shouted at the top of his lungs so he could be heard above the rain.

"As host of the games, I have decided to change the format," he called out, his voice strident. "In the next thirty minutes, you will see more action and bloodshed than any crowd in the history of the games has ever witnessed! I am ordering every gladiator except Flamma into the arena at the same time. The winner will be the last man standing. There will be no mercy extended to the others."

The crowd responded with a roar. The excitement was now palpable as the gladiators filed into the arena and found spots they could call their own. Many of them put their backs to the waist-high wooden walls that separated the arena from the bottom row of spectators. Others stationed themselves in the middle of the wet sand, their heads on a swivel.

The gladiators were using a variety of weapons, and it looked to me like some of the larger schools would be fighting in teams. Mansuetus and Cobius, the only gladiators from their school who hadn't already fought, stood back-to-back near the middle of the arena. I counted forty-two gladiators in total. Only one would survive.

The rain continued to pelt the spectators, but now nobody cared. Caligula stood on the Rostra, his arms spread wide—a god posing for his people. "Now who wants to leave?" he bellowed.

The crowd shouted its approval.

"And that's not all!" Caligula yelled. "In the history of the games, the *equites* have only fought each other. Today, that changes too!"

Caligula waited for the crowd to cheer itself out, and then he gave the order. "Bring them in!"

At his command, four mounted gladiators entered the arena. Each had the traditional round shield of the Republican Cavalry in his left hand, a lance in his right, and a sword at his waist. The *equites*, from their saddles, would be able to cut down the other gladiators and then turn on each other. In a few minutes, the whole scene would explode into chaos.

The sky thundered and the crowd thundered back. The spectators were on their feet, stamping on the wooden stands. Mansuetus looked this way and that, calling instructions over his shoulder to Cobius.

Caligula smiled at his deadly creation. "May the best gladiator survive!" he yelled. He raised his scepter and the fighting began.

†

The men surrounding Flavia were all shouting at once. She stood on her seat so she could get a better view, but others did the same. Her eyes were fixed on Mansuetus, and she mouthed a silent prayer to the gods.

Keep him safe. Give him strength. Allow him to emerge victorious.

She had seen him win so many fights, but she had never seen anything like this. She suspected Caligula had planned this type of spectacle all along. The storms were just an excuse to get back at Mansuetus. If it meant sacrificing the lives of forty-five other gladiators in the process, so be it.

Her heart was in her throat, and she could feel every beat in her ears. In the first few seconds of chaos, three gladiators went down, pierced by the lances of the *equites*. One gladiator was caught in a net thrown by a *retiarius* and then speared with a trident. But before the *retiarius* could exult in his conquest, another gladiator had sliced his neck from behind.

Mansuetus and Cobius were both engaged with a man in front of them when an *equites* came by and put a sword between the shoulder blades of their opponent.

Men were falling so quickly that it was hard to keep up. Flavia had her fists balled in front of her mouth, stifling her screams, hoping that Mansuetus would somehow be able to survive the bedlam.

— CHAPTER 59 —

The speed of the attacks caused Mansuetus to operate on pure instinct and adrenaline. He barely noticed the pain in his right foot or his inability to pivot and cut as quickly as normal. Right now everything was defensive. He just had to survive this initial melee.

He hunkered behind his heavy convex shield, putting his left foot forward and relying on Cobius to cover his back. He fended off an *equites* who came flying by and landed a blow that deflected off Mansuetus's shield and rocked him back. He quickly regained his balance and found himself and Cobius surrounded by four gladiators from a rival school. Mansuetus lashed out, taking on two men at once, undercutting one's shield and disemboweling the man with a single stroke.

He heard Cobius cry out behind him and quickly glanced around to see his friend bleeding where a blade had sliced his shoulder. Enraged, Mansuetus lunged at the remaining gladiator in front of him, raining down one blow after another on the man's shield until he lowered it just enough that Mansuetus could land a fatal blow to his neck.

He turned to help Cobius, and they finished off the other two gladiators in a matter of seconds. But there was no time to relax. A *retiarius*'s net entangled Cobius and dragged him to the ground. Before Mansuetus could react, the gladiator drove his three-pronged spear into Cobius's midsection, and Mansuetus's young friend let out a death moan.

Something snapped inside Mansuetus. He went on the attack again, this time recklessly, killing three more gladiators in less than a minute. His sword was red with blood as he flew forward in a rage, descending on anyone close to him. Bodies of men and horses now littered the arena floor, but Mansuetus didn't pause even for a breath. He turned and attacked, driving his sword through another man's side, then ripping it free so he could whirl and attack again.

His nostrils filled with the smell of blood and sweat and other men's fear. His chest heaved in great gasping breaths.

Rage fueled him. Rage at Caligula for this needless slaughter of valiant men. Rage at losing his friend Cobius. He had never fought this hard before, never been this rabid for more blood. He struck another man down, a thunderous blow that nearly took off the man's arm, then moved to the next gladiator. Someone else could finish the last one off.

With fallen gladiators all around him, he reared back, looked up to the heavens, and let out an insane roar. The rain pelted down, and there were still skirmishes throughout the arena. But who dared take on Mansuetus?

An impulse made him turn just in time to fend off another blow, his fury now kindled against the man who had sneaked up behind him. As he beat that man backward, he felt a searing pain in the back of his left shoulder. It staggered him but still he fought on. When the man in front retreated, Mansuetus glanced over his shoulder and saw the spear that had lodged there.

He dropped his sword, reached back, grimaced, and yanked the spear out with his right hand. The piercing pain turned the world black and made him momentarily dizzy. Disoriented, he managed to block another blow with his shield and then quickly crouched down and picked up his sword.

He fought on, but now he could barely carry his shield, and he was losing blood. There were only a few other gladiators left, and the roar of the crowd was deafening. Mansuetus tried to shake off the dizziness as the last two gladiators came at him. They were both from the same school and looked determined to finish off Mansuetus before they turned on each other.

He let his shield drop, his left arm useless as the gladiators circled to opposite sides of him. He was exhausted now, his one arm hanging at his side, his right foot throbbing. He had no way to defend his exposed body. He would lunge at the man on the right, try to make short work of him, and then pivot before he took a sword in the back.

Mansuetus made his move, but the gladiator deftly sidestepped, and Mansuetus stumbled. The gladiator swung his sword, but Mansuetus rolled just in time. He scrambled to his feet and wondered what had happened to the man who had been in position behind him. By all rights, Mansuetus knew, he should be dead by now.

When he looked, he saw the other gladiator tangled in a net, a three-pronged spear draining his lifeblood.

Cobius stood there, his midsection covered in blood, listing to the side, grinning. "You're on your own for the last one," he said.

Even without the use of his left arm, Mansuetus could not be stopped. He attacked the remaining gladiator, relentlessly moving forward until the man got too close and the swing of Mansuetus's sword sliced open his right arm. The man dropped his sword. Mansuetus grabbed the man's shield, pulled him close, and thrust his sword through the gladiator's chest.

When the man fell at his feet, Mansuetus stood there, staggered, surrounded by the carnage, wondering what had come over him. The crowd was cheering and stomping on the wooden bleachers. Cobius slumped over, his hand on his side, trying to stanch the bleeding.

Mansuetus was the last man standing.

The crowd began throwing *sestertii* into the ring. The bodies of forty-four gladiators and four horses littered the wet sand like a battlefield.

Caligula stood at the front of the imperial box, yelling, waving his arms, trying to make himself heard.

Mansuetus glared at him from the other side of the arena. He would never walk over and salute the emperor. If he managed to get close enough, with his dying breath he would kill the man.

When the boisterous cheering ebbed, the trumpets blew and the crowd quieted. The emperor could finally be heard through the driving rain.

"The fight is not over!" he yelled. "There are two gladiators left, not one! Whip them into action!"

Mansuetus couldn't believe his ears! Several of the men moaning in the sand were still squirming and hadn't yet bled out. His friend Cobius would be lucky to survive the night. Yet the emperor wanted more blood?

Mansuetus took a few staggering steps toward the middle of the arena. He stared at Caligula for a moment, raised his sword over his head, and planted it firmly in the wet sand. He took a step away from the weapon.

"You have seen enough death!" Mansuetus yelled. "Enough brave men have died so that cowards can be entertained!"

— CHAPTER 60 —

I could breathe again. I had watched in amazement as a wounded Mansuetus fought off one attacker after another. He moved with a fury and speed I had never witnessed before. The long sword sliced through the air and landed with such force that the other gladiators were helpless before him.

But now he stood there, in open defiance of the emperor, displaying contempt for every spectator who had enjoyed watching forty-five men fight to the death. Nobody around me knew how to react.

In the rain, Mansuetus took one last look at the carnage and began walking toward his friend Cobius. He reached the man and looped one of Cobius's arms around his own neck to prop him up. Together they headed toward an exit.

Caligula barked out orders, and his guards descended on the arena. Some of them grabbed the dead gladiators and started dragging them out of the arena to be discarded. Others surrounded Mansuetus and Cobius.

At Caligula's orders, they separated the men and forced Mansuetus off to the side of the arena. Blood was still spilling from the gash in his left shoulder. He was covered in wet sand, and the armor on his right arm was stained with the blood of his opponents. Cobius was left standing alone, barely able to hold himself up.

"A champion has not yet been crowned!" Caligula announced. "The two remaining gladiators have earned the right to fight the great Flamma!"

Even as the emperor spoke, Flamma entered the arena and headed straight toward Cobius. I heard Mansuetus cry out, "No!" as he tried to break free of the Praetorian Guards, but there were too many men holding him back. I turned in disgust as Flamma ran his sword through Cobius and spun to go after Mansuetus.

The fury returned to Mansuetus's face as he picked up a sword and marched forward to meet his fresh new challenger. Flamma threw down his shield, an attempt to even the fight. But Mansuetus was exhausted and injured, dragging his right foot and unable to raise his left arm.

Flamma let out a battle cry, gripped the hilt of his sword with two hands, and moved in for the kill. The two traded blows, but Flamma was striking with a speed and power that Mansuetus couldn't match with a single hand. One blow sliced Mansuetus across the back of his right hand, and he dropped his sword.

Flamma hesitated as Mansuetus fell to both knees. The wounded gladiator tilted his head back, and Flamma, whose face could not be seen through his helmet, put the tip of his sword against Mansuetus's neck.

Men throughout the arena turned their thumbs up, a tribute to the amazing valor that Mansuetus had shown throughout the day. Everyone looked at Caesar.

Like the others, Flamma turned to see what Caligula's verdict would be.

It was apparently the opening that Mansuetus was looking for. He knocked the sword away from his neck and lunged.

At first, he caught Flamma off guard and had his opponent in his grasp. But Flamma recovered quickly, pulled his right arm free, and drove his sword into Mansuetus's exposed side, burying it halfway to the hilt.

For a second, the entire world seemed to stop. Mansuetus leaned on Flamma, the sword piercing his side.

Flamma stepped back, and the great Mansuetus, just two fights away from earning his freedom, fell face-first into the wet sand.

This time Flamma took no chances. He pulled the sword out of Mansuetus's side, put his foot on the gladiator's neck, and finished the job.

The crowd was stunned. I was sickened. Mansuetus had seemed invincible. I never thought it would end like this.

Nobody cheered. No *sestertii* were thrown into the arena. An eerie stillness filled the place, the only sound coming from the driving rain.

Caligula stood at the edge of the imperial box and spoke into the silence, loud enough for the spectators to hear. "It's a pity Mansuetus took things into his own hands. I was about to extend him mercy."

✝

Flavia had tried to rush the arena floor when Flamma was brought in for the final fight. She screamed and battled, but the Praetorian Guards dragged her outside the arena. When her hood came off, one of them realized she was a woman.

"I won't kill you this time," he sneered. "But if you ever try to sneak into the lower stands again, I'll see to it that you are crucified with the prisoners."

She was still outside when the place went silent. She knew immediately that Mansuetus was dead.

She sobbed uncontrollably and made a vow to the gods that Caligula would one day pay.

✝

After Mansuetus died, I sprinted down the steps, pushed my way through the crowd, and ran as fast as I could to the exit where they were dragging out the bodies of the slain gladiators. By the time I got there, the spectators were leaving the arena, and I had to fight my way against the flow. Men seemed anxious to get out of the rain and shake off the disconcerting memories of the day's events. The games weren't supposed to conclude that way.

I elbowed my way through the spectators until I found the two guards who were disposing of Mansuetus's body.

"Where are you taking him?" I asked.

"He was an honorable contestant. We'll cremate him with the other brave ones."

The less courageous ones, I knew, would be dragged to the Tiber.

"I know him," I said.

"You and everyone else."

I reached into my pouch and pulled out two gold coins. "An *aureus* for each of you," I offered. Each *aureus* was worth more than a hundred *sestertii*. It was more than either of these soldiers would earn in the next three months.

"Where do you want him?" one of the soldiers asked under his breath.

I gave him a location in an alleyway near the shops at the foot of the Palatine Hill. "If you have him there in ten minutes, there will be another *aureus* for each of you."

✝

By the time I arrived, the soldiers were already there. A few minutes earlier I had purchased a horse at an exorbitant price. We now loaded the body of Mansuetus and tied it down. His hair was matted with blood, his body covered with dirt and sand. We wrapped the body with blankets I had brought, and I paid the soldiers. They left without saying a word.

I rode slowly down the cobblestone streets of Rome and ignored the looks of those who watched me pass. It was four miles to the estate of Apronius. Once there, I would build a funeral pyre from the driest wood I could find. I would place the body of Mansuetus on top of the wood and prepare it for a proper funeral.

I had spent a considerable amount to bribe the soldiers and buy this horse. But that was the last thing on my mind.

I was sickened by what had become of my country. A mad emperor was single-handedly destroying the greatest civilization the world had ever known. Good men like Mansuetus were paying with their lives.

My emotions swung between despair and rage. I thought about the heartbreak that today's events would cost Flavia. I thought about the complicity and cowardice of so many who allowed Caligula to continue his tyrannical ways. I thought about my own naiveté in thinking that good people doing things the right way would ultimately prevail.

I was supposed to be an unemotional Stoic, but every inch of my being was consumed with hatred and thoughts of revenge. That night I planned on lighting the fire and watching the flames rise and the sparks fly, carrying the body of Mansuetus to the heavens.

That fire would quickly go out. But a second one, burning hot within me, would not be quenched until Caligula was dead.

— CHAPTER 61 —

When I returned to Rome, I wrote a letter, sealed it with my signet ring, and took it to the temple of Vesta. I gave it to one of the guards who recognized me as Flavia's advocate. I asked if he would deliver the letter to Flavia, and he promised that he would.

Later, at midnight, Flavia met me under the Arch of Augustus just as the letter had requested.

She wore a hooded black cloak, and even in the torchlight, I could tell she was in deep sorrow. I was shocked to see her hair cut so close to the scalp. It made her look thinner than she had at the trial and gaunt, ghostlike in the dim light. Her big brown eyes were hollow, underscored by dark circles. They were red from crying. She carried herself with the same regal bearing as always, but it seemed to be at great effort.

She walked up to me, and we embraced. I could tell she was fighting back more tears.

"I have Mansuetus's body," I told her.

Her head jerked back at the news. "Where?"

"At the estate of Apronius. I've prepared it for a proper funeral."

She was anxious to go with me, and we rode out on the horse I had purchased, Flavia sitting behind me, her arms around my waist. The trip went slowly because I was not much of a horseman and because the steed I had paid handsomely for was not much of a horse. We talked very little, and occasionally I could hear her quietly crying.

The storms had passed, but when we arrived at our destination, the ground around the funeral pyre was still soggy.

I had done my best to prepare Mansuetus's body. I had washed his exposed skin and hair, cleaned out his wounds, and anointed him with oil. I left him in his gladiator's armor. He lived as a warrior; he would be cremated as one. I had created a wreath and placed it on his head.

I asked Flavia to wait for a moment before she approached the body. The night was pitch-black with dark clouds covering the moon and stars. I lit two torches, one on each side of the funeral pyre. Mansuetus actually looked peaceful lying there, his battles over.

I turned and nodded to Flavia. I stepped away so she could have a private moment with him.

She walked up to the body, removed her hood, and gently stroked his cheek. She leaned forward and kissed Mansuetus's forehead and placed a coin in his mouth, the cost for the gods to transport him in the next world. Her tears fell softly on his face. She ran her fingers over his eyelids, and I watched her body tremble with grief as she stepped away. I moved next to her and put an arm around her. She leaned into me and sobbed.

"I'm sorry," I said.

After a few minutes she regained her composure and wiped her eyes. "I'm ready."

Before I lit the fire, there was one more thing that needed to be done. Every great man was entitled to a funeral oration. I would give it my best shot.

"Mansuetus fought with great valor and dignity and skill," I said. "But more than that, he embraced life, even life in the arena, with the joy and passion of a true Roman. He fought to obtain Roman citizenship, and he fought for his brothers, the other members of his gladiator school.

"In a way, he gave his life for them—one man laying his life down for his friends. He knew when he stepped into the arena for the last time that he wouldn't just be fighting his fellow gladiators. He would be fighting the twisted schemes of the emperor himself. He did it anyway because his brothers needed him to. He did it because he thought it was the right thing to do."

I paused, unsure if my words were helping or hurting. I decided to plow ahead.

"He also knew how to love. He called himself 'gentle' because that's what he was. The same huge heart that made him courageous in battle made him tender in love."

Flavia gave me a squeeze with the arm she had wrapped around my waist, a small token of thanks.

"I could see in his eyes, Flavia, that he loved you more than life itself. I sometimes think that his great success in the arena was due in part to his visions of spending the rest of his life with you. Love is stronger than fear. Total love eviscerates fear.

"May the gods be merciful to his soul. May his spirit rise to the heavens. May the name of Mansuetus be praised and his memory be as fixed in our hearts forever as it is on this day."

I paused, but I knew I couldn't stop there. It would take more than mere words to honor the memory of the great Mansuetus.

"And may the gods give us strength to avenge his death and desecrate the memory of all those who caused it."

We waited in silence for a few moments, and I sensed that Flavia was summoning the strength to light the fire. "Thank you," she said softly.

She left my side, picked up a torch, and lit the wood.

We watched for a few minutes in reverent silence as the flames leaped to the sky.

"Did you mean what you said about avenging his death?" she finally asked.

I turned to her. Light from the flames seemed to dance on her anguished face. "Yes."

"Let me have your dagger," she said.

I handed it to her, and she wrapped her left hand around the blade. She pulled the knife through her hand, slicing her fingers and palm. She handed it back to me, her hand now bloody.

I did the same, doing my best to ignore the pain.

She placed her bloody hand under mine and her right hand on top. In turn, I placed my right hand over hers.

"I vow by the gods to avenge the death of Mansuetus," she said.

"Blood for blood, life for life. I will not rest until Gaius Julius Caesar Augustus Germanicus is dead. May the gods curse me and torment my soul if I do not fulfill this sacred vow."

I repeated the words while our blood ran together. When we were done, we rinsed out the cuts, and I sliced a piece of my toga into strips so that we could bandage our hands.

I had no remorse about what I was preparing to do, but I marveled at the person I had become. Theophilus, the lover of Roman justice, a man who saw the best in everyone, was now a conspirator intent on assassinating the Roman emperor.

We both knew, as we watched the flames die out on Mansuetus's funeral pyre, that other similar conspiracies had failed. Yet I had no doubt that ours would succeed. It wasn't just the look in Flavia's eyes. It was a sense that somehow the gods were with us. That despite the death of Mansuetus, the gods could not sit idly by and watch Rome be destroyed.

And if they did, we would succeed anyway. The gods be cursed. We were taking matters into our own hands.

PART VII

THE
CONSPIRATOR

For two weeks, Flavia and I met secretly every night and planned our conspiracy. We studied the failed attempts to take Caligula's life and learned from them. Other would-be assassins had enlisted too many conspirators. They didn't have a plan to get past the Praetorian Guard. They had underestimated Caligula's cunning and paranoia.

I told Flavia about the poison I now carried with me at all times, but we both agreed that Caligula wouldn't die that way. He never ate or drank anything that hadn't been tested by others. Plus, although Flavia never explicitly said it, I sensed that she thought poison would be too humane.

There were three major complications. The first was finding somebody close to Caligula to help pull this off. He had surrounded himself with trusted members of the Praetorian Guard and elite soldiers formerly from the Germanic tribes his father had fought against. Many of these men didn't even speak Latin, and all were fiercely loyal to Caligula.

Our second problem was the Senate. Flavia, who at one time had defended imperial rule, now agreed that the imperial system would be the death of Rome. We didn't just want to avenge Mansuetus; our goals were loftier. We would reestablish the Republic. But this would require decisive action by the Senate, and who could be trusted in that backstabbing body?

Even if we found a senator we could trust, we had to make sure he wouldn't be implicated in the plot. Caligula still had enough popularity among the freedmen and the military that the Senate would never be able to take back power if the people believed that a senator had been complicit in the assassination.

Our final challenge was the emperor's family. If all we did was kill Caligula, the Praetorian Guard would appoint another member of his family as emperor. We would have to arrest Caligula's family members as well, including his incompetent uncle Claudius— the butt of Caligula's jokes but still the most likely successor to the throne.

Yet none of these challenges would matter if we couldn't find a way to get Caesar alone.

After two weeks of planning, the idea for doing so came from an unexpected source.

†

The conversation took place at the conclusion of a lavish banquet hosted by a distinguished senator. I generally despised such affairs, but my station in life demanded I show up for this one. Seneca was there as well, reclining on the other side of the large banquet hall. We hadn't spoken to each other since our falling-out after Flavia's trial.

To my shock, he asked me to go for a walk with him in the gardens. At first the conversation was forced. But when he was certain that no one else was around, he opened up.

"Timidius has accused Senator Pomponius of conspiracy against Caesar," Seneca said. "Pomponius knows of our past friendship and asked me to intercede with you to take his case."

I was taken aback by the reference to our *past* friendship. And though I was flattered that Pomponius would turn to me, I was still inclined to say no. The very last thing Flavia and I needed right now, in the midst of our conspiracy to kill the emperor, was the attention of a *maiestas* trial.

"I want to say yes, Seneca, as a favor to you. But I can't."

I could sense his disappointment. He didn't immediately respond, and I knew he was too proud to beg.

His mood weighed heavy on me, and so I took a risk. If I couldn't trust Seneca, a friend and mentor who detested Caligula nearly as much as I, whom could I trust?

"You once told me that bold times require bold actions," I said, checking his reaction in my peripheral vision. "I'm tired of defending good men from *maiestas* charges. I'm tired of emperors who condemn valiant Romans to die just to amuse the people. I'm tired of senators who kneel down to kiss the foot of a man like Caligula, vote to bestow him with great honors, and then complain about the emperor behind his back."

We took a few steps in silence. I hesitated to get any more specific unless Seneca gave me a sign that he was sympathetic to our cause.

"You've always been an idealist," he said. "Idealists become teachers. Pragmatists become emperors."

It was typical Seneca. Vague and tantalizing. Not a word that could ever be used against him.

"I'm going to kill Caesar," I said bluntly. "I need your help to restore the Republic."

Instinctively, Seneca checked behind us. He frowned, making no effort to hide his concern. "I assume you have a plan to get him alone?"

"Not yet."

"I assume you are keeping your inner circle of trusted advisers small?"

"Yes."

"And who might they be?"

Again, I deliberated how much to say. "I'm not at liberty to tell."

"I see." He let out a big sigh, the same symbol of exasperation he had used years earlier when I had disappointed him. "So let me get this straight. You have decided to kill the emperor, but you have no plan. And for this reason you are rejecting my request to represent my friend Pomponius in his treason trial?"

"I am open to suggestions," I said.

Seneca smiled. "I suggest that this time you leave my name out of it."

I promised I would, and I apologized again for listing him as a witness in Flavia's trial. I then told him about the funeral I had arranged after the death of Mansuetus. I told him about the vow that Flavia and I had made. I tried to paint a compelling picture of Flavia and her overwhelming grief.

We were almost done with our walk, and Seneca lowered his voice. "I would never be part of a conspiracy against the emperor; I must make that clear. Yet I do worry about how long he will survive. I have heard that he has an insatiable lust for women, especially ones who are off-limits. He is never seen in public with his wife, Caesonia, anymore. If a beautiful woman lured him into a private place, I fear that the good emperor could be too easily disposed of. And if that happened, the Senate might even rise up and restore the Republic. There is nothing like the humiliation that's been imposed by Caligula to help senators understand the shortfalls of an imperial system."

Seneca stopped and looked up at the expansive estate in front of us. "That would be a shame, would it not? If the emperor got lured into a private meeting with a woman like that?"

"A real shame," I agreed.

"Then given the nature of our conversation, I don't think we should speak again for a good while," Seneca said. "But as your former teacher, I'll leave you with a reminder from history. On the Ides of March when Julius Caesar was assassinated, the Liberators thought that all of Rome would join them in exultation over his death. They marched through the Forum and called out to the masses, 'People of Rome, we are once again free!' But they were met with silence."

He put his arm around my shoulders, and it seemed for a moment like my old mentor was back. "You know what my point is, Theophilus?"

I waited.

"It is easier to kill a tyrant than to end a tyranny," he said.

†

Despite my mentor's dire warning, I was in too deep to turn back. Ironically, the missing piece fell into place shortly after the *maiestas* trial of Senator Pomponius. His accusers, including Caepio Crispinus as their advocate, had counted on the testimony of Pomponius's alleged lover, a beautiful actress named Quintilia, as their primary source of proof. To elicit incriminating testimony, she was tortured by the Praetorian commander Cassius Chaerea so badly that her face was permanently disfigured. Still, she refused to testify against Pomponius.

When Quintilia was dragged before Caligula and accused of conspiring with Pomponius, the emperor took great pity on her appearance and released both Quintilia and Pomponius. He gave the actress a present of eight hundred thousand *sestertii* for her steadfastness in the face of torture. He also berated the guard Chaerea in front of the entire Senate, mocking him for his effeminate ways and his pudginess and chastising him for torturing the helpless Quintilia.

That night Flavia and I decided that we should ask the humiliated Chaerea to join our cause.

Flavia began finding ways to bend his ear. A conversation here. A sympathetic look there. A request that the two of them meet in private. It took her ten days to woo him over.

We were both nervous about bringing him in, I more than Flavia, primarily because I hadn't had the opportunity to evaluate him face-to-face. But Flavia asked me to trust her, and besides, what choice did we really have? If we wanted to get close to Caesar, we would have to deal with one of the members of his despicable inner circle.

After Flavia brought Chaerea into the conspiracy, my job was to put Apronius, my former client, on notice. I spent three separate evenings at his countryside estate, discussing philosophy and our mutual love for the Republic. Finally, when the time was right, I hinted at what might be coming. "If anything happened to Caligula, the public mood would be ripe for restoring power to the Senate," I suggested.

We were sipping wine, and he eyed me suspiciously.

"It would take senators with great courage and conviction to make it happen," I continued. "The Praetorian Guard would have to be neutralized, and there could be no suspicions that the senators themselves had been part of the conspiracy to kill Caesar."

I watched as Apronius slowly nodded his agreement. "All of what you say is true," he said. "But I do have a question."

"I'm listening."

"Is Flavia involved?" he asked.

"Yes."

"Then tell her I will do my part," Apronius promised.

Two months after the funeral of Mansuetus, Caligula decided to move his palace to Alexandria. Chaerea secretly told us that the emperor was motivated in part by his increasing paranoia about possible conspiracies against him and in part by his dreams of exotic Egyptian women. He planned to leave on January 25. Just prior to his departure, he had scheduled three days of theatrical performances.

Our plan was to strike on the last day possible.

— CHAPTER 63 —

On the morning of January 24, two Praetorian Guards showed up at my house just after dawn and put me in shackles. I was being arrested on charges of *maiestas*, they said, and was accused of conspiring to take the life of Gaius Julius Caesar Augustus Germanicus. I would be held in the palace prison along with others who had been arrested on similar charges.

The temperature was barely above freezing, so the guards allowed me to put on my cloak before we left. I hung my head as they paraded me down the streets of Rome, my face hidden by the hood of my cloak. It was early, and there were few people in the Forum.

The guards marched me to the palace and placed me in a dark cell in the catacombs. I instantly recalled my visits with Mansuetus and Flavia. This wasn't the Tullianum—I supposed I wasn't important enough for that—but this place was depressing enough. There were no windows here. It had the same foul odor. I shuddered in the damp darkness.

They had taken my dagger, but I had managed to keep the small vial of poison. I fingered it now and thought about the hours ahead. I said a prayer to Apollo for Flavia to be protected. I sat down, leaned against the wall, closed my eyes, and tried not to imagine what was to come.

✝

The lavish, custom-built theater could seat nearly nine thousand patrons, another monumental waste of government funds. It was built on the Palatine Hill with several entrances from the Forum and an underground tunnel that connected it directly to Caligula's palace.

It opened the week before the emperor was scheduled to leave for Alexandria, and for the last two days, the festivities had been nonstop. On this, the final day of the plays, every seat was taken.

It was a command performance. When Caligula took his place in the imperial box—without his wife, Caesonia, by his side—he had insisted that Flavia sit next to him. Her hair had started to grow back, but she still used a black wig imported from the Middle East. It framed her face in ringlets. She had shaded her eyes with a bit of ash, straightened her eyelashes, and colored her lips with dark-red cinnabar. She had applied perfume generously. Rubria had told her how beautiful she looked.

Caligula opened the festivities by sacrificing a bull in honor of

Augustus. When he returned to the imperial box, his hands were covered in blood. He had his slaves throw expensive sweets to the spectators while he rinsed his hands in a basin and returned to his seat beside Flavia to enjoy a glass of wine.

As Caesar drank, Flavia took stock of the security precautions. Around the perimeter of the theater were no less than a hundred of Caligula's Germanic bodyguards. A similar number of Praetorian Guards were scattered throughout the crowd. There had been some speculation that conspirators might try to strike on the last day Caligula was in town.

"I'm told that you've been seen sneaking out of the House of Virgins again," Caligula said under his breath as the crowd scrambled for the sweets. "I'm told that this time the recipient of your late-night affections is none other than Theophilus."

"I am afraid Your Excellency has been misinformed."

"It may interest you to know that we arrested Theophilus this morning," Caligula continued, his voice cheery and casual. He was speaking softly enough that only Flavia could hear. "He's being held in the palace dungeon on charges of treason. I'd like to have his case resolved before I leave."

Flavia tried to keep her emotions in check. She cast a casual glance behind her and saw Chaerea standing in the back of the imperial box. She kept her voice low and steady as she responded.

"I know Theophilus well, Your Excellency. I can assure you that he would never be part of such a conspiracy. Who is it that accuses him?"

"A man I trust. A man who is willing to testify in the Senate about the details of the conspiracy. That's all you need to know."

The crowd had quieted again, and Caesar stood. "There will be three plays this morning," he announced to the audience. "The final two are based on the Greek tragedy of Cinyras and Myrrha. The other, the one that will open our show today, has been written especially for this occasion."

Caesar sat back down and said little else. His conversation with

Flavia was apparently over, and she watched in horror as the first play unfolded. It was a pantomime about a band of robbers who were arrested, their leader nailed to a cross. A large amount of fake blood covered the stage.

"A pity I can't crucify Roman citizens," Caligula said. He tossed a few grapes into his mouth. "But I can behead them. Which is what I have in mind for Theophilus, though I'm open to negotiations."

Flavia swallowed hard. "What types of negotiations?"

"I'll be back in my chambers for lunch," Caligula said. "If you were to meet me there, alone, all might be forgiven. I could give an order releasing Theophilus right after I leave for Alexandria. I'd be a safe distance away by then."

"How do I know that this time Caesar would keep his word?"

The actors took their bows, and the audience started clapping. Caligula stood, and the audience stood with him. Reluctantly, Flavia rose to her feet as well.

"Let's put it this way," he said, leaning toward Flavia so he could be heard over the applause. "You have my word that he will die if you do nothing. And since you obviously care for the man or we wouldn't be having this conversation, it would make sense for me to keep him alive as long as you play along. That way, I can invite you to my palace whenever I wish."

"What about Caesonia?"

"She's the mother of my child, nothing more."

They sat down as the theater readied for the next play. Flavia's skin crawled with contempt. She hated being this close to the man.

"Let it be done according to Caesar's wishes," Flavia eventually said. "Should I leave now?"

He reached over and put a hand on top of hers. She wanted to recoil but forced herself to stay calm.

"Your hands are cold, my dear," Caligula said.

"You make me nervous."

Caligula laughed, a disdainful chuckle that came from deep in his throat. "Maybe you should head back now," Caligula said. "I'll follow in a few minutes. In the meantime, it might be good for the citizens of Rome to see a Vestal give me the same kind of respect I'm afforded by Rome's greatest senators."

He bent over and unfastened a sandal. He held out his right foot and looked at Flavia.

The thought of it was revolting, and she couldn't bring herself to do it, to kneel and kiss the man's hairy foot as if he were some kind of god she needed to worship. Caligula was truly insane.

Instead, she leaned closer and whispered in his ear. "I don't kiss the feet of Caesar," she said. "But I'll be waiting for you."

He considered this for a moment and then lowered his leg. He turned and snapped his fingers, and Chaerea approached his seat.

"Flavia would like to see my chambers," Caligula said, keeping his voice low.

Chaerea nodded, and Flavia took his arm. Together they left through the exit that led to the palace.

— CHAPTER 64 —

I sat in the cell for what seemed like an eternity, plenty of time to consider all the options. The best case was that the plan was on track, just taking longer than expected. The worst case—Chaerea had double-crossed both of us, or perhaps the plan had otherwise been exposed and Chaerea and Flavia were now in prison too. There were a thousand other possibilities and nothing I could do about any of them.

And so I waited. The minutes passed like hours. At first, I couldn't shake the dark thoughts of everything that could go wrong. Yet there was also something about sitting alone in the cold darkness that strengthened my resolve. I fortified myself with vivid images I had stored in the recesses of my mind. Caligula as a teenager, spoiled and arrogant, laughing at me as I hung on the cross. Caligula as Caesar, scorning me while I made my case for Mansuetus and Flavia. A jealous Caligula presiding over the games, causing the deaths of brave men like Mansuetus. The hypocritical emperor shouting from the imperial box that he would have extended mercy to Mansuetus if only given the chance.

And the final image—the inconsolable grief of Flavia.

I convinced myself that we were doing the right thing. The emperor was a madman. Somebody had to stop him.

As the minutes marched slowly by, I replayed each of these images over and over, replacing every vestige of fear with a surge of rage and a steely resolve to exact our revenge.

✝

Chaerea whisked Flavia through the underground tunnels of the Imperial Palace, narrow hallways with pictures of Caligula and other emperors painted on the walls. She passed a painting of the emperor giving his first speech to the Senate and thought about those heady days when it looked like a young Caligula would usher in a new golden age. It was not even four years ago.

Chaerea was already out of breath when he led her into the small alcove at the foot of the steep stone steps that led to the holding cells. He grabbed a hooded brown cloak from the corner of the alcove and tossed it to Flavia. She put it on without speaking. He handed her a dagger.

They would free Theophilus first. Then the three of them would circle back and cross paths with the emperor in the single narrow passageway that led to his chambers. Flavia knew the emperor's chambers would be guarded by the loyal Germanic troops. The best place for an assassination would be in the passage before he got there.

As they climbed the steps, Chaerea told Flavia to take off her hood so the guards could see her face. He would explain that Caesar had told him to take Flavia back to Caesar's chambers. The guards would have no problem believing that story. He would also explain that Caesar wanted Theophilus there as well to be threatened in front of Flavia in case she didn't cooperate. Whether they believed it or not, the guards would obey Chaerea's orders.

When they reached the cell, Chaerea spoke to the guards in German, and Flavia had no idea what they were saying. A couple of times the guards looked at her, but eventually they handed the keys to Chaerea, and he opened the door.

✝

Chaerea jerked me out of the cell and pushed me down the hallway toward the stairs. He had his sword drawn, and Flavia was with him. I thanked the gods and descended the steps as quickly as I could.

At the bottom, Chaerea looked into the hallway and made sure the way was clear. He unlocked my wrist irons and handed me a brown cloak with a hood. He pulled an extra dagger from his belt and gave it to me.

"We don't have much time," Chaerea said. His puffy round face was red with exertion, his eyes narrow. I could see the fury in those eyes and a look that approached panic now that the moment had finally arrived. Once again, I wondered if we had chosen the right ally.

"Put your hoods up and let's go," Chaerea said.

We ran down one corridor and then another. Each time we made a turn, Chaerea stepped out into the new passageway and made sure nobody was coming. We moved quickly, hugging the walls. One time, a group of Praetorian Guards came from the opposite direction.

"Hold your wrists together," Chaerea whispered. I did as I was told, and Chaerea pressed the point of his sword against my back. Flavia followed behind. The guards stopped and asked if Chaerea needed help. He told them he was fine, and they went on their way.

We arrived at the one long tunnel that led directly to Caesar's chambers, and we waited at a corner of the passageway, where it intersected with some others. We were out of sight of anybody approaching from the theater. The minutes dragged by. There was no sign of the emperor.

"What if he doesn't come?" I asked.

"Then we kill him in the theater," Chaerea said. "I'll put the knife in his back myself. My men will either rally to support me or arrest me. Either way, you can be on your way to the Senate."

The three of us decided to give it another ten minutes.

From a hallway on our left, a group of young Greek choirboys passed by, their directors trailing behind them. They must have been scheduled to perform in the theater. They were singing a melancholy tragedy as they walked, their song echoing off the walls. I recognized the song from my days at the School of Molon, and I took it as an omen. The gods were smiling on us. It was a funeral dirge for Caligula.

"He's coming," Chaerea said. He had peeked around the corner after the Greek choir passed. "Come on."

We followed Chaerea down the tunnel about fifty yards behind the two dozen choirboys. I could see the heads of Caligula and two of his guardsmen on the other side of the choir. Why didn't we wait where we were? It seemed to me like Chaerea wanted to make this as dramatic as possible. Perhaps he actually wanted witnesses so there would be no doubt about who had killed Caesar. His name would be praised or cursed, but it would be his name on the lips of every Roman.

The choir stopped and bowed before Caesar. The three of us froze when they did so, but we were far enough down the hallway that Caligula didn't seem to notice us.

"Let me hear another song," Caligula said.

The boys broke into an upbeat melody. They sang at the top of their lungs, and the directors joined in. It felt surreal, pressing flat against the wall, hearing this energetic musical tribute while creeping up behind the chorus and ducking into an alcove just out of Caesar's view. Every nerve in my body was on fire. Within minutes we would make our move.

The choir stopped, and Caligula applauded them. He lavished praise on the boys and their directors. We could hear the boys thank him as they headed toward the theater. We knew that at any moment Caligula would be passing directly in front of us.

"The guard on the left is Sabinus," Chaerea said. "He's one of us. The guard on the right is not."

I had recognized the guard on Caligula's right. It was Lucian, still one of Caligula's closest friends. He was fully armed, but we would have the element of surprise.

"Put the dagger right here," Chaerea said to me, pointing to a spot next to his breastplate on the left side. "I'll take care of Caesar."

"Not if I can help it," Flavia said.

And just like that, the moment arrived. We stepped out of the alcove, directly in front of Caligula and his guards. The Greek choir was nearly fifty yards down the hallway behind them, turning a corner and disappearing.

"What is this?" Caligula asked.

Chaerea had drawn his sword, and he wasted no time. He swung at Caesar with a two-fisted strike, a mighty blow designed to decapitate the emperor.

Time seemed to slow in those pivotal few seconds. I saw the astonished look of the emperor, his mouth forming a small O, his eyes wide with fright. The sword struck his collarbone, opening a huge gash in the skin and cracking the bone.

Lucian leaped at Chaerea, and I delivered an underhanded thrust that buried my dagger in Lucian's ribs, just under his left arm. He turned on me as I twisted and sliced as hard as I could, feeling the shudder that told me my dagger had pierced his heart. He cried out, but before he could deliver his first blow, he reeled and crumpled to the floor.

Miraculously, Caligula had survived the initial attack, though it had seriously staggered him. Before he could regroup, Flavia lunged forward and plunged her dagger into his heart. The guard named Sabinus got in on the action as well, stabbing the emperor repeatedly from behind. As Caligula fell, Chaerea struck again, this time driving his sword into the back of the emperor's neck. Blood came gushing out. Caligula gurgled, and his body went limp.

I stared, frozen by the horror of the moment. Rome's leader was dead at our feet, a pool of blood spreading on the polished stone floor of the tunnel. His childhood friend and my onetime tormentor lay next to him, his eyes staring at the ceiling. I had dreamed many times of exacting revenge on the emperor. But I had never once intended to kill an innocent man along with him.

"It's done," I said.

"Not yet," Chaerea said.

I knew what he meant. He and Sabinus would now enter the palace and arrest Caligula's wife, daughter, and uncle. Flavia would stay here and let out a scream to alert the world that the emperor had died. She would claim that she was returning from the palace when she stumbled across him in the hallway. I would run through the underground tunnels to an exit that led to the Forum. It would be my job to inform the Senate and rally the people.

"May the gods be with you," Chaerea said.

Flavia took off her cloak and handed it to me. She took my face in both of her hands, leaned forward, and gave me a kiss.

"Play your part well," she said. "And be careful."

With that, I took off after Chaerea and Sabinus down the corridor and up the steps. Behind me, I heard a bloodcurdling scream.

Caesar was dead. The question now was whether the empire would die with him.

— CHAPTER 65 —

Flavia's scream brought the Greek choir back into the hallway—staring and stunned. A number of Germanic troops sprinted past them to where Flavia knelt over Caligula's body, covered in blood. She pointed in the other direction, and they took off. Praetorian Guards were not far behind, and soon the corridors underneath the palace were crawling with troops.

Flavia made her way back to the theater, where pandemonium reigned. Caligula's Germanic guards stood by the exits, swords drawn, forbidding anyone to leave. Flavia took a seat in the imperial box and wept aloud as she explained that Caligula had been stabbed to death. His attackers had apparently fled. Rubria knelt next to her, embraced her, and buried her head in Flavia's lap.

Some of the senators tried to leave the theater, but the guards held their ground. The senators protested loudly, yet the guardsmen just shook their heads, tensed their muscles, and pointed the senators back to their seats.

Some senators obeyed. Others approached the imperial box.

"I just came upon him in the hallway," Flavia explained.

"Are you sure he was dead?"

She nodded, started to say something, and broke down again.

Emotions quickly escalated. Some spectators wept openly, while others seemed pleased by the emperor's demise. A rumor started that Caligula had not actually died and that the whole thing was nothing more than a ruse to see who would celebrate.

When three of the emperor's closest bodyguards returned from the tunnel, things took a bloody turn. They had decapitated three senators they had discovered in the hallway, and they carried the heads of those senators into the theater. They placed the bloody heads at the front of the stage so that they stared out at the audience. The people shrank back in horror. Some of the freedmen threw themselves at the guards' feet, pleading their own innocence.

It sickened Flavia to see how quickly the violence had escalated. Apparently the three dead senators had just been in the wrong place at the wrong time.

Another fifty or so senators quickly huddled together near their seats as the Germanic guards surrounded them. Flavia grabbed Rubria's hand, and the two of them walked between the senators and the bodyguards. They stood there, facing the guards, shielding the senators. Two other Vestals came over and joined them.

"Move," one of the guards demanded.

"At the very least, these men are entitled to a fair trial," Flavia said, standing her ground.

The commander of the guards stared at Flavia for a moment, his nostrils flared with rage. "Nobody leaves!" he barked.

†

I sprinted to the house of Sentius Saturninus, one of Rome's two consuls, who would now temporarily rule until a new Caesar was selected by the Senate. I breathlessly relayed the news that Caligula was dead. I urged Sentius to convene the Senate or risk throwing all of Rome into chaos.

Sentius, a cagey old survivor, rose to his full height as if he had been expecting this all along. "Thank you for your service, Theophilus. You can rest assured that the Senate will be convened with the greatest possible haste."

I left Sentius's house and ran to the *doma* of Seneca. He was there waiting, along with Apronius.

"Caesar is dead," I gasped, standing in front of both of them. I bent over to catch my breath.

"How did he die?" Apronius asked.

"With much less pain than he deserved," I said.

†

Forty minutes after the death of Caligula, an envoy from the Senate entered the theater. His name was Arruntius Euaristus. He was dressed in black mourning attire, and he strode to the stage, taking a place behind the severed heads of the three senators. Euaristus was an auctioneer and possessed one of the most commanding voices in all of Rome.

He announced that Caligula had been murdered—stabbed to death by unknown assassins. By order of the consuls, the Senate was being convened to elect a new Princeps, and the theater was to be emptied. Mourning for the emperor was to begin immediately. The senators should report to the Capitol.

Though they didn't look happy, the guards threw open the doors of the theater. People nearly trampled each other in their haste to leave.

Flavia left with them and quickly headed to the House of Vestal, where she tried to scrub the blood from her skin and clothes. She had done her part to free Rome from the reign of a maniacal tyrant. Now it would be up to the Senate to do theirs.

†

For three hours, I watched the senators debate the future of the empire. Apronius was one of the first to speak. As I knew he would, he presented a compelling case to cast off the chains of the imperial system and return to a republic. He castigated the senators for their failure to take a stand against Caligula's abuses. He had prepared a list of insults and atrocities the Senate had suffered at the hands of Caesar, and he went through them now, one by one. "This is what happens when we give up our rights as Roman citizens and kneel to kiss the foot of a man who calls himself a god!" Apronius shouted.

I knew Apronius would be a strong voice for a return to the Republic, but I had no idea he would be *this* strong. His speech was interrupted by frequent applause, while opposing senators looked furious.

He was followed by Sentius Saturninus himself, the consul I had spoken to earlier, who carried forward the same theme. "The tyranny of Caesar was fostered by nothing more than our own indolence and failure to speak in opposition to his wishes. We succumbed to the seduction of peace and have learned to live like conquered prisoners. We have been afraid to die like brave men and have endured the utmost degradation."

When he finished, half the Senate was on its feet applauding, and the other half looked like they wanted blood. A member of the opposition leaped to his feet and walked up to Sentius. He pointed to the signet ring on Sentius's finger, holding up the consul's hand for everyone to see.

"Do you see what this man has?" the senator asked. "A signet ring with the likeness of Caligula. He upbraids us for being sycophants of the tyrant. But how do you think he got appointed as consul?"

As the debate dragged on, a huge crowd gathered outside the Senate doors. In the Forum, speakers mounted the Rostra and fired up their portions of the crowd. The city's police force, following strict orders from the consuls, stood guard close by. The Praetorian Guard was nowhere to be seen.

A few of the more outspoken proponents of the Republic came into the Senate chambers and asked me to take my turn outside on the Rostra. "People will listen to you," they claimed. "This is your chance to turn the tide of history."

At first I hesitated, wondering whether I should take such a public stand. Though the word was not yet out about my arrest, people would eventually learn that I had been charged with *maiestas* earlier that morning. But if the Republic was restored, that charge, like similar charges against other individuals, would be dismissed and likely considered a badge of honor. And if the Republic was not restored, the *maiestas* charge would be just one problem out of many. There was no middle ground.

I followed them outside, and when my turn came, I mounted the Rostra, the same spot where Mark Antony had eulogized Julius Caesar. With that famous eulogy, Mark Antony had demonized Brutus, Caesar's killer, and the power of the emperor had been solidified. Perhaps today, that same power could be broken.

—— CHAPTER 66 ——

"There will be a time for us to mourn Gaius Julius Caesar Augustus Germanicus," I said. "But that time is not now!"

I looked out at the thousands of people standing before me, at the magnificent temples of Rome, at the police lining the porticoes in the Forum proper.

"There will be a time when we recall fondly his early reign, the days when he disavowed the treason trials and walked among us as a fellow Roman citizen. The days when he treated everyone with decency and respect. But now is not the time for reminiscing."

My voice carried, and I didn't feel the least bit nervous. I had been preparing for this moment my entire life. My voice was strong, my gaze steady, my chin high.

"Today is a day for action. Today we must choose. On the one hand, freedom. A nation of laws. A nation where every man, whether born a freedman's son or a slave or a Roman equestrian, may ascend to the highest heights and achieve the greatest triumphs. If we follow this road, we choose the glory of Rome. The courage of a Roman legionnaire, the authority of a Roman magistrate, the ingenuity of a Roman architect.

"Rome civilized the entire world not because we had superior weapons but because we had a superior will. We are Romans. We bowed to no one. That is one road that lies before us—to recapture that glory.

"The other road is the road of the imperial system. We stumble over each other to kiss the feet of another man. We allow that man to mock our institutions by threatening to appoint his horse to the second-highest position in the land. We stand idly by as this man reaches out, takes the hands of our wives, and whisks them away to his chambers while we watch in shame. Saying nothing. Doing nothing. This is the road of the empire. One man becomes a god, and everyone else becomes his slave!"

A few people broke into applause while others hissed or shouted in protest. I knew I was now on dangerous ground, condemning the legacy of Caesar even before his body was cold.

"What is the cost of a Roman soul? Is it the price of free bread and entertainment at the Circus Maximus? Is that how much we charge to be debased like animals?

"Or does a Roman soul have infinite worth? Is the soul upright, good, and worthy? Should every citizen have a chance to rise to heaven from the very slums? This is what it means to be a republic. This is what it means to recapture the glory of Rome."

I paused, searching for a way to end.

"The founders of Rome gave birth to the greatest Republic in human history. It's time for a second birth; it's our turn to write a new chapter in Roman history—a chapter of dignity and opportunity and freedom."

People clapped; a few even cheered. But it wasn't the raucous reaction I had wanted—a crowd mobilized for action.

I walked down the steps of the Rostra disappointed in my own performance. My friends told me that my words were eloquent and moving, yet I knew I had not captured the imagination of the crowd. Perhaps they had been slaves to the emperor for so long that they no longer had a spark of freedom that could be ignited.

Augustus Caesar and his successors had cleverly wooed them, turning defiant citizens into submissive slaves, all in exchange for Roman peace, beautiful roads, free food, and entertainment.

For some strange reason, I thought of my conversation with Nicodemus. He had spoken of new beginnings, a second birth. Perhaps it only happened in Judea. Perhaps in Rome, where cynicism prevailed, the death of a republic could never be reversed.

†

It was two hours later when Herod Agrippa mounted the Rostra and quieted the crowd. He was a well-known friend of Caligula's and had been appointed tetrarch over Galilee and Perea. He had come to Rome to celebrate with Caligula in the last few days before the emperor moved to Alexandria.

He was a tall and distinguished man, fifty or so but with a face that looked ten years younger. He had a long, pointed nose and a protruding forehead and always wore a small laurel wreath half-hidden by his curly black hair. He also had that intangible presence that let everyone know he was a man in charge.

"A few hours ago, one of Rome's top advocates said that this was not a day to mourn Caligula. But I hope you will excuse those of us who loved the emperor if we cannot keep our eyes as dry as this day apparently requires."

Agrippa looked at me as if I had the power to give him permission to mourn. I stared back, unblinking.

"I also hope our friend Theophilus will forgive us if we shed a tear for the emperor's wife and baby daughter."

My breath caught in my throat at this mention of the emperor's family. Had they died as well? Chaerea was supposed to have arrested them.

An audible gasp went up from the crowd as they heard the news.

"Chaerea and Sabinus, the cowardly traitors who stabbed Caesar in the back, barged into Caesonia's room and told her to make her peace with the gods," Agrippa continued. "Caesonia faced the sword courageously and made only one request. She begged them to spare her two-year-old daughter, Drusilla."

Even before Agrippa finished the story, I knew in my gut that Chaerea had done something unspeakable. I could already sense the crowd's disgust at the merciless slaying of Caesonia. I braced for what was coming next.

"After killing Caesonia, Chaerea killed little Drusilla by banging her head against the palace wall. These are the great defenders of the Republic to whom Theophilus referred earlier."

The crowd was aghast, and so was I. My greatest fears had been realized. Chaerea was a monster, created by incessant ridiculing from Caligula. Now the monster had turned and destroyed every member of Caligula's family.

"The Praetorian Guard found Claudius secreted behind a curtain in the palace. They carried him from the Palatine Hill to their barracks, where they have crowned him as Rome's new emperor."

I couldn't believe what I was hearing! Claudius, the fifty-year-old uncle of the emperor, had only survived this long because he was widely believed to be wholly incompetent and no threat whatsoever to Caligula. He was clumsy, stuttered when he talked, and kept to himself as a reclusive scholar. Caligula had frequently made fun of him. Nobody considered Claudius to be emperor material.

"Chaerea and Sabinus have been arrested and executed," Agrippa announced. My heart dropped. Chaerea had told us that the rest of the Praetorian Guard would back him once Caligula was dead. He had grossly miscalculated.

"Men like Theophilus can long for a republic, but we must remember that it was the divine Augustus who found Rome built of stone and left it built of marble. Our greatest years have been our years as an empire! It is therefore right and just that we should mourn those emperors who are slain before they can show the benefits of their rule. Now, if you'll be so kind as to excuse me, I will go pay my respects to Caligula and Caesonia and poor little Drusilla."

Agrippa walked off the Rostra, and the crowd showed its respect by watching in silence.

I knew at that moment we were defeated. The Senate held out for a few more hours, but as the prospects for restoring the Republic became dimmer, senators started fleeing the chamber for fear of reprisal.

Agrippa became the unofficial envoy between the Senate and the Praetorian Guard. By early the next morning, he had negotiated a resolution. The Senate would recognize Claudius as the new Princeps. In exchange, there would be no further prosecution of those who were alleged to have participated in the conspiracy to murder Caligula. Those awaiting trial on *maiestas* charges were pardoned. My own arrest, orchestrated by Chaerea as part of the assassination conspiracy, would be one of many erased from the record books.

The next day, January 26, Claudius was escorted back into the Imperial Palace by members of the Praetorian Guard. He was crowned Caesar by the commander of the guard on the balcony of the palace. He immediately announced that the state would give every Praetorian soldier fifteen thousand *sestertii*, more than ten times a soldier's annual wages. The Praetorian Guard had made Claudius emperor, and now he was paying them back.

That same day, the Senate recognized Claudius as emperor and awarded him the customary rights and honors of the principate. Like his nephew before him, Claudius announced an end to the treason trials and said he would burn all criminal records associated with them. He stammered his way through his first speech, announcing his intentions to treat the Senate with great respect.

That night I lay in bed and tried to sleep for the first time in forty-eight hours. When I closed my eyes, I saw the bloodied corpse of Caligula. I felt my dagger ripping through the intestines of Lucian. I heard the words of Agrippa describing the violent death of a defenseless baby girl.

Was this what I had become? An assassin? A failed leader of a rebellion? A man who had unleashed horrible evil in the name of justice?

But what was the alternative? Somebody had to stop the madness. The speech in the Senate that day by Claudius sounded uncomfortably familiar, as if the words from Caligula's first speech four years earlier had been bottled up and then poured out one more time. Perhaps we had just traded one tyrant for another. Time would tell.

I dozed in and out that night, haunted by the way events had unfolded, trying hard to convince myself that I had done the right thing. How could Flavia and I have known that Chaerea would rampage through the royal family like a wounded lion? Was it our fault that the Senate had once again shirked their opportunity to seize a historic moment?

Maybe the Republic was forever dead. But at least I had tried.

I thought about Flavia. I reminded myself of the senseless death of Mansuetus. Flavia and I had fulfilled our vow. We had no other choice.

I cursed the name of Caligula and finally fell asleep.

— CHAPTER 67 —

I was on the ragged emotional edge for weeks after Caligula died. I couldn't sleep at night. I kept glancing over my shoulder during the day. I replayed the assassination in my mind a thousand times.

At first I was sure the Praetorian Guard would be coming for me. I worried that either Chaerea or Sabinus had said something before being executed. Or perhaps one of the Greek choirboys or their leaders could describe me.

I fretted about Flavia, too. Not only had we been coconspirators in the assassination, but we had both taken risky public stands immediately after Caligula's death—she in the theater and me at the Rostra.

Yet Claudius seemed to be an emperor of his word, and I began to think that perhaps there really wouldn't be more prosecutions for conspiracy or other acts of alleged treason. I began to wonder if I had totally misjudged Claudius. He was ungainly and had a trick knee that sometimes went out on him. His head shook when he got angry, and his voice wailed when he was excited. Yet there was something authentic about the man, and he slowly began winning over the senators. He sat among them when they debated legislation, waiting his turn to speak. He chided them occasionally about their reluctance to debate bills he had introduced. He didn't ridicule or abuse them. He didn't love the privileges of his position the way Caligula had.

Days turned into weeks and eventually into months. I kept my head low and focused on my clients, trying hard to avoid any political controversies. When Flavia and I had put together the plan to assassinate Caligula and restore the Republic, I had reconciled myself to the fact that either our plan would succeed or I would be a dead man. Instead, I was living in an outcome I had never envisioned. The Republic was still dead, but I was alive.

Even though I was barely in my thirties, I decided that my days attempting to influence Roman politics were over.

As time moved on, my thoughts turned more and more to Flavia. I would rearrange my schedule to attend the same public ceremonies I knew she would attend. We would catch each other's gaze, but we were both careful not to linger too long for fear that others might notice. I suspected she had the same concerns I did. If we were seen with each other too soon after the death of Caligula, people might put the pieces together and figure out our conspiracy.

I wondered if I would spend the rest of my life this paranoid, jumping at every knock at the door, fearing the men behind me on the street were there to arrest me. I started to understand how emperors could go insane.

It was in the springtime when I heard the shocking news. Seneca had been banished by Claudius. He had been accused of committing adultery with Caligula's sister, Julia Livilla. The word on the street was that Claudius's wife had insisted that Seneca be sent away from Rome.

The news saddened me, both because it demonstrated that Claudius was open to manipulation and because I had never reconciled with Seneca. I decided to show up on the day of his departure for Corsica. Perhaps I could restore our relationship before he set sail.

✝

When the day arrived, I was surprised that only a handful of Seneca's clients had made the trip to the harbor to see him off. I thought about the early morning *salutationes* at his house when dozens of clients had waited each day for his patronage. He was a popular man then. He was learning now who his true friends were.

I took a seat on a stone wall and waited patiently as he shared private moments with the others. At last, he walked toward me and I stood to greet him. We grasped forearms, and I was struck by the sadness in his droopy eyes. Behind him, his servants were loading crates of his possessions onto a boat. Nobody would ever accuse Seneca of traveling lightly.

"It was good of you to come," he said. There was none of the normal mirth in his voice. Of all men, Seneca would miss Rome the most. He thrived on the intrigue, the intellectual debate, and the raw power that settled like fog around the capital. Corsica was no-man's-land. A true Stoic would love it. Seneca would wither there.

"I'm sorry, Seneca," I said. "You deserve better than this."

"I'll have plenty of time to write. Every great philosopher needs time to write."

"I wish I could help in some way." I looked down and kicked a small pebble, wondering whether any of this had to do with the fact that I had named him as a witness in my case against Caligula.

"I know what you're thinking," Seneca said. "But it's not your fault, Theophilus. I brought this on myself."

There were always rumors about Seneca and the ladies. I never knew what to believe and what to ignore. It was one of the many contradictions in my friend's life. A man who preached morality yet evidently violated the marriage contract.

We talked for a few minutes before some men called out from the shore. It was time to set sail.

"Watch your back," Seneca said. He grabbed my shoulders the way a father would his son's. "And don't give up on Rome. Don't give up on the Republic."

I nodded. In truth, I had already raised my shield in surrender, but my mentor didn't need to know that.

He embraced me and whispered something in my ear that left my jaw hanging open. "I've talked to Flavia. She asked me if you were going to propose a marriage to begin after she finishes her duties as a Vestal."

I leaned back, my eyes wide. "What did you tell her?"

"I told her I didn't know. But if you did, I told her she would never find a better husband."

"You told her that?" In my excitement, I raised my voice, and it drew a few stares.

Seneca kept his voice low, conspiratorial. "Bold times call for bold action," he said. He slapped me on the arm and turned to leave.

"Did she say what she would do if I asked?"

Seneca stopped, pivoting slowly. "She didn't say, Theophilus. But if you want my advice, you ought to find out."

I thanked him for everything. As he walked away, I thought about how much I would miss him.

He stopped before boarding the ship. He turned and looked at his assembled friends.

"I'll be back," Seneca promised. "Take care of the place while I'm gone."

✝

I didn't waste any time before writing a letter asking Flavia to meet. I sealed it and found a way to slip it to Rubria. She promised she would give it to Flavia.

A day later, a courier came back with the reply, sealed with Flavia's own ring. It contained only directions to a place by the Tiber River along with a date and time. We were to meet in two days at the eighth hour of the night.

I knew immediately that I wouldn't be able to eat or sleep for the next forty-eight hours.

— CHAPTER 68 —

I went through more parchment in two days than I had when Seneca and I wrote the letter to Tiberius urging him to shut down the games. I tried humor. I tried heartfelt. Next, a combination, resorting to the old formula of making her laugh, then making her cry. But nothing seemed to adequately describe my feelings for Flavia.

I realized eventually that my feelings couldn't be scripted. I would have to speak from the heart. Yet even for a trained orator like me, the prospect made me weak in the knees.

I decided not to bring a ring. It was traditional, once a man and woman were engaged for marriage, to have the woman wear a ring on her third finger. Yet there was nothing traditional about this. A Vestal Virgin couldn't wear a ring until she had completed her service, could she? For Flavia, that would be six more years. If she said yes, we would have to keep our engagement a secret until just before Flavia finished her term. Her obligation right now was to be married to Rome.

When I arrived at the designated spot on the night of our meeting, Flavia was already there. I heard her voice as I was picking my way through the trees and underbrush on the banks of the Tiber.

"Theophilus, over here."

I stepped into a small clearing where there were some logs with the sides flattened so they made nice seats. There was a fire pit filled with ashes, and someone had strung a canopy at the side of the clearing to provide shelter from the rain.

I gave Flavia a kiss on both cheeks. "Is this where you and Mansuetus spent time together?"

She nodded. "This place is filled with memories," she said sadly. "I probably should have picked a different spot."

We sat on one of the logs. There was a chill in the night air and we moved next to each other, sharing a blanket Flavia had brought.

"Do you want me to start a fire?" I asked.

"Better not. It might draw too much attention."

The stars were out, and a full moon danced off the ripples of the Tiber. This night and this spot were nearly perfect except that the memories of Mansuetus hung in the air, as tangible and strong as the ancient trees surrounding the clearing. It would feel awkward and disloyal to ask her to marry me *here*. But I thought about my exchange with Seneca, and I knew that this might be my one and only chance.

We talked for a long time first. We were both cautiously optimistic that our role in the conspiracy against Caligula would never be discovered. She told me firsthand about the horror in the theater that day and the way Rubria and others had helped her protect the senators.

"If Chaerea hadn't executed Caesonia and Drusilla the way he did, we might have pulled it off," I said. "Sentiment was beginning to turn our way."

"We unleashed a lot of anger that day," Flavia said. Her voice was melancholy, and I wondered if she was having second thoughts.

"Would you do it again?"

She thought about it for a while. In her eyes I could see the memories darken her thoughts. "For the sake of Mansuetus, yes. But I wouldn't enlist the others. I wouldn't try to restore the Republic."

A million thoughts danced across my mind as we talked. I thought about the first time I had laid eyes on her, my will melting as she discussed the games with Seneca and me. I thought about how my feelings for her would never go away. I remembered that night at the funeral of Mansuetus when our blood mingled and I saw a steely determination harden her face. Her eyes were sadder now, more resigned to the pain of life, but every bit as hauntingly beautiful.

I wanted to change the subject to something more uplifting. "What are you going to do when you finish your service as a Vestal?" I asked.

She had been playing with a twig, and she tossed it into the ashes. She reached over and took one of my hands, a natural and small gesture, but it made my heart race.

"I'm not sure yet. For the last year I've just been hoping to survive. I'd like to travel. The Parthenon in Greece. The pyramids in Egypt. The ruins of the hanging gardens in Babylon. I'd like to see the world. I'd like to taste the wines in the four corners of the empire."

There was an awkward silence as I tried to figure out what to say next. Part of me wanted to tell her those were my dreams too, but the truth was that I had a strong and visceral love for the city of Rome. I had been to the provinces, and they didn't live up to expectations. But I would follow Flavia to the ends of the earth if that's what it took.

I expressed none of those thoughts. Instead, I asked a single question that mattered more to me than anything else. "Alone?"

"I guess. I don't know."

I was so nervous, I shivered in the cold. I was a twelve-year-old schoolboy again, raising my hand for the first time to answer a question posed by Seneca. An uncertain young advocate with buckling knees arguing his first *maiestas* trial. A lowly equestrian meeting a beautiful Vestal.

"We could travel together," I managed. Since the earth didn't swallow me and Flavia didn't bolt away, I decided to continue. "I'm not sure how to say this, and I've actually tried to write it down a hundred ways, so I guess I'll just blurt it out."

I looked at Flavia and she turned to me. I couldn't read her expression and decided to speak before I lost my courage.

"I want to marry you, Flavia. So I'm asking you to be my wife once your time as a Vestal is over."

And there it was. The world's most inelegant proposal. A man who had studied advocacy his entire life, and the one little speech that mattered more to him than any other could have been scripted by a seven-year-old.

"Marry you?" she asked, her eyes wide.

"I've loved you since the first time we met," I admitted. "I never said anything because I knew you were in love with Mansuetus. And maybe I should hold my tongue now. But, Flavia, I would never be able to forgive myself if I didn't at least try. And when Seneca told me a few days ago that you had asked about my intentions—"

"Seneca? What does Seneca have to do with this?"

It took my nervous mind a split second to process what she had just said. She had no idea what I was talking about—she hadn't said anything to Seneca! This was truly catching her off guard. I wanted to strangle my mentor, but that thought could wait.

"Nothing," I said. "Except that sometimes Seneca has this knack for saying profound things. Like marriage should be a matter of the heart and not a contract for social status."

"Seneca said that?"

"Well . . . not really. But he should have."

She smiled, and the look relaxed me.

"I think Seneca is right, or at least he could have been right if he had said that," she said, looking down at the ground in front of her. "But I'll be thirty-nine when my time as a Vestal is over. I knew as a young girl that my life would be spent in service to Rome. That being a Vestal meant I would likely never be a matron of my own family. Childbirth at thirty-nine is no small thing."

"But not impossible," I said quickly. "And what does it matter? There are plenty of young women with whom I could start a family.

But I don't love *them*, Flavia. I love *you*. Even if it were just the two of us, I want to grow old with *you*."

"A lot could happen in six years."

"I've waited eleven. I can wait six more."

She looked at me with those dark-brown eyes, and I wanted to believe she was softening. I gently placed my hand under her chin and leaned in so our lips were just a few inches apart.

"Forget about children and our age and how many years it will be until we are joined as husband and wife, and just answer one question," I said. "Do you love me? Maybe not the same way you loved Mansuetus. But do you love me?"

In response, she leaned in and gave me a kiss. She placed her hand on the back of my head, gently holding me until I relaxed and enjoyed the greatest moment of my life.

When we pulled back, she shivered a little as if overcome with emotion. She wrapped her arms around herself and leaned against my side, and I held her there. In the silence I could tell she was thinking, and my own mind raced with visions of what those thoughts might be.

When she spoke, her voice was barely above a whisper. "I remember the last night I was with him," she said. "Right here. Just the two of us. He said he'd quit fighting as soon as he earned his freedom. We made plans together. On these same logs. We promised each other I would walk out of the House of Vestal on my last day and follow him to his own home, where we would consummate our marriage. All of Rome would talk of nothing else. A Vestal and Rome's most popular gladiator. And now he's gone."

Her voice broke, and I knew that she was crying. I reached over and wiped away a tear.

"You're a good man, Theophilus," she said. "But this is all happening so fast. I need time. Even our kiss felt like some kind of betrayal."

The words tore at my heart. Not because she still loved Mansuetus but because I had been so blinded by my own desires that I hadn't understood that. Maybe she would never love me. How could I compete with a ghost?

"I'll never be able to take his place," I said softly.

"I know," she said. "I'm not asking you to."

I probably should have left it there. But I had already risked everything, and my heart was speaking now. "We could have something different. Special in our own way. Surely Mansuetus would want you happy."

She brushed her tears away and gave me a kiss on the cheek. "I just need time," she said. "Thank you for understanding."

— CHAPTER 69 —

"If you wish to be loved, love."

That *was* Seneca. And it became my mantra for the next six months as I pursued Flavia with renewed zeal. We would meet at night, our locations varied. The banks of the Tiber. Lying on our backs, gazing up at the stars in a meadow on the Esquiline Hill. Huddled next to each other, leaning against the Servian Wall. Staying warm by the fire at my family's estate.

We talked about Mansuetus—his heroism and bravery, his love for the arena, the way we had honored his memory. We shared our own dreams and hopes and frustrations. We talked about religion and our families. I told Flavia about my time in Judea. My regrets at the trial of the Nazarene. She regaled me with stories about the intrigue in the House of Vestal. She admitted that she didn't really remember me from that first meeting—the scared young equestrian anxious to impress one of Rome's famous Vestals. "I am sure you were charming," she offered.

During those months, we both developed a grudging admiration for Claudius as emperor. He was more concerned with running the empire than with his own comfort or popularity. "It's refreshing not to worry about somebody looking down on us from the Palatine Hill when we're in the baths," Flavia said.

Every hour we spent together seemed like seconds to me. My life was divided into segments of days—countdowns until my next evening with Flavia. I *lived* for those moments, and I relived them for days afterward.

There were times—some of my favorite times—when she leaned into me and I pulled her close and we both said nothing. I had learned to relax with her and forget that she was a Vestal. We parted each time with a kiss.

On one of those nights, when I sensed the mood was just right, I asked the question again. This time I told Flavia that I couldn't imagine living without her. Six years of waiting would be a single day if she said yes. But I only wanted her to be happy. And I would understand if she didn't have the same feelings toward me. I held my breath and waited for a response.

She took my hand and looked me in the eye. "What took you so long?" she asked.

I smiled, and she gave me a long kiss. It reminded me of the kiss we had shared six months earlier, but this time it was more relaxed, and neither of us wanted it to end.

"Is that a yes?" I asked.

"It's a yes that I love you, Theophilus. But on a matter as important as marriage, I'll need to check with the gods."

The *gods*? Who cared about the *gods*?

"What if the omens are bad?" I asked.

"If we are meant to be together, the omens won't be bad."

Unless the gods are asleep or the entrails are ambiguous or a thousand other things go wrong, I thought. But how could I argue with a priestess who wanted to check with the gods?

"Just remember, the heart should triumph over the entrails."

"Seneca again?" she asked.

"You should know by now that my quotes are better than Seneca's."

✝

The next day, Flavia sacrificed a fully grown bull. She slit its throat and carved it open. She spread the liver, intestines, and kidneys on the altar. She poured out the incense and the wine and prayed that the gods would be pleased with her sacrifice.

But the gods were not pleased. The liver was damaged. The intestines scarred. She spread them gently with her fingers, flipped them over. She tried to separate them, but the scar tissue held them together. The kidneys and heart were the only organs not damaged.

What did it all mean? Certainly there would be no children. The scarring promised heartache, but the liver was the most disturbing omen of all. She stared at it, trying to reconcile her feelings for Theophilus with this foreboding message.

Until now, she had not realized how much she wanted the gods' approval. She had stayed awake at night thinking about her relationship with Theophilus. It was certainly different from what she had shared with Mansuetus, but that no longer bothered her. Was it better? That was impossible to say.

Theophilus was a kindred spirit. He had a keen mind and a good heart, and she felt her own heart race when he was around. Her love for Mansuetus had been the kind that made her risk everything, putting her life on the line to make love with him. These feelings she had toward Theophilus, this new love, was very different. Not as reckless, but just as real. It felt so natural to be around him, as though they were created for each other. He was tender and focused on her. He *believed* in her. He was the kind of man who would make twenty years of marriage seem too short a time.

Yet it seemed the gods were having none of it. She could break his heart now and tell him the truth about the omens. Or they could marry, and his heart would someday be broken just the same, his death painful and anguished.

Perhaps the gods were wrong. But could she take that chance?

Maybe this was their punishment for conspiring against Caligula, a man who claimed to be a god himself. She and Theophilus were both strong. But were they strong enough to defy the will of the gods?

She pondered these things as the flames flickered up and charred the entrails. She watched the flames grow and engulf the organs, disintegrating each of her offerings.

Who can allay the wrath of the gods? she wondered. The gods were angry, and the entrails of a bull were not enough to satisfy them.

Well, she had her answer. The gods had spoken.

She wished she had never inquired.

CHAPTER 70

SIX YEARS LATER
IN THE SEVENTH YEAR OF THE REIGN OF
TIBERIUS CLAUDIUS CAESAR AUGUSTUS GERMANICUS

For Flavia, at thirty-nine years old, it was a day of bittersweet emotions. She had all but forgotten life apart from being a Vestal. She would miss the others, miss the privileges and responsibilities of her exalted office, and she would desperately miss Rubria, who was growing into a beautiful young woman.

On her last day as a Vestal, she spent as much time as possible with Rubria. The younger Vestal helped Flavia fix her hair in the traditional style worn on such a special day. Using just the point of a spear, Rubria divided Flavia's hair into six braided locks that were then coiled and held in position by ribbons on top of her head. For extra flair, Rubria wove several flowers and sacred plants into the hairstyle.

Late in the afternoon, Flavia put on a hemless white tunic with a band of wool tied in the knot of Hercules around her waist. She had dyed her sandals saffron for the occasion. She and Rubria spent nearly an hour on her makeup.

Finally Rubria held the mirror and Flavia nodded in approval. She put on a flaming-orange veil that covered her head and face, along with a saffron *palla*, a sleeveless flowing cloak worn over her tunic.

Now ready, she spent time in the garden of the House of Vestal, saying good-bye to the other Virgins. There were six of them leaving that evening. In a few weeks, Claudius would select six more.

When Flavia had finished her good-byes, she moved to the portico of the house, where she waited for her groom. She looked out over the Forum and saw the upturned faces of her admirers stretching as far as she could see. It seemed all of Rome waited with her.

Nobody could remember a spectacle like this—a Vestal being taken away in marriage the same day she finished her service. Flavia stood there patiently, surrounded by friends and adoring Roman crowds, and she couldn't keep herself from smiling.

†

It was the happiest day of my life, and there wasn't even a close second. I arrived at the House of Vestal and sang the traditional marriage hymn while a few thousand onlookers and friends joined in.

I climbed the stairs and stood next to Flavia and the other Vestals on the portico as we watched Rubria sacrifice the pig and spread the entrails on the altar. Adrianna came over, pushed the intestines and liver around, and nodded her approval. A few years ago, she and Flavia had ended their feud, and everyone knew the omens would be favorable on this day.

Still, I had a catch in my throat. I remembered the look on Flavia's face when she first told me that the original omens had been bad. She had agonized for months about whether we should even move forward while I carefully built my case. I claimed that the omens had been wrong on so many occasions it made one wonder what the gods were doing. I told her of my own personal experience with the oracle and the prediction of a noble prince. "Is that what you would call Caligula?" I asked. We both recounted other times when the omens had been good and disaster had followed. She admitted that she had sometimes questioned the entire ceremony herself.

But most important, she eventually agreed that I had been right from the very beginning. The heart triumphed over the entrails. The prospect of spending our lives together was worth whatever heartache might come our way.

We decided not to go through life looking over our shoulders. We made a pact not to mention the bad omens again.

When the marriage sacrifice was complete, we signed the contract. I wrote my name with a flourish, and ten friends sealed it with their signet rings. In a traditional wedding ceremony, I would yank the bride away from the arms of her mother. But because Flavia was a Vestal, I pulled her away from the arms of Adrianna, the Vestal matron.

From the portico, we followed three young boys who led a procession from the House of Vestal to my own newly purchased *doma* on the Esquiline Hill. The crowd shouted and sang and straggled behind us. I occasionally turned and tossed nuts, sweetmeats, and sesame cakes. Along the way, whenever we went by a temple, Flavia dropped coins in tribute to the gods. Maybe the omens couldn't be trusted, but it wouldn't hurt to keep the gods appeased.

When we arrived at my house, Flavia spread wool over the doorposts and anointed the door with oil and fat. She turned to me, pulled back her veil for the first time, and I picked her up and carried her over the threshold.

Once inside the atrium, I placed her gently on her feet and handed her a pitcher of water to signify that she would be the giver of life in my household. Next I handed her a torch to represent her role as the matron of the house. I watched as she lit the hearth.

The place immediately warmed with Flavia's presence. The crowd that had squeezed into the atrium behind us cheered. She turned her back to them, blew out the torch, and tossed it over her shoulder. The gods would smile on the man who caught it.

After a lavish banquet that lasted well into the evening, the moment I had been craving finally arrived. Flavia and I retired, alone, to our chambers. We talked about the day's events and our future together. I told her I was ready to step away from the stress of being an advocate in the Roman courts. I had spent years dedicating myself to my clients. I was ready to dedicate myself to my family.

"I want to teach. Maybe set up my own school of rhetoric. I want to spend time with you and travel."

"Where to?" Flavia asked.

"Everywhere. Let's start with Greece and go from there."

She gave me a kiss, and it was clear our travel plans could wait. "You know what I want to do?" Flavia asked.

"Tell me."

"I want to have a family. I want to give you a son."

And so we tried. On a day that couldn't possibly get any better, the omens were the furthest thing from my mind.

PART VIII

THE
APOSTLE

— CHAPTER 71 —

Fifteen-year-old Mansuetus, my only son, dragged his crossbeam down the Appian Way alongside twenty-one of his classmates. I was now fifty-three, but the memories came flooding back as if it were yesterday. It helped that the weather was every bit as dry and miserable as I remembered it from my own childhood. My students and I choked on dust the entire way, and my skin was covered with a thin film of dirt. I kept the pace brisk, much faster than Seneca ever walked, and my students struggled to keep up. Of course, I was the only one not dragging a crossbeam.

Unlike my own class nearly forty years ago, Mansuetus and his schoolmates did not complain. My son was built like me—thin and wiry—but he had his mother's nose and eyes. I kept an eye on him, watching as he grimaced and changed the crossbeam from one side to the other. I smiled to myself because my son was determined to stay a few steps ahead of his classmates, the same way I used to when I had followed so closely behind Seneca. The only difference was that Mansuetus was not self-conscious about it.

After a few hours of walking, we arrived at the same clearing, several miles outside Rome, where Seneca had taught my classmates and me about crucifixion. I had the boys gather around and sit on their beams. I kept glancing down the Appian Way, hoping that Seneca himself would soon appear as he had promised.

I let the boys get a drink of water and waited a few more minutes before I started. I told them about the rebellion of Spartacus and the slaves. How Crassus had crucified the rebels along the Appian Way from this clearing all the way to Rome. How the slaves had cried out for mercy, begging to be thrust through with a spear. I described the crucifixions I had witnessed myself in Judea and at the games in Rome.

Just when I was ready to engage the students in dialogue, I saw Seneca's litter approaching in the distance. I strung out the story a little so he would have time to reach us.

It had been no small feat getting someone as famous as Seneca to address my school of rhetoric. But he owed me.

He had returned from exile during the eighth year of the reign of Claudius. The emperor's notorious fourth wife, Agrippina the Younger, had requested that Seneca tutor her son, Nero. Five years later, Claudius died under suspicious circumstances, shortly after consuming a bowl of mushrooms. Nero became emperor, and Seneca served as his chief adviser.

Early in Nero's reign, Agrippina lost favor with the spoiled young emperor. When she was bludgeoned to death, most Romans suspected that the emperor had ordered it done. But Seneca drafted a letter to the Senate claiming that Agrippina had first conspired against her son and that the men who killed her had saved the emperor's life. Seneca's letter carried the day in the Senate, though public suspicions against Nero never faded.

With Agrippina out of the way, the impulsive young emperor had proven impossible to control. Several months ago he had limited Seneca's own influence by accusing him of embezzlement. Seneca turned to me, even though I hadn't served as an advocate for years. I negotiated a deal that allowed Seneca to retire from public life peacefully with the embezzlement charges dropped. In exchange, he was required to publicly show his support for Nero in the final days prior to leaving office.

"How can I ever repay you?" Seneca had asked.

That's when I first thought of having him address my students on the Appian Way.

When his entourage stopped at the clearing, Mansuetus and his schoolmates were enthralled. They knew somebody of great importance had arrived. The litter opened, Seneca stepped out, and I watched their jaws drop.

The reign of Nero had aged my old mentor noticeably. He was mostly bald with just a few tufts of gray hair over his ears and a ring of hair around the bottom of his head in the back. His teeth had yellowed, and he'd lost so much weight that I worried about his health. His skin was wrinkled and spotted, and excess amounts of it hung on his bones as a reminder that he was not the man he once was. Veins protruded in his forearms and legs and formed spiderwebs on the backs of his bony hands.

He apologized for being late.

I introduced Seneca to the students and told him where we were with the lesson. I asked if he would take it from there.

He began by detailing the horrors of crucifixion as only a man who had witnessed it up close could do. His grim descriptions and hollow eyes drove home the point in a way that I had failed to accomplish. Mansuetus soaked up every word.

When Seneca posed a question—"Was Crassus right to crucify the slaves?"—I was not surprised that Mansuetus was the first to raise his hand.

"I would side with Spartacus and the slaves," he said. He stood ramrod straight and looked Seneca directly in the eye, just as I had taught him. "Why should we allow crucifixions of everyone except Roman citizens? It is either an effective form of punishment or it is not. If it is, Romans should be prepared to reap what we sow."

Seneca's lips formed a bemused grin. I knew what he was thinking. He was seeing me all over again—an idealistic young man, someone who had not yet been marred by evil, someone who saw the world in black-and-white.

"Spartacus and the slaves are the heroes in this story because they found a cause worth dying for," my headstrong son continued.

"The slaves fought for freedom and equality. In Rome today, Master Seneca, we have nothing that inspires us to sacrifice. We live for entertainment and pleasure. We value life for its own sake and prolong it at all costs."

I almost felt sorry for Mansuetus because I knew what was coming next. Nobody could use the Socratic method of teaching more lethally than Seneca. He would ask a few pointed questions that would cut my fifteen-year-old son down to size. It would be a good lesson for the confident young man.

Instead, Seneca just nodded, his expression pained. "You have spoken well," he said. "The real danger in life is not to die a painful and humiliating death while you are young. There is no shame in dying like the slaves did. The shame is dying young yet living to be old. That, my son, is a fate worse than any crucifixion."

CHAPTER 72

Nero loved the theater. In that way, as in so many others, I could see the influence of Seneca in his life. Seneca had encouraged Nero to embrace music and the arts, de-emphasizing the games and their symbolism of military conquest. At Seneca's urging, Nero had built theaters and gymnasiums. Romans followed the emperor's lead and flocked to Greek sports like gymnastics and wrestling. Greek plays dominated the theaters.

But Seneca had created a monster. It was one thing to embrace music and theater. It was another to obsess over being the star.

Nero first performed on the lyre during the Juvenalia games, instituted in the fifth year of his reign to celebrate the first shaving of the emperor's beard. Ever the center of attention, the young Caesar collected what he shaved and placed it in a golden container that was offered as a sacrifice to Jupiter.

At age twenty-two, Nero had competed as a *citharede*, playing the lyre and singing a ballad. When he finished his song, he knelt next to the other contestants in front of the judges. Naturally, he was awarded the wreath of victory. The crowd erupted into raucous applause.

From that moment, Nero focused more on his career as a *citharede* than he did on running the empire. He hired voice coaches and practiced singing every day. He seldom addressed a large gathering without an intermediary who would shout out his speech so that Nero could preserve his voice. When he got angry and erupted into a rage, Seneca would calm him down by reminding him that he might hurt his voice if he wasn't careful.

"Nero is a performer at heart," Seneca told me. "An emperor in an artist's body. For Nero, the empire is a stage, and he has the leading role."

Flavia and I had never seen Nero perform and had no desire to do so. But on the tenth day of October in the ninth year of his reign, we found ourselves among the patrons sitting in a glistening new nine-thousand-seat theater, waiting for the twenty-five-year-old emperor to take the stage.

Part of the deal I had struck for Seneca required that my mentor attend tonight's performance and lavish praise on the emperor. Even for a narcissistic man like Nero, the requirement seemed strange. I was suspicious of what the emperor had in mind.

I stole a glance at Flavia as we waited for the featured performance. At fifty-five, my wife still had the graceful lines and piercing eyes that had mesmerized me thirty years ago. Her high cheekbones gave her an aura of sophistication and classic beauty. Tonight her hair was braided in a way that made me remember her days as a Vestal and my starry-eyed dreams of how we might one day be married.

Her face was not without wrinkles, and men no longer turned and stared when she passed. But her outer beauty was still the equal of women half her age, and nobody could come close to the beauty of her soul.

"He reminds me so much of Caligula," Flavia said, leaning toward me as Nero took the stage. "Young. Spoiled. Lustful."

"Who do you think is worse?" I asked. To me it seemed like a choice between the beasts and the cross.

"I knew Caligula better, so I hated him more," Flavia said grimly. "But I think Nero is actually more dangerous."

"Especially with Seneca out of the way."

Flavia shrugged. She was no great supporter of Seneca since his defense of Nero after Agrippina's death. "I don't see how it could get any worse."

Just wait, I wanted to say. But I had learned to give Flavia the last word.

On this night, Nero wore a long, flowing white robe patterned after the garb of his patron god, Apollo. He carried his lyre to the stage, and the place grew quiet with anticipation.

Unlike Caligula, Nero had the visage of a god. His jaw was chiseled, his hair curly and blond. His steel-blue eyes danced with mischief. He worked out in the gymnasium every day, and his body was lean and muscled. Those who flattered the emperor by comparing his looks to Apollo were not far off.

I had heard that Nero wrote his own poetry. On this night, he sang an original ballad that he claimed he had composed. His voice carried well, and though I hated the man as an emperor, his onstage presence was actually quite impressive. To everyone, that is, except Flavia.

"That's horrid," she whispered. "He never hits the right notes. Look at the way he twists his face in an effort to express feeling." She frowned and shook her head.

She had a point about the contorted facial expressions. Unlike the best *citharedes*, who allowed the music to carry the emotion, Nero felt obliged to help it along by squeezing his eyes shut as if in ecstasy or overplaying an expression to show his emotion.

He sang for thirty minutes and seemed to have the entire theater enthralled. His ballad ended with the suicide of its main character, and somehow Nero coaxed a tear that coincided with the last note. When he was done, the crowd sat reverently in stunned silence for a moment, reflecting on the sad nature of the song.

And then I was treated for the first time to the delirious praise of Nero's famed Augustiani, a group of hundreds of freedmen paid to praise the emperor for his performances. They stood and cheered wildly, and within seconds the rest of the theater joined them. Nero acted pleasantly surprised by the warm reception and stood next to his lyre, bowing slightly at the waist. The cheers from his claque grew louder, and they began chanting Nero's name.

Flavia and I stood as well and brought our hands together in what appeared to be clapping. She looked at me and rolled her eyes. I returned a knowing smile.

Five minutes turned into ten and then nearly fifteen before the crowd finally tired. Just as the noise was beginning to die down, one of the claque members raised his voice and shouted loud enough to be heard over the continued clapping.

"Beautiful Caesar, Apollo, Augustus, another Pythian! By yourself we swear, Caesar; no one can defeat you!"

When he finished shouting, the crowd roared again, and Nero patiently absorbed their praise and adoration. Even the seasoned veterans of the Praetorian Guard joined in the emotional response. Seneca was right there with them, in the front row, cheering enthusiastically.

"You would think that would be beneath the dignity of a man like Seneca," Flavia said into my ear.

"You just don't appreciate talent," I said.

She elbowed me in the ribs as the crowd continued to cheer.

†

The real theater began an hour later. Professional actors performed Greek tragedies, most of which were familiar to the audience. But tonight, they were just the warm-up. The last tragedy starred Nero himself. It was the first time he had ever donned the mask of an actor and performed in public.

For his inaugural performance, Nero had chosen the tale of Orestes, one of the best-known and most complex Greek tragedies. Nero appeared in the costume of the Greek prince, but his mask was a duplicate of Nero's own handsome features.

For the next hour, surrounded by a cast of professional actors, Nero played the title role of Orestes, the legendary Greek hero who slew his own mother to avenge the death of his father and to save his kingdom. After the slaying, Orestes was pursued by the Greek Furies, who were spurred on by the ghost of his mother. Orestes then became the defendant in a famous Greek murder trial at Athens and was acquitted by a single vote from a divided jury, the vote of the goddess Athena. The homicide was justifiable, the jury ruled, because Orestes had to save the kingdom from the treachery of his own mother.

Flavia and I watched in stunned silence and understood immediately what Nero was doing. In the court of public opinion, this was Nero's defense for his murder of Agrippina.

The events of her death were well chronicled. When Nero became resentful of Agrippina's attempts to control him, he had hatched a scheme that would have ended her life by shipwreck. But she survived the near-fatal experience at sea, so Nero dispatched his soldiers to club her to death. When they appeared where she was staying, Agrippina reportedly bared her womb and told them to strike her there because her womb should be cursed for giving birth to a creature as vile as Nero.

Most people, including me, believed that Seneca had been no part of this plot. But he had helped Nero rationalize Agrippina's death to the Senate. He had concocted a story about a conspiracy against Nero headed by Agrippina, and the Senate had passed resolutions in celebration of the fact that the emperor's life had been spared.

Now, five years later, Nero's first public performance as an actor had a nefarious subscript. *Yes, I killed my mother. But it was justifiable matricide, and Rome should thank me for it.*

In the play, just as Orestes was preparing to slay his mother, she bared her breast and told her son to strike her there because she regretted that she had ever nourished him. A bare breast, a bare womb—everyone in the theater made the connection.

"I can't believe Nero has the audacity to do this," Flavia whispered.

When the play was finished, the Augustiani burst into wild applause, and the patrons joined them for a second time. Flavia and I stood, but we both refused to clap.

Nero ripped off his mask and beamed at the cheering crowd. It was said that his mother's death had haunted him and caused him nightmares for years. Perhaps this was his way of exorcising those ghosts.

But the greatest horror of the night was still to come. After the applause had died down, the last word belonged to Seneca. This was the venue we had agreed upon for Seneca to announce his resignation. And now I understood full well why Nero had insisted that Seneca praise his performance as part of it.

After Nero's nauseating debut, I wondered if my mentor would refuse to do his part.

To my disappointment, Seneca took the stage, looking stooped and frail. He sounded embarrassed as he announced his resignation and what a privilege it had been to serve under Nero. He stole a few furtive glances at the emperor and paused as he surveyed the assembled patrons. His gaze landed for a moment on me and Flavia, as if he was apologizing in advance for what he was about to say.

"Take nothing away, Fates," Seneca said, his voice now loud and sure. "Let the duration of all human life be surpassed by the one who is like Apollo in looks and grace and the equal of Apollo in voice and song. He will guarantee an era of prosperity to the weary and break the silence of the laws. Like the morning star as he rises, scattering the stars in flight, like the gleaming sun as he gazes on the world, such a Caesar is now at hand, such a Nero shall Rome now gaze upon. His radiant face blazes with gentle brilliance, and his shapely neck with flowing hair."

This brought another round of wild cheering, which Flavia and I again refused to join. "I'd like to wring his shapely neck," she whispered. "As far as I'm concerned, he and Seneca deserve each other."

✝

On the way home, I found myself defending Seneca. He was to be pitied, I told Flavia, not condemned. He was a victim of his lifelong pursuit of power and luxury. He had bargained away his soul, one compromise at a time, until he no longer controlled his own fate. Heaping praise on the emperor was now part of the deal, his only way out. He hadn't known that Nero would be performing a tragedy about killing his mother.

Flavia was having none of it. "'Take nothing away, Fates,'" she said, her voice mocking and snide. "'Like the morning star, such a Caesar is now at hand. His radiant face blazes with gentle brilliance, and his shapely neck with flowing hair.'"

She was right, of course. And even as we spoke, I promised myself that I would never fall into the same trap as Seneca. Power and influence were empty promises. Like drinking the salt water of the Mediterranean, they only made you thirsty for more.

Flavia grunted her displeasure at the thought of my mentor's performance. "Remember your question about which Caesar was worse?" she asked.

"Yes."

"I've decided Seneca is worse than either of them. Men who know better but still help rulers get away with murder are the most deplorable men of all."

— CHAPTER 73 —

I hadn't heard from Pilate's wife in years, so the letter came as a total surprise. Procula said she was doing well and had finally found peace with the events that had transpired in Judea and afterward in Rome. She had also found forgiveness.

A few months ago I met with a prisoner named Paul of Tarsus, an apostle in the movement called the Way.

After listening to him and learning about the miracles he has performed, I have become convinced of something so astonishing that I hesitate to even write it down. Jesus, the man called Christus, whom Pilate ordered crucified, came back to life three days later! He was seen by hundreds of witnesses, Theophilus, and his Spirit is what allows men like Paul to perform miracles.

I would love to talk to you about this when you have an opportunity, but I also have a request. Paul is in need of his own miracle now. He has been accused of propagating an illegal religion and of sedition against Rome. As a Roman citizen, he has appealed to Caesar.

Paul has been under house arrest for over a year, and he needs an advocate worthy of the cause. Needless to say, my thoughts immediately turned to you. I know that you are no longer actively taking cases, but I was hoping that you might

consider making an exception. I have been baptized into the
Way. I have experienced what I can only describe as a freedom
and forgiveness I have never before known. I am willing to pay
you whatever it takes to retain your services.

Forgive me for being so forward. Please give my respect and
love to Flavia.

Thirty years earlier, I might have said yes. But that was when I dreamed of becoming Rome's greatest advocate. I was wiser now. Flavia and I had fought one emperor and barely escaped with our lives. Now we were spending our energy on the next generation. The students I taught today would be the leaders of Rome tomorrow. It was the only hope we had left.

It had been more than fifteen years since I had tried a major case. Times had changed. Styles had changed. Even my stamina and energy were not what they used to be.

I sat down and began writing my reply. Halfway through, I decided that I should at least discuss it with Flavia first.

✝

At dinner, Flavia had her own objections to Procula's bold request. Followers of this new sect had already created a stir in Rome. Flavia saw them as a threat to Rome's combination of emperor worship and obeisance to the Roman and Greek gods.

"Look at the repercussions from allowing the Jews to worship their own God," she pointed out. "They have never become a part of the Roman culture. I cannot imagine you helping to authorize another religious sect that would further weaken public devotion to the gods we've spent our entire lifetimes serving."

What Flavia said made sense, but Mansuetus had a different take. "What if the man's innocent? And, Mother, are the Roman gods not strong enough to defend themselves?"

Flavia gave me a look as if I had somehow instigated the question. I knew what she was thinking. *He's too much like his father.*

"If he's innocent, he needs an advocate who actually believes in his cause," I said.

"Maybe he just needs somebody who won't let him rot in prison," Mansuetus countered.

"What difference would it make in front of Nero?" Flavia asked, ganging up on our son. "Even the best advocate wouldn't stand a chance in front of the emperor. He's more concerned with practicing for his next *citharede* competition than meting out proper justice."

I nodded. "She's right."

"That's all the more reason you should do it," Mansuetus argued. "The toughest cases need the best advocates. Isn't that what Cicero said? Isn't that what *you* taught me?"

I made a face. How do you explain the real world to a fifteen-year-old?

"I've heard all the stories about what a great advocate you were, but I've never seen you try a case," Mansuetus continued. "What happened to the man who took on a crazed emperor to save a Vestal Virgin's life?"

"That's no way to talk to your father," Flavia said sharply.

"It's all right," I responded. This was exactly what I had taught my son—ask the hard questions. Challenge things. Besides, there was truth in what he was saying.

"I'll talk to your mother about it after dinner," I said. I used my fatherly tone of voice, the one that signaled an end to the conversation.

I could tell from looking at him that Mansuetus still had a hundred other reasons why I should investigate Paul's case. He had been taught respect, so he held his tongue, but the flash in his eyes betrayed his real feelings. He was a young man. He was itching for a battle. He wanted to see me take a stand for the principles I had been teaching him.

He ate the rest of his meal in silence.

Later that night, Flavia and I talked. The idea of representing Paul had started to intrigue me. I will always consider that conversation with Flavia to be one of my greatest oratorical triumphs. Flavia eventually agreed that I should at least meet with Paul and hear his story. I decided I would take Mansuetus with me.

But Flavia also made me promise that I wouldn't take the case if it would be impossible to win. We both knew that once I signed on for a client, I was committed to do whatever it took to prove his innocence. That might mean incurring the wrath of Caesar and putting my family at risk.

"We don't even know this man," Flavia said. "Why should we put our lives on the line for him?"

"Let's just take it one step at a time," I suggested.

I didn't tell her that I was now looking forward to the meeting. Throughout my life, the Fates had not always been good to me. But perhaps here, in a twisted way, they were giving me a chance to right a wrong. If Paul had been a leader of some other religious sect, I never would have given the case a second thought. But he wasn't. He was a leader of the Way, the followers of a man I had helped put on a cross during Passover week thirty years ago.

The Nazarene had haunted my thoughts since that day. He had inspired my best work as an advocate. His trial had exposed a weakness in my moral fiber that still made me ashamed when I thought about it.

I was glad I could pin some of the blame on Mansuetus for suggesting this meeting. But in truth, I was more than a little curious. I was anxious to hear what Paul had to say.

— CHAPTER 74 —

Paul did not look anything like I expected. We met at a house he was renting in the Jewish section of the city. It was near the grain storehouses, east of the Tiber, close to the curve in the river that formed Tiber Island. The walls of the house were thin, and you could hear the cacophony of pedestrians and merchants on the streets outside. Paul's left wrist was chained to a Roman soldier. When I entered, the soldier stood to attention and introduced himself as Sergius Fabius Cossus.

The apostle, as Procula had called him, was about my age or maybe slightly older. He was slump-shouldered and short with a wiry black beard, a balding pate, and small eyes that frequently squinted. He seemed to have boundless energy, though he stood with difficulty, straightening slowly, as if he had a bad back. He walked with a noticeable limp and couldn't seem to raise his right arm much above his shoulder.

Ours was not a private meeting. Mansuetus had tagged along with me. Sergius was, of course, chained to Paul, though the soldier didn't act like the stiff-lipped jailer I had expected. A young, bright-eyed physician named Luke was also in attendance. Procula was there to make the introductions. Rounding out the group was Onesimus, a runaway slave whom Paul introduced as "my brother in Christ." It was an eclectic bunch.

I felt uncomfortable discussing Paul's legal problems in front of Sergius, but Paul didn't seem to mind. "This man has heard more preaching and praying than anybody in Rome," he said, jangling the chain on his left arm. Sergius smiled as he did so, showing an obvious affinity for his quirky little prisoner. "I've got no secrets from him or my other jailers," Paul added.

In her introduction, Procula had referred to me as one of Rome's greatest advocates. I deflected the praise with a self-effacing comment. I had asked Procula not to tell Paul about my role in the trial of Jesus. On the off chance that I did take Paul's case, I didn't want him to resent me for not stopping the Nazarene's execution. More importantly, I also wanted to test Paul's knowledge of the historical events that I had witnessed firsthand. I knew from talking to Procula that Paul had not been in Jerusalem himself during the critical few days surrounding the death of Jesus. I wanted to know if his sources were accurate.

I began by asking Paul to tell me about the charges against him and the legal proceedings that had taken place in Jerusalem and Caesarea. I reminded him that Sergius was duty bound to report any incriminating conversations to his superiors.

Brevity was not Paul's gift. He took his time and told his life's story from the beginning while Mansuetus took notes on his wax tablet.

Paul had originally persecuted the followers of the Way until his own dramatic conversion. He talked about his subsequent attempts to convert more followers to the Way. He described the various places he had visited and the many people he had told about Jesus' death and supposed resurrection. He spoke fondly of those who had believed. It was quite a tale, filled with healings and jailbreaks and miraculous conversions.

I watched the animated little man and tried to evaluate whether he was telling the truth. In the past I had appraised hundreds of clients this same way. There were mannerisms that betrayed a lie. A furtive glance here or there. Hesitation just before a deception. Details that didn't match up. I noticed none of that with Paul.

The apostle clearly believed everything he said with every fiber of his body. He exuded passion, sometimes jerking his left hand up and drawing a smile from Sergius, whose right hand would go with it. Procula listened with a half grin. She must have sensed that I was already enthralled by the man.

He was definitely persistent, I would give him that. Everywhere he went, he had preached about the Nazarene. He seemed to have a determined group of enemies that followed him from city to city and stirred up trouble. He had been beaten with rods three times, stoned once, whipped with thirty-nine lashes on five separate occasions, and imprisoned so many times I lost count.

"Show him your back," Luke suggested.

Paul shrugged it off. "I think Theophilus gets the picture."

Over the years, I had learned to take my clients' stories with a grain of salt. Especially ones as dramatic as Paul's. In my mind, I discounted most of the miraculous. An earthquake in Philippi when Paul and his friend Silas were in prison, resulting in a jailer who was baptized. A proconsul in Cyprus who became a believer because Paul spoke a curse against a sorcerer and the man was immediately struck blind. A man named Eutychus who had fallen asleep when Paul preached in Troas and fell from a third-story window ledge to his apparent death. Paul allegedly threw himself on the young man, and Eutychus came back to life. "Some say my sermons are a bit long," Paul deadpanned.

The story that intrigued me most was the one Paul told about going to Athens, the very center of Greek culture.

Flavia and I had visited there as well. Paul's description of the place rang true, especially the story about being called to address the Areopagus, where he had been asked to explain his new religion to the city's great philosophers. "I quoted a few of their own philosophers," Paul said. "Men like Epimenides. I told them I would reveal the unknown God they had been worshiping in ignorance."

"How was that received?" I asked.

Paul made a face. "Sometimes, great learning can be a stumbling block when it comes to what is true."

I loved the man's frank style. And I don't think I had ever met anyone more convinced that he had found the truth.

I could tell by the look on my son's face that Mansuetus was totally captivated by these stories. What fifteen-year-old wouldn't be? Time sped by, and I realized that after two hours with the apostle, I still didn't have a solid understanding of the evidence that might be used against him. But the man's plight interested me, and I had an idea.

I had watched Luke as Paul talked. The doctor was levelheaded and focused on details. He had been with Paul through some of his journeys and had interjected names and places during Paul's narration. He seemed to have an indelible memory and a compulsion to get the facts straight. He thought like a Greek, something that would resonate with Nero. Plus, testimony from an independent source would have more credibility.

"To get this appeal heard, you need to grab the emperor's attention," I said. "Written submissions have the same force as oral testimony."

I had to be careful here. I didn't want Paul to think I was committing myself to his case.

"Here's what I'm proposing," I said. "I would like Luke, as an independent witness commissioned by me, to chronicle this entire story. Address it to me, and I'll submit it to those who are investigating the case for Caesar. Start at the beginning, and don't leave anything out. Luke, you need to emphasize that this faith is an outgrowth of the Jewish faith and not something different and therefore illegal. You also need to demonstrate that nobody is trying to start an insurrection against Rome."

"Will Nero read the manuscript?" Paul asked.

"I don't know. And please understand, I'm not committing to your case. Not yet. I'll decide after I have a chance to digest the manuscript."

Luke seemed intrigued by the idea, but Paul looked troubled. When he spoke, he was less animated than before, his face somber, his forehead wrinkled with concern. "I appreciate your advice," he said. "But you must understand, Theophilus, that when I first met with Ananias thirty years ago and the scales fell from my eyes, he left no doubt about my mission. He told me that I would be a chosen instrument to proclaim the name of Jesus to the Gentiles and their kings as well as to the children of Israel. He said I would have to suffer much for the sake of Jesus."

Paul looked around the room, and his eyes landed on the chains that bound him to Sergius. "If this letter is to be read by Caesar, the most important thing is not that the letter proclaims my innocence but that it proclaims the good news about the Messiah."

His words, though noble and heartfelt, heightened my concerns. If Paul was intent on dying for the sake of the Way, he could do that without me. I wanted clients who would listen to my advice and help me set them free.

For the time being, I kept those concerns to myself. We agreed that the manuscript would be a group effort. Mansuetus would work with Paul and Luke in the process. Nothing could better help prepare the young man for a life of advocacy than working on a real case. I promised to read every word of it when they finished.

"Keep in mind this will be read by some very influential people," I said.

"I'll remember," Paul said quickly. He rose and limped to a corner of the room, dragging Sergius with him, and pulled out some fragments of an old papyrus manuscript. "We already have some remnants of an account of the life of Jesus written by a young disciple named John Mark. Perhaps we can start with that."

Before we left, Paul asked whether I would mind if we all prayed. How could I object? I had prayed thousands of times to dozens of Greek and Roman gods. What was one more?

I told Paul it would be fine with me, and he dropped to his knees. Sergius smiled as he went down with him.

Paul's prayer that day made a lasting impression. He talked to his God as if speaking to another man in the same room. He called on the power of the Holy Spirit to help Luke write this testimony that I had requested. And he asked that the Spirit of God would open my eyes and enter my life. That part was awkward. The man needed to work on his social graces.

On the way home, Mansuetus couldn't stop talking about Paul. "You've got to help him," he said.

"You don't know what you're asking," I told my son. "For now, let's just focus on the manuscript. We can decide what to do next after it's completed."

— CHAPTER 75 —

Mansuetus took to the task with a level of enthusiasm I had not anticipated. His own studies suffered because he spent so much time with Paul and his companions. When he was with them, my son took notes, much as he did when I taught him, on wax tablets. He would bring his notes home, read them to me, smooth over the wax, and get ready for the next day. He somehow talked me into buying stacks of parchment sheets for Luke's final manuscript even though papyrus would have been much cheaper.

I saw in his eyes the spark of idealism that had fueled my younger years. For me, it had been about restoring the Republic. For Mansuetus, it was this new movement called the Way, with its talk of a different kind of Kingdom. I hurt for my son, knowing that his dreams, like mine, would one day shipwreck on the hard, jagged rocks of Roman reality.

After two months of making notes and rewriting drafts on papyrus, Luke was finally ready to fill the parchment with the stories of Jesus and of Paul. Mansuetus couldn't wait for me to read it.

✝

They were in the final stages of the project when Mansuetus came home one night clearly distressed. He said hardly a word and kept his eyes on his food. Flavia and I exchanged concerned glances.

"What is bothering you?" I asked.

He shrugged. "Nothing."

It was the response of a son who had been trained in Stoicism but could never hide his true feelings.

"I'm your father. You can talk to me."

Mansuetus pushed his food around on his plate without speaking. It pained me to see him so reluctant to share something obviously weighing on his heart. It occurred to me that I might be losing his affections to Paul.

"Paul sent Onesimus home today," Mansuetus eventually said.

"Onesimus the slave?"

"Yes. Paul called him a brother, but he still sent him back."

"Back where?"

"Back to Philemon of Colossae," Mansuetus said. "It doesn't seem right."

"He had to send him back," I said. "The man belongs to Philemon. Paul's in enough trouble as it is."

"How can one man own another?" Mansuetus asked.

The blunt question caught me a little off guard. What kind of ideas was Paul planting in my son's head? We treated our slaves with great respect, paid them a fair wage, and eventually set many of them free. But until they earned their freedom, they belonged to us.

"Fate determines who is born free and who is a servant," I said. "Our job is to play either role well."

"That's not what Paul says. He says in his religion everyone is equal. There is no Jew or Greek or male or female. No slave or free, either."

I noticed Flavia suppressing a smile. She had been trying to tell me that our son was becoming his father, that he had an answer for everything. But on this issue, he shared his mother's views. Flavia's first love had died trying to earn his freedom. For that reason, and a thousand others, she hated the whole notion that one man could own another. She was always pushing me to set more of our slaves free.

Mansuetus looked at me with his big brown eyes to see how I would react. Flavia gave me a subtle twist of the head.

"He says all that, yet still he sends Onesimus home?" I asked.

"Hold on," Mansuetus said. He left the dining room and brought back one of his wax tablets. "Can I read you part of what Paul wrote to Philemon?"

I shrugged. What could it hurt?

"He starts by telling Philemon how much he thanks God for

him and for his faith in Jesus. Then he says this: 'Although in Christ I could be bold and order you to do what you ought to do, yet I prefer to appeal to you on the basis of love. It is as none other than Paul—an old man and now also a prisoner of Christ Jesus—that I appeal to you for my son Onesimus, who became my son while I was in chains. I am sending him—who is my very heart—back to you. Perhaps the reason he was separated from you for a little while was so that you might have him back forever—no longer as a slave, but better than a slave, as a dear brother. So if you consider me a partner, welcome him as you would welcome me.'"

Mansuetus flipped over one piece of wood and continued reading from the next. "'If he has done you any wrong or owes you anything, charge it to me. Confident of your obedience, I write to you, knowing that you will do even more than I ask.'"

He finished and waited for me to respond. But Flavia jumped in first. "I think I'm beginning to like this man," she said.

We reclined there for a long while that night, discussing the way we treated our servants even as they cleared our plates and performed the household chores. I agreed that we had an obligation to treat them fairly and help them earn their freedom. If they did, their children would also be born free.

But my radical son was not satisfied. "Paul treated Onesimus as a brother," Mansuetus argued. "Why should it only be Romans who have rights?"

I reminded myself that I had been the same way at his age. As his instructor, I had spent the last two years teaching him to ask questions and challenge traditional wisdom. I wanted Rome to change, but I wanted it to go back to the days of the Republic. Mansuetus wanted something new and totally different.

I had done my best to teach my son the value of a human soul. Perhaps I had taught him too well.

⟶ CHAPTER 76 ⟵

Nearly three months to the day after my initial meeting with Paul and his companions, the physician Luke came to my house in the early evening and delivered the requested manuscript in two parts. Mansuetus stood by watching, arms behind his back, proud of the role he had played in developing the evidence. As was the custom, Luke had sewn the pieces of parchment together with vegetable fibers, making two long strips that he had rolled into separate scrolls. Each was far longer than I had ever anticipated.

"You did all this in three months?"

"We worked with great urgency, day and night. We had no idea when Paul might go to trial."

We celebrated the accomplishment with a glass of wine, and Luke detailed all the help he had enlisted in compiling the two books. He lauded the assistance of Mansuetus, who had served as a sort of secretary, taking notes as the others talked so that they would have something to reference as they transcribed the final text.

"The first book describes the life of Jesus," Luke explained. "Good portions of it are based on John Mark's work. It will prove that Jesus is the Jewish Messiah and not the founder of some strange new religion.

"The second book is the story of the followers of Jesus. Naturally, I have emphasized Paul's ministry, and I've provided a detailed account of each of his trials. It ends with his imprisonment here in Rome."

I played the gracious host and listened patiently to Luke. I didn't say anything, but I was secretly anxious for him to leave so I could begin reading his masterpiece. When the process had first started, I had expected maybe thirty or forty parchment pages. But as I watched Mansuetus engage with Luke, Paul, and their companions, I knew the manuscript would grow much larger. Still, I had never expected *this*. I didn't have the heart to tell Luke, but I doubted whether Nero or his *assessores* would ever take the time to read something this long.

Nevertheless, it was exactly what *I* needed. There was more than enough here for me to decide whether Paul would become my first client, other than Seneca, in the last fifteen years.

✝

As soon as Luke left, Mansuetus urged me to start reading. I thought he might stand there and look over my shoulder as I did. To get him out of the way, I gave him some assignments for the next day and sequestered myself alone in my study.

Luke was a good writer. He was straightforward, paid attention to detail, and knew how to tell a story. My instincts had been right.

He started off with a formal and confident introduction. To his credit, in the very first sentence he mentioned the things that had been "fulfilled," a reference to Jewish prophecies and a tie-in to the Jewish faith.

> Many have undertaken to draw up an account of the things
> that have been fulfilled among us, just as they were handed
> down to us by those who from the first were eyewitnesses
> and servants of the Word. With this in mind, since I myself
> have carefully investigated everything from the beginning,
> I too decided to write an orderly account for you, Most
> Excellent Theophilus, so that you may know the certainty
> of the things you have been told.

He began his story with a dramatic account of the birth of Jesus. With the precision of a historian, he pinpointed the exact time of the Nazarene's birth.

> In those days Caesar Augustus issued a decree that a census
> should be taken of the entire Roman world. (This was the first
> census that took place while Quirinius was governor of Syria.)

He claimed that Jesus had been born of a virgin and was some kind of child prodigy. He skipped quickly into the Nazarene's three years of ministry. Page after page, Luke told of the teachings and miracles of Jesus. He healed people. He challenged the conventional thinking of the Jewish religious leaders. He spoke of the Kingdom of God.

I was most intrigued by the final pages of the first scroll, where Luke described Jesus' last days. By the time I read that part, it was late at night, and Mansuetus had long since gone to bed. But I couldn't stop reading. It was as if Luke had been there himself.

I read the story of Jesus riding into Jerusalem on a donkey, and I recalled the way Pilate had sneered when he heard the news. I thought about the contrast of my own entrance that week, trailing the great caravan of soldiers. A few pages later, when Luke described Jesus driving out the traders who sold pigeons in the Temple courts, I closed my eyes and could still visualize the scene.

I was pleased to see that Luke included the incident where the Pharisees' spies asked Jesus whether they should pay taxes to Caesar. This was, I knew, a critical part of our defense. Luke quoted the rabbi's question: *"Show me a denarius. Whose image and inscription are on it?"*

I remembered what my friend Nicodemus had told me, how the words actually played on two levels. But Nero wouldn't need to know that. The words of Jesus were plain enough: *"Give back to Caesar what is Caesar's, and to God what is God's."*

I loved what Luke wrote next:

They were unable to trap him in what he had said there in public. And astonished by his answer, they became silent.

It was surreal, reading about these events as if Luke had been standing right next to me. Every detail was correct.

When I got to Luke's description of the night before Jesus' death,

I could no longer sit still. I picked up the scroll and began pacing back and forth, reading the words intently. So much had been going on behind the scenes that I didn't know about. Jesus had predicted his betrayal. That same night, he had prayed to the Jewish God that he could somehow escape his destiny but then had ultimately submitted himself to his fate.

Next came the trial of Jesus.

Then the whole assembly rose and led him off to Pilate. And they began to accuse him, saying, "We have found this man subverting our nation. He opposes payment of taxes to Caesar and claims to be Messiah, a king."

So Pilate asked Jesus, "Are you the king of the Jews?"

"You have said so," Jesus replied.

Then Pilate announced to the chief priests and the crowd, "I find no basis for a charge against this man."

I had to set the scroll down and walk away from it for a few minutes as the events and all the emotions that went with them came flooding back. Pilate's agonizing attempt to declare Christ innocent. Sending Jesus to Herod. Jesus coming back dressed in that ridiculous purple robe, the victim of Herod's insults and torment.

When I picked up the scroll again, I read the words I had been dreading.

But the whole crowd shouted, "Away with this man! Release Barabbas to us!"

Wanting to release Jesus, Pilate appealed to them again. But they kept shouting, "Crucify him! Crucify him!"

Emotions overtook me as I contemplated the enormity of what I had done—and not done. I had suggested the gambit with Barabbas. I shuddered as I recalled the chants of the crowd to crucify

Jesus. Hearing them, I had remained silent instead of urging Pilate to do what we both knew was right.

"What is truth?"

At the time, I knew we had executed an innocent man. But if Luke was right, it was much more than that. If Luke was right, we had crucified the Jewish Messiah and the very Son of God.

I sat down again and read about the crucifixion. The words of Christ echoed back to me, piercing my conscience.

"Father, forgive them, for they do not know what they are doing."

So did the words of those who taunted him.

"He saved others; let him save himself if he is God's Messiah, the chosen one."

I remembered the woman caught in adultery and how she had told me about Jesus defending her. It gave me chills to think about how I had used that same strategy to rescue Flavia.

Luke described the darkness that came over the land at noon and how the Temple curtain was torn in two. He even mentioned the centurion, though he was careful not to name the soldier who cried out to God at the foot of the cross.

By all rights, that's where the first scroll should have ended. From my perspective, that *was* the end of the story. A righteous man unjustly killed. The gods were angry. Even nature protested.

But Luke was not finished. He went on to describe the events I had heard rumors about for the past thirty years. Three days after the Nazarene's crucifixion, his tomb was empty. He came back and walked among his disciples, ate with them, and appeared to numerous witnesses.

Jesus reminded them that he had predicted both his death and his resurrection. *"The Messiah will suffer and rise from the dead on the third day."* He had done exactly what he said he would do.

His followers remembered those words and found a cause worth dying for.

After teaching them, he "left them and was taken up into heaven."

It was all scintillating stuff. But was it true?

Paul and Luke sure seemed to think so.

— CHAPTER 77 —

After a few hours of sleep, I woke up and started on the second scroll. Luke had done a masterful job on the first one, and the story of Jesus was compelling. But I was not being asked to defend Jesus. Paul was the one under house arrest. Book two contained his story.

The second book began right where the first one ended, with Jesus leaving his disciples and the beginning of the movement I knew as the Way. Rather than fading away after Jesus disappeared, his followers began preaching with renewed fervor. I found it astonishing that more and more people in Jerusalem and the surrounding areas continued to believe in this Messiah even after he was gone.

Paul made his first appearance as a man named Saul, a persecutor of the church. Luke then described Paul's vision of Jesus on the road to Damascus. After becoming a follower, Paul changed his name and went from persecutor to preacher. From enemy of the Way to its foremost advocate. By doing so, he became a target. In the following years, he suffered many things at the hands of those who wanted to silence him.

I was troubled by the last several pages of this second manuscript. Paul was a brilliant man, but he had no sense of how to defend himself. He seemed intent on converting anyone who sat in judgment of his case. King Agrippa, for example, who was now serving as the prefect over the entire area of Syria (including Pilate's former territory), seemed insulted by Paul's approach. "Do you think that in such a short time you can persuade me to become a Christian?" he had asked.

Paul's reply was not exactly astute: "Short time or long—I pray to God that not only you but all who are listening to me today may become what I am, except for these chains."

The trial ended when Agrippa declared that Paul had not done anything deserving of death but sent him to Rome anyway. "This man could have been set free if he had not appealed to Caesar."

I could see it coming. I would be standing with Paul in front of Nero, and Paul would tell the arrogant young emperor that he must repent and worship the Jewish Messiah. It seemed that Paul's sole objective was to stir up trouble everywhere he went. He certainly wasn't afraid to suffer for his beliefs. Perhaps he was so enchanted with the Nazarene that he felt called to die a violent and noteworthy death too. But I was not willing to go down with him.

In my younger years, I had been driven by the same kind of fierce idealism. I was willing to die for my principles when Flavia and I took on Caligula. Yet all that had been for naught. We risked our lives, the emperors changed, and now Rome was worse off than before.

Paul could sacrifice his life for the Way if he wanted. But unlike Paul, I had a family now. Flavia and Mansuetus needed me alive.

Still, I couldn't stop my mind from working through the possibilities. Perhaps there was a clever way to establish Paul's innocence. Perhaps Nero had an Achilles' heel the same way that Caligula did years before.

If he did, there was one man who would know. I packed up the parchments and went to visit Seneca.

✝

"You don't know what Nero's doing right now, do you?" Seneca asked.

I shrugged. I had quit trying to keep track of the emperor and the backstabbing politics of the capital.

"He's extending his palace," Seneca said. "He's bringing in gold from the four corners of the empire so that the edifice will be blinding. He's draining a lake at the foot of the Palatine Hill to build a racetrack for the chariots that will be ten times larger than the Circus Maximus. He's planting a forest on his property, fencing it in, and stocking it with wild game so he and his friends can hunt."

Seneca got up from his seat and stoked the fire in the hearth. He moved slowly, his body stiff, his spine curved.

"For Saturnalia, he's preparing the most lavish and spectacular party the Roman Empire has ever seen."

I shuddered at the thought of it. Saturnalia was the annual celebration that took place in December, starting on the shortest day of the year. For six days, society threw off its constraints, roles were reversed, and anything went. Masters were expected to serve dinner to their slaves. Gangs of boys looted homes and assaulted pedestrians. Sexual depravity found new depths.

It all started with a sacrifice at the temple of Saturn followed by a great banquet open to the people of Rome. Schools, courts, and businesses closed. Togas were stuffed away and replaced with a loose Greek garment called a *synthesis*. People started drinking in the morning and partied until late at night. For days, banquets were held all over the city, with a "king" of Saturnalia chosen by lot for each banquet.

Seneca returned slowly to his seat and caught his breath before continuing. "Nero has appointed his friend Tigellinus to be the chief entrepreneur for Saturnalia this year."

There could not have been a more troubling choice. During Caligula's reign, Tigellinus was suspected of having an affair with

Agrippina the Younger and was banished to Greece. At the request of
Agrippina, he was allowed to return to Rome when Claudius became
emperor.

Tigellinus eventually inherited a vast sum of money and invested it
in breeding horses for the chariot races. When Nero became emperor,
he installed Tigellinus as prefect of the Praetorian Guard, making
him the second-most-powerful man in all of Rome. Though he was
old enough to be the emperor's father, he was also the emperor's main
instigator, partying with Nero indiscriminately.

He was known to be both brilliant and ruthless.

"And that's not all. The case of your friend Paul has finally garnered the emperor's attention," Seneca informed me. "It seems the
followers of the Way are refusing to show the emperor proper respect.
Tigellinus has been appointed to prosecute Paul's case and make an
example of him."

Tigellinus had little experience in court and had never studied
under the great rhetoricians. But he had something that all the eloquence in the world could not overcome. He was a fellow rabble-
rouser with Caesar. He could whisper in the emperor's ear at night
as they frequented the brothels together and thought up new ways
to shock Rome's aristocracy.

Paul would become their plaything.

"Are you saying the case has already been decided?"

"I'm saying Paul is fortunate to be a Roman citizen. Beheading is
much quicker than crucifixion."

✝

Paul took the news that I could not represent him with great equa-
nimity. He thanked me for reading every word of the manuscripts
Luke had authored. He also thanked me for allowing Mansuetus to
spend so much time with him. I told him I would make sure the
scrolls made it into Nero's hands.

Before I left, Paul and his friends laid hands on me and closed their eyes while Paul prayed for me. I was more than a little uncomfortable, finding myself in the center of this prayer circle, and I inquisitively opened my eyes to catch a glimpse of the others. They all seemed to be taking this exercise very seriously, their eyes closed tight in concentration, murmuring their agreement with Paul.

Paul thanked his God for sending me and Mansuetus into his life to help him prepare for his trial. He prayed for God's blessing on me and my household. He asked that I might see the message of the cross of Jesus not as foolishness but as the power and wisdom of God.

On the way home, I had to remind myself that there was nothing I could do. Augustus Caesar himself could come back from the dead to represent Paul, and the apostle would still be sentenced to death.

It was one thing to be noble; it was another to be foolhardy. Nero had killed his own mother. He would not hesitate to destroy me if I stood up for a cause that was undermining his authority.

When I told Mansuetus, he took it hard. I tried to explain, but he retreated to his room. For two days, he only spoke to me when I spoke to him first. He never smiled, and he refused to look me in the eye.

I remained troubled but undeterred. I knew I had made the right decision. I would not risk my own neck for a man with a death wish. Still, in quiet moments, doubts nagged. What was it that Seneca had said? *"The real danger is not to die while you are young. The shame is dying young yet living to be old."*

On the third day, I read through Luke's first manuscript a second time. I was drawn to the Nazarene again just as I had been thirty years ago in Jerusalem. I loved his stoicism, his teachings, the way he silenced his critics. Even his shameful death on the cross seemed to have a deeper meaning—a way to somehow appease the wrath of God. When I finished, I knew what I had to do.

On the day before Saturnalia, against my own instincts and Flavia's strong advice, I told Paul I was taking his case.

— CHAPTER 78 —

Flavia stayed away from Rome during the week of Saturnalia, but the reports she heard were horrifying. The center of festivities was the great artificial lake known as the Stagnum Agrippae, which was fed by an aqueduct and flowed into the Tiber through an eight-hundred-foot canal.

The lake was surrounded by woodlands that Nero had stocked for the occasion with exotic birds and animals. Taverns and brothels had been built on the shores, and large torches ringed the lake, giving the water an eerie glow.

For two days, thousands of Romans gorged themselves on food and wine, supplied free of charge by the emperor. Nero, of course, took center stage, floating on a huge luxury raft covered with purple carpet and plush beds. Male and female prostitutes rowed out to the raft day and night so the emperor and his inner circle could entertain all of Rome on their floating stage.

On the third day of Saturnalia, the news was no better. Nero had moved the drunken festivities to the palace, where an elaborate wedding ceremony took place. It would be Nero's third and most controversial marriage.

As a young man, Nero had consented to marry Claudia Octavia, the great-niece of Tiberius and Nero's own stepsister. She was elegant, aristocratic, and loved by the populace. Nero found her boring. While married to Octavia, he fell in love with the beautiful Poppaea Sabina, the wife of one of his friends. At Nero's suggestion, Poppaea obtained a divorce. When she subsequently became pregnant with Nero's child, Nero divorced Octavia and married Poppaea two weeks later. Octavia was banished from Rome, accused of adultery, and forced to commit suicide. The child born to Poppaea died four months after birth.

Nero was still married to Poppaea when he decided to get married again during the Saturnalia festivities. According to eyewitness reports, Tigellinus gave the bride away. Pythagorus, a former slave and a member of Nero's inner circle, was the groom. And the drunken emperor, dressed in a bridal gown and veil, was the glowing bride.

The palace court celebrated the marriage with great enthusiasm, not sure whether the emperor was serious or acting as *Rex Saturnalia*, the king of irony, confounding all of Rome with his practical joke.

For Flavia, word of Nero's latest stunt merely increased her gratitude that she was no longer a part of Rome's inner court. The emperor had systematically attacked every traditional pillar of Roman society. She was relieved when the orgy of Saturnalia finally ended. Perhaps now Nero would get back to governing the empire.

✝

The day after Saturnalia, Flavia journeyed into the city and heard the news that pierced her heart. Rubria was dying. The night before, while tending the eternal flame alone in the temple, she had been assaulted. Her clothes were torn, her face bruised and bloodied. She had apparently hit her head on the marble floor.

The guard outside the temple had been ambushed from behind and rendered unconscious. A trail of blood could be traced from the inner court of the temple out the front door. There were pieces of flesh under Rubria's fingernails. She had fought back.

Flavia was allowed into the House of Vestal, where she stood vigil with the others. Rubria was lying in her bed, attended by the best physicians in the empire, but she wasn't moving. She had marks on her neck where the assailant had tried to choke her. Her left eye was dark and swollen nearly shut. Her lip was swollen; there was dried blood in her hair. She was breathing and her heart was beating, but there were no other signs of life.

Sacrifices were made. Prayers were offered. Omens were consulted.

Whispered suspicions focused on the emperor himself. He and Tigellinus had been overheard in their drunken stupors the night of Rubria's attack, talking about the Vestals to other revelers. It was the one sexual barrier nobody had dared cross during the festivities. It would make a fitting capstone for the last night of Saturnalia. Tigellinus had even proposed a toast.

Nobody in the House of Vestal now felt safe. The matron of the house decided that the Vestals would tend the flame in pairs. More guards were stationed all around the property.

Later that afternoon, the Vestals breathed easier when Rubria's attacker was identified. He turned out to be a servant in the palace, his face bloodied from Rubria's fingernails. Though he loudly proclaimed his innocence, he was executed before dark.

Rubria still had not moved.

✝

Flavia stayed next to Rubria's bed for the next two days, praying to the gods that the Vestal would recover. Rubria was the closest thing Flavia would ever have to a daughter. She could still picture Rubria when the girl first came to the House of Vestal, wide-eyed and innocent, enthusiastic and anxious to please. Now she was a beautiful woman, thinner than ever, far more jaded and cynical but still possessing a great love of life.

At least that's the way she had been a few short days ago.

Flavia watched her friend breathe, in and out, her bony chest rising and falling. A few times Flavia thought she heard Rubria mutter something. She leaned close to her friend and watched her lips. "It's me, Rubria. Can you hear me?"

But there was no response. Flavia decided she was just imagining things and leaned back and prayed to the gods again.

Flavia slept in short stretches and refused to eat anything. At times she wept bitterly and cursed Nero under her breath. Other times she was too drained to shed even a single tear.

She held Rubria's hand. She washed the Vestal's hair. She dipped her finger in water and spread it on Rubria's lips.

By the end of the second day, the doctors were not hopeful. They had drained plenty of blood, but it didn't seem to be helping. They couldn't use their herbal remedies because Rubria couldn't swallow anything. They checked her pulse, watched her shallow breathing, and shook their heads.

How long could somebody go without water? Flavia wondered.

As evening approached on the second day, Flavia talked to the matron of the Vestals. The women agreed it was time to take Rubria to the temple of Aesculapius. It had worked for others. Certainly the god of healing would show mercy to a Vestal Virgin.

— CHAPTER 79 —

The servants from the House of Vestal carried Rubria to the temple of Aesculapius and placed her gently on a pile of blankets near the altar, her arms at her sides. She was wearing her Vestal garments. The matron of the house gave her a kiss on the forehead, and everyone except Flavia left the temple.

Flavia knelt next to her friend, said a prayer, and poured the wine on the altar. She placed the bread cakes on the marble floor and looked up at the statue. "Heal her, O god of eternal life."

Flavia released the snake from the burlap bag and watched as it slithered across Rubria's body, up one arm and shoulder, across her neck, and down the other side. Flavia knew better than to touch the snake. Like the temple, the snake was now sacred. It could go wherever it wished.

She sat down next to Rubria on the cold stone floor and waited. Perhaps she would have a vision of what needed to be done. Perhaps she would fall asleep and learn in a dream.

She placed a hand on Rubria's forehead and felt the heat radiating. It was not a good sign. Rubria's lips were cracked and dehydrated. Her closed eyes sunken. Her body unmoving.

"Heal her, O god of eternal life."

Just a few short weeks ago, Flavia had met with Rubria and talked about life after the House of Vestal. Four more years and Rubria would have her freedom. She had thanked Flavia for being a model, for demonstrating that you could still have a family after serving the state. Rubria already had a few ideas about who the lucky man might be. As Flavia listened, she flashed back to her early years with Theophilus. The romance before their marriage. The first few months of married life. The joy of learning she was pregnant. The miracle of Mansuetus.

Now Rubria might miss all those things and more.

Flavia yawned, her eyes heavy. She fought to stay awake. She needed to pray. She needed to beseech Aesculapius on behalf of her friend. She needed to be watchful so that when the miracle occurred, she would see it. . . .

†

Flavia jumped, startled by the hand on her shoulder. She scooted quickly back and looked up at the three men standing in the shadows. It took her a few seconds to remember where she was.

Next to her, Rubria was still lying there with her eyes closed, her chest moving up and down.

"I'm sorry to startle you," one of the men said, his voice soft.

In the shadows Flavia recognized her son. "What are *you* doing here?"

Mansuetus was standing next to an older man who was mostly bald, his face weathered and angled. He was chained to a Roman soldier. Flavia assumed it was Paul of Tarsus.

"I brought Paul to pray for Rubria," Mansuetus said. "He has the power to heal her, Mother."

"Does anybody know you're here?" Flavia asked sharply, glancing at the door.

"I don't think so," Paul said. "If they did, both Sergius and I would pay with our lives."

He was right, of course. Sergius was risking punishment just as much as Paul.

"I'll explain it all later," Mansuetus said, his voice a mixture of nervousness and excitement. "But we don't have much time. Paul needs to pray and get back to his house."

In Flavia's mind, it wasn't that easy. She stood and thought about the best way to phrase this. They were in the temple of a Roman god. A jealous Roman god with power to heal and power to grant eternal life. They couldn't insult Aesculapius by praying to the Jewish God, or worse yet, a dead Jewish rabbi.

But Paul was already kneeling, taking Sergius with him. He placed his right hand on Rubria's forehead.

"I don't think this is a good idea," Flavia said.

Paul looked up at her with understanding eyes. "Your friend is very ill," he said. "Aesculapius has had his chance. What's your friend's name?"

Flavia was still waking up and struggling to think clearly. She couldn't just kick these men out. If she called for help, Mansuetus would be in trouble along with Paul and his guard. But she had never heard of praying to the Jewish God inside a Roman temple.

"Her name?" Paul asked again.

"Rubria."

That was apparently all he needed. He closed his eyes and began to pray. To Flavia's surprise, Mansuetus knelt down next to him and placed his own hand on Rubria's shoulder.

Paul's voice was sure, his words eloquent. "Heavenly Father, just as you raised Jesus up on the third day, so raise up Rubria, full of life and hope and understanding that she has been raised by your grace. Open the eyes of her heart that she might learn the depth and breadth and height of your love. Strengthen this woman with the power of your Spirit and fill her with all the fullness of God."

Mansuetus followed with a halting prayer of his own. He asked God to demonstrate his power by healing Rubria. Like Paul, he mentioned the name of Jesus and the resurrection that Luke had written about.

Flavia decided she would have a serious talk with her son later.

When they were done, all three visitors said, "Amen." Paul thanked God for the miracle he was about to perform. He traced the figure of a cross on Rubria's forehead and then he stood.

Rubria lay still.

"She will live," Paul said as if he somehow knew this for a fact. "God will raise her up."

He thanked Flavia and prepared to leave.

"Be careful," Flavia said. This was serious; they were violating the laws of Paul's arrest. "And, Mansuetus, we *are* going to talk."

†

Rubria didn't move the entire night. She never sat up. She never moaned or twitched or mumbled even a single word.

But the next day, just before noon, as Flavia was sitting in Rubria's room again, keeping her vigil next to Rubria's bed, the most amazing thing happened.

Rubria opened her eyes.

—— CHAPTER 80 ——

It took Rubria a few days to regain her strength. At first she was disoriented and had a hard time recognizing people. She couldn't remember a thing about what had happened to her. Over time she became more lucid and could follow conversations, though she still had a constant headache. She remembered everything up to the night of the assault but could not recall anything about the attack in the temple that had caused her injuries.

She drank lots of water and began eating small pieces of bread, fruit, and cheese, along with a little bit of honey. She gained strength and took short walks with Flavia. The swelling on her face receded.

Flavia told her about the servant of Nero who had been punished for the assault. But she also whispered her own suspicions. "Nero and Tigellinus were heard talking about violating the Vestals during Saturnalia. Nero hasn't been seen since the last day of the festival, and I think he's trying to let the scratches heal."

Rubria took the news in stride. She tried harder to remember the events of that night but would get frustrated, shake her head, and apologize when she couldn't.

"It's not your fault," Flavia said. "It will come back someday."

Five days after Rubria awoke, her blazing headache finally vanished and her spunkiness returned. Flavia knew it was time for her to leave the House of Vestal. But first she wanted to share one last walk with her friend.

They were in the gardens under the statues when Flavia told Rubria what had happened that night in the temple of Aesculapius.

"Do you think that's why I was healed?" Rubria asked.

"I don't know," Flavia said thoughtfully. "All I know is that when Paul left, I felt different. His faith gave me hope that night. For some reason, it still does. When you opened your eyes, the first thing I thought about was his prayer."

Rubria furrowed her brow, an expression Flavia had seen hundreds of times before. "Everything seems so confusing," she said.

"I know," Flavia said. She reached out and touched her friend's hand. "I'm just grateful that you were healed."

✝

For Mansuetus, defending Paul became a personal crusade. My son was certain that Paul had healed Rubria. He was convinced that we had all now witnessed the same type of miracle Luke had written about in his manuscripts. How could anyone not believe?

Flavia eventually began thinking the same way. She found excuses to spend time at Paul's house, listening to him preach. She became good friends with Procula, who told her about her own experience in the temple of Aesculapius. Flavia started suggesting that we give money to the followers of the Way who were struggling to put food on the table.

Flavia and I had more than a few arguments about how much we could help them. I was already handling Paul's case without charging a fee. What more could she ask?

I was struck by the similarities between Rubria's healing and Procula's. Both had occurred in the temple of Aesculapius when all else had failed. One involved a vision of Jesus; the other involved a prayer to him. In Luke's manuscript, Jesus had not only healed people but had supposedly raised some from the dead.

But questions still lingered. If Paul had healed Rubria, why didn't she awake right after his prayer? And if Jesus was so powerful, why hadn't he saved himself?

For the sake of my client, I tried to remain objective. The man needed an advocate who could convince Nero. To be that person, I would need to regard this new strand of religion with the same skepticism that Nero would bring to the trial. Flavia and Mansuetus could react emotionally. I could not. Not yet.

As I continued to analyze Luke's manuscripts and the merits of our case, I realized we were going to need a lot of witnesses. To prove that the Way was an outgrowth of Judaism and not some new and dangerous religion, I needed an expert who could talk about the Jewish Messiah. Nicodemus, a member of the Sanhedrin, would be ideal for that.

Luke had also described two centurions who became followers of Jesus. The first was the man whose servant Jesus had healed. The second was Quintus, the centurion in charge of Jesus' crucifixion. I wanted the first man to testify that Jesus never told him to leave the Roman army. If Paul was on trial for insurrection as a follower of Jesus, that would be strong testimony. With regard to Quintus, whom I knew from my time in Judea, he could testify about the earthquake and darkness that accompanied the crucifixion of Jesus. Even Nero would have to admit that these were strong signs that the gods had sided with the Nazarene.

I also wanted someone who had personally heard Jesus tell the Jews to pay their provincial taxes. Then there was that jailer in Philippi who could talk about the way Paul and his friend Silas had remained in prison even when they had a chance to escape as a result of another earthquake.

Nero loved the Greeks, and I thought it would be great to have Dionysius, a member of the Areopagus, talk about how he became a follower of Jesus after Paul preached in Athens. The city clerk in Ephesus could provide an affidavit describing how Paul's enemies, not Paul, had stirred up trouble in that city.

I put together a long list of witnesses who could certify the truth of the events recorded in Luke's manuscripts. I wanted as many witnesses as possible who had seen Jesus walking the earth in the days after his crucifixion.

Three months before trial, we met at Paul's house. I had gone over my list with Paul, and he had called in every favor he could to make it happen. His house was packed that night with men who had been part of his ministry or had become followers of Jesus under Paul's preaching in Rome. These men had already agreed to go wherever it took to bring the witnesses back to Rome. There was no time to waste.

We sent Tychicus to Ephesus, Crescens to Galatia, and Titus to Dalmatia. I met John Mark for the first time that night. He was young and healthy, and we sent him to Jerusalem to find witnesses who had seen the risen Christ. Aristarchus was dispatched to Greece and told to look for Dionysius.

It was an amazing sight, each of these men willing to pack up and leave on a moment's notice for the sake of Paul and the cause of the man they called Christus. Paul prayed for each of them before he sent them out.

After they left, the house seemed quiet and deserted. Luke stayed behind because I needed him to verify the manuscripts. Procula, Mansuetus, Flavia, and I were there as well. Sergius, who had switched places with another soldier so he could be there that night, had tears in his eyes.

I thought about how different this was from the *maiestas* trials. Even a good man like Apronius had been abandoned by his colleagues. When the wrath of Caesar came down on someone, his friends ran for the hills.

Not so with Paul. The men who had gone out that night were standing with him, willing to put themselves in harm's way for the sake of the apostle.

"How many do you think will return?" I asked.

"All of them," Paul said.

The little man had no doubt. And nobody in the room would have expected him to say anything different.

CHAPTER 81

Nobody came back.

Even though Paul prayed for a safe and speedy return for his friends, those prayers apparently went unheeded. We received word from John Mark that he was having difficulty persuading witnesses to make the journey with him. He asked if we could delay the trial. We never heard from Crescens, Tychicus, Aristarchus, or Titus.

The day before trial, even Paul conceded that the witnesses were not going to show. "My friends deserted me," he said. It was the only time I saw the dark clouds of doubt color Paul's countenance.

By the next day, any hint of self-pity was gone. Always a bundle of energy, Paul was more upbeat than ever.

He prayed before we left his house. "Lord, give me strength to share the gospel boldly, as I ought to share. Let Nero hear and repent. Today, let your glory shine in the judgment hall of Caesar!"

He finished his prayer and stood. Sergius, still chained to his wrist, rose with him.

"You don't think you should pray that we win?"

I was half-joking, but Paul took the comment seriously. He looked at me with those intense brown eyes, sheltered by his bushy eyebrows. "When I was arrested in Jerusalem, the Lord appeared to me to encourage me. He told me that just as I had been a witness in Jerusalem, I would also preach the Good News in Rome. That was my mission from the very start. To preach the Good News to the Jews and the Gentiles and their kings. What greater earthly king is there than Caesar?"

This was the running debate Paul and I had been having for the last few months, and I knew there would be no point in rehashing it now. Paul saw his trial as an opportunity to preach the gospel in the highest court in the world. But I wanted to win. I tried to convince Paul that he could preach until he died of old age once we gained his freedom. But his reply was always the same. "God is in control. If God gives me a chance to preach to Nero, how can I not take it?"

We had a two-mile walk from Paul's rented house to Caesar's palace, and the apostle spent most of the time leading our small troop in songs of praise. Luke sang along, obliterating the tune. Mansuetus chimed in as well. He only knew about half the songs and even fewer of the notes, but that didn't stop him. Even Sergius sang a little under his breath, and I found it impossible not to be buoyed by the spirit of this small gang, though I was too sophisticated to join in the singing.

We drew a few strange looks along the way, but Paul ignored them. I grinned at the irony of it all. Paul, an incessant singer of praise songs, a man who never met a tune he couldn't butcher, was about to be tried by a man who cared more than anything else about how well he sounded on the lyre.

✝

Flavia spent the morning at the House of Vestal. She saw no other option. Paul's witnesses were nowhere to be found, and he was determined to confront Caesar and tell him to repent. *That* was not going to end well. She loved Paul's tenacity, but on this point she agreed with her husband.

She had waited this long because she struggled mightily with asking Rubria to inject herself into this fight. Flavia recalled her own struggle twenty-seven years earlier when she had decided to free Apronius. She knew then that she was putting her life on the line. The same would be true of Rubria now.

Flavia explained the situation and told Rubria she would leave the decision entirely up to her. "I believe this man healed you by the power of God's Spirit," Flavia said. "And I believe that same Spirit can protect you. But you're the only one who can make this decision, and I'll understand either way."

Rubria was smart enough not to promise anything. They both

knew that the Vestal's shadow had to fall on a condemned prisoner accidentally or he would not be set free. But Rubria did inquire about the timing of the trial and the route Paul might take afterward.

"I'm afraid they'll take him straight to the Forum for beheading," Flavia said. "I sense that Caesar wants to make him an example."

Rubria lifted her eyes to the window, and Flavia knew immediately what she was thinking. It had been drizzling all morning. The sky was full of clouds. If things didn't clear up, there would be no shadows.

"I know," Flavia said. "I've been praying about that."

✝

It felt strange to be in the same enormous judgment hall where I had defended Flavia and Mansuetus so many years ago. The place seemed even larger today because there were no crowds pushing for room and chanting my client's name. Instead, the hall was populated by about fifty Praetorian Guards, a half-dozen prisoners who would have their appeals heard, and another fifty or so members of Caesar's court.

"Impressive," Paul said, looking around.

Like everything else in the palace, Nero had overhauled and upgraded this room since the days of Caligula. The judgment seat was now covered in gold, and ivory statues of former Caesars lined the walls. A golden statue of Nero himself, larger than life, towered over the dais where the emperor would sit. The statue was designed to evoke images of Nero as Apollo, the muscle-bound and handsome god who granted health and life and pulled the sun in a chariot.

Nero entered with the usual fanfare and made quick work of the cases that preceded Paul's. Most of the prisoners either defended themselves or were poorly represented. Nero was more engaged than I thought he would be, asking questions and making snide comments. At the end of each case, after the prisoner or his advocate made the final argument, Nero wasted no time passing judgment.

"Guilty. The prisoner is sentenced to beheading at the Rostra at noon."

Each verdict made me shudder, but Paul seemed to take it all in stride, his intellectual curiosity in full bloom. He would lean over and whisper questions about the legal procedures or the background of the various defendants. At times, it looked like he was silently praying.

At other times, he kept his eyes glued on Nero as if he could somehow gaze into the dark soul of Rome's young ruler.

"Next case!" Nero announced.

Sergius leaned over and unlocked the shackle on Paul's left wrist. Paul rubbed the wrist and smiled.

My stomach was in knots, just as it had been years ago. But Paul seemed to be nothing but excited.

"Rome versus Paul of Tarsus," the clerk called out. Paul rose from his seat, as did I.

"Praise God," he said under his breath.

CHAPTER 82

Tigellinus, Nero's friend who was prosecuting the case, was just a few years younger than me, but his hair was still dark black. From a distance he appeared to be no more than thirty-five or forty. Up close, his true age was betrayed by leathery skin and a large red nose that was the product of too many nights of uncontrolled drinking. He was widely reviled as a man who acted half his age and only held power because of his inherited wealth and carousing friendship with Caesar. He was especially hated by the senatorial class because he was not one of them.

Nobody underestimated the man. Reviled him, yes. And also feared him for his ruthlessness and cunning intellect. But he was not to be taken lightly.

He stood when our case was called and moved next to Paul, putting his arm around the small apostle.

"This man," he said, turning and looking at Paul as they both stood together in front of Caesar, "appears to be harmless. But he is in fact an insidious threat to the empire."

He patted Paul on the back a couple of times, patronizing gestures that were already getting under my skin, and sauntered toward Nero's dais. "I know Your Excellency doesn't like long speeches, so I will get right to the point. Paul of Tarsus is on trial because he wants to start a new religion and because he refuses to worship Your Excellency or any other Roman gods. He's also on trial because of his treasonous teachings."

Tigellinus cast a condescending glance at the apostle. Paul returned the look with a serene stare, more pity than contempt.

"He certainly doesn't look like much," Tigellinus said with a dismissive wave of the hand. "I'll grant Your Excellency that. But in fact he is one of the most dangerous men in Rome. He has thousands of followers, and he teaches them all that there is a power greater than you, Caesar. He speaks of a Kingdom that will defeat yours.

"I could present a thousand witnesses, but I will need only two. The first is Alexander the metalworker from the city of Ephesus. The second is Demas, a follower of the Way who has spent many hours with Paul in Rome. Together, they will tell Your Excellency everything you need to know about this new movement that seeks to undermine your authority. And because I know that Caesar likes to act swiftly, I will keep my case short. There will be plenty of time for Paul's beheading before lunch."

As Tigellinus returned to his seat, he stared at Paul. His statement of the case had surprised me. Several Jewish leaders had made the trip from Jerusalem to testify against my client and this strange new "superstition." But Tigellinus had apparently decided to ignore them. Instead, he would focus mostly on the treason charge.

"Does the advocate for the defense wish to present a brief opening argument?" Nero asked.

"I do."

Nero flipped his wrist, a signal to do so quickly.

I stood and took a deep breath. This matter was too important to rush.

"Before you start," Nero said, "you should know that I have read the testimony submitted in two manuscripts from a witness named Luke. As a student of Greek drama, I must say that I found the good doctor's story highly entertaining."

Nero said it with a half smirk, and I already resented his attitude. He was trying to get a reaction out of me and put me on the defensive. I wouldn't let him knock me off stride.

"As Caesar is well aware, neither Governor Festus nor Governor Felix nor King Agrippa found any fault with my client. It took them years just to settle on the charges. Agrippa said he would have released Paul himself if my client had not appealed to Caesar."

Nero whispered over his shoulder to one of his *assessores*, and I wanted to strangle the man. He had paid perfect attention during Tigellinus's short speech.

I decided to wait until I had his full attention.

He stopped whispering and turned back to me impatiently. "Go on," he said.

"From reading Luke's testimony, Your Excellency knows that these charges originated with the Jewish Sanhedrin in Jerusalem. A great dispute broke out when Paul testified in front of that body that he believed in the resurrection of the dead. That's when they threw him in the barracks. That's what started this entire case."

Nero whispered over his shoulder again, and my blood ran hot. A man's life was at stake! The least he could do was listen.

"Is it a crime in this empire to believe in a resurrection?" I asked.

"What about Augustus? Did not the Romans see the soul of Augustus rise like a spark to the heavens?"

Caesar wasn't listening. I was speaking to the back of his head.

"What about Agrippina?" I asked.

Nero's head jerked around at the mention of his mother. "What *about* Agrippina?" he responded irritably.

"Is she gone forever?" I asked. "Or does her soul live on?" There were reports, I knew, that Nero had been haunted by his mother's tortured soul. "How can my client receive the death penalty for preaching a doctrine about life after death that every Roman knows is true?"

I let the question hang there for a moment, and Nero stared angrily. At least now I had his attention.

"As for treason, nothing could be more ridiculous. I have personally heard the defendant teach the followers of Jesus to obey every authority. They are taught to give to all what is owed them. If they owe taxes, pay taxes. If revenue, then revenue. If respect, then respect. If honor, then honor."

Paul was nodding. It was the one part of his testimony I knew Nero would like.

"Thirty years ago, I served as *assessore* to Pontius Pilate in Judea. I was there, Most Excellent Caesar, for the trial of the man called Jesus of Nazareth. The Jewish leaders accused him of blasphemy and treason, but Pilate knew he had done nothing wrong.

"I knew that too. I had personally heard him preach in the Temple. The Pharisees asked whether the Jews should pay taxes to Tiberius Caesar, and Jesus asked for a coin and then asked them whose image and inscription was on it. When they said Caesar's, Jesus told them, 'So give back to Caesar what is Caesar's, and to God what is God's.'"

I lowered my voice. "On the day of *that* trial, Pilate worried more about keeping the peace than he did about whether the Nazarene was innocent. I stood behind Pilate, just as your own *assessores* are behind you today, and I gave him legal advice on the best way to contain the fury of the Jewish leaders. On that day, we ordered the crucifixion of an innocent man. It was more than thirty years ago, Caesar, but if I close my eyes, I can still see the stoic face of the Nazarene waiting for us to judge him rightly.

"That moment haunts me. If I could live one day over in my life, it would be that day. I allowed fear and ambition and politics to smother justice. And because I believe in the immortality of the soul, I know that I will one day give an accounting for what I did.

"Don't make the same mistake, Your Excellency. Before you stands Paul of Tarsus, an innocent man. Do not allow his blood to stain your own soul."

CHAPTER 83

"Well," Nero said when I had finished, "that was quite the dramatic speech. Perhaps you could join me on the stage sometime, Theophilus."

To me, this was no laughing matter, and I did not grace the emperor with a smile.

"What did you think of the Greeks?" Nero asked Paul affably. "I read about your little presentation at the Areopagus."

Paul stepped forward, but a big guard came over and held out his hand.

"The Greeks worship reason," Paul said. "I preach that we are saved and forgiven by the sacrificial death of Jesus on a Roman cross. To the Greeks, that seemed like foolishness."

"Not just to the Greeks," Nero quipped.

Paul smiled. Unlike me, he looked relaxed. "At first it seemed like foolishness to me as well," he admitted. "That's the power of the gospel. It seems foolish to the intelligent but profound to the simple. It is said in the Jewish prophecies that God will destroy the wisdom of the wise and frustrate the intelligence of the intelligent."

"Yes, yes," Nero said, his voice dismissive. "But I prefer the Greek philosophers to the Jewish prophets."

"'Whoever yields willingly to fate is deemed wise among men,'" Paul said.

"The Stoics?"

"Precisely. May I explain how that kind of fate intervened in my life?"

"I'm not interested in the words of the Stoics. I tend to favor the Epicureans—men who appreciate the role of pleasure and sensuality."

I watched this exchange in amazement—Nero and Paul discussing Greek philosophy as if they were sharing a glass of wine over dinner. I couldn't tell how this impacted our case, but I had to think that Caesar was at least impressed with the breadth of knowledge possessed by the tattered man in front of him.

"'When we say, then, that pleasure is the end and aim, we do not mean the pleasures of the prodigal or the pleasures of sensuality, as we are understood by some through ignorance, prejudice, or willful misrepresentation,'" Paul said, keeping his eyes fixed on Nero. "'By pleasure we mean the absence of trouble in the soul. It is not through an unbroken succession of drinking bouts and revelry, not by sexual lust, nor the enjoyment of a luxurious table that we achieve a pleasant life.'"

Paul stopped for a breath, and I noticed that Nero's face had darkened, his chin propped on his fist.

"Those are the words of Epicurus himself," Paul said. "They have been largely forgotten."

Caesar reached for a sip of wine. Paul took it as a cue to continue.

"There was a time," Paul said, "when I was convinced I ought to do everything possible to oppose the name of Jesus of Nazareth. I had lived my life as a Jewish Pharisee and thought the followers of

Jesus were a threat to the religion of my fathers. On the authority of
the chief priest, I put many of the Lord's people in prison, and when
they were sentenced to death, I cast my vote against them. I was so
obsessed with persecuting them that I hunted them down in foreign
cities."

Nero leaned back as Paul recited his tale, regarding the prisoner
with a mixture of disdain and curiosity.

"On one of those journeys I was going to Damascus with the
authority and commission of the chief priests. About noon, Your
Excellency, I was blinded by a light from heaven brighter than the
sun. I heard a voice saying to me, 'Saul, Saul, why do you persecute
me?'

"I asked who was speaking to me, and I heard an audible response,
Caesar. The voice said, 'I am Jesus, whom you are persecuting. Now
get up and stand on your feet. I have appointed you as a witness
to open the eyes of your own people and the Gentiles so that they
might be delivered from the power of Satan and receive forgiveness
for their sins.'"

Paul was animated now, his enthusiasm contagious. This was
what he had dreamed of doing for the past two years. I could see the
excitement in his eyes.

"From that day forward, I obeyed this vision from heaven. I was
told later by a man named Ananias, a man who prayed over me and
healed my blindness, that I would be a chosen vessel to bear the name
of Jesus to the Jews, the Gentiles, and the Gentile kings. Since that
day, I have preached everywhere that men should repent and turn to
God. And now . . ."

Paul hesitated, overcome by the moment. He choked back his
emotions and continued. "And now God has brought me here to
testify to the most powerful king in the Gentile world about the
truth, great Caesar. The Messiah suffered and died, but on the third
day he rose from the dead. He has brought a message of light to you
and all the Gentiles.

"He has set a day when he will judge the world with justice, and he has given proof of this to everyone by his resurrection from the dead. Now is the day of salvation. Now is the day for all men to repent."

The speech moved me. Paul's passion. His courage. The blunt truth that echoed in the great judgment hall.

But it was also a strategic blunder—the one thing I had warned Paul against. He had challenged the man who would decide his fate. He might as well have wagged his finger at the great emperor and accused him by name. He had claimed that there was a judge greater than Nero who would punish the emperor and everyone else who didn't repent.

Nobody spoke to Nero that way. And you could see the derision in the humorless smirk that curled his lips.

After a few seconds of silence, Nero managed a wry smile. "I noticed from the manuscripts that during one of your trials Governor Festus called you insane. I'm beginning to think the man had a point."

A few servants in Nero's court snickered.

Then Nero leaned forward, and the smile disappeared. His eyes were cold and black. "Do I understand you correctly, Paul of Tarsus? Are you saying that I should repent as if I've somehow wronged your God? Is the prisoner accusing his judge?"

Paul didn't hesitate even for a moment. "Yes, Your Excellency. You, of all men, should indeed repent."

— CHAPTER 84 —

From that moment, I knew the trial was over. Everything else was just for show.

I saw Nero's face tighten to constrain his emotions. At the very least, he wanted to give the appearance of impartiality.

"Does the prosecution wish to call any witnesses?" he asked coldly.

"We would, Your Excellency," Tigellinus said. "Our first witness is Alexander the metalworker."

Paul watched with empathy as Alexander stepped forward and took the oath. Paul apparently recognized him from Ephesus.

Alexander testified about what happened when Paul preached at Ephesus. Over the course of two years, many had become followers of the Nazarene. Paul had preached that gods made by human hands were no gods at all. The great goddess Artemis was discredited, and worship at her temple largely dried up. People lost their jobs. A riot ensued, and Paul was forced to leave the city.

Tigellinus walked over to a box of scrolls and pulled one out. He handed it to Alexander and asked if the witness recognized the papyrus.

"Yes. Recently, during Paul's imprisonment in Rome, he wrote a letter to the believers at Ephesus. Copies were made, and I brought one to Rome."

Paul showed no reaction, but my heart dropped. I knew my client was a prolific writer, and I was certain that this letter wouldn't help our case.

Tigellinus pointed to a spot on the manuscript. "Please read what the defendant wrote here."

Alexander took the scroll and began reading, his voice shaky and uncertain. "'That power is the same as the mighty strength he exerted when he raised Christ from the dead and seated him at his right hand in the heavenly realms, far above all rule and authority, power and dominion, and every name that is invoked, not only in the present age but also in the one to come.'"

He finished and looked up at Tigellinus.

"Do the followers of the Nazarene in Ephesus claim that the name of Jesus, also known as the Christ, is above the name of Caesar?"

Alexander's eyes flitted around. He was tense as a caged bird. "Yes, they do."

"And where did they get that idea?"

"From that letter."

Nero watched dispassionately, but I knew he couldn't allow such doctrines to go unpunished.

When Alexander finished testifying, Nero asked me if I had any questions.

"No, Your Excellency." What was the point in drawing more attention to what Paul had written?

The next witness was more of the same. Demas meekly joined Paul in the center of the floor below Nero's judgment seat. Under questioning from Tigellinus, he testified that he had once been a member of the Way and a disciple of Jesus in Rome. Another scroll was unrolled. This one was a letter to the believers in Rome, written by Paul before his recent imprisonment. It took Tigellinus a few minutes to find the passage for Demas to read, but when he did, the words were deadly.

"'If you declare with your mouth, "Jesus is Lord," and believe in your heart that God raised him from the dead, you will be saved,'" Demas read. "'For it is with your heart that you believe and are justified, and it is with your mouth that you profess your faith and are saved.'"

Everyone in the judgment hall knew the import of the words, but Tigellinus drove them home anyway.

"Are you aware of the custom of Roman generals when they conquer a new province?" he asked Demas.

"Yes, I have heard the stories."

"And what is it that they make the subjects say as a sign of their subjugation to Rome?"

"That Caesar is lord."

"Have you ever heard the defendant teach the followers of the Way?"

"A few times at his house."

"During those times of teaching, have you ever heard him acknowledge that Caesar is lord?"

"No. He taught us that Jesus is Lord."

"And what about Caesar?"

Demas looked down and hesitated.

"What about Caesar?"

"We were taught that one day, at the name of Jesus, every knee in heaven and on earth would bow and acknowledge that Jesus is Lord. That would include Caesar."

Nero's lips were tightly pressed, his eyes narrow. "Is this true?" he asked Paul.

"Perhaps my words are being taken a bit out of context," Paul replied quickly. "God is merciful and long-suffering. He is rich in grace and anxious to forgive. But his grace is manifested through his Son, Jesus. And yes, that is the only name under heaven through which salvation is possible."

Nero snorted. "I've heard enough evidence," he said, standing. His eyes blazed. "I will return with my ruling."

With that, he left in a flurry. His *assessores* and clerks trailed in his wake.

I stepped forward and stood next to my client.

"I have preached the gospel to Nero himself," Paul said, his voice filled with melancholy. "It's in God's hands now."

"The emperor has no power except what is given him from above," I said.

Paul looked sideways at me—the knowing look of a proud mentor. "The words of Jesus," he said.

I nodded. "It's what he said to Pilate in the Praetorium."

"Do you believe it?"

"How could I not? He came back three days later, didn't he?"

Paul grinned. "That's what I've heard," he said.

✝

Flavia stepped outside the judgment hall and looked up. Not a hint of blue sky anywhere. The menacing clouds on the horizon were the darkest of all, and the wind was blowing them directly over Rome.

There would be no sun today. No shadows. No chance that a Vestal Virgin could cross paths with a guilty man and set him free.

It didn't seem like Paul cared. She had heard it in his voice. His prayer that morning had been that God would give him the courage to speak the gospel boldly. His prayer had certainly been answered.

Now, if God would only answer hers.

— CHAPTER 85 —

Nero returned in a foul mood. His jaw was firmly set as he took his seat and the clerk called the session back to order. His *assessores* shuffled into their places behind him, their eyes darting around the judgment hall. I wondered what they had talked about during the break.

I hoped that I would get a chance to give a closing argument before he ruled. I knew that I at least had to try.

"Before the court pronounces judgment, I believe I'm entitled to provide Your Excellency with a closing argument."

Nero scowled at me. "The defendant seemed quite capable of speaking for himself."

"Still, if Caesar pleases, the defendant is not a trained advocate. He is not versed in the intricacies of Roman law that might determine whether he lives or dies."

"Perhaps he should have thought of that before he spoke."

"With respect, Caesar, you asked him questions. It is traditional in cases of this nature—"

"Enough!" Nero barked.

"But, Caesar, there are procedures. Time-honored rights—"

"I said enough!" Nero stood and glowered at me. His guards took a few steps forward. I felt my face flush with anger.

"My *assessores* have informed me of your history of advocacy," Nero said, practically spitting the words out. "You defended Apronius when he heaped vile insults on Tiberius. 'Mere words,' you called them. Later, the body of Caligula was not even cold when you mounted the Rostra and rallied the citizens against the principate. You said that emperors turn Romans into slaves."

Nero's face was tight with rage, the veins in his neck bulging. I stared back at him, unapologetic.

His anger simmered for a moment before he spoke again. "Perhaps you should be the one on trial rather than some deluded Jewish madman with his strange new superstition."

"I have a job to do as an advocate," I said. My voice was steady though my throat was tight, my mouth suddenly dry. "Our Roman system of justice requires that I do it well."

This seemed to appease Nero, if only a little. He relaxed and sat back down, his fierce stare still fixed on me. In that moment he seemed to remember that he was there as a judge, not my adversary.

He took a sip of wine and surveyed the judgment hall, taking in the ostentatious beauty that reflected his unlimited power. There were pearls from Persia lining the walls. Colored marble from Egypt on the floor. Intricately carved columns from Corinth. His own gold statue looming over the defendant. Who could stand up to his power?

He looked at Paul with an expression that worried me. A glint of irony in the small blue eyes. The faintest hint of a smile. A wave of premonition swept over me. Nero was up to something that couldn't possibly be good.

"You claim to believe in a resurrection," he said. His voice was less acerbic and more playful now. "I should give you a chance to prove it at noon."

Paul, for once, had the good sense not to respond.

"Tigellinus has proven his case that you are a danger to Rome. You call on Rome's emperor to repent. You say there is a God greater than the Roman gods. You swear allegiance to another king.

"But maybe Festus had it right. Maybe you are simply out of your mind. Visions of a dead man. Speaking to Caesar as though I were a common slave. You seem to believe that with just a few sentences you can convince me to throw away the power of Rome and become a convert to a religion founded by a Jewish rabbi. What sane man has such thoughts?"

For a moment, the smallest flicker of hope kindled inside me. Was he going to call Paul a madman, punish him for insanity, and set him free? Yet even as Caesar took this unexpected path, my instincts were telling me something more insidious was at play. Nero, the great actor, was playing a part. This trial was a scene in a larger play. But I had no idea what that larger play was about. And why did it matter as long as Paul was ultimately set free?

"You have spoken of a God who shows great mercy and grace," Nero said. He rose and stood to his full height, chest out, chin up, a specimen for the world to admire. "Today you will know that Caesar is the greatest god of all. I find you guilty of sedition. I find you deserving of death. But by the grace and mercy of Caesar, you shall be released."

The ruling stunned the entire judgment hall and took a moment to sink in. A quick glance at my client told me that Paul was troubled by it and wanted to speak. I placed my left hand on his arm to keep him from doing so.

"Thank you, Your Excellency," I said.

"Now get out of my sight before I change my mind," Nero said.

✝

Against my strong advice, Paul proceeded directly to the Forum and preached like he had never preached before. He didn't say a word about the trial, but he still drew quite a crowd. He talked about the crucifixion and resurrection of Jesus. He told the well-worn story of his own conversion on the road to Damascus. If anybody deserved to be punished, Paul said, it was him, the greatest of all sinners. But he had found forgiveness and so could everyone else.

At noon, he was shoved aside by the Roman soldiers, who dragged the condemned prisoners to the Gemonian Stairs for their ceremonial beheadings. I thought this might sober Paul, but it only seemed to invigorate him. He directed his preaching at the prisoners and spoke with a greater sense of urgency. The condemned men just stared at him as if he were some kind of lunatic.

When the executions were over, Paul invited everyone to the Tiber for baptisms. I followed in his wake along with Flavia and Mansuetus. At the dawn of this day, being baptized was the furthest thing from my mind. I was an advocate, not a disciple. But so many things had changed in the last few hours.

Sometime during the trial, though I couldn't say precisely when, the jumbled pieces of my life all came together. I suppose they were there all along, these discrete blocks of evidence from an Advocate far greater than I, building a case I could no longer ignore.

My face-to-face meeting with the Nazarene. His sacrifice. The anguished protest of nature at his death. The growing proof of his resurrection. The supernatural power of his followers.

Paul had made the choice magnificently stark. Who was Lord—Nero or the man called Christ? Whose kingdom would prevail?

As Romans, we were fascinated with death, inventing the cross as the ultimate tool of pain and humiliation. I had hung there once, feeling the full force of the shame.

But now, in this new movement, the cross was an instrument of power. Humiliation became strength. The blood that flowed from the Nazarene created a river of forgiveness and freedom and hope. Death was no longer something to be feared but a passageway to new life.

"What is truth?" Pilate had asked.

His wife, Procula, had discovered the answer. So had my son, Mansuetus, and eventually even Flavia, when the healing power of Jesus had brought a Virgin back from the brink of death.

It was only fitting that I would find the answer in the middle of a trial, through the brave words of a client who cared more about truth than freedom, more about the souls of kings than the chains that bound him.

For whatever reason, in spite of Paul's blunt words about Caesar's need for repentance, the emperor had sided with the apostle. The verdict was wholly unexpected and nothing short of a miracle.

Paul was guilty, yet still he was free.

And now, as I followed him to the banks of the Tiber River, for the first time in my life, so was I.

—— CHAPTER 86 ——

That day, only a few hundred yards from where I had first proposed to Flavia, I walked down the muddy banks of the river, holding her hand. Mansuetus was on Flavia's other side. We had watched Paul baptize more than forty new believers, men and women of every stripe. Each one of them had come out of the water smiling and looking to heaven. They all embraced Paul when they were done.

Paul had intentionally saved us for last. The others watched as one of Rome's storied advocates and a former priestess from the temple of Vesta, along with their son, entered the waters to symbolize our commitment to our new faith. About halfway to Paul, I stepped on an algae-covered rock and slipped, pulling Flavia down with me. We laughed, and the believers cheered. Mansuetus just shook his head.

As the three of us approached Paul, he was beaming like a proud father. Mansuetus went first, which was only fitting, because he had been the first to believe. When he came out of the water, Paul threw his arms around my son and patted him on the back. I saw tears glistening in Flavia's eyes.

"Your son is a good man," Paul said to us.

"I know," Flavia replied. I simply nodded, at a loss for words.

Flavia went next. She stood in front of Paul and grasped his left hand. He placed his right hand on the small of her back.

"Are you willing to die to yourself and follow Jesus of Nazareth as your Savior and Lord?"

The question was not just an academic one. Everyone knew we had escaped Caesar's judgment hall that day by the narrowest of margins.

"I am," Flavia said.

And with that simple declaration, Paul leaned her back under the muddy waters of the Tiber and then raised her out. Water dripped from her long dark hair, and she brushed it out of her eyes. It reminded me of the first time I had seen her, drenched in the blood of a sacrificed bull, her face glistening and beautiful and magnetic. I had loved her from that moment, but I had never loved her more than I did right now.

She walked over to me, and we embraced for a moment before I stepped forward to take my turn.

The entire experience was a blur. Paul asking me if I was ready to put my life on the line. A quick look at Flavia and Mansuetus before I went under. The breathtaking exhilaration of coming out of the water and looking up at the sky. Experiencing the pleasure of God.

By nature, I had never been an emotional man, but I suddenly wanted to shout or cry or raise my arms in celebration. I settled for a slap of the water.

When we were done, the three of us walked out of the river together, climbing up the slippery bank without saying a word.

I didn't know what Flavia and Mansuetus were thinking, but as for me, I went back to that evening I spent with Nicodemus just a few days before the troubling events in Jerusalem. At the time, the words made no sense, but I understood them perfectly now. Back then they were concepts. Today they described my feelings and my life.

"Unless a man was born of water and the Spirit, he could not enter the kingdom of God. . . . What was born of the flesh was flesh, but what was born of the Spirit was spirit."

That day, on the banks of the Tiber, I felt the cool wind on my skin. We were all soaking wet, and there was a bite in the early spring breeze.

"How do you feel?" Flavia asked me.

I thought for a moment before answering. The guilt I had lived with for so long—guilt for my cowardice at the trial of Jesus, guilt for conspiring against Caligula and for killing Lucian, guilt for a thousand other acts of selfishness and greed and deceit—all of it was now gone.

"Forgiven," I finally said. "Forgiven and fully alive."

✝

Six days after our baptisms, Paul and Luke set out for Hispania. Paul had long been determined to share the good news about Jesus with the Celts and Iberians there. It was part of his quest to take the message to the very ends of the earth. Beyond the Roman region of Hispania lay only the sea.

He promised to return, but that didn't make his departure any easier. Mansuetus took it especially hard. He begged me and Flavia for permission to go with Paul, but we all agreed he wasn't yet ready. Besides, Paul told him, he was needed in Rome.

I wanted to see my son complete his training in rhetoric. I had no doubt that somehow God would use him to spread faith in the Nazarene, but not in a remote province like Hispania. I had always dreamed of Mansuetus following in the footsteps of great orators like Cicero right here in Rome. Maybe he and his generation could usher in a return to the values of the Republic based on the principles the Nazarene had taught.

Besides, I needed Mansuetus with me. I wanted us to learn about this new faith together.

As we watched Paul and Luke walk away, I felt a mixture of bemusement and loneliness. Paul's brisk pace, limp and all, made me smile. I imagined that the much-younger Luke would be the one suggesting that they stop for the night. We had offered to help them buy horses, but Paul told us to use the money for the needy believers. He preferred to walk.

I also felt a profound sense of loss. Paul was the unquestioned leader of the believers in our city, and I had spent most of my waking hours the past few days soaking in his wisdom. Now the man who had led me to faith and inspired me to be bold in Nero's court was leaving. I still sensed the Spirit at work in my life and in the lives of the other believers, but that did nothing to dissipate the sadness. The apostle, the man who had performed so many miracles and endured so much suffering, was walking down the road, leaving the rest of us behind.

Dozens of us watched them leave, but Paul never turned to acknowledge us a final time. He had obviously done this before.

Last night he had met with Flavia, Mansuetus, and me privately. He had prayed for us. He had thanked me again for delivering him, as he put it, "out of the mouth of the lion." He had encouraged us to become leaders among the believers in Rome.

And now he was fading into the distance. As he and Luke disappeared, one of the believers broke out in song. It was a song of praise, taught to us by Paul, one he said he had used in the jail at Philippi. I joined in as best I could, though the lump in my throat made it hard to participate.

"Now to him who is able
To do immeasurably more than all we ask or imagine,
According to his power that is at work within us,
To him be glory in the church and in Christ Jesus
Throughout all generations, forever and ever! Amen."

PART IX

THE
WITNESS

TWO MONTHS LATER

— Chapter 87 —

It was one hour before dawn, nearly two months after Paul had departed, when Theophilus put down the reed pen, his eyes bleary and moist, his memoirs finished. The others in the house were fast asleep, and he contemplated his achievement in weary silence. He had ended the memoirs just the way he wanted them to end—with a fitting doxology to the power of God and the glory of Christ.

The idea for the memoirs had come from Paul. An accomplished writer himself, the apostle believed in the power of ink on parchment to inspire people and capture ideas with a permanency that the fleeting rhetoric of speech could never match.

It had taken Theophilus nearly one month less than it had taken Luke for his writings, but then again, writing one's own memoirs required less research. During the day, Theophilus had continued to teach Mansuetus and the other students in his school of rhetoric. But he toiled on his manuscript deep into the night, hunching over the parchment by candlelight as he summoned the memories and emotions of every life-changing event. For eight weeks he ate little and barely slept. On several occasions he was still hard at work when the cock's crow signaled the start of a new day.

There were times when he had called on Flavia, asking her to recount some of the events she had experienced. She had wept when she described the day Mansuetus the gladiator died. She alternated between smoldering rage and lingering shame when she recalled her interactions with Caligula.

But it was more than the urging of Paul that had kept Theophilus awake at night, painstakingly transcribing his life's story. Cicero had done this, and to a certain extent so had Seneca. It was a way of impacting future generations, of passing values from father to son. The soul was immortal, outliving the body. In some ways, a story might live forever as well.

On top of this, Theophilus had a sense of foreboding after Paul's trial, the same dark emotions he had experienced after the assassination of Caligula. He had a premonition that he and the other followers of the Nazarene would soon experience the full brunt of Nero's wrath. For whatever reason, Nero was toying with them. Eventually, like the exotic animals at the games, he would hunt them down.

The day after he finished his writings, Theophilus carefully placed the parchment scrolls in a box. He sealed it with wax and, accompanied by Flavia, carried the box to the temple of Vesta. The Virgins were the custodians of Rome's most important documents, including the wills and memoirs of its most prominent citizens.

They entrusted the memoirs to Rubria and gave her strict instructions. If both Theophilus and Flavia died, the memoirs should be given to Mansuetus and no one else. Mansuetus could decide whether to release part of them, all of them, or none. He could decide, for example, if he wanted it known that his parents had been coconspirators in the assassination of Caligula. As it stood now, those who had opposed Caligula were considered heroes. But Rome was a fickle mistress, and today's heroes were tomorrow's villains.

If Mansuetus did not survive them, Rubria was to release the memoirs to the public. But neither she nor Mansuetus should release them at all until after the death of Seneca, in order to protect the man from any retribution.

Theophilus had prayed that the memoirs might somehow, someday, shine a light on the corruption of the imperial system and foster a movement to restore the Republic. But even if that never occurred, even if the memoirs were read only by Mansuetus, they had been worth every minute he had slaved over them.

In truth, they were written for an audience of one. Perhaps it was just the dark mood that seemed to follow Theophilus after every major victory, but he worried that he might never see Mansuetus grow fully into manhood. It was why he and Flavia had put a letter to their son in the same sealed box, explaining that there were things about their past they had never told him but now wanted him to know. The memoirs contained that story. They had told Mansuetus about his namesake but wanted their son to someday read a firsthand account of the courage and dignity with which Mansuetus the gladiator had faced death.

Theophilus had included the raw details of his own greatest failings as well—his cowardice at the trial of Jesus, his drunken ranting after the trial of Apronius, his plotting to assassinate Caligula.

"Your son needs to see your failures as well as your triumphs," Paul had counseled. "Our weaknesses make room for God's power."

And there were plenty of weaknesses. Theophilus decided to write with brutal honesty, reflecting the one question that Seneca had long ago taught him to ask, the same question that Pilate had so flippantly posed at the trial of Jesus: *What is truth?* The words would lose their power, Theophilus believed, if he strayed from the truth to protect his own reputation.

Flavia had insisted on baring her own soul as well, sometimes over the protests of Theophilus. She had violated her vows as a Vestal yet had ultimately found forgiveness. That had to be part of the story. "The whole truth," she said, "is more powerful than a partial lie."

When they delivered the scrolls, they made Rubria promise to safeguard them with her life. Afterward, they left the temple without speaking. There was something about leaving the completed memoirs with the Vestal that seemed to heighten the danger around them. While writing his story, Theophilus had a sense of invincibility—that God wouldn't let him die without completing this important work. But now that the memoirs were done, he felt a certain vulnerability, the shadow of a seething emperor looming large over every step.

"I feel like I left a piece of my heart in that box," Flavia said.

Theophilus felt the same way. "It's been quite a journey."

"And it's not over yet," Flavia quickly responded. "Not even close."

Theophilus couldn't be so sure. He said nothing.

But as usual, Flavia could read it in his eyes. "You worry too much," she said, moving next to him. He put his arm around her as they walked.

"Maybe," he said unconvincingly.

"'Life, if well lived, is long enough.'"

The quote surprised him. "I thought you didn't like Seneca."

"Despise the man; embrace the teachings."

They had been married more than sixteen years, and she still had a knack for throwing him off-balance.

The words she had quoted were true enough. Seneca knew how to turn a phrase, how to inspire people toward an exemplary life. But it was Flavia, at least in the eyes of her husband, who best knew how to live one.

CHAPTER 88

In the ensuing weeks, Theophilus kept up with developments in Rome by sending one of his servants into the city each day to transcribe relevant portions of the *Acta Diurna*—the official daily news sheets posted by the emperor's clerks in the Forum. The *Acta* contained the latest information about military campaigns, trials, scandals, and Caesar's various exploits. Each report was, of course, personally approved by Nero himself.

Even after editing, the reports made it clear that Nero was becoming increasingly narcissistic and unpredictable.

The emperor had apparently decided that his artistic talents should be shared with a wider audience than just the citizens of Rome. Greece, the cradle of the arts, was calling.

Nero's premier event took place on the stage of a packed theater in Naples, where the audience, spurred on by the wildly cheering Augustiani, lavished praise and a standing ovation on the emperor.

According to the *Acta* reports, an earthquake rocked Naples later that evening, and the theater collapsed. If the earthquake had occurred a few hours earlier, thousands would have died. It was, in the eyes of Nero, a sign of blessing from the gods.

A few months after Caesar returned to Rome, the *Acta* announced his plans to again travel abroad. This time he would visit Alexandria. The trip was scheduled to take place during the first week in June. Nero issued a public proclamation, assuring Roman citizens that things would remain "unchanged and prosperous" while he was away. He would not stay long, and when he returned, there would be a great celebration. He was the father of Rome, and the city would always be first in his heart.

But two days later, Nero canceled the Alexandria trip. The reason had a familiar ring and made Theophilus more suspicious than ever. It was almost as if Nero, like a trained actor improvising from a script, had taken Paul's Damascus Road experience and made it his own.

According to the *Acta*, Nero had been making the rounds of the temples to sacrifice to the gods before he left for Alexandria. It was the start of the Vestalia celebration, and the festival would begin with a simple ceremony at the temple of Vesta, which Nero would grace with his presence.

But when he entered the temple, the hem of his robe caught on something, and he couldn't move. He was immediately seized with trembling and a sense of imminent danger. Without warning, everything went dark.

Blinded, the emperor was carried in a litter back to his palace. His sight was miraculously restored later that night when someone laid hands on him, the same way that Ananias had laid hands on Paul.

For Nero, the experience constituted a kind of spiritual awakening, and his plans abruptly changed. The day after his sight was restored, he issued a decree, carried word for word in the *Acta* and copied by the servants of Theophilus:

> I have seen the sad countenances of our citizens. I have heard their secret complaints at the prospect of my undertaking such a long journey, when they cannot bear even my briefest excursions, accustomed as they are to being cheered in their misfortunes by the sight of the emperor. Therefore, as in private relationships, the closest ties are the strongest, so the people of Rome have the most powerful claims and must be obeyed in their wish to retain me.

The *Acta* praised the emperor for his decision to remain in Rome. The omen from the temple of Vesta could not be ignored. Misfortune lurked on the horizon, and Rome needed him. The emperor would be there for his people.

Theophilus read the breathless account and scoffed at Nero's newfound benevolence toward his people. The emperor was making plans. For some unknown reason, he had concocted a spiritual excuse to remain in the capital city.

†

Nero's pledge to remain in Rome notwithstanding, the emperor and his huge entourage of bodyguards, servants, and magistrates left the stifling city on July 14 and headed to Antium, a coastal city thirty-five miles away. Nero had an elaborate palace there that sprawled along the coast for eight hundred yards, cooled by the westerly winds that skimmed across the surface of the Mediterranean.

Theophilus was one of the few aristocrats who did not make the trip to Rome to watch Caesar leave. Those who did told Theophilus it was quite a procession, at one time stretching all the way from the Via Sacra to the Esquiline Hill.

According to reports, Nero did not plan on staying in Antium long. He would be back in time for the final festivities of the scheduled games honoring Julius Caesar and his patron deity, Venus. Those games would climax with three days of chariot races in the Circus Maximus, and Nero, who never missed a race, would be there.

But first he was scheduled to take the stage at his own personal theater in Antium, dressed in the unbelted tunic of a *citharede*, to perform a ballad in front of many of Rome's most prominent citizens. The *Acta* even mentioned the title of the ballad—"The Sack of Ilium"—a melancholy song about the destruction of Troy by the Greeks during the Trojan War made possible by the shrewd deployment of the Trojan horse.

It was a complex and technical piece, one that would call upon the full range of Nero's acting and vocal abilities. But there seemed to be little doubt, at least among those who wrote for the *Acta*, that Rome's greatest performer would pull it off brilliantly.

—— CHAPTER 89 ——

Theophilus was roused from his sleep by a servant who had in turn been alerted by a runner coming from Rome. It was the middle of the night, and when Theophilus stepped outside, he could see the flames even from his portico two miles outside the city. Fires were common in Rome, but he had never seen one of this magnitude. The flames leapt into the sky as if reaching up to torment the city's gods, sparks flying in every direction. He quickly woke Mansuetus and the household servants. They all grabbed buckets and shovels and together headed to Rome to see if they could be of any help.

On the road they passed thousands of panicked residents running for their lives. Most were frantic, occasionally glancing over their shoulders at the orange flames dancing in the night. Others hysterically searched for loved ones. Some passed with blank-faced stares, trudging forward as if half-dead. They had probably seen all of their possessions go up in flames.

Theophilus pieced together what had happened from the harried stories of those he met on the way. The fire had started near the Circus Maximus, where thousands of slaves had been preparing the stadium for the *Ludi Victoriae Caesaris*. Fed by cooking oils, lamp fuel, hay, straw, and wood, the flames had turned the Circus Maximus into a huge, crackling inferno.

From there, the fire had spread quickly, consuming hundreds of shops and apartment buildings. The narrow streets served as wind tunnels to fan the flames. Huge vats of oil and tar had exploded. Sparks floated on the wind and found new sources of fuel in other sections of the city.

As Theophilus, Mansuetus, and their servants approached the city, the smoke and smell of the fire hit them before the heat. At first it smelled of oil, tar, and paint. But as they grew closer, they could pick up the more putrid odor of the burning flesh of animals and humans. Thick smoke blinded and choked them, but they forged ahead, searching for bands of *vigiles*, the trained firefighters responsible for extinguishing the flames.

Theophilus had expected a more organized firefighting effort, but chaos ruled. Here, a woman ran through the streets carrying a baby, screaming as she looked for her other children. There, an entire family huddled together as buildings collapsed around them. People jumped from the top floors of apartment buildings, crushing bones as they landed in the streets. Theophilus and his servants were able to drag some to safety. Others were consumed by the raging fire.

The flames spread, destroying the great granaries on the lower slopes of the Aventine Hill and the abandoned marketplace on the Caelian Hill. Worried that he and the others would soon be surrounded by the flames, Theophilus ordered his group to retreat to the Forum. There, they joined *vigiles*, slaves, and Praetorian Guards who worked feverishly to empty the great temples of their sacred objects. Surely the fire couldn't spread *here* to the great stone-and-marble center of civilization, to the ancient temples of the Roman gods.

But within hours, the ravaging beast proved them wrong. Theophilus stood next to Mansuetus and watched slack-jawed as Nero's enormous *Domus Transitoria*, a new wing of his palace, became kindling for the hungry blaze. Expensive works of art, precious artifacts from the four corners of the empire, Nero's wardrobe, lyres, and self-aggrandizing statues—everything was devoured in a matter of minutes.

Unstoppable, the flames spread down the Via Sacra, like a great leviathan lapping at the Forum. It rained a million sparks and embers as Theophilus and his team retreated.

The travertine stone became a bed of lava. The temple of Vesta, containing Rome's mother hearth, was itself consumed by flames. The Vestals had already fled their nearby house, carrying as many precious artifacts with them as they could. With a triumphant roar, the fire engulfed the House of Vestal and seemed to feast there for a moment, hungry, looking for its next prey on the Forum.

As Theophilus watched from a safe distance, he heard the *vigiles* lament the loss of so much of Rome's history. Only the most precious artifacts had been removed from the temple in time. So many other sacred objects and virtually every important document in the city of Rome had now been reduced to ashes. There was talk that a few of the most precious documents, like the last wills of Julius Caesar and Augustus Caesar and Nero himself, had been rescued. But Theophilus knew that his own memoirs, which he had obsessed over for the past two months, had likely been consumed in an instant.

The thought made him sick to his stomach, but he had no time to dwell on it.

He and the others worked feverishly with the *vigiles* ahead of the flames, pulling down row after row of buildings, flattening the structures in an effort to starve the fire. At times they worked so close to the fire that the heat singed their hair and eyebrows. To Theophilus, it seemed the flames might melt their faces. Great walls of fire towered over them, forcing them to retreat and set up new lines of defense as sparks were carried by the wind beyond their hasty demolitions.

Sometimes rivers of fire would flow past them to other sections of the city. Buildings behind them would begin to burn and other structures would glow with embers. Someone would shout an order and another hasty retreat would occur. Theophilus and his companions would weave their way out of the labyrinth of flames—exhausted, choking, bewildered, and half-blind from the smoke. Staggering, they would find another line of defense and help to demolish more buildings only to have the fire overtake them again.

Halfway through the night, Theophilus and his team decided they could be more useful helping residents flee ahead of the flames. The elderly, disabled, and sick littered the roads, crying for assistance, desperately trying to avoid being trampled by the mobs. Small children who had been separated from their parents roamed aimlessly, panicked and sobbing. Theophilus, Mansuetus, and their servants saved as many as they could, escorting them to a safe hill nearly a mile outside the city.

As dawn broke, the team regrouped on that same hill to rest. Great regions of the city had been reduced to ashes. In others, billows of smoke wafted to the sky. The fire continued to spread in all directions, devastating everything in its path. The wind seemed to have changed directions, and streams of flames branched out everywhere. Thousands of firefighters continued to demolish great portions of the city in a desperate attempt to head off the flames.

As they surveyed the damage, Theophilus and Mansuetus realized that the regions of the city that housed many followers of the Way were in real danger now. Though they were both exhausted, they rallied their servants and decided to fan out to those areas and let the believers know that they could take temporary residence at the estate of Theophilus, located a safe distance from the flames.

†

For five days and five nights, the fire feasted on Rome. During the days, Theophilus and Mansuetus helped fight the relentless flames and then retreated to their estate each night to feed and care for the refugees. Nero and his entourage returned from Antium and directed that the public buildings in the Campus Martius be thrown open for refugees who had been burned out of their homes. Because so much of Rome's supply of grains and breads had been consumed by the fire, the emperor ordered that new shipments be brought in immediately from the great granaries in the coastal city of Ostia.

After five days, the *vigiles* finally contained the flames with a fire break that held at the foot of the Esquiline Hill. Large areas of the city still smoldered, and small fires broke out here and there, but the ferocity of the blaze had been brought under control. People returned from the fields surrounding Rome to gingerly search for loved ones. The smell of death hovered over the city, mingling with the swirling smoke. Some of the decaying bodies had been nearly consumed by the flames, while others were left to rot in the sun. Grieving mothers wailed as they searched for their children.

But just as everyone began focusing on the massive rebuilding and relief efforts ahead, the fire broke out again. It began in the shops of the Basilica Aemilia on property owned by Tigellinus, Caesar's friend and confidant who had been Theophilus's opponent at the trial of Paul.

As before, the fire spread at an uncontrolled speed toward the

Capitoline Hill. This time Theophilus stayed at his estate outside the city, too exhausted to respond. He learned from those who ventured into the city that temples spared in the first blaze went up in smoke this time around. More sacred objects and gold melted away. Even the ancient temple of Jupiter, the patron god of Rome, was engulfed by fire, its roof collapsing in ruins.

By the time the flames died down after the second wave of fires, all of Rome was on edge. Of the fourteen regions of Rome, three had been totally destroyed and another seven were badly damaged. Only four of the fourteen regions had escaped unscathed.

— CHAPTER 90 —

Theophilus and Flavia opened their home to refugees from the fire, most of whom were followers of the Way. Many had lost family members. The majority had seen the flames wipe out every possession they had ever owned. They slept in every room of the house, and Theophilus stepped over people when he rose in the morning. Some of them he did not recognize—new refugees who had just found this haven the night before.

Everybody's clothes smelled like smoke, mingling with the odor of dozens of unwashed people crammed into tight quarters. During the day, the refugees ventured back into the city to comb through the rubble where they had once lived or to search in vain for family members. Theophilus and Mansuetus often joined them. At night, everyone regathered at the house, where Flavia and the servants rationed out food and found places for people to sleep for a few hours.

The crowd seemed to grow daily because there was fresh water, small portions of grain, and a safe place to sleep. Every piece of clothing Theophilus owned except the tunic on his back was given to the men who took refuge in his house. Flavia's garments adorned the women. It was, she said, the least she could do.

The first few days after the fires were full of grief and mourning. The believers held services for loved ones who didn't survive the blaze. Stories were told about the lives of those who had died too young. Men and women were overcome with sadness and would go for long walks so they could mourn privately.

Marcus stopped by each morning to treat the burn wounds of those who had gotten too close to the flames. The rest of the refugees, along with Theophilus and Mansuetus, coughed and hacked from inhaling so much smoke. Everyone was hungry and anxious about the future.

Yet even in the midst of grief, rays of hope emerged. Children played with each other outside during the day, their squeals and laughter reminding everyone that life would go on. The third day after the fires, a mother found her two children among the hundreds of thousands of refugees at the Campus Martius complex. It was like they had come back from the dead, she said. Two days after that, a pregnant woman gave birth to a healthy child.

Theophilus leaned hard on God. He and the others started each day with prayer and teachings about the faith. They read from the manuscripts Luke had written about the life of Jesus and the journeys of Paul. Sometimes they read portions of Paul's letters to the churches at Rome or Ephesus or Philippi. They discussed what it meant to be followers of Jesus and how his resurrection offered hope for those who had died—hope that the rest of Rome was not experiencing.

In the weeks after the fire, Theophilus noticed a real difference between those who were living at his house and the other bands of refugees staying in the public buildings. He had heard reports of constant fights and the hoarding of scarce resources. On the contrary, though there were still disputes at the house of Theophilus, the words of Jesus and the work of his Spirit pushed everyone toward selflessness. When food was short, there were always volunteers who said they could go without.

A spirit of togetherness and resiliency began to spread. The believers talked about rebuilding the city and how it could be better than before.

In the city itself, the fire brought out the worst in the criminal elements. A vast underground network of thieves spread like a swarm of locusts, looting and stockpiling stolen goods. Bands of delinquents attacked helpless victims, sometimes killing for a plate of food. The estates of some senators, untouched by the fires, were pillaged by gangs who knew that Rome's police force was otherwise occupied.

Nero tried hard to rally his subjects. Each day in the *Acta Diurna*, he published details about his plans to rebuild. He set up a relief fund and required all the provinces to contribute. He enlisted prisoners from Rome and surrounding cities to clear out the rubble. He announced a new style of architecture. When Rome was rebuilt, its streets would be laid out in straight geometric patterns. Streets would be wide, and there would be restrictions on the height of private buildings. Apartment owners would be required to provide courtyards for their properties and erect colonnaded porches to serve as platforms from which fires could be fought. Lower floors of buildings had to be constructed of stone or other material impervious to fire. Water from the city aqueducts would be available at the courtyards of every new apartment building.

Rome would be rebuilt better and more elegant than before. The slums would give way to architectural wonders. Rome would be transformed—a phoenix rising from the ashes. Nero's palace would be the centerpiece, the *Domus Aurea*, a great golden house that would span three hundred acres. Nero would forever be proclaimed as the father of the new Rome.

Perhaps, Theophilus thought, Rome's great fire had sobered the emperor and focused his attention on running the empire. The believers at Theophilus's house made it a point to pray for Nero each day during their worship time. Rome was at a crossroads. Maybe the great fire could melt the emperor's hedonistic heart.

If nothing else, it had already galvanized the nascent group of believers, who began, for the first time, to refer to themselves as Christians.

— CHAPTER 91 —

After three weeks of people crawling all over his house, including at least a dozen who slept in his bedroom, Theophilus needed a respite. His makeshift refugee camp was doing better than most, but it was still a refugee camp. There were people everywhere, unsupervised children running about, broken vases, furniture that couldn't hold up under the constant barrage.

Theophilus had to keep reminding himself that, compared to others, he was blessed just to have a house still standing. Even so, it came as a relief when a messenger arrived from the household of Seneca, requesting a meeting with Theophilus at Seneca's country estate. The messenger said it was urgent.

Theophilus saddled one of the family's three horses and started out just after breakfast. Seneca's estate was a two-hour ride by horseback, and the journey gave Theophilus plenty of time to think.

Things were getting intense in the city. Theophilus had been there two days earlier, and rumors were running rampant. Stories persisted about men who had kept others from fighting the flames. When challenged, these men had allegedly claimed they were under orders to prevent the fire from going out, though they wouldn't reveal the source of their orders. Other citizens claimed they had witnessed men running into structures with torches and setting them on fire.

Much of the city's anger was directed at the emperor. Despite the testimony of thousands who had seen Nero in Antium the night the fire started, a rumor made the rounds that Nero had watched from the rooftop of his palace and played the lyre while Rome burned. Graffiti sprang up all over the unburned sections of the city, labeling Nero as an arsonist and worse. Many citizens believed Nero had ordered the city destroyed in order to create room for his expansive new palace.

When tragedy hits, people need someone to blame. And who could be better than the man in charge?

When Theophilus finally arrived at Seneca's estate, he was struck by how peaceful things seemed. This far removed from the city, there were no refugees. No smell of smoke. No clothes hanging everywhere, drying out in the sun. No shortage of food or space or fresh water.

Seneca greeted Theophilus warmly, and the two men settled into Seneca's office. Theophilus noted with dismay how much his mentor had deteriorated since the last time they were together. Seneca's back was more rounded, his head sticking out from hunched shoulders like a vulture's. His wrinkles had deepened and he had great bags under his eyes.

After they exchanged pleasantries, Seneca told Theophilus that Nero had sent a messenger inquiring whether Seneca might come out of retirement. Nero needed help raising funds to rebuild the city. Seneca had politely demurred. A few days later, Nero had sent a second messenger. This time, Seneca claimed ill health that rendered him incapable of traveling.

"I haven't heard back since," Seneca said.

But that was not the reason he had called Theophilus to his house. There were more urgent matters. Seneca was concerned about the safety of Theophilus and his family.

"According to my sources, Nero has decided that he needs to deflect blame for the fire," Seneca said. "He has found a convenient target in the followers of the Nazarene. Apparently some of the leaders of that movement have given speeches about a God who judges places like Rome with great fire. After Nero's Saturnalia celebrations, those leaders claimed that Rome was like the ancient cities of Sodom and Gomorrah, which were consumed by fire from heaven."

As Seneca spoke, Theophilus felt a dull pain besieging him, a gnawing in the pit of his stomach. Maybe Nero had this fire planned all along. Maybe he had released Paul so he could use that act of mercy as evidence of his impartiality toward followers of the Way. Maybe he was just setting up the Christians to ultimately take the blame.

"Have you heard about such speeches?" Seneca asked.

"Not specifically."

"In any event, I know you are close to the leaders of this new movement. Your defense of Paul was admirable, but your client was more than a little reckless. If Caesar did not despise the followers of the Way before that trial, he surely did after Paul condemned him."

"What is Caesar planning?" Theophilus asked.

"I know that Tigellinus has already arrested thirty followers of the Way and put them on the rack. They've extracted a list of names from those men, and they're prepared to arrest everybody on that list and accuse them of arson." Seneca gave Theophilus a look. The philosopher could convey more with his eyes, weakened and narrowed as they were, than most men could convey with a thousand words. The look forecast what was coming next.

"Your name is on that list, Theophilus."

Theophilus swallowed with some difficulty, trying without success to keep the fear at bay. "What about my family?"

"Flavia and Mansuetus, too."

✝

Thoughts of his family consumed Theophilus on the way home. Nero and Tigellinus were ruthless in the best of times. They would be grotesquely sadistic now. Somehow, Theophilus had to protect his wife and only son.

The rack Seneca had referred to was a rectangular wooden frame slightly raised from the ground with a roller at each end. Tigellinus had invented the device. He would chain the victim's ankles to the roller at one end and his wrists to the roller on the other. Using a handle and ratchet, he would gradually increase the tension on the chains as he interrogated the victim. Eventually, if the victim didn't cooperate, his or her joints would be dislocated and separated. Muscle fibers would be stretched to the point that they could no longer function, finally snapping with a loud pop.

Theophilus doubted he could withstand such torture. But one thing he knew for certain—he would do whatever it took to spare his wife and son that kind of pain.

By the time he returned to his chaotic house, the things that had bothered him just a day earlier now seemed trivial. He gathered the adults who were staying there and put together a list of known and reputed leaders of the Way. He pulled out the epistle that Paul had written to believers in Rome and worked his way down the list of names Paul had mentioned.

Paul had referenced Priscilla and Aquila as coworkers in Christ Jesus. They had already risked their lives for Paul, according to what he wrote. Theophilus knew they needed to be warned. The same was true for Epenetus, a man whom Paul called the first convert to Christ in the province of Asia and who was now living in Rome. Then there were Andronicus and Junia, Jewish believers who had been imprisoned with Paul and were called "outstanding among the apostles." The list went on: Ampliatus, Urbanus, Apelles, whose fidelity to Christ had withstood the test. The entire household of Aristobulus was mentioned, together with many others.

The community of believers in Rome was tight-knit, and many of the names were familiar ones. Theophilus and Flavia added others whom they knew personally, including Procula, the widow of Pilate.

Theophilus drafted a letter, and his servants spent the night making copies. Early the next morning, Theophilus and Flavia sent out volunteers with instructions to locate these leaders and invite them to an important meeting. In the letter, Theophilus said he could not yet share the details but assured each of the leaders that it was a matter of life and death. The believers prayed fervently that the leaders would respond.

━━ CHAPTER 92 ━━

They started arriving the next day at noon. Priscilla arrived first and explained to Theophilus that her husband, Aquila, had been trampled during the first night of the fire. Procula appeared an hour later, and Theophilus was relieved to find out she had survived.

Andronicus and Junia came in the middle of the afternoon and told stories about the early days of what they called the *ecclesia*, the assembling of Christians. They were old and gray, the grandparents of the group, and they brought a calming influence with them. They had physically seen Jesus after his resurrection and had been in Jerusalem to hear the first message preached by Peter the fisherman. They said that people from all over the empire had been there. They described how the disciples of Jesus had begun speaking in strange languages, yet everyone had heard the words in their own tongue. Theophilus watched as Mansuetus soaked in their stories and asked questions throughout the afternoon.

As each new set of leaders arrived, Theophilus pulled them aside and told them what he had learned from Seneca. Everyone agreed that they would meet together later that night to discuss how to proceed.

Not all of the leaders showed up. Some sent explanations that they couldn't leave what they were doing to make the trip. Others had simply disappeared.

Some of the guests brought their own supplies of bread and wine, which Flavia pooled with what she had on hand. By dinner, there were more than two hundred people at the estate. Following directions from Flavia, the servants did their best to feed everyone, parceling out the limited provisions as far as they would go.

After dinner, the leaders crammed into Theophilus's study to debate the next move. They all agreed that they should tell the people what they knew.

Before the meeting of leaders adjourned, Junia had a suggestion. "Our Lord Jesus told us that when we assembled together, we should break bread and share a cup of wine to remember his sacrifice. I think we should do that first."

The others agreed.

Flavia and Theophilus set up the atrium for the occasion, though the crowd overflowed out the front door. Everyone sat as close together as possible while Andronicus, Junia, and Priscilla led the ceremony. They recounted the story of the Passover meal that Jesus had shared with his disciples the night before his crucifixion.

Andronicus held up a loaf of bread. "Jesus broke the bread and gave pieces to his disciples and said to them, 'This is my body given for you; do this in remembrance of me.'"

Andronicus broke the loaf in half and gave one piece to Theophilus and another to Flavia. He broke other loaves and distributed those to the other leaders.

Theophilus joined Priscilla and Procula as they walked around and broke off pieces of the bread for the people sitting on the floor. It was such a simple ceremony, yet there was something profound about the looks on the faces of the Christians as they thought about the broken and bruised body of Jesus.

Many of them cupped the small piece of bread in their hands for a few moments, staring at it as if it were a sacred object. Some were openly crying.

When the leaders had finished distributing the bread, Andronicus took a cup of wine. "When he drank the wine after the Passover meal, Jesus said, 'This cup is the new covenant in my blood, which is poured out for you.'"

Andronicus took a sip of the wine and then nodded at Junia. She stood in front of him and shared a drink from the same cup while others lined up.

Theophilus took his place in line with Flavia and Mansuetus. When it was his turn, he looked into the eyes of Andronicus, a man who had actually seen the risen Christ.

Nero's threat seemed far away. Theophilus's fellow believers were close, and Jesus was even closer.

He watched Flavia close her eyes as she drank, letting it all sink in. Mansuetus looked as serious as Theophilus had ever seen him.

It took three or four cups, but when everyone had finished, Andronicus closed the ceremony with a prayer. Only then did he turn it over to Theophilus so that the host could tell the others about the new danger from the emperor.

Without mentioning Seneca's name, Theophilus explained that several followers of the Way had already been arrested and were prepared to testify falsely against the rest of the believers. Theophilus told everyone that he would help defend them if they were charged.

The entire room was silent for a few minutes after Theophilus finished. Eventually, those who had been believers the longest stood up to share their experiences. The stories were different, but the themes were always the same. Christ had suffered. His disciples had suffered as well. Now it was their turn to stand strong in the faith. A few shared their own stories of being thrown into prison for nothing more than believing in Christ.

"We should not fear an emperor who can only harm our bodies,"

Priscilla said. "We should only fear the one who has authority over both body and soul."

Theophilus gained strength from this time of sharing. He had expected that they would all discuss strategies for protecting themselves and their families. Instead, person after person talked about the will of God and their belief that God could deliver them if he chose to do so. If not, they were prepared to suffer for their faith.

Somebody's remarks brought to mind what Paul had said in his letter. It had been an exhibit in Paul's trial and Theophilus had kept it. He quietly instructed Mansuetus to retrieve the scroll from his study. Within a few minutes, Mansuetus returned.

As host, Theophilus had the last word that night. He told the others about his role in the trial and crucifixion of Jesus. Twice he choked up and had to regain his composure before he continued. Procula was nodding along. Everyone listened intently as Theophilus described the suffering and passion of Jesus.

He ended by taking the scroll that contained a copy of Paul's letter to the believers in Rome and read his favorite passages.

"I consider that our present sufferings are not worth comparing with the glory that will be revealed in us. For the creation waits in eager expectation for the children of God to be revealed. . . .

"What, then, shall we say in response to these things? If God is for us, who can be against us? He who did not spare his own Son, but gave him up for us all—how will he not also, along with him, graciously give us all things? Who will bring any charge against those whom God has chosen? It is God who justifies. Who then is the one who condemns? . . .

"Who shall separate us from the love of Christ? Shall trouble or hardship or persecution or famine or nakedness or danger or sword? . . . No, in all these things we are more than conquerors through him who loved us. For I am convinced that neither death nor life, neither angels nor demons, neither the present nor the future, nor any powers, neither height nor depth, nor anything else in all creation, will be able to separate us from the love of God that is in Christ Jesus our Lord."

When Theophilus finished, there was hardly a dry eye in the room. He closed the scroll and handed it back to Mansuetus. The believers sang a hymn, and because it was late, the other leaders stayed for the night.

— CHAPTER 93 —

They left at three in the morning. Mansuetus made it clear to his father that he was not happy. He saw this as running from danger. "How can you read Paul's words about God's love and protection like you did last night and then send me off to Greece?" he asked.

But for Theophilus, the matter was not open for discussion. He and Flavia were of the same accord. There were those who were called to stay in Rome and face the wrath of Nero. Others were called to spread the faith to the rest of the empire.

It had been a quiet but tearful farewell when Mansuetus said good-bye to his mother. The two of them had always connected at the heart, and at times Theophilus envied that relationship. He was his son's teacher and disciplinarian. His job was to mold Mansuetus into a man. But Flavia had always been much closer. She and Mansuetus had a comfortable and jocular relationship—as much friends in the last few years as mother and son.

Mansuetus had held his mother for a long time while she cried quietly on his shoulder. He tousled her hair, kissed her on the forehead, and told her how much he loved her. She pursed her lips and nodded, unable to speak.

Neither Mansuetus nor Theophilus looked back as they rode away. Theophilus knew it was one of the hardest things his son had ever done.

An hour into the ride, Theophilus began to talk about his time in Greece as a boy. The School of Molon had given him confidence and purpose. He told Mansuetus about the strenuous physical training and the voice exercises by the Aegean Sea.

"Until I married your mother, those were the best days of my life."

For most of the ride, Mansuetus didn't talk much. It was apparently his way of protesting the decision to send him away. But in the last hour or so, he admitted he was nervous about being on his own. He had never known life outside Rome. More important, he didn't know what he would do if anything happened to Theophilus and Flavia.

Theophilus kept his chin up, his tone positive. He told Mansuetus how proud he was of the man he had become. Mansuetus had been the first to embrace the faith that now sustained the entire family. God had given him gifts of leadership and intelligence and passion. Those things would be needed for this new movement of faith. But Mansuetus also needed to be trained in rhetoric, and no place could do it better than the School of Molon.

The two of them arrived at the port of Ostia an hour before dawn. Theophilus gave his son a large portion of the money the family had so carefully saved from his wages as an advocate and then a teacher.

Mansuetus appeared shocked by the amount. "What are you and Mother going to do?" he asked.

"There's more where this came from," Theophilus said casually. How much more, his son didn't need to know. Living in Greece and attending the School of Molon was not cheap. Mansuetus would need almost everything the family had saved.

While father and son waited, watching the workers load the ship on which Mansuetus would sail, Theophilus decided it was time for a story. It was something he had heard a few weeks ago as the Jewish believers talked about the Hebrew Scriptures. It was the story of a famous Hebrew prophet named Elijah and his young protégé, Elisha. Before Elijah was to depart and be taken up to heaven, he asked Elisha a question: "What can I do for you before I am taken?"

Elisha's reply was that he wanted a double portion of Elijah's spirit. Elijah told his young disciple that if he saw Elijah when the old prophet was taken away, a double portion of Elijah's spirit would stay with Elisha.

Theophilus explained how Elisha was indeed there when his mentor was taken up to heaven. Elijah left behind his cloak and Elisha picked it up. He then struck the waters of the Jordan, and the waters parted just as they had with Elijah. And that was only the start of the miracles done by Elisha, miracles that were far greater than those of his mentor.

"God has favored me, Mansuetus," Theophilus said. "He has allowed me to be part of some of the greatest trials in the history of the Roman Empire. But I believe he has greater things in store for you."

He gazed at his son, his heart swelling with pride. Then he took his sleeveless cloak out of his bag and handed it to Mansuetus.

"It gets cold in Rhodes at night," Theophilus said.

Mansuetus took the cloak in his hands, his eyes moistening. Theophilus placed his hand on his son's shoulder and prayed that God would do greater things in his son's life than God had done in his own life.

When Theophilus finished praying, both of them sat in silence for a few moments, watching as the rising sun at their backs shimmered on the sea before them. Theophilus thought about his own hasty departure from Rome nearly forty years earlier and the adventures that had awaited him in Greece. Mansuetus would take that school by storm.

But before his son boarded the ship, there was one more thing Theophilus wanted him to have. He took out the most precious possessions he owned—the copies of the two manuscripts written by Luke—and put them in Mansuetus's bag.

"Guard these with your life," Theophilus said. "And let your life be guarded by the words in these books."

Mansuetus stared at his father, his jaw set. He nodded, and Theophilus knew the manuscripts couldn't be in better hands.

"I love you, Father," Mansuetus said.

"I love you too, Son."

They embraced and fought back the tears. Theophilus watched his son walk onto the ship and had a horrible feeling he would never see him again. He remembered what Luke had written about the baptism of Jesus, how a voice had filled the air after Jesus came up out of the water. *"You are my Son, whom I love; with you I am well pleased."*

That was the way Theophilus felt at that moment. He sat down on a stone and observed the final preparations for the voyage. He watched the ship sail away until it became a dot on the horizon. Then he tied Mansuetus's riderless horse to his own, mounted his tired animal, and wept as he headed home.

── CHAPTER 94 ──

Theophilus took his time on the way home. He stopped at an inn for breakfast and watered the horses. He wasn't anxious to get back to the suffocating chaos that had overtaken his house.

By the time he hit the rolling hills near his estate, it was early afternoon, and the sun was bearing down. The horses' hooves kicked up dust, and Theophilus was parched. The grain fields of the neighboring estates were brown from the late summer heat. He crested a hill and looked out to the horizon, where he could see his estate about a half mile away.

His heart caught in his throat. There was smoke drifting into the sky.

He kicked his horse into a trot and squinted into the distance. Had the place caught fire while he was gone? He rode quickly around a curve and crested another long hill, aghast at the horror that lay before him. White and black smoke billowed from the next hill over—his house and fields seemingly on fire. He unhooked Mansuetus's horse and spurred his own into a gallop—past the statues at the entrance gate and down the long path lined with grapevines, through the orchard and onto his property.

Fire had destroyed everything.

He dismounted a few hundred feet from his home and stepped through fields that were still smoldering, small pockets of flame and smoke scattered everywhere. His sandals burned from the heat.

He ran up to the portico and gaped at the rubble before him. All of the wood from the house had been reduced to ashes and soot. Concrete statues had been tipped over and smashed. Portions of the house were still standing, sturdy stones that had only blackened in the blaze. But the entire roof had caved in, and large sections of his house were nothing more than a smoldering heap of charred remains.

"Flavia!"

No answer.

"Flavia!"

He walked around the exterior, trying not to burn his feet. He screamed his wife's name and the names of the others who had been staying at his house. He found a long pole and tried to move some of the materials in search of charred bodies.

"Flavia!"

He searched frantically, pushing debris aside with the pole. He found no one.

Everything Theophilus owned had gone up in flames. His books. His clothes. The furniture and utensils in the house. Everything a total loss.

He returned to the front of the property and retrieved his horse. Panicked, he rode to a neighbor's house where he learned the awful truth. The Praetorian Guard had arrived right after dawn. They had arrested everyone and torched the house before they left. They had told the neighbors to stay away.

His neighbor, a friend for the last several years, had at one time risen to the rank of *tribunus* in the Roman legions, fighting distinguished campaigns in Germania and Britannia. He gave Theophilus a sword, along with his own breastplate, belt, and a new pair of sandals to replace the damaged ones Theophilus was wearing. He insisted that Theophilus take his horse and eat something before he left.

Theophilus refused the food, drank a glass of wine, mounted the horse, and headed for Rome. He had no idea what he would do when he got there.

✝

They were waiting for him.

As Theophilus neared the city, spurring his horse as fast as she would go, he ran into four members of the Praetorian Guard. Theophilus reined his horse to a stop.

"It took you long enough," the commander said.

"Where's my wife?"

"She's been charged with arson."

Theophilus hadn't slept the entire night. He was exhausted, not processing things very quickly. He sized up his options. They were trained soldiers. Four against one. But he was furious and willing to die if he could only rescue Flavia.

"What are you doing with that sword, graybeard?" one of the soldiers sneered.

"Somebody burned down my house and kidnapped my wife. I've come to set her free."

Too late, Theophilus heard hoofbeats behind him. He turned and saw another half-dozen guards coming down the road. They brought their horses to a halt and blocked his path of retreat.

"Toss your sword on the ground," the commander in front of him said. "I understand you've got a reputation as one of Rome's best advocates. You won't be able to help your wife if you're dead."

"Will you take me to see her?"

"Throw down your sword!"

The soldiers all drew their own swords. Behind Theophilus, an archer strung his bow. The commander was right—Theophilus couldn't help Flavia if he was dead.

Furious, he pulled out his own sword and speared it, tip first, into the ground.

"Dismount the horse," the commander ordered.

Theophilus obeyed, dismounting slowly, staring at the soldiers the entire time. When his feet hit the ground, the soldiers quickly dismounted and swarmed over him, shackling his wrists together so they could lead him off to prison. "What am I being charged with?" Theophilus asked.

"Arson. Setting fire to the city of Rome."

Anger clouded his thoughts as the soldiers pushed him along the road. They seemed to find great enjoyment in parading him through the city.

Theophilus kept his head up, determined to act like the inno-cent man he was. Parts of the city were still ash heaps, while other areas had been cleared so new construction could start. Thousands of slaves stirred up dust and ashes. It seemed everyone was covered in a thin layer of black soot.

The guards walked Theophilus through the ruins of the Forum and past the burned skeleton of the temple of Vesta. At the foot of the Palatine Hill, they threw him into a dungeon with about thirty other prisoners.

Andronicus and Junia were there, calm and reassuring. This wasn't the first time they had been imprisoned. Epenetus and Priscilla were in the cell as well.

Theophilus asked if anyone knew what had happened to Flavia. The others explained that about five hundred soldiers had shown up at Theophilus's house right after dawn and arrested everyone. Two men had resisted and were killed on the spot. Their bodies were dragged inside the house before the soldiers started the fire.

Flavia had fought back and had been overpowered, though nobody knew where she was being held. The soldiers had given the prisoners in this cell no information about the evidence against them or when they might stand trial.

The cell had no windows and no light except a single torch that flickered on one of the walls. The floor and walls were made of stone. The place was damp, and it stank.

"What do you think will happen?" Priscilla asked Theophilus.

"They'll put us on trial. They've probably got witnesses who will say they saw us start the fires."

The others had lots of questions about how the trials might work, and Theophilus did his best to explain the process. But after a while it became obvious that the more they talked about the possible arson trials, the more everyone began to worry. It was Junia who changed the whole tone of the conversation.

"I think we ought to pray," she said. "God can take care of the trials."

For the next two hours, the believers prayed as they had never prayed before.

— CHAPTER 95 —

The torch flickered and went out during the night, leaving Theophilus and the other prisoners in total darkness. Early the next morning, two soldiers walked into the cell, and light came streaming through the door. Theophilus squinted while his eyes tried to adjust. The soldiers pointed to a young woman named Julia, who had been separated from her two children when she was arrested.

"Come with us."

They jerked her to her feet, and Andronicus rose as well. He began praying loudly for Julia's safety.

"Shut up, old man," one of the soldiers said. He pushed Andronicus in the chest, forcing him back against a wall. Angered, Theophilus stood, as did a few other men. But a hard look from the guards kept them at bay. Julia sobbed as they led her away.

The prisoners sang hymns and prayed while she was gone. A few hours later they brought Julia back and threw her on the floor. Her limbs were dislocated and she could no longer stand. Her face showed the shock and horror she had been through, her eyes vacant and distant.

The soldiers looked around the cell, and Andronicus stood slowly. "Take me next," he said.

Junia stood with him, and then a young, muscular man named Urbanus joined them. "No, take me first." Next came Apelles and Priscilla, joined by Theophilus. They each told the guards that they wanted to be the next one to go.

The guards looked past the standing prisoners and grabbed a man named Phlegan from the floor. Again Andronicus prayed loudly while some of the women sat down with Julia to give her comfort.

Phlegan never returned.

For two long days, the guards repeated the routine, taking prisoners out of the cell one at a time. Some, like Julia, refused to tell the guards what they wanted to hear. Those prisoners were tortured mercilessly and thrown back into the cell with their faith intact. Others didn't come back. Theophilus knew those prisoners had confessed to arson and agreed to testify against the rest of the believers.

The prisoners quit singing when Phlegan didn't come back. The optimistic belief in a miracle that had pervaded the cell earlier was replaced by a grim desire to survive.

They were given no food or water, and Theophilus felt his strength ebbing away. His tongue swelled, his thirst so bad that he had difficulty swallowing. One of the believers found a small puddle in the corner of the cell, and Theophilus and the others took turns lapping at the wet stones.

For Theophilus, the worst part was the waiting. Waiting for someone to return from the torture. Waiting to see whom the guards would choose next. His anxiety was compounded as he wondered what had happened to Flavia.

His emotions swung from vicious thoughts of revenge to resignation that the end was near. He might have gone insane had it not been for Andronicus and Junia. They were old and frail, but they were stronger in spirit than the others. They had seen the risen Christ. They reminded the others that God could deliver any of them with just a word. And if he didn't, their task was to persevere and bring honor to his name.

Even when the guards brought Andronicus back from his time on the rack, his spirit was unbowed. "I told them it wasn't too late to repent," he gasped. He moaned for a while and eventually passed out from the pain.

Theophilus was the last to be taken. He knew when the doors opened that it was his time, so he stood and walked toward the guards. They chained his manacled wrists to a burly guard and escorted him out of the cell.

"Be strong in the Lord!" Andronicus shouted out.

Theophilus stumbled along, his eyes stinging from the light. He was weak and tired and fearful that he wouldn't be able to stand the test. Every time he had closed his eyes in the past two days, he had seen visions of the hated torture device. He could almost feel his bones being dislocated and his muscles popping. He had seen the defeated looks on the faces of those who had returned. Some could no longer walk or even stand.

The soldiers dragged him along, and he prayed for strength.

A half-dozen soldiers joined the others and took him outside. He squinted in the bright sunlight. They escorted him down the Palatine Hill and along the Via Sacra toward the Forum. People stepped out of the way and stared at the pitiful sight. Theophilus couldn't even imagine how pathetic and unkempt he must have looked.

He tried to keep his eyes up, but it was a chore to do even that. He was still amazed at the nightmare that Rome had become. So many of its beautiful public temples had burned to ashes. Some of those temples had now been demolished, and enormous new stones lay in great piles next to the foundations, ready for the rebuilding process.

Without talking, the soldiers led him through the Forum to the Gemonian Stairs at the foot of the Capitoline Hill. It was here that foreign emperors were strangled before their bodies were thrown down the stairs and left for the dogs. Sejanus had been executed here after his trial in the Senate. Death on these stairs was considered the greatest of all Roman insults.

Theophilus knew this might be the end. He didn't think they would torture a Roman citizen in the open, but it seemed that with Nero, the traditional norms no longer applied. Were they going to execute him without even a trial?

He waited for several minutes, the sun baking down on him, before he heard a voice from behind.

"My old friend Theophilus," the man said, his tone mocking. Even before Theophilus turned, he knew it was Tigellinus.

The prefect of the Praetorian Guard stood on a perch a few steps above Theophilus, a cold smile playing on his lips. He reeked of stale perfume, and his eyes looked bloodshot. Theophilus could tell he enjoyed seeing the prisoner in such a desperate state.

"Have a seat," Tigellinus said.

"I'll stand."

"So be it," Tigellinus sneered. He came down and stood next to Theophilus. He put his arm around the prisoner's shoulder.

"Can you see it, Theophilus?" he asked, motioning to the Forum. "Rome rebuilt like never before. Nero's *Domus Aurea* connecting the Palatine and Esquiline Hills. A golden statue of our emperor 120 feet high. A magnificent lake for staging mock naval battles and for hosting more Saturnalia parties."

He squeezed Theophilus's shoulder. Theophilus wanted to spit in the man's face.

"You could have been Rome's wealthiest advocate," Tigellinus continued. "You could have helped rule all this. But you had to throw it away on this Christus fellow. A rather foolhardy gamble for a man of your intelligence."

Tigellinus removed his hand from Theophilus's shoulder and lowered his voice. "Your wife sends her regards."

Theophilus turned and stared at his tormentor but said nothing.

"If you confess, I'll spare her the rack. In fact, if you confess that you and the other leaders of this new superstition started the fires, I'll let Flavia go. She can walk out of prison today, and she'll never hear another word about it. You saved her once, Theophilus. Save her again."

In his weakened state, Theophilus was drawn to the possibility. He loved Flavia more than life itself. But he also knew that this man could not be trusted. Theophilus would have told Tigellinus anything if he really believed it would help set Flavia free. Yet he knew that the whole thing was just a mirage. He reminded himself of that as Tigellinus talked.

"I'll make it quick and painless for you as well," Tigellinus promised. "A beheading fit for a Roman. Far less pain than a crucifixion."

"You can't crucify Roman citizens."

"Interestingly, that's not entirely true," Tigellinus said as if he were discussing an academic question in a courtroom. "The law says we cannot *execute* Romans by crucifixion. His Excellency has interpreted that to mean that Romans can still be hung on a cross so long as they die by other means."

He looked at Theophilus as he said this, apparently searching for weakness or fear.

Theophilus stared straight ahead, anger heating his body. "Does almighty Caesar believe he can dispense with trials as well?"

"On the contrary, almighty Caesar thinks the trials should start right away."

It was the first slim ray of good news Theophilus had received in days. Perhaps he would have a chance to defend himself and others in open court.

"Twenty-four hours," Tigellinus said. "If you don't confess within twenty-four hours, you won't recognize your wife when you see her again."

He let that threat sink in for a moment, then walked down the stairs. The guards parted to let him by.

"Tigellinus!"

The prefect paused before reaching the bottom.

"I want to represent my wife," Theophilus said. "Don't put her on trial without me there."

The comment produced a mirthless chuckle. "You must think me a fool," Tigellinus said. Then he walked away.

✝

When Theophilus returned to the cell, he felt ashamed that he had not been tortured like the others.

"We should praise God for your protection," Priscilla said.

"Perhaps they know that all of Rome will come to see your trial and Flavia's," Andronicus suggested. "They know better than to torture either one of you before you have your day in court."

Theophilus clung to that hope because it meant that Flavia would be spared, at least for the moment.

But that night, he felt his strength fading fast. He wasn't sure that he would even be coherent by the time his case was heard. He prayed that regardless of what happened to his body, his faith would remain strong.

There was moaning and labored breathing in the cell that night by those in so much pain. But there was also an inexplicable feeling of triumph. Everyone still there had been steadfast. Everyone but Theophilus had withstood agonizing torture.

The next morning, as the prisoners woke from their fitful sleep, they prayed for strength and courage to face another day.

— CHAPTER 96 —

The trials began on the third day of his imprisonment, and Theophilus begged the guards to let him represent his fellow prisoners.

His pleas fell on deaf ears. The guards were under strict orders. A man accused of arson could only represent himself.

The trials were run with typical Roman efficiency. From the reports of those who left the cell and returned as condemned arsonists, the prospects of acquittal were nonexistent. Dozens of trials were held simultaneously in the Basilica Julia, and each one featured numerous witnesses who claimed to have firsthand knowledge of a plot by followers of the Way, including Theophilus and his fellow prisoners, to burn down the city. Those who had been formerly imprisoned with Theophilus but had confessed under torture were among the informants.

As each prisoner returned from his or her trial, Theophilus asked about Flavia. Nobody had seen her. He prayed she was still safe. He couldn't get her out of his mind, and he didn't want to. He thought about the early months of their marriage. The joy at learning that Flavia was pregnant. A young Mansuetus, innocent and playful. Mansuetus as a teenager, becoming serious about his studies. Theophilus longed for those days again. Why did following Jesus have to be so hard?

Julia's report was the most disheartening of all. Just before her case started, the prosecutor approached her and offered a deal. If she would testify against her fellow prisoners, the authorities would release her children. If not, she would watch her six-year-old son and four-year-old daughter be fed to the beasts during the private games in Nero's gardens. She rejected the proposed deal, clinging to her faith that Jesus would somehow spare her children.

When she returned to the cell, she was inconsolable. "What have I done?" she sobbed. "What if I've condemned them to death?"

As time marched on, a sense of despair invaded the cell. The trials were a farce. Nobody would be spared.

Theophilus was not called for his trial that day, and he wasn't surprised. They would want him to go last so they could accumulate as many witnesses as possible before they allowed him into the courtroom.

As evening approached, the prisoners were given something to eat for the first time in three days. The guards shoved bread and water inside the door, and the believers split it up evenly. There was barely enough for each of them to have a small morsel of bread and a few swallows of water. Theophilus wondered how long some of the prisoners could last under these conditions.

That night, he slept fitfully. He was hungry. Some of the prisoners were crying. Others prayed quietly. Urbanus, who had been found guilty that day, was snoring.

The dream came just before morning. The figures were ghostlike, shrouded in fog. Theophilus couldn't see their faces. They were young, some holding their parents' hands as they walked toward the giant ship waiting in port.

Mansuetus was there, waving at Theophilus while boarding the ship with the others.

Theophilus reached out, but he couldn't touch his son. Parents cried, but the children didn't seem to notice, smiling as they climbed on board one by one.

Theophilus heard the thunderous pounding of horses' hooves behind him. He turned to see the dust kicked up by a thousand Roman soldiers. His fellow prisoners turned with him to bravely face their executioners. With quiet dignity, they stood shoulder to shoulder as the soldiers drew nearer, swords drawn, hatred flashing in their eyes.

Before the slaughter began, Theophilus glanced back at the boat. Its sail was full, catching the wind, leaving port. The children, Mansuetus among them, leaned over the boat's railing, staring at their parents.

"They're safe," the woman next to Theophilus said. Theophilus turned and looked into the eyes of Julia. "Now I can die in peace."

When he woke, Theophilus knew immediately what the dream meant. God had given him a purpose for his trial and with it he felt a renewed surge of strength. Somebody had to speak for the children. He had been taught advocacy by the best tutors in the world. Now he would face his final test.

†

Plautius Lateranus was a large man with a bull neck, puffy cheeks, and small slits for eyes. His infamous past included an alleged affair with Messalina, the third wife of Claudius Caesar. He had been exiled and spared the death penalty because he had a famous uncle who had been granted an ovation after his conquest of Britannica.

When Claudius died, Lateranus was fully pardoned by Nero and restored to his former rank and position.

Despite the man's history, Theophilus was not at all distressed when he was dragged into the Basilica Julia and realized that Lateranus was the *praetor* who would decide his case. Lateranus was reputed to be a stubborn judge, an independent thinker, and no great fan of Nero despite the pardon Nero had granted him.

The prosecutor, of course, was Tigellinus himself, splendid in his broad-striped toga, his hair perfectly coiffed. Theophilus, on the other hand, had grown a short and unkempt beard peppered with gray and wore the same tunic he had been wearing since the day of his arrest. His wrists were manacled together. He had no notes, no exhibits, no witnesses. He felt like he could barely stand, and he knew his voice would be raspy.

Before the trial started, Tigellinus came up to Theophilus and renewed his offer to release Flavia if Theophilus would only confess.

"Has she already been found guilty?" Theophilus asked.

"Of course. She confessed after a few hours of stretching the truth out of her."

Theophilus wouldn't allow the image to take root in his mind. He knew he couldn't trust a word this man said. He chose not to believe him.

"I'm innocent," Theophilus said, though the words lacked force. "I intend to prove it if given the chance."

Tigellinus pointed behind him to a row of a dozen men and women. "I have some witnesses who might say otherwise."

A few seconds after Tigellinus stepped away, Theophilus felt a tap on his shoulder. He turned and found Marcus standing there, holding a flask of water.

"What are you doing here?" Theophilus asked. He took a quick drink and coughed from gulping it down too fast.

"I'm a doctor," Marcus said as if Theophilus might have forgotten. "The guards let me through."

Theophilus took another swig but saw Tigellinus approaching from the side. "Get away from the prisoner," the prosecutor sputtered, his eyes burning through Marcus.

"I'm a doctor," Marcus said. "This man is sick."

"Guards!" Tigellinus called.

The guards stepped forward and Marcus held up his hands. "I'm leaving," he said.

He looked at Theophilus before stepping away. "May the gods be with you," Marcus said.

A guard grabbed his arm but he shook it off.

"I was here for Flavia's trial," Marcus said quickly to Theophilus. "She looked fine, though she was found guilty. Rubria tried to help but is being held under house arrest."

"Thank you," Theophilus said to Marcus as the guards shoved his friend away. Marcus stiffened, but they pushed him harder and made him stand back with the rest of the crowd.

"Loyal to a fault," Tigellinus said, staring after him. "He'll pay, Theophilus. Just like all the others."

✝

Lateranus called the proceedings to order and recognized Tigellinus first. The man spoke at length against the Christians and painted Theophilus as one of the chief conspirators in the great fire of Rome.

"Did not the fire destroy many temples in Rome, temples that honored the same gods the Christians refuse to worship? These are the people whose leaders compare Rome to the immoral ancient cities of Sodom and Gomorrah, claiming that their God will judge such cities with fire from heaven. Well, it appears the followers of Christus decided their God needed a little help."

As he had during the trial of Paul, Tigellinus strutted around while he talked. "I heard it myself during the trial of Paul of Tarsus. He claimed that every man and woman in the Roman Empire, including even the great Caesar himself, would one day fall on their faces and worship Christus. Exercising great grace and restraint, Nero freed Paul even though he found Paul guilty. But that didn't stop this new superstition from spreading. Nor did it stop its adherents from deepening their hatred of the emperor and this city.

"Witnesses will describe secret meetings of this sect where the followers of Christus are instructed to eat his body and drink his blood. They foment rebellion among our slaves and claim that the lowest slave is equal to the highest Roman citizen. More than that, you will hear witnesses testify that Theophilus and other leaders plotted the fiery destruction of his own city. The prisoner has long been an enemy of Roman emperors, and today the blood of ten thousand Romans is on his hands."

Theophilus took it all in, his eyes fixed on Lateranus. The *praetor* seemed unmoved by the rhetoric. Perhaps it was only Theophilus's tired and disoriented mind engaging in wishful thinking. Or perhaps the *praetor* would actually consider the evidence impartially.

When Tigellinus concluded, the *praetor* asked if Theophilus wished to speak in response. Theophilus declined, stating that he would wait until Tigellinus had presented his evidence.

For the next three hours, Theophilus listened wearily as Tigellinus called his witnesses. They testified exactly as Tigellinus had predicted they would. Former slaves of Christian households testified that Theophilus had counseled them to rise up against their masters. Believers who had been imprisoned with Theophilus claimed that they had heard him and Andronicus discussing the rumors the two men had started and spread—rumors against Nero for allegedly causing the fire.

Other witnesses, men and women whom Theophilus had never seen before, claimed they had been in the room with Theophilus when he helped plan the great fire. With a touch of flair, one witness said that Theophilus planned on mounting the Rostra after the fires to give a speech against Nero and advocate a return to the Republic.

"He gave the same type of speech after the assassination of Caligula," the witness said.

One brave man refused to indict Theophilus. The man had apparently confessed when the guards tortured him, yet when Tigellinus called him forward, he had a change of heart.

"That man is innocent," he said, pointing to Theophilus. "And putting me back on the rack will not make me support your lies."

It was the sole bright spot in three hours of testimony. The crowd grew restless, murmuring their disapproval every time Theophilus declined to cross-examine a witness. They had apparently expected a spirited defense. Instead, Theophilus stood there stoically, never asking a single question.

Lateranus periodically looked at him, his eyes filled with curiosity. Theophilus suspected that his judge was wondering the same things Theophilus himself had wondered so many years ago about the Nazarene.

Why don't you defend yourself? Don't you hear all these things being said against you?

But Theophilus continued to bide his time.

Finally, at the end of Tigellinus's case, an exasperated Lateranus turned to Theophilus. "Does the defendant have *any* evidence?" Lateranus asked.

"I do."

"You may proceed," Lateranus said, relief evident in his voice.

The spectators seemed to shuffle a little closer, leaning forward to hear what Theophilus had to say.

"I am innocent," he began. "You have the wrong man on trial today."

~ CHAPTER 97 ~

"There are rumors, Your Excellency, about who started the fire. Today I will say in the open what others whisper in the shadows. I will argue in court what others are silently thinking. I will ask the question on everyone's mind."

Theophilus licked his lips. His mouth was dry and he felt a little unsteady. But his strength was surging, as if he were somehow drawing energy and intensity from the crowd.

"Was the fire started by the Christians or was it ordered by Nero?"

The blunt question caused a stir in the crowd, and Theophilus glanced over to see the face of Tigellinus darken.

"That's outrageous!" the prosecutor said to Lateranus. "You *cannot* allow the emperor's name to be defiled in open court."

"And you *will not* tell me how to run this court," Lateranus snapped back, lowering his chin in a look of stubborn defiance. He was one of the few *praetores* with enough courage to allow this type of defense to proceed. It didn't hurt that the crowd was edging in even more, anxious to hear Theophilus argue the one question everyone cared about most.

Tigellinus snorted but did not respond. He apparently didn't want to anger the *praetor* too much and risk a not-guilty verdict.

"A few months ago, I represented a man named Paul of Tarsus in his appeal to Caesar," Theophilus said. He cleared his throat. "He was accused of starting this new religion you've heard so much about and of stirring up trouble against Rome. Tigellinus prosecuted that case and did an outstanding job even without using tortured witnesses."

Out of the corner of his eye, Theophilus noticed Tigellinus shaking his head.

"At Paul's trial, the defendant testified that he had been converted to this new religion when a bright light appeared to him on the road to Damascus, striking him blind. When Paul recovered his physical sight, he was given miraculous spiritual insight. Paul testified that from that day forward he became a follower of the man named Jesus, who was crucified and rose from the dead. Paul even told Nero that one day every tongue would confess that Jesus is Lord."

Lateranus listened with an expression that was hard to read. Perhaps he was curious about the relevance of such testimony at this trial. Perhaps he was thinking that the disheveled advocate before him was as insane as he looked. Perhaps he was just going through the motions, determined to hear Theophilus out so he could declare him guilty.

"Imagine my surprise when Nero released Paul," Theophilus continued. "Even though it seemed like an incredible gift to my client at the time, I was troubled by the outcome. Nero said that Paul was guilty but nevertheless wanted to show Paul grace. Yet I could tell that the emperor was seething at this new philosophy spreading throughout his city."

"That's outrageous!" Tigellinus roared. "How can this man speak for the emperor?"

Lateranus frowned. "The defendant is entitled to make his arguments. I will be the judge of whether they are persuasive."

The dismissive tone of the *praetor*'s comments signaled to Theophilus that he was facing an uphill climb. Lateranus would allow Theophilus to make his case, but persuading him would be a different matter.

"Paul's release was not the last time Caesar surprised me," Theophilus continued, undaunted. "Months later, as he was preparing to leave for Alexandria, Caesar was himself struck blind in the temple of Vesta. Like Paul, Caesar had his own spiritual revelation. The people of Rome needed the gift of his presence so that they might be 'cheered in their misfortunes by the sight of the emperor.'

"Perhaps this was a genuine spiritual experience that just happened to mimic the story of the apostle Paul. Or perhaps our emperor was already setting the stage for an event that he would instigate to make his reign complete. A great fire that would destroy Rome so he could rebuild it in his own image . . . and a group of people he could blame for the fire—people who claimed that a greater ruler than Nero had already walked the face of the earth."

Those accusations brought some shouts from the crowd and another strong protest from Tigellinus. It took Lateranus a few minutes to calm things down.

"It may be that the defendant is mad," Lateranus said gruffly, once order had been restored. "But even madmen are entitled to state their defense. You may continue, Theophilus, but I hope you have more evidence than these empty accusations I have heard so far."

It was, Theophilus knew, the best he could hope for. He might never persuade Lateranus, but the public would be the ultimate judge of whether Nero or the Christians were to blame.

"A few weeks passed, and then the same emperor who issued a decree proclaiming that we needed his virtuous presence in Rome departed for the nearby city of Antium. All of Rome witnessed his spectacular departure. Who could count the number of aristocrats, freedmen, secretaries, servants, barbers, cooks, waiters, and wine tasters? Who could forget the hordes of harpists, flautists, cymbal players, *citharedes*, trumpeters, dancing girls, actors, and groomers? The procession lasted for hours."

Theophilus looked around at the crowd. "How many of you were witnesses to the fact that Nero was leaving—far enough away that he couldn't be accused of starting the fires but close enough to ride swiftly to the rescue?"

Theophilus stopped for a breath and to regain his strength. He could tell by the faces that he was gaining sympathizers. He was articulating what many Romans had been thinking all along.

"Is it a coincidence that the fire started on July 19, the exact anniversary of the fiery destruction of Rome by the Gauls more than four hundred years ago? Is it a coincidence that the destruction would give Nero a chance to rebuild the city just as it was rebuilt once before, but this time in his own image, with his own great palace dominating three hundred acres of land that formerly hosted warehouses and apartment buildings?"

In his excitement, Theophilus had raised his scratchy voice and motioned with his manacled wrists. It dawned on him that he was beginning to resemble a student of the Asiatic school of rhetoric, which he so deplored. He took a deep breath and lowered his tone.

The crowd was hushed, anxious to hear every word.

"On the night of the fire, there were numerous reports of men running around the city, preventing other citizens from putting out the blaze. They said they were operating on orders. And what was our great emperor doing on the night the fire started?"

Theophilus paused because everybody already knew the answer. "He was displaying his gift of music to the inhabitants of Antium. What a giver of gifts this emperor is! He gave Paul the gift of freedom. He gave Rome the gift of watching his beautiful entourage head to Antium. He gave the people of Antium the gift of watching him play the lyre.

"And his gifts don't stop there. He gave Romans who became refugees the gift of staying at the Campus Martius, public property that Nero opened up to the people. Not only that, but he brought in free grain from the port of Ostia and promised to subsidize the building process for all Romans. Will his gifts never cease? How could anyone not love such a generous emperor?"

Theophilus knew that his sarcasm was not lost on the crowd. They were engaged now, maybe even enthralled by the brazenness of someone who dared to criticize Nero so openly.

"Yet where was this giver of gifts when Rome started burning? He was on the stage of a theater in Antium, singing about the sack of Ilium.

"Think about it, Your Excellency. Our emperor, on the night the fire started, was intentionally singing about the destruction of another city long ago that occurred because the Trojans wheeled a large wooden horse inside their own city walls. The bowels of that horse hosted an enemy that would bring about the destruction of Troy.

"The city was destroyed because the Trojans didn't listen to their own prophets—men who told them to beware of Greeks, even those bearing gifts."

Theophilus paused, knowing he had made the accusation plain enough—Caesar was Rome's own Trojan horse. Now he would drive the point home.

"Perhaps Caesar is prophetic after all," Theophilus said, his voice dripping with mockery. "What a prophetic song he chose to sing. Perhaps we should fear our own emperors just as the Trojans should have been wary of the Greeks. Perhaps we should especially fear emperors bearing gifts."

Theophilus glanced at the intent crowd. Some were whispering to their friends and family members. Others were nodding. Still others were riveted, hanging on every word. They had never heard it stated quite this way—the damning evidence so carefully arranged in the open for all to see.

"And so, Your Excellency, you must choose between the witnesses, who have testified about a conspiracy of Christians who started the fire, or the evidence, which points to a more insidious cause. But so too must all of Rome choose. And I acknowledge that valid differences of opinion may honestly exist.

"Yet I submit that there is one final question that must be asked. The answer to this question will determine which side is right.

"And the question is this: Whose blood runs so cold that they would sacrifice innocent children? Because whoever ordered the fires had to know that the most vulnerable persons would be the ones most likely to die. As we know, thousands of infants did indeed die, sacrificed to the flames.

"Could Nero have done such a thing? He alone knows. We can only be sure of this—that even as I speak, the children of Christians are being held captive by the emperor's forces.

"Did children start the fires? Did two-year-olds who are barely able to walk torch all of Rome? Have we ever as Romans punished children for the sins of their fathers? Did we hold Nero accountable for the actions of Agrippina? When Drusilla, the two-year-old daughter of Caligula, was killed by Caligula's assassins, did not the whole city of Rome turn against those men? When did we decide that it is acceptable to kill innocent children?"

Theophilus was winding down, his strength fading. He thought about poor, tortured Julia and her precious little ones. There were hundreds of others like them, children who at best would be orphaned and at worst would be sacrificed along with the rest of the Christians.

"If Nero and Tigellinus are ruthless enough to condemn the children of Christians to the beasts, then who could say they weren't ruthless enough to start the fires?"

Tigellinus could stand it no more. "Your Excellency," he scoffed, "we are not here to put Caesar on trial, and we are certainly not here to condemn innocent children. We are only here to pronounce the guilt or innocence of a man so desperate to save his own skin that he would accuse our beloved emperor of arson."

Theophilus chose not to respond. He would let his adversary have the last word. He had said everything he came to say, and his energy was spent.

"I've heard enough," Lateranus said. He glanced at both Tigillenus and Theophilus. Then he stood, ready to pronounce judgment. A cold chill went down Theophilus's spine. It was one thing to be the advocate, quite another to be the defendant.

"I find the defendant guilty of arson and murder," Lateranus said abruptly. "I find his attacks on Caesar to be without basis and scurrilous." He narrowed his eyes. "If you had been charged with treason, I would have found you guilty of that as well."

It was the ruling Theophilus had expected, but it still felt like a hammer to the gut. Like his cellmates, Theophilus would return to the dungeon with the penalty of execution hanging over his head.

But Lateranus was not yet done. Instead, he showed at last why Theophilus had drawn the perfect *praetor* for his final trial.

"The lengths of your paranoia, Theophilus, are aptly demonstrated by your fears that our beloved emperor would somehow execute children for the crimes of their parents." Lateranus turned from the defendant and fixed his icy stare on the prosecutor. "Tigellinus, can you assure this court that there are no plans for that? I would not want the populace to leave here believing a single word that Theophilus has said."

Tigellinus hesitated, and Theophilus could see that the prosecutor's mind was spinning. He had probably already concocted the most gruesome deaths imaginable.

But he played his part well. Tigellinus stood to his full height, the picture of indignation. "As all of Rome knows, Nero spent the days after the fire sacrificing to the gods. He has shed endless tears on behalf of the little ones consumed by the flames. Propitiation requires that the guilty parties be punished most severely. But Nero will, by his benevolent grace, spare the children. After all, grace is the emperor's defining characteristic. And that truly is a gift, Your Excellency, for which all of Rome should rejoice."

— CHAPTER 98 —

When Theophilus returned to the dungeon, he told the others about his trial. Julia and three other women wept with joy at the knowledge that their children would be spared. Andronicus thanked God for the deliverance of the little ones. It was a rare victory in an otherwise-vile situation.

Now, with guilty verdicts hanging over their heads, there was nothing left for the prisoners to do but wait. Conditions in the cell were intolerable. Nobody cleaned out the human waste, and the place grew putrid, the air so thick with stench that Theophilus could taste it. The guards shoveled in small amounts of food and water at unpredictable intervals, and the prisoners divided up the provisions and gave thanks.

Theophilus clung to thin reeds of hope. Maybe Seneca would reach out to Nero and talk him out of this madness. Maybe some of Theophilus's former clients or friends in the Senate would take action. Maybe the people of Rome wouldn't stand for a mass execution of Christians when the evidence all pointed back to the emperor. Or maybe—and this was the hope that kept Theophilus alive—God would provide a miraculous escape. He had done it before, and he could do it again.

The prisoners had no contact with the outside world, no way of monitoring the events that would dictate their fate. Each day Theophilus could hear less optimism in the others' voices, less will to live, less expectation of a miracle. They tried keeping sane by remembering parts of Luke's books or Paul's writings. They sang hymns and songs they had sung before their arrest. Theophilus and three other prisoners whose limbs had not been dislocated came up with small and subtle exercises they could do. Those who couldn't move enough to exercise simply tried to survive and heal.

With no light in the cell, it became hard to distinguish day from night. The prisoners lost all track of time. A week passed. Perhaps two.

The day came without warning. Finally, mercifully, it would all soon be over.

The metal door of the cell was flung open, and the guards barked at the prisoners to stand up and hold out their wrists. They put shackles on the prisoners and then chained them together in a long line. Theophilus made sure Julia was between him and Urbanus so that the men could carry her.

They were all led down some steps, through a long corridor, and out into the street. Those like Julia who had trouble walking were whipped by the guards and then carried by their fellow prisoners.

It was late at night, and the procession moved slowly by torchlight. The guards pushed and prodded the prisoners to the other side of Rome, across the Tiber River, to the private stadium built by Caligula in the Vatican Gardens. It was not as big as the Circus Maximus, but it had been constructed in the same grand style. There was a large track for chariot races and a center obelisk that reached toward the sky. The wooden bleachers could hold nearly seventy thousand spectators.

From the activity that was taking place when they arrived in the middle of the night, Theophilus knew preparations were under way for a day of races and games.

The prisoners were herded into an underground crypt that already contained dozens of other Christians. The guards said they would be back for them in the morning.

✝

A few hours after dawn, the guards emptied the all crypts and lined up the prisoners. They hung a *titulus* around each neck, declaring each prisoner to be an arsonist. There were too many prisoners to easily count, four or five hundred at least, and Theophilus searched the ranks for Flavia.

He spotted her, along with Procula, a hundred feet behind him, and his heart jumped. When her eyes met his, he drew strength from her. Her clothes were tattered, hanging from her emaciated body, but she was walking on her own. She mouthed, "I love you," and Theophilus mouthed it back.

The guards herded the prisoners together outside the stadium and put them on display in the unrelenting sun as Roman citizens streamed past. There were thousands of people entering the stadium, carrying bundles of food and jars of wine, their togas clinging to their sweaty bodies. They pushed and shoved as they squeezed through the entrances and crossed the bridges that brought them to the Vatican Gardens. Most ignored the prisoners, but some stared, and others couldn't resist a few mocking comments.

Theophilus stared back, realizing that he had once been one of them. He looked for faces of friends, though he wondered if they would even recognize him with his hair disheveled, his beard grown thick, and his skin blackened and scaly.

He picked up on bits and pieces of their conversations. These were no ordinary games. Nero had apparently promised that he would, in the most spectacular fashion, punish those who had set fire to Rome. There would be no gladiators or chariot races today; the Christians were the only show in town.

At least, Theophilus thought, there would be no children.

✝

Before they paraded Theophilus and the others in front of Nero, a phrase was passed down the line from one prisoner to the next. The woman in front of Theophilus turned and whispered it to him.

"Be strong in the Lord."

Theophilus repeated the phrase to the man behind him. He nodded and passed it to the next man back.

Trumpets blared from inside the stadium, and Theophilus knew that Nero was taking his seat at that moment. The crowd roared, and the guards started whipping the prisoners forward. One by one, the prisoners were unchained from the next person in line and marched into the stadium.

It was only while he was being unchained that Theophilus saw him—Marcus was the very first prisoner being forced to march around the oval track! Theophilus had a sickening feeling that Marcus had been arrested solely for helping at Theophilus's arson trial. He had always been there for Theophilus, time after time, since child-hood, and now that loyalty had become his undoing. Guilt-ridden and helpless, Theophilus prayed that one of Marcus's cellmates had led him to faith.

With the line of prisoners stretching behind him, Marcus stopped in front of Nero's box. He looked up at the emperor but didn't say a word. The guards glared at him as if by sheer willpower they could force him to grace Caesar with the traditional greeting of honor.

But Marcus refused to speak. A guard stepped forward, took the blunt end of his sword in its sheath, and drove it into Marcus's midsection.

Marcus doubled over and knelt on the ground.

"Say it!" the guard demanded.

Thin and frail, Marcus lifted his head, stared for a moment at the emperor, and spit in the sand.

Theophilus wanted to break free and somehow help him, the same way Marcus had come to his aid so many times before. But his wrists were shackled together, and he was too far down the track. All Theophilus could do was watch helplessly as the guard lifted his sword, swung it in a gigantic arc, and severed his good friend's head.

Theophilus stared in disbelief. Vomit caught in his throat, and he turned away. Marcus, of all people, was the first to die.

With tears blurring his vision, Theophilus looked back as the next prisoner refused to salute Caesar as well. This time it was a young woman. Nero cursed at her and ordered the guards to take the pris-oners back to the crypts without further ceremony. The crowd jeered as the guards marched Theophilus and his fellow prisoners out of the stadium to await their turn for execution.

∼ CHAPTER 99 ∼

On the way back to the crypts, the prisoners marched past the cages of wild animals. For Theophilus, it was a harrowing experience, walking close enough to touch the cages holding the snarling lions and leopards, brooding bulls, and howling packs of wild dogs. The lions especially seemed so much bigger this close, their eyes bloodshot and yellow, their manes gnarled and matted. Theophilus knew they had been starved the last twenty-four hours, and when they opened their massive jaws and roared, it seemed the ground shook under his feet. The soldiers banged on the cages as the prisoners passed by the animals, riling up the beasts, and laughed as the prisoners shuddered or shrank away from the animals.

The prisoners were thrown back into their cells, and Theophilus was again separated from Flavia. Left alone, the Christians quickly rallied. They had been inspired by Marcus's brave stand and the refusal of the next prisoner to bow her knee to Caesar. Andronicus and other leaders who had the gift of encouragement were exhorting their fellow prisoners. "Let us show the Roman people how to die! The Spirit of the Lord casts out fear! Let us meet God with praises on our lips! All of Rome is watching!"

Others echoed the words of Paul: "Have the same mindset as Christ Jesus, who made himself nothing and became obedient to death—even death on a cross!"

Though he felt abject fear coursing through every vein in his body, Theophilus joined his voice to those preaching courage. "I was there at the trial of Christ," he said, pivoting so he could look all the prisoners in the eye. "I heard him tell Pilate that he was born for that moment. This is *our* moment! May we meet it with the same resolve!"

A long time passed as they waited for the soldiers to come for the first victims. Perhaps Caesar was giving a speech or playing the lyre or sacrificing to the Roman gods. Whatever the reason, it gave Theophilus and his cellmates sufficient time to regroup.

When the guards returned, Theophilus stepped to the front of his crypt along with half a dozen other men, shielding the women and older prisoners. The guards pushed Theophilus and the men standing with him aside and dragged out several others.

A few of the selected prisoners protested, but their words were interrupted by a lone voice from another crypt echoing through the underground tunnels, singing a hymn of praise. Other voices joined, rough and hoarse, but the words lifted the spirits of the prisoners. Soon everyone was singing, their voices rising louder.

The iron-barred doors to the crypts were slammed shut, and a gang of slaves fastened animal skins to the first set of victims, tying the skins around the shoulders of the manacled Christians so they couldn't shrug them off. The guards then took out knives and sliced the skin of the Christians so the beasts would smell the fresh blood. Theophilus stood at the front of his crypt, his fists clenched around the bars, searching for Flavia. To his great relief, she was not among the first group selected.

"Let's go!" one of the commanders barked. With that, the Christians were pushed and prodded down the long, dark corridor and disappeared out the other end of the tunnel.

When Theophilus could see them no longer, he joined the others in prayer. They heard the cheering of the crowd as the victims entered the arena. They heard the clang of the cages farther down the tunnel and the great roar of the lions as they were whipped into the arena. In the next few minutes, they heard moments of relative silence, followed by cheers or gasps of excitement and then resounding applause.

Theophilus could see the scene unfolding in his mind. He knew his own turn would come soon enough.

For hour after grisly hour, the process was repeated as the guards came for more victims. Sometimes, after the prisoners left, Theophilus would hear the growls of the wild dogs. Other times he heard the roar of the lions. Sometimes he heard nothing but the rattling of cages and the sound of the whips, and he knew they had loosed the leopards.

The guards took fifteen or twenty prisoners at a time, but as far as Theophilus could tell, Flavia was never among them.

By noon the crowd was not nearly as enthusiastic as it had been earlier. Maybe they were finally growing weary of the mindless slaughter.

Theophilus just wanted it to be over. He was sick with fear but also determined to finish well. The examples of those who had gone before him would have inspired even the most insipid of men. Though Theophilus had eaten and slept little, he was no longer tired. Every time the guards returned, adrenaline rushed through his body, preparing him for the agony that lay ahead. He had determined that he would at least go down with a fight. He would attack the beasts—enrage them if he could. That way they would make short work of him and the others.

He didn't allow himself to think about what would happen to Flavia.

By midafternoon, the crypt housing Theophilus had only three prisoners left. The singing and speeches had long since ceased. Defiant resistance had been replaced by a grim acceptance of fate. The soldiers and prisoners had both learned the routine. Guards would enter the crypt and tap the selected prisoners on their shoulders. The Christians would leave the cell willingly and begin their silent death march to the stadium. Those left behind would shake their heads and wait their turns.

But sometime in the late afternoon, the soldiers stopped coming. An hour passed. Two hours. Theophilus strained to hear, trying to determine if the crowd was still there. He didn't hear the cheering he would have expected if the emperor had moved on to other events like gladiator fights or chariot races.

He allowed a brief flicker of hope to reignite. The executions had stopped, at least temporarily. He and the other prisoners wondered aloud at what it could mean.

Then he heard it, unmistakable, echoing in the twilight air. Something far more sinister, a rhythm that pierced his soul.

The crowd noise had been replaced by the distant sound of hammering.

CHAPTER 100

After darkness fell, the guards emptied the remaining cells and lined the prisoners up again. Theophilus still had his wrists shackled, and they placed him at the very end of the line. Andronicus and Junia were just ahead of him. He heard the voice of Procula a little farther up.

"Procula, do you know if Flavia is still alive?" Theophilus asked.

"She's at the front," Procula replied.

He was both relieved and pained at the news. Absent a miracle, they would die together, a thought that created a deep ache in his body, a gashing of his heart.

He walked with the other prisoners past the cages of animals, but this time the beasts seemed more docile, as if they had had their fill.

The procession stopped just before the opening of the tunnel. From his vantage point at the end of the line, Theophilus could see little but could hear the bustling and murmur of the crowd. They had apparently regathered in the darkness.

Trumpets blared and a lictor announced the entrance of the great Nero Claudius Caesar Augustus Germanicus. The spectators quieted, and it sounded like Nero was giving a speech. It was not his voice, of course, because he couldn't risk damaging his vocal cords by shouting to such a crowd. But Theophilus could pick up bits and pieces from the crier who was relaying the emperor's words. *"Punishment fit for the crime . . . The law prevents death by crucifixion. . . . It does not prevent the use of the cross altogether. . . . The emperor has consulted with the fire god, Vulcan. . . . The gods must be appeased."*

Theophilus expected the crowd to roar when the speech was over, but the arena was largely silent. He shifted his weight anxiously from one foot to the next, imagining the ghastly new torture that Nero had in mind. He found himself wishing he had simply been fed to the beasts.

When the prisoners emerged from the tunnel, Theophilus's heart melted like wax. He had expected this from the hammering, but it was another thing to see the sight with his own eyes. The oval-shaped track had been cleared of all the mutilated bodies, and the sand was freshly raked. Lying on the ground on both sides of the track, all the way around the oval, were dozens and dozens of crosses. Perhaps two hundred in total. One for each prisoner still alive.

The entire place was lit by torches positioned between the crosses. Theophilus remembered the teachings of Seneca on the Appian Way, the images of Crassus crucifying thousands of slaves. Now Nero was trying to top that—fewer bodies but a more gruesome spectacle, one that included women.

"Be strong in the Lord." The mantra came down the line of prisoners again. Theophilus realized that Flavia, as first in line, had probably started it.

The guards shoved the prisoners forward, leading them to their individual crosses. The cross for Theophilus was located directly in front of the imperial box. When the procession stopped and the front of the line had circled the entire track, he realized that Flavia would be next to him.

They looked at each other again, their eyes conveying what words could not. She was still regal, even with her hair gnarled, her eyes hollow and gaunt, her skin covered with sores and grime. *Be strong,* she said with her eyes. *Finish well.*

Tigellinus came down from the imperial box and stood in front of Theophilus. A sheen of sweat covered his brow.

"Confess your crimes and worship Caesar," he said to Theophilus. "And Flavia walks away."

"Don't do it," Flavia warned. "Don't betray our Lord. Don't betray *me*."

Theophilus looked at his wife, then back at his tormentor. Behind Tigellinus, Caesar sat victoriously in the imperial box surrounded by his court. Theophilus noticed the Vestal Virgins were not in their places. Perhaps they were protesting the execution of Flavia.

"Jesus is Lord," Theophilus said.

Tigellinus slowly nodded. "We'll see how Jesus helps you now."

He turned on his heel and walked across the sand, back to the imperial box. He climbed the steps, thrust out his chin, and took his place next to Caesar.

The emperor raised his hand. "Let the sacrifices begin!"

Driven by rage and adrenaline, Theophilus lashed out. He balled his fists together and swung his arms, landing a blow against the jaw of the guard on his right. Another guard jumped him from behind and took him down. Somebody kicked him in the stomach, knocking the wind out of him. They were all over him, grunting and cursing. He heard Flavia scream in the background. *"Theophilus! Stop fighting!"*

There were powerful arms everywhere, and they quickly subdued Theophilus, pinning him on the ground as they removed his shackles. They rolled him on his back on top of the cross and pried his arms apart, positioning them against the wooden crossbeam. A guard on each side placed the tips of the spikes against his wrists. He squirmed but they wrenched him in place. The commander nodded, the guards swung the hammers, and Theophilus cried out as the spikes pierced his wrists.

Other guards held his feet against the angled footrest attached to the cross. He felt the point of the nail on top of his foot, the skin and tendons tearing as the spike was pounded through his feet. When the hammering stopped, he swallowed his screams and moaned. He had never experienced such pain in all his life.

Before they lifted his cross, the guards coated it in resin and nitrates, sulfur and pitch. They wrapped soaked linens around Theophilus, and the smell of oil filled his nostrils.

The pain and odors made him nauseous. He felt like he might pass out at any moment.

Three burly guards lifted his cross and jammed it into place, causing the nails to tear his wrists and feet, sending bolts of excruciating pain through his body. He looked over at Flavia, who was nailed to her cross as well. She was gritting her teeth, her eyes closed in prayer, her face lifted to heaven.

Theophilus tightened his muscles and pushed himself up so he could take a deep breath, the pain again ripping through his arms and ankles. "I love you, Flavia," he said.

She smiled, a half smile filled with pain. She formed a few words without speaking aloud.

In agony, Theophilus looked at the emperor's box. He would draw strength from the face of Nero—perhaps the rage could block out some of the pain. But the man was gone! He hadn't even stayed to see the culmination of his own gruesome creation!

A searing, painful moment passed, and then Nero reemerged in the imperial box. He was wearing the green uniform of a charioteer. He left the box and mingled with the patrons in the stands for a few minutes, then jumped the rail and landed on the track. He walked over and stood in front of Flavia.

As he looked up at her, he shook his head and made a *tsk* noise as if he couldn't understand how she had gotten herself into such a position.

"In a few minutes, we will extinguish the oil torches and light the human ones," he said. "A fitting punishment for those who torched our city. I will ride Rome's finest chariot down the middle of the blazing gauntlet. I'd hate for you to miss a spectacle like that."

Flavia said nothing. She stared down at him, her expression seething with contempt.

"You were a Vestal once," he said. "Married to Rome. Embrace her again, Flavia. Confess your role in the fires, your love for your emperor, and I will order my men to take you down."

"I will make a confession," Flavia managed, struggling to get her breath.

Nero looked surprised. "Go on," the emperor said.

Jerking violently, Flavia raised herself up. "You raped Rubria." She drew in a breath. Tears of rage filled her eyes. "You set fire to Rome," she gasped, "raping your own . . . city."

She stopped for breath, and Nero's face darkened. He sneered in hatred, but Flavia was not yet done. Theophilus watched in stunned admiration as she fought bravely for another breath.

"I have sinned . . . too." She let out a moan, and this time she couldn't seem to find the strength to rise again.

"It's all right, Flavia," Theophilus managed.

She shook her head, her face a picture of determination. She lifted herself up one more time. "I clapped . . . in the theater. . . . In truth . . ." She grimaced. Gasped. And then there was a smile. "You were *horrible* on the lyre."

She sagged back down, her energy spent. Nero's soldiers stood there speechless. Perhaps they wanted to laugh. Theophilus knew this much—Flavia's dying insult fueled his own resolve. It was her way of saying that they had nothing to fear from this man. The emperor could destroy the body, but he couldn't lay a finger on Flavia's indomitable spirit or incorruptible soul.

Without warning, Nero grabbed the torch from the man next to him and lit the flame himself.

"Nooo!" Theophilus cried out. He twisted violently and strained against the nails holding him to the cross as if he could somehow break free. Pain pierced him.

In horror, he saw the wood of Flavia's cross light instantly and act like a candlewick, setting on fire the linens wrapped around her body. Theophilus turned his head, unable to watch as Flavia suffered. He would not look at her again in this world. The next time he saw her, she would be as she once was—radiant, flawless, totally at peace.

He shut his eyes but could not block out the sounds. She screamed in agony. He felt the heat and smelled the burning flesh. Her cries became muted as she choked on the smoke. But then he heard a gasp and words forming again.

"Look. . . . He is risen!"

She must have regained her strength even as the flames consumed her. "It's real, Theophilus!" she cried. And then she shrieked in pain.

There was another anguished yell, nothing Theophilus could decipher, and then her voice softened almost to a whisper. It seemed that perhaps the pain was gone.

"It's real," Theophilus heard her say again.

—— CHAPTER 101 ——

Flavia's death fueled Theophilus's own commitment to die well and at the same time extinguished his will to live. For him and the others, it wouldn't be long now.

He struggled for breath as he had on another cross so many years ago. He watched Nero walk down the length of the track and disappear out the doors that led to the stables. The stadium stilled as the crowd waited with anticipation for the moment to arrive. The only sound came from Theophilus and the other Christians straining to breathe. Some moaned in pain; others sobbed quietly.

One by one, the soldiers covered the oil torches. The entire stadium complex turned black, the light from Flavia's cross the sole exception. Theophilus knew that in a moment his cross would also be lit, and his life would soon be over.

He hung there, his thoughts muddled by the horrific pain radiating from the nerves in his wrists and ankles. He tried to remember the example of Jesus. Hanging on the cross at the place of the skull, the Nazarene had prayed that God would forgive those who killed him.

Theophilus couldn't bring himself to do the same. Instead, he hung his head and prayed for Nero's punishment. But as he prayed, his heart was convicted of his own role in the death of Jesus. He remembered the Nazarene's eyes of compassion even in the midst of his trial, the look that told Theophilus he was loved.

Tears streamed down his face as he somehow found the will to pray for Nero. *Convict him, Lord. Convert him to your cause or raise up another who will take his place and lead all of Rome to you.*

His thoughts and prayers were disrupted by the sound of a disjointed chant. Whose voice started it, Theophilus couldn't say. But the familiar words were picked up by the others. First one prisoner, then another, hoisting themselves up and carrying on the jagged refrain.

"Now to him . . . who is able . . .
To do more . . . than we ask . . . or imagine . . .
According to his power . . . at work in us . . ."

The words, breathless and forced as they were, reverberated in the darkness of the stadium. A few patrons booed, but the prisoners could still be heard.

Theophilus lifted himself up and added to the refrain. "To him be glory in the church!"

"And in Christ Jesus!" somebody else added.

They never finished. A light erupted at the far end of the stadium as the stable doors opened. On cue, the soldiers simultaneously lit two hundred crosses, and each burst into flames.

Nero came thundering out of the stables, riding down the gauntlet of human torches, his chariot drawn by four white stallions.

The tongues of fire climbed up Theophilus's cross and lapped at his legs. Within seconds, the linens they had wrapped around him ignited. He gasped for breath and inhaled black smoke. The blaze seared him and consumed him, every inch of his skin on fire.

There were a few seconds of suffocating pain as Nero flashed by. A bright-white light exploded and Theophilus cried out, a prolonged scream of unbearable agony, and then . . .

It was over.

✝

Instantly, there was peace.

Calm.

Silence.

A radiant white light.

The tender face of the Nazarene.

Flavia was there as well, smiling. So was Marcus.

"Well done, good and faithful servant."

The Nazarene held out his hand and welcomed Theophilus. And in that moment, the advocate knew that all of his Savior's promises were true. Every word he ever spoke.

As were the words of Seneca that had followed Theophilus throughout his life.

What we have to seek for, then, is that which is untouched
by time and chance. And what is this? It is the soul that is
upright, good, and great. . . .

A soul like this may descend into a Roman equestrian or
a freedman's son or a slave. . . . They are mere titles, born of
ambition or of wrong. One may leap to the heavens from
the very slums. Only rise and mold thyself into kinship with
thy God.

IN THE THREE HUNDRED THIRTY-FIRST YEAR
OF OUR LORD AND SAVIOR, JESUS CHRIST

The commission went out from Constantine, the first Roman emperor who had converted to the cause of Christ, the same ruler who had abolished the ancient punishment of crucifixion. He wrote the letter to Eusebius, the bishop of Caesarea in Palestine, a respected leader in the church. The emperor needed the bishop's help.

I have thought it expedient to instruct your Prudence to produce fifty copies of the sacred Scriptures, the provision and use of which you know to be most needful for the instruction of the Church, to be written on prepared parchment in a legible manner, and in a convenient, portable form, by professional transcribers thoroughly practiced in their art.

Eusebius started immediately, assembling the books that had proven most useful in the instruction and encouragement of the church, the books that had shown themselves to be inspired by the Holy Spirit. He enlisted the most diligent scribes to copy the sacred pages. They wrote each word carefully on new parchment, counting the letters and words on each page, dividing the pages into three or sometimes four columns. They bound the books with sturdy leather and inscribed the cover with gold letters.

The sacred Scriptures.

✝

Four years after their delivery, Eusebius and the other bishops were called to Constantinople to deal with a heresy being espoused by Athanasius of Alexandria. During his time there, Eusebius was granted a private audience with the emperor.

He was pleased to see that Constantine had kept a copy of the Scriptures for himself and even more pleased when he learned that Constantine had read every word. The emperor had some vexing theological questions about the divinity of Christ and other weighty matters that had troubled the church. Eusebius answered as best he could.

But the emperor had a practical question as well. It was about the books written by Saint Luke.

"Who is this man Theophilus?" the emperor asked.

"Nobody actually knows, Your Excellency. His identity has been lost to history. There are some theories, however."

Constantine waited, and Eusebius took it as a cue to continue.

"Some say he was a generous benefactor of Luke. Others suggest he may have been an investigator for Nero in preparation for Paul's trial. Still others believe the name is a code word for Nero himself."

Constantine seemed to consider this, though his expression soured with the thought that the notorious Nero might have been Luke's intended audience. Like every other Roman, the emperor was well aware of Nero's infamous reign and cowardly death. Repulsed by the people, condemned by the Senate, and hunted by the Roman legions, Nero had struggled to even muster the nerve to take his own life. When he finally did, with the help of a servant, his last words were fittingly narcissistic: "What an artist dies in me!"

Following his death, the Senate had issued a *damnatio memoriae*, condemning even the memory of the man, erasing his name and visage from all public documents and places.

It was no wonder that Emperor Constantine recoiled at the thought of such a man being the intended recipient of Saint Luke's writings.

"What is *your* thought on the matter?" Constantine asked Eusebius.

The bishop mulled the question for a moment. "The name Theophilus means 'lover of God,'" he eventually replied. "In that respect, it may be that the Gospel of Luke and the Acts of the Apostles are general epistles, addressed to every believer who loves our Savior."

The emperor walked to his desk, opened the sacred volume, and read the words again. "'Most Excellent Theophilus,'" he murmured. He looked at Eusebius, pinning the bishop with his incisive eyes. "Is that the view to which you subscribe, Eusebius?"

"Yes, Your Excellency, though it's difficult to prove such a thing. Still, it's my belief that there is a small part of Theophilus in all of us."

Author's Note

I have never felt more indebted on a book than this one. Five years is a long time to work on a project, and I've required more than the usual help along the way.

My team at Tyndale has been beyond patient. We delayed the release of this book a few times, even completing a contemporary legal thriller while I continued to work on this one in the background. I am so grateful for Karen Watson, Jeremy Taylor, Jan Stob, and the rest of the team who believed in this book and helped make it exponentially better than the raw manuscript I first submitted. In addition to that, a team of advance readers and transcribers, including Mary Hartman, Robin Pawling, Mike Garnier, Jana Hadder, Alisa Bozich, and my wife, Rhonda, (the ever-fastidious teacher of grammar) weighed in with helpful thoughts and feedback.

I have newfound respect for authors of historical fiction. Learning how to speak, write, live, and think like a first-century Roman has not been easy. To the extent this book feels authentic, I owe enormous debts to the sources and people who helped me understand what the world was like when the Son of Man chose to invade history.

The seed for this book was sown when I read *Paul on Trial*, a nonfiction book by a friend and fellow lawyer named John Mauck. In it, John argues that the books of Luke and Acts are written like legal briefs that were intended as evidence in Paul's trial in front of Nero. I took that premise and ran with it, developing the fictional story of Theophilus, the intended recipient of those two books of Scripture.

I am a former history teacher, and the historical details are both fascinating and important to me. Unfortunately, space does not allow me to sift the real from the fictitious here. Suffice it to say that I attempted to remain true to the historical accounts to the extent possible. I have put a full list of my sources, along with detailed notes about what is real and what is fictional, on my website. However, a few of the more prominent sources bear special mention.

This period in history came alive through two main sources. The first was a wonderful tour guide I had in Rome named Cinzia Cutrone. She was a first-class historian who patiently answered every question, never injecting her own opinions but always taking me back to the original sources.

The second is an author named Ann Wroe, who wrote a magnificent nonfiction book titled *Pontius Pilate*. Her vibrant writing made the events surrounding the trial of Christ leap off the page and helped me see the first-century world through a Roman's eyes. In particular, scenes in my book where Theophilus visits Nicodemus and where Procula, the wife of Pilate, is healed in the temple of Aesculapius were inspired by Ann Wroe's descriptions of that temple and by her vivid imagining of a possible meeting between Pilate and Nicodemus. She also did an excellent job describing the details of Pilate's life, the politics that confronted him, and the quotes from Roman philosophers like Cicero and Seneca that would have helped him process the trial of Jesus, all of which impacted my story. I believe I used no fewer than five historical quotes that I first discovered in Wroe's book, including a quote from Seneca that played a large part in the life of my fictional Theophilus and is the concluding quote for his story.

On the life and times of Nero, a book of the same name by Edward Champlin was most helpful. His insightful writing helped me understand the events during Nero's reign and see the ruler as an actor trapped in an emperor's body as opposed to just a one-dimensional persecutor of the early Christians.

In the same way, three sources brought to life the epic fire that destroyed most of Rome. *The Flames of Rome* by Paul Maier, *The Great Fire of Rome* by Stephen Dando-Collins, and *The Apostle* by Sholem Asch all contain gripping accounts of what that tragedy was like. These accounts formed the basis of my own description. Also, the novel *Imperium* by Robert Harris did a wonderful job describing what life was like for an advocate in ancient Rome—in particular for Marcus Cicero, a hero of my book's protagonist. I relied on several of Mr. Harris's insights when I wrote about the training of Theophilus and when I described the role of an advocate in the Roman legal system. For example, the life of Theophilus at the School of Molon and the description of the Asiatic School instructors as "dancing masters" were based on Mr. Harris's book. In a similar way, I am indebted to Jeffrey Barr for his insightful analysis of the episode where Jesus was asked about paying taxes, an analysis I relied on in this book.

I tried to stay true to the original historical sources, and you can be the judge of whether I succeeded. I started with the writings of Luke and the other New Testament books including, of course, the letters of Paul. I also found great value in the ancient historians—Tacitus, Josephus, Suetonius, Cassius Dio—and in the writings of Seneca, who waxed eloquent on a great variety of topics.

I'll end my thanks with the man who has guided my writing career for most of the past decade—my former agent, Lee Hough. I'm pretty sure there was nobody more excited about this book than Lee. After a long and courageous battle with brain cancer, he passed away just before the manuscript was submitted. Nevertheless, this book has his fingerprints all over it. They are prints of encouragement and persistence and faith.

And as good as Lee was as an agent—which was pretty darn special—he was even better as a friend. I miss him a lot. And I hope this book will make him proud.

About the Author

Randy Singer is a critically acclaimed, award-winning author and veteran trial attorney. He has penned more than ten legal thrillers and was a finalist with John Grisham and Michael Connelly for the inaugural Harper Lee Prize for Legal Fiction sponsored by the University of Alabama School of Law and the *ABA Journal*. Randy runs his own law practice and has been named one of the top 100 lawyers in Virginia by *Super Lawyers* magazine.

In addition to his law practice and writing, Randy serves as teaching pastor for Trinity Church in Virginia Beach, Virginia. He calls it his "Jekyll and Hyde thing"—part lawyer, part pastor. He also teaches classes in civil litigation at Regent Law School.

The Advocate is Randy's first work of historical fiction. His fans will enjoy Randy's trademark legal suspense in a first-century setting.

Randy and his wife, Rhonda, live in Virginia Beach. They have two grown children.

Visit his website at www.randysinger.net.

ALSO BY RANDY SINGER

Fiction

Directed Verdict

Irreparable Harm

Dying Declaration

Self Incrimination

The Judge Who Stole Christmas

The Judge
previously published as The Cross
Examination of Oliver Finney

False Witness

By Reason of Insanity

The Justice Game

Fatal Convictions

The Last Plea Bargain

Dead Lawyers Tell No Tales

Nonfiction

Live Your Passion, Tell Your Story, Change Your World

Made to Count

www.randysinger.net

CP0232

Keep in touch with author
RANDY SINGER
at RANDYSINGER.NET

→ Sign up for Randy's newsletter

→ Download discussion guides

→ Read first chapters

→ Have Randy speak to your book group

→ Discover his latest releases

→ Connect with Randy on Goodreads

CP0650

Have you visited
TYNDALE FICTION.COM
lately?

YOU'LL FIND:

- ways to connect with your favorite authors
- first chapters
- discussion guides
- author videos and book trailers
- and much more!

PLUS, SCAN THE QR CODE OR VISIT BOOKCLUBHUB.NET TO

- download free discussion guides
- get great book club recommendations
- sign up for our book club and other e-newsletters

Are you crazy for Tyndale fiction? Follow us on Twitter **@Crazy4Fiction** for daily updates on your favorite authors, free e-book promotions, contests, and much more. Let's get crazy!

CP0541